'Tracy's met ... ... reader with the complete experie... ... glorious'
Kathryn Hughes, bestselling author of *The Letter*

'I loved the evocative atmosphere of the 20s,
the lovely characters and gorgeous descriptions of
nature/turning of the seasons'.
Lucinda Riley, bestselling author of *The Pearl Sister*

'I love Tracy's writing; it's full of colour and atmosphere,
with sparkly dialogue and just the right pace
to keep you turning the pages'
Gill Paul, author of *Another Woman's Husband*

'A clever book that's a joy to read . . . These three
women will stay with you for a long, long time'
Claire Dyer, author of *The Last Day*

'Completely delightful . . . Tracy writes with a warmth
and authenticity that draws her readers into
the delicious world she has created'
Rosanna Ley, author of *Her Mother's Secret*

'Full of vitality and warmth, *Darling Blue* is delightful'
Tor Udall, author of *A Thousand Paper Birds*

'It's a simply glorious read . . . A truly stunning novel'

Also by Tracy Rees

*Amy Snow*
*Florence Grace*
*The Hourglass*

# TRACY REES

# DARLING BLUE

Quercus

First published in Great Britain in 2018
This edition published in 2018 by

Quercus Editions Ltd
Carmelite House
50 Victoria Embankment
London EC4Y 0DZ

An Hachette UK company

A CIP catalogue record for this book is available
from the British Library

PB ISBN 978-1-78648-668-4
EB ISBN 978-1-78648-667-7

10 9 8 7 6 5 4 3 2 1

Typeset by CC Book Production

Printed and bound in Great Britain by Clays Ltd, Elcograf S.p.A.

*For the jolly old parents, with love as always. You're the tops!*

# Part One

## Summer

*As hot as Hades and twice as stuffy*

# Chapter One

All through that shimmering riverside summer of 1925 there seemed to be only one question on everybody's lips: who was Blue Camberwell going to marry?

'Jolly well *everybody* wants to know!' squealed Juno Forrester in the *Richmond Gazette*.

Blue dropped the newspaper onto a side table and rested her brow against the window. The lawn was abuzz with preparations for her twenty-first birthday party. Waiters were lining up diamond-bright champagne glasses on long tables spread with white tablecloths smooth as icing. Servants hired for the evening perched on ladders, stringing fairy lights through the trees and looping ribbons from trellis to trellis. In the summerhouse, Midge was carefully positioning a gramophone in readiness for the half hours when the jazz quartet would take a breather. Blue's father was nowhere to be seen.

Unable to resist what she knew to be a depressing impulse, Blue picked up the article again.

Could that question be answered tonight, at her coming-of-age party? Nothing confirmed, remember! But it *is* a special occasion, and at *least* three gentlemen of my acquaintance are head over heels with the young lady.

Three? In love? It was news to Blue.

Whether or not an engagement is announced, this promises to be the party of the year. The guest list includes some of our most distinguished neighbours and yours truly has been privileged with an invitation which I'm clutching in my little paws *right now* (coloured nail polish – *naturally*). Dear readers, I promise you a full and faithful account tomorrow. But for now, must dash – time to get my glad rags on!

With a low growl, she dropped the *Gazette* into the wastepaper basket – a gesture only, since Midge would certainly fish it out later and paste the article into her scrapbook. Blue was used to having her life described in extravagant terms: beautiful Blue and her charmed life; beautiful Blue who lived in a castle with her handsome father, her virtuous stepmother and the elf in the garden . . . She *was* blessed, that she knew, but life was never just one thing nor the other, not for anyone. As for 'jolly well everybody' – they would have to face disappointment. They wouldn't learn who Blue was going to marry for one simple reason – she didn't know herself. Blue was far more preoccupied by how she could achieve her dream of becoming a writer than she was by thoughts of romance. But that didn't make good gossip.

Hours later, gauzy twilight hung over the long garden of Ryan's Castle, which was in fact not a castle at all but a terraced Georgian house on Richmond Hill. A previous owner had named it thus, his reasons now lost in the mists of time. But the name had stuck – quirky and rather gorgeous, Blue always thought, her imagination tantalised by who Ryan might have been and why he saw fit to dub his home a castle.

Blue had swapped her habitual daily garb of three-quarter-length skirt, blouse and lace-up shoes for the obligatory glamour. She wore her signature colour – the misty yet brilliant powder blue of the butterflies in Richmond Park. Midge had made her dress – a silk underlay with dropped waist and fringed hem and a chiffon top layer scattered with thousands of tiny blue beads. The chiffon was so sheer, and the beads so heavy, that dancing was sure to wreck it. This was a dress for just one night; a real labour of love.

Blue's older sister had styled her. Merrigan might be the married lady now, with a home of her own and a small daughter (eighteen-month-old Cicely of cherubic face and foghorn voice), but she was still the fashionable sister. Blue's outfit was completed by silver shoes with clippy little heels and a silver headband worn low over her brow, an elaborate seashell-shaped embellishment sitting just above her right ear.

'But you're the *beauty*,' Merrigan had scolded when Blue questioned the seashell. '*I'm* only ever attractive at best; *you're* the one all this jazz isn't wasted on!'

Blue had scoffed. 'Attractive at best' was not a phrase anyone else would apply to Merrigan. Her sleek, nut-brown hair was perfect for the new bob, she had wicked dark eyes that could slay a beau at a hundred paces and she carried herself with aplomb, as though trouble were waiting only a corner away. In contrast, Blue sometimes felt old-fashioned and pallid. She was tall and slim; the new dresses hung on her as though she were just an old coat hanger inside them. (This, Merrigan asserted, was *exactly* what they were supposed to do.) Her eyes were brown, like her sister's, but her hair was blonde and meandered across her forehead in a languid wave. Now it was tucked up at the back to imitate a bob, but during the day she often wore it long and loose over her shoulders, a habit that caused Merrigan to shudder. Her mouth was generous, and she had inherited a more feminine version of her father's aquiline nose, a thing for which she occasionally resented him. It was a nose she often bemoaned as Roman.

'Roman!' Merrigan would jeer. 'It's not *Roman*. Darling, it's barely even Italian!'

Now the guests were arriving and the Camberwells clustered on the threshold to greet them *en famille*. Blue's arm

6

was tucked through Merrigan's. Lawrence Miller, Merrigan's husband, stood behind his wife, gripping the ankles of their child, who rode on his shoulders and drummed her feet rather determinedly against his chest. Behind Blue stood her father and next to him was Midge.

Blue murmured and smiled as the familiar faces filed past; faces she had seen all her life, people she had grown up amongst. For a moment, as she looked at the glittering, gossiping crowd, all she could see were losses and scars. These were people who had suffered through the war and recovered from it, to a greater or lesser extent, each in their own way. For a moment it was as if her own casings had dissolved – the fabulous house, the sparkling dress, the happy family – leaving her wounds exposed. These moments often took hold of Blue, allowing her to take nothing for granted. Then she shook herself. Tonight was not the night for feeling like that; tonight was for celebrating. Dear Midge had gone to so much trouble, as usual. Blue reached for her hand and squeezed it. Midge squeezed back.

When most of the guests had arrived, Blue began to circulate. She accepted kisses, gifts and compliments. She shouldered enquiries about her love life with patient smiles and gracefully fielded Juno Forrester's avid request for an 'inside scoop'. As far as she knew her, Blue liked Juno, a fast-talking, determined woman in her thirties with a penchant for turbans. *But really*, Blue thought, *are women's marital prospects all that interest the* Gazette *readers, even these days?*

It wasn't that Blue wasn't interested in love. Heavens, who was more romantic than a writer? An *aspiring* writer, she corrected herself hurriedly. Juno had told her once that *aspiring* writers were the most romantic people in the world. But *real* writers didn't have time for romance, she'd added, blowing out a long, philosophical plume of cigarette smoke. They were too busy meeting deadlines. So Blue had never allowed herself into any situation that might hinder her pursuit of her goal. And she didn't intend to now.

'Hello, Blue, old chap. Golly, you look smashing!'

Blue turned to see Foster Foxton, her childhood friend, and gave him a happy hug. The Foxtons and the Camberwells went way back – two fine families, living just around the corner from each other. Foster's older sister, Tabitha, was Merrigan's best friend and had virtually lived at Ryan's Castle before Merrigan married. Foster was a few years younger than Blue.

'You look rather sharp yourself, Floss,' she remarked, using his old childhood nickname. 'Lovely party, isn't it?'

Foster nodded, looking around. Seventeen now, but still as shy as ever.

'How's school?' asked Blue.

He sighed. 'Oh, you know. Fellow's got to get a decent education and all that.'

'Golly, that doesn't sound very chipper. Everything all right?'

There was a little pause. Then he gave a trembly smile. 'It's fine.'

'And how about your music?' asked Blue. Foster played rather wonderfully, according to Tabitha. Blue wouldn't know; she'd never been treated to a performance. 'Oh, Floss, you wouldn't play something for us tonight, would you? At the party? It would be so splendid if you did.'

Foster looked alarmed. 'Oh no, I couldn't. Please don't even think of it.'

'*Please*, Flossy, dearest.'

'I'm sorry, Blue.' Conflict was writ large upon his face. 'I'd love to do something like that for *you*. I mean you're so . . . But I just can't. Not with . . . all these people . . .'

There was such fear in his eyes that Blue took pity on him. 'Never mind then, let's just enjoy ourselves.'

The night whirled on. Blue danced until her feet ached, including several with Dorian Fields, the most dashing man in Richmond. She laughed and hugged everybody and smiled at the comments she overheard when no one knew she was listening.

'Who's Father *Time*?' breathed one young woman whom Blue didn't recognise, and of course, when Blue followed her gaze, it was Blue's father who had caught her eye.

Kenneth Camberwell – decorated war hero, Cambridge scholar, devoted father – was one of those men. Somehow, the war and the subsequent tragedy of his first wife's death had not blunted his appreciation for life. He was the sort of person that other people wanted to be around because he always seemed to be living larger than anyone else. Panache, charisma and *joie de vivre* were all words used frequently by Juno in the *Gazette*. Occasionally she lapsed into vocabulary like 'cat's particulars' and 'drool-worthy'.

Blue adored her father; no question of that. But as the night went on and he drank more and more, she exchanged exasperated looks with Merrigan and Midge. Yes, it was his beloved daughter's twenty-first. Yes, he was presiding over a splendid soirée, the king of the castle. And no, there wasn't a malicious bone in his body. But his outspoken, boyish charm grew increasingly reckless. Kenneth Camberwell, like a sudden squall at sea, could sometimes wreak devastating effects. Blue was used to it, but even she couldn't have predicted what he did next.

'Ladies, gentlemen and those of you who haven't yet made up your minds!' he announced, provoking laughter, ringing one of Midge's crystal bells to summon the revellers from the garden. The bell broke and a servant shot forth with a dustpan and brush. Midge closed her eyes. Kenneth sprang onto the fifth stair. 'Your attention, please! As you all know, tonight is my best, my most beautiful, daughter's birthday!'

Blue sighed. Her father's tact diminished in exact correlation with his consumption of gin cocktails. Beside her, Merrigan snorted. She'd be having words with him tomorrow.

'Twenty-one today and the loveliest young lady imaginable!' beamed Kenneth from his podium. 'Darling Blue, would you please come up here?'

Blue threaded her way through the crowd. Of course he would make a speech. Of course there would be a toast. She just hoped that it wouldn't be *too* cringe-making. She joined her father, accompanied by applause and a few whistles. She grinned and bobbed a little curtsey, concentrating on the good feeling in the room rather than on her embarrassment. Midge came to the foot of the stairs, a reassuring presence.

'Twenty-one years ago today,' announced Kenneth, 'my wife Audra – that is, my *first* wife, Audra – presented me with a squirming, squawking bundle of joy . . .'

If he was starting from her babyhood, Blue had time to day-dream. She let her gaze wander. Juno was scribbling avidly by the aspidistra. Avis, the family's one remaining servant, gleamed in her best dress. Foster was gazing at Blue with all the ardour one freckled, adolescent face could express, his Adam's apple prominent even from this distance. His sister, Tabitha, stood beside a handsome newcomer, and if Blue wasn't greatly mistaken, was sliding her hand beneath his coat-tails in the general vicinity of his rear parts. Blue quickly looked away. She caught Dorian's eye and he gave her a wink. And over there was dear Elf, a family friend of such long standing that it was hard to remember he wasn't really family at all. He was beaming with paternal pride second only to Kenneth's own.

Then something her father said caught her attention. 'Here at Ryan's Castle, we are aware that there's considerable speculation about whom Blue will marry. We speculate ourselves!'

He paused and nodded, enjoying the mirth. Blue frowned. This wasn't her idea of a birthday speech.

'The inside scoop is . . .' said Kenneth, and a hush descended. He lowered his voice confidingly. 'That there *isn't* an inside scoop! There is currently no front runner for my lovely daughter's affections.'

A groan ran through the gathering. Juno's pen hung from listless fingers.

'But,' he went on, 'I have come up with a scheme! There is no finer state than matrimony and I want Blue to know the happiness that I have known, the happiness I shared with her dear mother.'

Horrified, Blue elbowed him in the ribs.

'What?' he asked, peering at her. 'Oh yes, *and* that I share now with my new wife, of course.'

Blue dared a glance at Midge, whose game face was firmly in place and gleaming.

'Yes, yes, jolly lucky, second time around and all that . . .' Kenneth continued, clearly not quite understanding what he'd said amiss. Blue nudged him again.

'Quite so, quite so. Yes, well, earlier today I was looking through some of Blue's old things, sentimental and all that, and I happened across some of her childhood books. She adored fairy tales – like most children, I suppose. Though Merrigan was always more interested in books about steam trains.' He paused to chuckle. 'I found Blue's favourite, in which an old king promises his daughter's hand in marriage to whichever young buck of the kingdom can slay the dragon. Well, no dragons in Richmond, of course! Only a few geese and some cows in the meadow yonder! But it got me to thinking. What test of merit could I devise in these modern times? What gauntlet could I lay down to suitors aspiring to win my daughter?'

'Daddy!' exclaimed Blue. *Surely* he couldn't be going where he seemed to be going? Juno was scribbling like fury, a bright light in her eye. Foster was swallowing madly, Adam's apple bobbing; she could see it from here. She had a horrible feeling he had a small crush. How uncomfortable; Floss was like her little brother.

'Hope is, as Pliny the Elder said,' intoned Kenneth, 'the dream of a waking man. What qualities do I, doting father, hope for in a son-in-law? Well, they may be easily hazarded. Honour, kindness, strength and so forth – all fathers must feel the same. But *she* must make the choice, *she* must find someone with whom she is happy to live for the rest of her life. And Blue, as you all know, is a writer.'

Blue poked him. She didn't want her private aspirations discussed in public. But Kenneth was in full flow.

'Writers are a rare breed,' he continued. 'On the one hand, deeply engaged with the world around them; on the other, reclusive sorts when the mood takes them. Sensitive, changeable, and frankly baffling most of the time! The hopeful suitor wishing to captivate such a woman must set out to capture not only her heart, but also her *imagination*. My proposal therefore is that anyone who wishes to woo her does so by letter.'

'Daddy! Shut up, there's a dear!' gasped Blue.

'Kenneth, darling . . .' cautioned Midge, coming to lay a hand on his arm.

'An anonymous letter,' Kenneth rolled on, 'so that whatever she might know of you cannot prejudice or predispose her. Her choice will be based on nothing but the bond your words can forge. And on this day next year, we will announce her decision.'

'No, we bloody won't!' exclaimed Blue.

'You have the turning of the seasons,' concluded Kenneth poetically, 'to woo and win my daughter. So, as we approach midnight on this special occasion . . .'

Blue glanced at the clock. God help her, it was indeed just approaching midnight. Her father's flair for the dramatic had surpassed itself.

'I make this vow. Whoever can win Blue's heart through a letter can have her hand in marriage. What? Oh – yes, Midge, right ho. And now I propose a toast. To my daughter, on the occasion of her coming of age.' He lifted his glass. 'To Ishbel Christina Camberwell. Known to us all as darling Blue.'

The clock began to strike midnight, as if casting some sort of spell on what should have been nothing more than drunken foolery. The guests raised their glasses, the rims glinting in the light like fairy dust. 'Darling Blue!'

# Chapter Two

The following morning, Kenneth's womenfolk were dreadfully cross with him. When he hadn't surfaced from his gin-laced slumbers by noon, they stalked from the house without him. Soon, the ladies of the family, plus Tabitha, languished on a picnic blanket in Richmond Park. It was hot as Hades and twice as stuffy, complained Midge, fanning herself with *The Ladies' Quarterly* and retreating further into the shade of her parasol. The heat, the anticlimax, the champagne and annoyance had all combined to put them in bad moods.

The park *was* diabolical in this weather, but the garden at home was out of the question with the servants clattering and calling as they cleared last night's debris. And there would be too many people at the river . . .

It was nearly two before Kenneth staggered up the hill to join them.

'Oh, it's *you*,' said Merrigan with a curl of her upper lip. 'Shall I scooch over so you can sit beside your *best* daughter?'

Kenneth groaned. 'So sorry, Merry, darling. You're my other best daughter, of course.'

There was no room on the blanket so Kenneth sat on the grass beside them. He was wearing cream slacks, from which any grass stains would be loathsome to remove. Midge compressed her lips and he cast her a harried look.

'Simply too hot and tired to stand, Midge, poppet.' He sighed. 'Even if it were three inches of mud.'

'Too hot and tired and *drunk*.' Blue scowled. 'I bet you haven't sobered up yet. How much does a father have to drink to sell his own daughter?'

'To be accurate, oh furious daughter, no sum of money or exchange of goods was mentioned, so I can't fairly be accused of *selling* you . . . Oh Lord.' He sighed, observing the disapproving faces around him. 'I've dropped a stinker, haven't I?'

'Yes,' said Blue, 'you have.'

Tabitha gave him her green-eyed grin. 'Call me old-fashioned, but I think it's romantic. I rather wish *my* father would do something like that for me.'

'But you're hardly short of beaux,' said Midge. 'I never knew anyone so popular with the gentlemen.'

'But not for *marriage*, darling,' explained Tabitha. 'Who on earth would marry me? I simply behave too, too badly.'

'Then stop?' suggested Merrigan.

'Oh, I can't, Merry, bad behaviour is too much fun. Still.

Don't be *too* crushing to your handsome Papa, Blue. He meant well, and it was rather sweet.'

'*Sweet?* I don't call it sweet. It's 1925, for heaven's sake! Except in Ryan's Castle, where we've apparently returned to feudal times. Marriage isn't the be-all and end-all for women any more. We work! We have the vote! Well, not *us*, we're too young. But some do. Midge does! Times are changing.'

'Changing, yes,' conceded Tabitha, 'but not *changed*. That's an important difference. Most parents still want to see their offspring married well. In families like yours and mine, anyway. I know Mother and Father have high hopes for Foster and me. At least one of us is sure to disappoint.'

'Either way, a girl can't be blamed for hoping her own father won't auction her off like a cow at market! Whatever came over you, Daddy?'

'You know perfectly well,' said Kenneth, wincing as he raised his sunglasses, and quickly lowering them again. 'A perfect cacophony of gin came over me, laced with some good old brain-bashing bubbly. That and a fit of nostalgia, I suppose, for simpler days, for romance. I think, in my giddy, impetuous state, I wanted to do something dashing, to get the gods to sit up and take notice of you, to send you someone . . . special.'

Blue frowned. 'I don't know how you do it. You can do the most outrageous things and then make them sound almost endearing. The point *is*, Daddy . . .'

'I know, fat-headed. But really, darling, as Aristotle said, "No excellent soul is exempt from a mixture of madness."'

'"It is a characteristic of wisdom not to do desperate things,"' countered Blue.

Kenneth squinted. 'Socrates?'

'Thoreau.'

'Ah. Anyway, it wasn't an auction. It was just an . . . *invitation* for young men to make their intentions known if they wanted to.'

'An invitation that should have come from *me* if anyone! It makes me look incapable of attracting a mate on my own, when in fact various people have described me as . . . Well, I'm supposed to be quite fetching, aren't I?'

'Not in *that* skirt,' muttered Merrigan.

'Of *course* you're fetching! And everyone knows you're not just some dolly holding out for a husband. That's why I said the thing about the writing and the letters . . . I was *trying* to say that not just anyone – no ordinary situation – would do. For you. Only I made the devil's own carcass of it.'

He rolled onto his stomach with a groan.

'Kenneth, darling, put your hat on,' said Midge. 'You don't want sunstroke.'

Tabitha tossed his panama so that it biffed him on the back of the head. He groped for it and jammed it in place.

Blue could never hold a grudge for long, especially when it came to her father. 'Well, I suppose the good thing is that no one will take any notice,' she said. 'Everyone knows you get overexcited and spout nonsense when you've had a few. They'll all talk about it for a bit and then it'll go away. And I'll be left in peace to get on with my own priorities.'

'Which are what, exactly?' wondered Merrigan, rummaging in the picnic hamper. Merrigan had opinions about Blue's life choices.

'I'm afraid I think you're wrong, Blue, old thing,' mused Tabitha. 'I think your Papa has done something he didn't set out to do.'

'Make a fool of me?'

'No. Capture people's imaginations. *Everyone* there perked up when he made that speech. It may have been foolish, old-fashioned, downright unrealistic and all that – but isn't that just what everyone's secretly craving? Golly, if I were a man, I'd take up writing to you myself! We need a quest. We need meaning. And the times we live in aren't giving us that. I think young men are going to rise to the challenge. And I think all of Richmond is going to live vicariously through you for the coming year.'

'What rot,' scoffed Blue, throwing a bread roll at Tabitha. It bounced off her cheek and landed in the grass. 'Of course no one's going to write! If anyone wants to . . . Oh Lord, *woo* me, to use an absurd phrase, they'll just knock on the front door and ask me to take a turn along the river! No one writes letters any more; Juno Forrester said so in the *Gazette* a couple of months ago. And romance is dead! She said *that* just the other day.'

'Juno Forrester looked more excited than anyone. Sweetie, I think romance might just have been resurrected.'

Blue lay down, shielding her eyes with a hand and gazing up into the cloudless sky. 'Rot,' she said again, uneasily.

# Chapter Three

By the following morning, everything had returned to normal. The temporary servants had departed, back to their agencies and whatever assignments next awaited them. Merrigan had returned to her marital home. And Kenneth's brain cells were rehydrated and restored to a coherent, functioning arrangement.

Blue had been determined that today she would at last conduct the perfect writing day. In her imagination, this involved rising at dawn, sipping a cup of something fortifying whilst gazing at the dew on the lawn, then setting to at seven for some hard graft before breakfast. But she overslept, then she felt ravenous, and now here she was at eleven, wrapped in her new floral dressing gown, reading the paper over kippers and toast.

The gap between intention and reality, between her expectations of the world and the way it really was, had always troubled her. Her mother had possessed the wonderful gift of filling the world with magic. It was easy to long for those vanished years, but when Blue found herself doing it she stopped.

Nothing could bring back the past. Blue had learned this the hard way.

She was only ten when the war came and shattered everything. Suddenly her father was gone. Her friends' fathers were gone. Audra was careful with what she told the girls, but Blue's imagination filled in the gaps. She could feel the storm clouds that hung over the world; she knew the carefree days of searching for fairies in the garden, of her parents singing her to sleep in harmony, were over.

She learned that her father was away protecting their country, because the nature of the world was such that thousands upon thousands of people were deliberately and systematically killing each other. That reality, combined with fear for Kenneth, turned Blue from a cheerful child who saw magic in everything into a silent presence who watched from the corners, or vanished into a book, where everything was more bearable. There was nothing Audra could say to protect her from the reality of war, because Blue could feel it.

'Such a sensitive child!' Avis would whisper.

By the time the war ended, Blue was fourteen. Richmond had changed. The banqueting room of the Star and Garter hotel, where Blue used to go to parties, had been turned into a hospital. Many of the people she had known were dead. Households had been dismantled because servants could earn better pay in munitions factories during the war. Blue became prone to long fits of despair. She felt that the happy world she had known wasn't real.

Then Kenneth came home, safe and sound, despite everything. 'Don't let despair claim you, Blue,' he implored her. 'I understand the temptation, believe me, but every life destroyed that way is a small victory for the enemy. What triumph exists in winning the war if only to afford them victory after victory after the fact, one man or woman at a time? That is not what we fought for. What we had before *was* real. Reality has room for a lot of things in it, good and bad. Make sure yours is as marvellous as possible. It isn't easy, but it's our task. *Now* is the moment, my darling, not the past and not the future. The war was horrendous. It's over. Now we live our next days.'

But almost at once, the Spanish influenza broke out and soon Audra was dead because of it. Audra, the last holder of magic and sweetness – or so it seemed to Blue. She thought the grief might end her. But gradually Blue came through – changed, but in some ways for the better. Now she knew the depths of her own resilience, when she had never thought of herself as strong before. So she survived, although at first that was the best that could be said of it; she didn't believe she could hope for more.

Eventually she started to experience the magic again. It would be very fleeting, just the trill of a bird or a particular beam of sunlight falling in a comforting way. Blue started to write all these things down, collecting them, gathering treasures. And life went on. Blue would always yearn for enchantment, and she would choose, whenever there was a choice to be made, to draw on every small beauty rather than succumb to that old despair.

It was hard work sometimes, but here she was, twenty-one – all grown up! – and with so much, still, to be thankful for. Here she was, procrastinating over her work, having succumbed to temptation and read Juno's latest piece about her party. The long version had run yesterday, with a full and enthusiastic account of her father's speech. Now there was an excited summary. If it had bypassed anyone on the grapevine, they certainly wouldn't miss it in the paper.

'Letter for you, Miss Blue.' She was interrupted by dark-haired Avis, plump and still pretty at fifty, bringing her a white envelope on a silver tray.

'Thanks, Avis. How are you today?'

'Well, thanks, Miss Blue. Always puts a smile on me face, the sunshine.'

'Me too. Time for a cup?'

'Not me, Miss Blue. I've got a tart in the oven,' protested Avis, hurrying out. Blue smiled. Any time of day was a good time for baking with Avis at the helm. She slid the onyx-handled letter opener under the fold of the envelope and read the letter.

'Oh Lord,' she said, and read it again.

*Darling Blue,*

*Golly, you're swell. Oh Lord. I've gone right in there and said it and I meant to be ever so elegant! But I've already ripped up five sheets and this is the last one in my sister's case. So I'd better make it count.*

*Blue, you are dearer to me than the nest to a bird, than the song to a sparrow, than the udder to a cow. You're the most beautiful girl I ever saw and I worship you.*

*If you would consent to write back to me, and maybe, some day, to be my girl, I'd be the happiest boy that ever lived. I know I could make you happy, Blue. Without giving away who I am, because your father said I mustn't, my family and yours are the same sort of family, we go back a long way. It would be the most natural thing in the world for us. I think we could be inseparable. I'd love to be inseparable with you. I'd let you write, Blue – I wouldn't mind a wife of mine working. I'm young and modern and I'd want nothing more than for you to be happy. I'd even play the violin for you, if it were just you and me.*

*Please write back, darling. If you leave your letter in the hollow in the old apple tree in your garden, I'll pick it up from there. That's romantic, isn't it? Tell me you think so.*

*I think I may have given away too much. You might even have guessed who I am. But all I could think, that night of your party, was that I had to write. I had to tell you how I feel. So for now I shall simply confess myself,*

*An ardent admirer*

Blue realised she was biting her lips as she read, and stopped, blowing out a long puff of air. So much for anonymity! She refolded the letter and put it back inside the envelope. She felt hot and trembly. Then she stood and went storming through the house in search of her father.

'*Daddy!*' she yelled.

# Chapter Four

Delphine Foley was dreaming of her sister. In the dream, the girls were around eight years old, bobbing on a calm blue sea in a rowboat, a thing they had certainly never experienced in their real childhood. Little dream Delphine closed her eyes, marvelling at the loving scorch of the sun on her face and the tender rocking of the ocean. She felt as if she were safe in a giant cradle, being watched over by a kind presence. She wanted to stay there forever, but a hand seized her shoulder, shaking her from the boat.

But she couldn't swim; she would drown! She struggled, she pleaded, but the words wouldn't sound. She was tipping into the water, and a voice was shouting at her that it was the end of the line . . . Foley!

Her eyes flew open and she awoke, screaming. But it wasn't Foley. It was an uncomfortable-looking young man in a flat cap. He let go of her shoulder and stepped back, raising his hands as though under arrest.

'Sorry, miss, didn't mean to alarm. Only it's the end of the line, see? Richmond. I thought it best to wake you.'

Delphine looked around, bewildered. Not eight years old, but twenty more than that. Not a boat but the underground. She was slumped in her seat and she sat up hastily, trying to look more composed.

Richmond?

'All right, miss.' The young man backed away as if she were a violent criminal. 'I'll just be on my way then.'

'Oh,' said Delphine. She always struggled for words these days. 'Th . . . thank you,' she called after him. 'Kind of you.' She was relieved to see his nod of acknowledgement, because she really *was* grateful. If he hadn't woken her, she might have travelled all the way back to where she started – imagine *that*! But still. Richmond?

'Honestly, Delphine, you're so stupid,' she muttered. The only words that came easily these days were self-berating ones.

She got to her feet and grasped her bags, because that was what everyone else was doing. But this wasn't what she had planned. The unexpected detour had rattled her. She longed to drink a cup of coffee and dredge up whatever shreds of her conviction remained. Perhaps she might find them in her handbag among the other inadequate items she had brought to equip her for the future: an insufficiently bulging purse; a ham sandwich, a well-washed hanky and similar. The sensible thing would be to go straight back; her ticket was only valid as far as Victoria. Otherwise, at worst, she might get into trouble. At best, she would have to pay an excess fare she could ill afford.

She stepped off the train. Sunlight and shadow lay in stripes on the tracks, courtesy of some overhanging trees. Delphine looked up in a kind of wonder. She'd never seen trees at a station before. Folk walked across an airy concourse, smiling as they presented their tickets to ticket collectors. Delphine swallowed nervously.

The station clock showed that it was shortly after ten. She'd waited until Foley left for work, and then a further hour in case he arrived home unexpectedly. He'd done that once – confused his shifts, gone to work on his day off and returned to find her sitting on the doorstep chatting to Muriel, their over-the-street neighbour. Delphine was saying something about men being helpless when it came to making their own meals. It was only a throwaway remark, made to sympathise with Muriel, whose husband Frank needed feeding every four hours without fail. Muriel, to whom cooking did not come naturally, struggled to rise to the challenge.

Foley had hauled her indoors, screamed at her for disrespecting him (as if he'd ever so much as buttered a slice of bread!) and berated her for passing the time idle. She wanted to say that she'd already swept all through the house and made a pot of stew ready for his dinner that night, and that she'd only sat down for a minute because Muriel was a chatterbox and once she got a hold of you, you'd be a long time standing. But this was after she'd started to lose her words so all that came was, 'F . . . Foley, I swept . . . I . . . I . . . m . . . made stew. M . . . Muriel . . .'

And he'd laughed and done his impression of her, hunching one shoulder in a parody of the slight imbalance in hers and cringing the way she shrank from him, so that he looked like some grotesque fairy-tale goblin. He mimicked her stammer: 'I . . . I . . . I . . . Foley, Foley, Foley.'

Then he'd picked up the simmering stew in the heavy iron pot and thrown it all over her. He hit her with a solid fist. She lost a tooth. She learned not to trust that when Foley was gone, he was really gone. A useful lesson.

This morning, after an hour, she'd set about packing quickly. She hadn't dared do it before, in case he happened across the bag, but she'd rehearsed it many times in her mind. She knew exactly where everything was; no time wasted in dithering or searching. Five minutes, then she was out the door. Muriel had popped up like a jack-in-the-box. Really, weren't all the women round there the same? Stuffed between four walls, crushed down and spring-loaded.

'Delphine! Wherever are you off to so early? Foley gone for the day, is he? I'd hoped we could have a cuppa this morning.'

Delphine knew that if she just hurried off, it would look suspicious. Not that the neighbours would stand in the way of an escape from Foley. They'd probably applaud it. But the less anyone knew, the better, as far as Delphine could see. Better all round. That's why she carried only a large handbag in addition to her usual shoulder purse.

'Hullo, Muriel. Covent Garden. S . . . sur . . . surprise for F . . . F . . . Foley. Secret. W . . . won't be long . . . Pop in?'

'Oh, all right! I've got a nice plum cake. I'll treat you to a slice if you show me the surprise. His birthday, is it? What time will you be in then? About twelve? Or later?'

'About twelve. L . . . love plum cake. Ch . . . ch . . . so long, Muriel.'

'Cheerio, Delphine.'

And she'd hurried to the tube. Now, in this strange new land of Richmond, she moved slowly, unsure of the wisdom of lingering within a ten-mile radius of Foley at all. Though she couldn't imagine a less likely setting in which to encounter him. It might not be very far away, but it felt like another world.

# Chapter Five

The photograph in the oval silver frame showed Margaret Faw-cett on 10 December 1920, the day she became Midge Camberwell. A woman of thirty-nine, then; tall, angular and, until very recently, perfectly entitled to the virginal white she wore. Her veil hung in neat scallops from a low headband, three or four years before low headbands were the rage. Kenneth's girls – *her* girls, now! – had insisted on it.

Apparently, somehow, she was fashionable. Becoming Midge Camberwell had magically recast her. Her long, unlux-urious body was suddenly enviable because she could hang an array of perfectly modish clothes from it. And now she had an abundance of them, though she still, five years on, struggled to think of her figure as an asset and not a liability.

There she was on her wedding day: worried-looking brown eyes; a nose so slender it looked as though an artist had sketched it in with a single hasty line; clutching the hand of her new groom like a child of five, not a woman in middle age. And he so handsome, so gloriously, opulently *handsome . . .*

Midge sighed, setting the picture back on the pianoforte, returning to the lilies she was arranging. An odd-looking pairing, she and Kenneth. How she of all people had managed to land *Kenneth Camberwell* was one of life's happy, lucky mysteries, and she knew that every other woman in Richmond was similarly baffled. There was only one problem with a stroke of luck *that* great: it left you reeling, off balance, so you could never really trust in it. So that you lived in constant fear that it would be taken away again. Fear – crawling, chronic, all-pervasive – took hold of you from the inside and sank invisible claws into your soul . . . It drove you to think terrible thoughts. Worse, it drove you to do terrible things.

The lily trembled in her hand, its ochre pollen showering onto the piano top. Midge stuck it quickly into the vase, then wrapped her arms around herself, went to the window and took a deep breath.

'Midge?'

She whirled round at the sound of Kenneth's voice in the doorway. He was looking especially elegant in a light linen suit and a blue satin waistcoat. His eyes were sparkling and Midge's heart fluttered, though she knew she really should be too old and sensible for fluttering hearts.

'Darling, why aren't you ready? We have to leave in five minutes.'

Midge's heart stopped fluttering. Sank. Roberta Grady's fiftieth birthday breakfast. Long dreaded, miraculously forgotten today, suddenly upon her, like the plague. 'Oh no. Kenneth, I'm so sorry, I totally forgot.'

He looked incredulous. Kenneth never forgot a social engagement. 'Gracious, darling, I don't know how you do it. You'll have to change ever so quickly. It wouldn't do to be late.'

Midge grimaced. 'Do I have to? Couldn't you go without me this once? Say I've got a headache or something? I'll never make myself beautiful in time and I'm not looking forward to it at all.'

His eyes widened. 'Why not?'

'Well, for one thing, I still don't know them very well. And that crowd can be a little . . .' *Critical. Superior. Intimidating*. Not to mention the fact that all the women found it impossible to resist flirting with her husband.

'Oh, they're fine, really. And you're *always* beautiful. Just stick a frock on and let's hoof it, Midge!'

'Oh, Kenneth, I really think . . .'

But he was across the room and holding her hands, smiling down at her. 'Please, darling. For me?'

Midge was powerless to resist. 'Five minutes then,' she agreed, and was rewarded by his beam of pleasure. 'Only . . .' She stopped. How to ask for what she wanted without sounding like a child of five? 'You will . . . keep me company, won't you?'

'Keep you company? We'll be with about thirty other people!'

'I know. But when we're there, and everyone wants to talk to you . . . just keep an eye on me a little, will you?'

'Darling, of course! I want you to have a splendid time! Old Bobbie's a bit of a dragon, it's true, but the rest are decent enough and it's bound to be a feast.'

Midge resisted the urge to drag her feet as she left the room. Upstairs, she threw on a mushroom silk shift, mid-calf, with a scatter of tiny seed pearls sweeping across the bodice. Her hair was fairly tidy, thank God, but it was that indeterminate length just a few inches longer than a bob, frowned upon by fashionistas and traditionalists alike. Well, she certainly didn't have time for a haircut! She patted a little red onto her lips with a fingertip, then rubbed it off – she still hadn't got the hang of make-up – and she was ready!

The breakfast was being held in the Peach Tree, a popular restaurant with a vast dining room in the centre of Richmond. The first things Midge saw when they crossed the threshold were two enormous bosoms, clad in emerald green, but only barely. Behind the bosoms stood Roberta, aiming her slightly feral grin at Kenneth.

'Kenneth, *darling*!' she cried, stalking towards them. 'You're here! Now it *really* feels like a party! I got in some of that gin you like, especially for you. Kiss for the birthday girl!'

It was a command, and Kenneth obliged, aiming for her cheek. He was caught out when she turned her head suddenly and he landed on her slippery red lips. 'Bobbie, you fiendish creature!' he chided, rubbing his mouth and looking perplexed at the bright smear on the back of his hand. 'Happy birthday, old girl. You look magnificent.'

He was very chivalrous. It was a quality Midge liked. Still, she enjoyed watching Roberta Grady kissing her husband and thrusting her chest against his as she murmured in his ear as much as any red-blooded woman might. And she did *not* look magnificent! Her hair was several shades blacker than the last time they'd seen her. She was dressed like a . . . Well, Midge stopped that train of thought. That was uncharitable. Roberta couldn't help how she looked. She could only help how she acted, though unfortunately that was far worse. She had angled herself with her back to Midge and was delivering a long, cosy monologue peppered with phrases like, 'And do you *remember* that time when we . . .?'

Midge was absolutely delighted when Kenneth reached out and pulled her close. 'And here's Midge, too!' he pointed out. He *would* look after her!

'Oh yes,' said Roberta, her expression blank, even though they'd met several times and she had been at their wedding. 'Hello.'

'Happy birthday, Bobbie,' said Midge warmly. 'Hard to believe that you're fifty.' It was true. She didn't look a day under sixty. 'I'm looking forward to celebrating with you.'

'Splendid,' said Roberta, glancing around. 'Ah, there's Eva-line Robinson and Millie Cuthbert. You'll like them.'

Midge looked over to see two impeccably dressed women,

heads bent together like willows, whispering scandal. 'Oh good,' she said politely. 'You must introduce us when we've settled in.'

'Lord, you're so old-fashioned, Midge! No need for introductions here – we don't stand on ceremony. Just pootle over and tell them who you are! Come with me, Kenneth, darling. Midge will have a hoot with the girls. Let *me* settle you in . . .' And she physically hauled him away, like a baker hefting a sack of flour.

Midge watched them go, open-mouthed. She'd never known what to make of women like Bobbie. She simply couldn't behave in such an obvious manner herself. Kenneth cast her a look over his shoulder that was at once apologetic, comically scared and amused. And Midge was alone. She hesitated. Whatever Bobbie said, Evaline and Millie didn't look as though they'd welcome interruption. As she surveyed the crowd, an older gentleman with a salt-and-pepper moustache very like Kenneth's badger-hair shaving brush threw a coat at her. It was a reflex to catch it, but she stared at him in confusion.

'Well, don't just stand there, gal!' he barked. 'Put it in the cloakroom.'

Midge's forehead crinkled. 'Sir, I don't work here,' she said. 'I'm a guest.'

'You are? Devil take it,' he sputtered, purple with embarrassment, snatching the coat and hurrying off.

Wonderful. When a passing waiter offered Midge a glass

of bubbly, she took one, even though she wasn't much of a drinker. And it was half past ten in the morning. She bore it off to a quiet corner from which to look for familiar faces, wait for Kenneth and ponder her lot.

On the outside, few women were more fortunate than Midge Camberwell. Her happiness had come to her relatively late in life, long after she had ceased to hope for anything of the sort, and it was all the more golden for that. But people said the same thing about Blue – a charmed life and all that – and it wasn't so straightforward. Blue had many blessings, certainly, but she carried her wounds, too.

Not only had Blue's girlhood been stained by war, but then her mother had died, devastating the little family on the hill. And it was this terrible and tragic event that had enabled Midge's own great happiness to take place.

If Audra had lived, Kenneth would still be the happiest of husbands; he would still be head over heels in love. Merrigan and Blue would have their mother, Elf would have his dear old friend and Midge would still be Margaret, living in East Dulwich, with her mother, in genteel mediocrity and suffocating chastity. If Kenneth hadn't been bowled over by grief, he would never have looked twice at her. She was plain where he was beautiful. She was ordinary where he was accomplished. Her life had been colourless while his was vibrant.

Yet it only took for them to be present at the same party one night to change all that: she a distant acquaintance of the hostess, invited to make up numbers; he present at the insistence of the host. Even widowed, broken and aimless, Kenneth added lustre to any event. They found themselves on the balcony at the same moment, taking refuge from the crush despite the cold. He found her a sympathetic listener and a bond was forged. He said afterwards that her impartial kindness made a refreshing change from all the women who pretended to care about his plight whilst really hoping their own chance would come if they hovered long enough. Women like Roberta. And it was true that Midge's concern was selfless – she would *never* have set her cap at Kenneth Camberwell. Even if she hadn't given up all hope of marriage, she would never have aimed so high.

They struck up a friendship, which quickly became more. Even when he took her to bed, she had no designs upon him. She didn't flatter herself that he found her beautiful. She didn't delude herself that he loved her. It was the need for physical comfort after so long celibate; it was the need for emotional closeness to fill the dark rift of Audra's loss. It was just one of those things.

Margaret was an old-fashioned sort of girl. Woman. Never the sort, by temperament or upbringing, to engage in a carnal dalliance. Yet that was exactly what she chose to do with Kenneth, because she loved him so much. And because she couldn't bear the iron-cold weight of her virginity one moment longer. It's often the atypical choices that bring us face-to-face with the bottom line of who we are; the shadows that mark out the light and make it clearer. Yes, Margaret Fawcett was wholesome, virtuous and ladylike. But on the night that Kenneth turned to her, his lovely face streaked with tears, his hands clumsy with need, she chose to say yes, because she knew she'd regret it for the rest of her life if she didn't.

She told herself not to expect more than one night. As he loosened the pins from her hair, she lectured herself sternly: *Even when life goes back to normal tomorrow, you must feel lucky, for at least you'll have had this*. Not sensible but sensual. An expanded Margaret, lusted after, even if temporarily, by an eligible man like Kenneth Camberwell. A Margaret who could give succour in unconventional ways, instead of merely toeing the line. This new sense of herself was as intoxicating as his hands peeling back her stockings, as heady as his breath on her lips. And life never did return to normal.

The following morning, she immediately broke her pact with herself and started yearning for more. She didn't feel lucky – she felt furious that she'd had to wait thirty-nine years for this, that life had withheld it until now.

From meeting to marriage took Kenneth and Midge just ten months. When he proposed, she tried to talk him out of it. She loved him too much to want him trapped through his own good manners, and she had too much pride. But he insisted.

And her life had transformed utterly. Suddenly she had not only a husband, but two wonderful stepdaughters. She lived in a house that seemed nothing short of luxurious to her. She was at the centre of a social circle that she would once have found aspirational, had she ever dared to aspire. Now that she was in it, she felt like a fish out of water.

A bell sounded to indicate that the pre-brunch mingling was at an end. Midge went to the table with relief; at least she'd be sitting beside Kenneth for a couple of hours. She saw him emerge from the other side of the bar, with not Roberta but the beautiful Cassandra Tilley attached to his arm. So he'd managed to escape the clutches of the dreaded Bobbie, but still hadn't come to find her. Midge sighed. She wasn't worried: Kenneth was an honourable man and Cassandra was the same age as Blue. But she couldn't deny that she found his enjoyment of the attention irritating.

At the table, another disappointment awaited her: there was a seating plan. Midge was seated between two men she barely knew. *And Bobbie'll be next to my husband*, she fumed as she took her seat. She wasn't, but she'd arranged the next worst thing. Kenneth was seated at the head of the table, for all the world as if he were presiding over the event, as if he were a special figure in Bobbie's life. And Kenneth loved to preside! So he did, keeping the top end of the table in stitches. Midge was too far away to hear the jokes. It was like sitting in a chilly spot, out of reach of the sun.

Well, it was only a breakfast, only one morning. Midge set

to and applied herself to making polite if pedestrian conversation with those around her. They all turned out to be perfectly pleasant. But from the corner of her eye she noticed that the seat next to Kenneth appeared to be a revolving door. Every time she looked, a different woman had secured it.

Finally it was over. Kenneth came and claimed her at last, in high spirits.

'Oh, I've missed you, Midgey.' He beamed, sliding an arm around her waist. 'Did you have a good time? I told you it'd be splendid fun, didn't I?' He nuzzled her neck.

For once, she pulled away. She was in no mood. They collected their coats and left among a flurry of goodbyes that set Midge's teeth on edge with impatience. On the walk home, Kenneth recounted all the gossip from his end of the table and Midge gritted her teeth and listened. Perhaps she should have said something, but women her age weren't brought up to criticise their husbands. Besides, Midge had grown very accomplished at guarding her tongue. Everything depended on it, after all.

Returning to Ryan's Castle was like returning to a world where everything made sense. Midge's haven. From the first moment she'd set foot in Ryan's Castle, she felt she belonged, even though Audra had been mistress here before her. Midge had fallen in love, hard, with Kenneth, and then she did so again with this house.

She didn't ever want to leave it, or Kenneth or the girls.

Though it was irrational, she couldn't help fearing that one day she would be cast out. She feared it so keenly that it threw a pall over her days, a shadow that dogged her every waking moment.

# Chapter Six

Delphine had a stroke of luck – her first in a very long time – at Richmond Station. The guard was involved in a heated dispute with a round lady in a lavender blouse, and he waved everyone else through impatiently. So she found herself leaving the station and following the crowd, soon arriving on a pretty side street lined with jewellery shops and hat shops and a chocolate shop – all manner of beautiful luxuries she would never be able to afford. It took her far too long to tear herself away from the lovely sights, and when she did she discovered more loveliness: a sunny green surrounded by beautiful old red-brick houses covered with misty purple flowers. Men in white were playing cricket; the polite thwack of ball on bat punctuated the morning air.

She spotted a tea room and went in and had a cup of tea and a pastry, even though it used up some of the hard-saved money she needed for . . . well, her life. Still, to allow herself this short respite, to set down her fears, even for one hour, felt like an unspeakable luxury, a luxury she *could* afford. Escape was dangerously euphoric.

It also allowed her to compose herself a little. She had been blown off course. She consulted her tube map and saw how it had happened. She'd meant to get off at Victoria, but she'd obviously fallen asleep and missed her stop. It was hardly surprising: she hadn't slept properly for years. It must have been the relief of being away from Foley and that house. It had been far too soon to let her guard down.

She checked the clock on the wall. It was still early; Muriel wouldn't even be wondering where she was yet. It wasn't too late to resume her original plan, which was to go to Victoria and from there catch a train to Sussex, where an old schoolfriend lived. So old a friend, in fact, that Delphine had never even mentioned her to Foley, which was perfect. She hadn't heard from Betty in years, but she'd never forgotten the name of her village, so she planned to go there and make enquiries. Betty had always been close to her family, so she wouldn't have gone far – Delphine hoped. As long as she could find Betty, surely she would be safe. Foley was clever and he was determined, but once she was out of London, how could he know where she was? It would be like picking a name out of a hat. She was sure Betty would help her. They'd been good friends, once.

This diversion, though, had caught her in an unexpected way. She would never have thought she'd be so affected by beauty and affluence – she'd had twenty-eight years without any, after all! Stupidly, she found herself wishing she could stay, but her only option was to stick to the plan. She could still be on a Sussex-bound train by midday, while Muriel was slicing plum cake and expecting her any minute.

'Visiting for the day are we, miss?' asked the waitress when she brought Delphine the bill.

Of course she didn't look like a local. Delphine nodded.

'Off to the river next?' the cheerful girl asked, as though that was the next thing visitors always did.

'Wh . . . wh . . .?'

'Where? Just cut straight across the green, miss, and follow that path. Five minutes, if that.'

Delphine nodded again, for simplicity's sake, and scrabbled for some coins. 'Th . . . th . . . thanks,' she said as she left.

'Oh, the poor lamb!' exclaimed the waitress, before Delphine was quite out of earshot. Delphine felt one side of her face flush.

She should go straight back to the station. The only sensible thing was to get far away from Foley, as fast as possible. But she wanted to see the river. She wanted to know if, like the houses, the people, the air, it was somehow different here in Richmond. The loop of the Thames that Delphine knew best, near her mother's home in Aldgate, was a brown, silty, sullen worm that writhed beneath Tower Bridge.

It *was* different. She emerged onto a wide, sunlit walkway, edged with large, white buildings that looked impossibly grand. Here, the river was green. It was spanned by a number of bridges and thick-clustered willows grew along the banks.

A heron, slate-grey and prehistoric, rose from the leafy cover and glided downriver. Ducks quacked and swans honked, for all the world as though passing the time of day. It was *beautiful*. Delphine had never known she so hungered for beauty until now. Heaven only knew she had little enough of her own.

She pulled her scarf up around her face to hide it. It wasn't scarf weather, but she'd worn a few extras that didn't fit in her bags. She was horribly hot, but she preferred to be covered up anyway.

Now that she'd seen the river, it was time to walk away, but still she lingered. What must it be like to live here? How did it dictate the shape of a life, to wake every morning to beauty, to spend your days surrounded by pump houses and palaces, by willows and dreaming water?

So she permitted herself one last luxury. She would take a short walk along the river, just as far as that graceful white bridge, then turn around and go back. She would walk as slowly as she possibly could, and concentrate with all her might on every inch of the way, on every footstep. Maybe if she did that, this place would imprint itself on her being. That way she would never forget it. And maybe, too, she would somehow imprint herself upon the place . . . and maybe that mutual impression would bring her back here one day, when everything was different. Like magic. But to make that happen, she would have to concentrate *very* hard.

# Chapter Seven

'It's Foster, of course!' said Blue, somewhat heatedly, after Merrigan and Tabitha had read the letter and dissolved into mirth, which Blue could not share. They were sitting by the river on yet another burnished late summer morning. Merrigan's little Cicely dozed in a basket, like Moses. Willows dipped wistful fingers into the water, which mirrored trees and sky and eternity.

'Yes, it's true,' gasped Tabitha, laughing so hard she was nearly sobbing. 'That is, in fact, his handwriting, and this is my letter paper. So he's left me an empty stationery case, has he? Gosh, little brothers are vile. Be glad you don't have one . . . Oh!' She straightened up. 'I'm so sorry, girls. Gracious, how *could* I say such a thing? I didn't mean . . .'

'It's all right, Tab, we know what you meant,' Blue placated her. 'This is about your brother, not ours. Really, this Foster business, it's not funny.'

'It jolly well is,' Merrigan argued.

'It's *not*! The poor boy! His *feelings*! I've already told Daddy.

Thanks to his breezy whim, a good friend's heart is about to be bruised. Thanks to Daddy, all and sundry think they have a shot at me, and they *don't*!'

'Foster is seventeen years old,' observed Tabitha, narrowing her eyes. 'His heart's not the organ he's concerned with.'

'*Tab!* You are shameless!'

'Well, it's true. No offence, darling, but once you put him straight he'll find someone else to pine after. It's not the end of the world. He'll bounce back.'

Blue remembered his yearning eyes at her party, his bobbing Adam's apple, and wasn't so sure. She hoped Tab was right, but seventeen was a tender age, at which feelings burned all the brighter for being discounted by everyone around. She liked to be careful with people. You never knew what they were dealing with.

'If you're that concerned, Blue, give him a try!' suggested Merrigan with an evil smile. 'As he says, he's from a good family. *And* he'd let you work!'

This time Blue permitted herself a smile. The thought of gauche, gawky Foster, whom she'd known since infancy, *letting* her do anything was quite *amusant*. 'No,' she said, watching a trio of ducks landing on the river, three overlapping wakes feathering behind them.

'Are you saying you don't find Tab's brother attractive? Are you insulted, Tab?' asked Merrigan, always happy to stir up mild levels of trouble.

'Not in the least,' said Tabitha, lying back on her elbows. 'He's a dear, but he's gormless. He doesn't have half my wit, looks or charm – thank God the pie sliced in my favour, say I! And honestly, he was meant to capture her *imagination*, for goodness' sake! Who woos a girl with talk of udders? I wash my hands . . .'

'I udderly agree,' cackled Merrigan, waking Cicely, who squawked and eyed them rather crossly.

Blue rolled her eyes and turned her back on them. They were a hilarious double act, but they could be wearing when one was preoccupied. She'd commanded her father to collar Foster at the next opportunity and explain – *clearly* – that it was all nonsense and not to be engaged with. It was Daddy's mess, he could clear it up. *And let that be the last of it!* she thought.

She loved watching the birds. Swans, geese and ducks congregated here in their dozens. *Birds of distinction*, she thought idly, then fished for her little notepad and pencil, liking the phrase. Impossible to imagine where it might come in handy, of course. She had notebooks full of such phrases – striking in the moment and applicable to nothing whatsoever when it came to writing anything useful.

'Squadron Leader Goose!' Kenneth used to say when Blue was small and used to wave in delight at geese flying overhead. She smiled at the memory.

A figure caught her eye, just along the river in the direction of the old Victorian lock. It was a woman, and she struck Blue as visibly, unbearably lonely. Blue sat up and shielded her eyes to look better. Perhaps it was the shabby coat that made her noticeable, or maybe it was the fact of a coat at all when the weather certainly didn't demand one. As for the *posture* of the poor thing! She shuffled along as if putting one foot in front of the other was an insurmountable difficulty. Her head was bowed and, if Blue's eyes weren't playing tricks, her shoulders were set at an odd angle. *Dejected*, decided Blue, her heart filling.

'I say, look at the . . .' she started to say, when a cacophony erupted. A clattering and shouting and then, of all things, a *horse* burst into sight. It was Albert the dairy horse, she saw at once, white coat churned to cream with sweat, his harness and one broken shaft waving wildly as he cantered towards Richmond Bridge. A few shrieks arose from various strollers and picnickers, who peeled out of Albert's path. But not the stranger. She continued shuffling along as though completely deaf to the furore.

'Is she *drunk*?' demanded Tabitha, following Blue's line of vision. 'Why doesn't she move? I say! I say!' she cried, waving furiously. But the woman carried on her plodding course while Albert thundered along on his, hooves skidding on the cobbles, the splintered shaft waving dangerously close to his own legs.

'He's going to fall,' cried Blue, leaping to her feet. 'Or knock that woman over.' She ran, shouting as she went. 'Hi! Move! Move! Runaway horse!'

At the very last minute, the woman snapped out of her

reverie and startled sideways. But she startled the wrong way and tumbled into the river with an almighty splash.

Blue hesitated. Falling into the water fully clothed wasn't ideal, but it wouldn't hurt, whereas Albert was stumbling now, the loose shaft checking his headlong flight. If the horse fell on these cobbles, it would ruin its knees, and ruined knees had spelled the end of many a horse's career. And Paul, who worked for the dairy, would be held to account for the loss. She leapt in front of Albert, vaguely aware of her sister's screams somewhere behind her, and waved her arms determinedly before the snorting animal.

'Stop, Albert!' she shouted, as he tittuped and slithered and made a half-hearted attempt at rearing. His front hooves waved somewhere around Blue's face and she heard Merrigan shriek again, but she ducked between his legs and rammed her shoulder into his massive chest. Then she grabbed the reins, close to his chin, and pulled down hard. 'Stop!' she commanded again, and was relieved when she felt all the fight go out of him. 'There, there,' she murmured. 'Silly chap. You're safe now. Stand easy, stand easy.'

'Thank you, Miss Blue, thank you!' called Paul, running towards them. Blue held the reins while he ran his hands over Albert's legs. 'I think we got away with it, miss, he seems fine. I owe you . . .'

'You owe me nothing, Paul. I'm only glad he didn't fall.'

'Me too, miss! I might've lost my job. Still, it's not every young lady would've stepped in there.'

Then Blue was crushed by a sisterly embrace and Merrigan was holding her close, saying, 'Oh, Blue' again and again.

'Where's that woman?' demanded Tabitha, following Merrigan, the baby basket swinging from her hand like a conker. 'The one who fell in the river?'

'Oh Lord, yes!' exclaimed Blue, running to the water's edge. For a horrible moment, she could see nothing besides the boats and birds, and envisaged the green waters closing over the stranger's head. Then Merrigan pointed and Blue saw a dark, sleek head bobbing like a seal. She was hanging on to the side of a rowboat for dear life, looking absolutely petrified. It must have been a devil of a shock.

'Are you all right there?' called Blue. 'Swim over! It's not far. We'll help you out.'

The woman didn't reply, but kept clinging and bobbing. 'She can't swim,' said Paul. 'I'll bet you. Hold Albert, if you please, Miss Blue. I'll go and help her.'

He jumped into a boat and thence to another until he reached the one to which the woman clung. It rocked as he climbed aboard, and the woman screamed, losing her grip. Blue's hands flew to her mouth, but Paul was on his knees in a trice. He seized the woman's coat, holding her by the scruff of the neck like a kitten. 'Take my hand, miss,' they heard him say.

'Golly, how fearfully exciting,' murmured Tabitha, dumping the baby basket on the cobbles, the better to concentrate.

'That's my child, not a bucket,' protested Merrigan.

'Your child is *heavy*! She's a small rhinoceros.'

Paul somehow manhandled the woman from boat to boat to the stone wall, where Blue and the others were waiting. With Paul hoisting her from below and Tabitha and Merrigan hauling at her arms, they wrestled her onto dry land. She collapsed in a soggy, shapeless heap on the cobbles. Paul hauled himself out and, thanking Blue again, led Albert away.

Blue crouched beside the stranger. 'Are you all right, dear? You're quite safe now. We'll take care of you. What's your name?'

The woman sat up and looked around. She opened and closed her mouth a few times but no sound came out. Stunned, Blue supposed. She noted the sodden, heavy clothes, the uneven shoulders and a large, roughly triangular pink stain covering her left cheek – a birthmark, perhaps. It marred an otherwise pretty face, the striking features of which were long dark hair, now a wet ribbon, and wide blue eyes which looked as if they had seen too many horrible things.

'What's your name?' asked Blue again, gently. 'I'm Ishbel Camberwell, but my friends call me Blue.'

# Chapter Eight

Gradually Delphine came to herself again. She'd survived the tumble into the river after all. The headlong flight towards the water, the fear of drowning, had been uncannily like her dream on the underground earlier. River water, thick and pungent, saturated her. She had wanted the place to imprint itself on her, but this was taking things a little far.

Three strange faces, all belonging to beautiful, elegant young women, were staring at her. Now was not the time to be thinking what Foley called her 'dopey Delphine thoughts'. One in particular – golden hair, dark eyes, pale skin – was looking at her in the most compassionate way.

'My friends call me Blue,' she was saying.

'D . . . D . . . Delphine,' said Delphine at last, holding out a wet hand. The golden girl – Blue – shook it.

'What a pretty name,' she said. 'And such a terrible fright,' she added. 'Do you live nearby?'

*Worlds away.* Delphine shook her head.

'Then you must come home with us and dry out. You can't possibly go on your way like that.'

'No!' The prospect of a further delay when she had already dallied too much, of dripping all over a stranger's home, parrying questions, shocked her into brief eloquence. 'It's warm.' She'd learned that short, simple phrases were best. It gave her a rather abrupt manner, but the gentler phrases she preferred were always just out of reach. 'I'll dry. But thanks.'

'Nonsense,' said a second young lady, who looked much like the first but with brown hair instead of fair, a stockier build and a formidable expression. 'You might not catch cold, but you'll be dreadfully uncomfortable, all damp and squidgy. Besides, you look a fright! Come along, it's not far.'

'I say!' said the third girl – black curls, eyes as green as grass. 'Where's your stuff? Delphine, was it? Did you have a purse or anything? Only . . . that's not it there, is it?'

Delphine looked, and to her horror saw her handbag floating away down the river. Behind it, if she wasn't mistaken, was the long, eel-like strap of her shoulder purse. She started to wail. She couldn't help it.

'Golly,' said Grass Eyes. 'I deduce it is then. Dash it all, girls. Shall I go and ask one of the boat men if they can punt after it or something?'

'Worth a try,' said Merrigan. 'Scootle off, love. Only don't waste time flirting!'

Then there were two. Sisters, Delphine felt sure, not only

because of the resemblance but because of the ease between them, the way they tucked their hands beneath her armpits and helped her to her feet without agreeing to do it out loud.

'Now don't worry!' Blue was saying. 'Tab will get your purse back – she thrives on a challenge. Even if she can't, it's not the end of the world, we can easily lend you money to get you home. You'll be quite safe. Where is it that you live?'

She was, quite literally, speechless.

*I've left home and I can't go back. I ain't been safe for five years. It's not just today's money, it's* all *me money. And it is, it really is the end of the world* . . . All these thoughts ran through Delphine's head, but that's where they stayed.

'Never mind,' said Blue, as if she sensed all was not as it should be. 'We'll get you clean clothes and a hot drink, that's the first thing. Tab can follow. But you're *not* to worry.' She said it rather determinedly, and stuck her arm through Delphine's, ignoring the stain of river water that spread from Delphine's coat across the sleeve of her pretty lemon dress. Then they set off, climbing some stone steps and then up a hill.

The house was worse than Delphine had feared, which was to say that it was far grander and lovelier.

'Thi . . . this is where you l . . . live?' she asked in wonder as they stepped into the cool, airy hall.

Blue nodded. 'Lucky, aren't I? I say *I*, not *we*, because Merrigan's married now and she doesn't live here any more. But she's only round the corner. That's her daughter, Cicely.'

Delphine hadn't noticed the baby basket before. She peered in and was again moved to words. 'Oh! What a dear little girl. What a cherub. C . . . c . . . could I . . .? Oh, I'm sorry, that wouldn't do. I'm w . . . wet.'

'Hold her?' asked Merrigan. 'Of course you can. Well, we'll maybe get you dry first. But then be my guest; she's an absolute hound for cuddles.' She wandered off, calling for someone called Midge.

'Come on,' said Blue, holding out a hand. The gesture was so natural and sisterly, and Delphine had missed all that so much, that she took it.

'This is my room,' said Blue, leading her into a room painted the powder blue of butterflies' wings, a shade that made Delphine think of palaces and princesses and all manner of things she never normally had cause to think about. White muslin curtains hung at the window, which overlooked a garden. Delphine could see a flash of green lawn, and leaves fluttered around the casement. There were round bowls of heaped flowers – blue, pink, violet and cream – and a light fitting made of crystal droplets. An involuntary sigh escaped from Delphine. Such loveliness had power; she could feel it.

'I wonder . . .' mused Blue, eyeing her. 'Merrigan's closest to you in height, but I think her things would be terribly loose on you. You're slender like Midge and me, but we're taller. Let me have a rummage.'

She opened a large cupboard and Delphine marvelled at the spill of colour that shone out.

'This might do,' Blue said, handing a rose-pink dress to Delphine. 'And perhaps this . . .' A cream cardigan followed. 'Undies . . .' muttered Blue, producing some, and finally a fluffy white towel. 'I'll give you some privacy. Help yourself to the washstand and just come down when you're ready. I'll get some tea going. Anything else you need?'

Delphine shook her head. 'You're s . . . s . . . so kind. I don't l . . . like to . . .'

'But you must.' Blue gave her arm a squeeze. 'Take your time.' And she vanished.

Alone in the blue bedroom, Delphine felt all at sea. To be so trusted! She was a complete stranger and it must be apparent that this was not her usual milieu. Necklaces and earrings were strewn over a dressing table on top of a white crocheted cover, along with knick-knacks and books and scarves . . . Such temptation! Of course, Delphine was no thief, but how could Blue know that? *Not everyone is like Foley*, she thought, moved. Then she took off her wet clothes and set about making herself clean and dry.

# Chapter Nine

What a day! As if Bobbie's birthday hadn't been excitement enough, Midge had scarcely changed out of her silk dress when her stepdaughters returned from the river with a stranger in tow and a story about a runaway horse. *Only at Ryan's Castle*, thought Midge fondly, coming to see what could be done.

But when the poor waif the girls had fished out of the river came downstairs, Midge merely brought tea and crumpets, with a tot of brandy for the newcomer, then left them to it. Such a pitiful-looking creature, shrinking inside Blue's old rose dress as if she didn't deserve to wear it. The poor woman looked as though having a third person fussing over her might just about finish her off.

She returned to the drawing room, where she had arranged lilies only a few hours ago, glad to have a little time alone after the excitement of the morning. The creamy blooms glowed in the afternoon sun. And Audra, beautiful Audra, smiled down from her frame above the fireplace, a painting which put the wedding photograph of Kenneth and his funny-looking second wife to shame.

Midge stood before the painting, as still as a churchgoer before the Stations of the Cross. Audra had such a pretty face, and a generous smile just like dear Blue's. She had brown, wavy hair which glinted like sunlight dancing off conkers. She was absolutely the sort of woman men would fall in love with. The stupid thing was, sometimes Midge wished she were still here. Not as Kenneth's wife, of course, but as Midge's friend. Midge had never had a great many friends.

She had Kenneth now, of course. But it wasn't easy to share her vulnerabilities or her darker feelings with him. And there was Elf. It was easier to approach the shadows with him, but still, he was a man and it wasn't the same.

As for Merrigan and Blue, they were just adorable, but Midge was their stepmother and she didn't think it fitting to wail on their shoulders. Besides, the things that troubled her the most were things that they, of all people, must never be troubled with. For Midge loved them – absolutely loved them.

She'd been so nervous about meeting them. Two accomplished, sophisticated young ladies – how would they judge her? Two girls who had lost their mother tragically young. How would they feel about her coming into their midst? It had been only two years after Audra's passing.

But they had welcomed her more warmly than she could ever have hoped. They were happy that their father wouldn't be alone any more, and excited to meet her, glad to have a mother figure again. They were perceptive, too: they could see that Midge felt insecure and took pains to make her feel valued. They were a trio now, the Camberwell girls. She hoped Audra would be happy about that.

She turned away sharply. She spent too much time gazing at that painting. It was no oracle. It couldn't offer her redemption.

And with that, an idea came to Midge. A way to forget about everything that had happened once, and all that was not quite right now. A way to feel a sense of purpose, like the young women of today, with their plans and ambitions. Something all for her. She looked around, wondering if she dared. It was a lovely room, unchanged in all the time Midge had been here – for how could you improve upon perfection? Even so, change was good, wasn't it? The essence of life itself, Elf said. A project might be good for her, carry her forward through the days, perhaps ease the fear. Yes, a project. She would redecorate.

# Chapter Ten

'I can't go home! I can't, I can't!' exclaimed Delphine. She stopped in astonishment. Not only had she said it without stammering, but she hadn't meant to say it at all.

There were three of them again now. Tabitha Foxton, the friend, had come in with the news that Delphine's bags were lost to the Thames. All three were peppering her with questions. They didn't know her circumstances. To them it was the most natural thing in the world to want to help her home, as if that would solve everything.

She hadn't wanted to explain. Years of living with Foley had left her incapable of confiding in *anyone*, let alone strangers. And she was afraid. What if leaving a husband was frowned upon in a household like this? It might be the twenties, but marriage was still sacrosanct to most people. What if they insisted on taking her back? You never knew with people, that's what Delphine had learned. But they were relentlessly, exhaustingly caring.

'Do you have a phone at home so we can call your husband?'

'Where do you live? How much is a ticket?'

'Would you like one of us to go with you, to explain to your husband that you need a lot of looking after?'

'That *is* what husbands are for!'

'Not *all* they're for, darling.'

'*Tab!*'

In the end Delphine cracked. And now she had to explain. She hadn't taken more than a polite sip of the brandy that Mrs Camberwell had brought her – she didn't like the taste and she'd never been a drinker – but she swallowed the rest now for its fiery vigour. Then, haltingly, she told them the bare facts of her situation. It took a painfully long time, and they sat very still, mouths slightly open as they listened. She almost felt sorry for them when a particularly tricky consonant held her up at a crucial moment, but to their credit they didn't interrupt. At last she came to the end of her story, to Richmond, and sat for a moment staring at her hands.

In the silence that followed she looked up. 'If y . . . you c . . . could lend me the . . . m . . . m . . . money to get to Sussex, I p . . . promise I'll pay it back as soon as I can. I'd need to get a job. But I swear I w . . . w . . . wouldn't forget.' She hardly dared to hope.

'Well, yes, of course,' said Blue immediately. 'And a change of clothes. And a book to read on the journey and something to eat on the train and whatever you need. Only . . .'

'Only what?' asked Merrigan, looking at her sister as if she were reading her mind.

'Isn't there some other way we could help?' Blue reached out and took Delphine's hand. 'Call the police? Support you? Let you stay here with us. A man like that should be behind bars!'

'Blue,' said Merrigan in warning tones. Despite Blue's kindness, Delphine felt her spine pressing into the back of the chair. Even the *thought* of confronting Foley, or telling anyone official what he'd done, was too terrifying for words. Blue might live in a world of right and wrong and justice being done, but it wasn't like that where Delphine came from.

'Sorry,' said Blue. 'I know very little about it, of course. Only I hate to think of you being alone and so far away. What if you don't find your friend? What if she's moved away?'

Delphine didn't have answers because these were questions she'd had to ignore in order to leave at all – along with other worries, like whether she would be welcome in Betty's new household. It had been sixteen years. Betty must be married by now. What would her husband think? What would he be like? Would there be any room to stay with them, even for a few nights?

It was all very well to throw herself on their mercy until she found a job, but unemployment was much worse in other parts of the country than in London – everyone knew that. She didn't even know what Betty's own financial situation might be. What if she imposed herself on an overstretched, overburdened family of – effectively – strangers? What if there was no work and she couldn't pay back the Camberwells? What then?

'That's quite a good point actually, dear,' said Merrigan, in a voice more gentle than her usual tone. The endearment was aimed at Delphine, and it surprised her. 'I understand it was the best plan you had, but it's not fool-proof, is it? Not without its holes?'

Delphine's eyes filled. She realised suddenly that it had been a very long day – and it was only lunchtime. It seemed a lifetime ago that she had woken beside Foley after her usual fitful sleep, then risen in silence when he poked her, to make his breakfast and see him off to work at the docks.

She looked around the room: tall sash windows with curtains the colour of old gold drawn back with fat swags; a thick rug on a polished floor; an ornate fireplace with a marble mantel scattered with ornaments and pictures and bits of life thrown down hastily – keys, notes, an earring. Birds chattered in the garden. A grandfather clock ticked the ponderous moments away. Peaceful. She felt a thousand miles from home. But Foley was just a tube ride away. Delphine shivered.

'There, there. It was the best plan you had,' said Merrigan again. 'Your only option, I suppose?'

Delphine nodded.

'But perhaps not any more?'

Delphine hesitated. She couldn't imagine what was being suggested. Only short minutes ago, even coming home with them had seemed too excruciatingly presumptuous. Yet now she was here, though it felt strange and imposing, it also felt safe. And since her meagre threads of independence had disappeared down the Thames, she'd have to accept help from *somebody*, or she'd be in a proper pretty pickle. Perhaps they weren't strangers any more than Betty was now.

'Exactly!' said Blue, shooting her sister a look of gratitude. 'Not any more.'

The plan in the short term was for Delphine to stay at Ryan's Castle for a couple of nights while they all had a good think about what could be done. For Delphine, the sense of safety was overwhelming. There was no way Foley could find her here. The same surge of relief she'd experienced on the train that morning came over her like a fog. She wanted nothing more than to lie down and sink into a deep sleep.

But the first thing was to explain the situation to Midge, whom they found looking very pensive in a room along the hall. She gave Delphine a warm handshake of welcome. 'We'll have a special dinner for you tonight, Delphine,' she promised.

Next in the order of business was for Delphine to meet her host, Mr Camberwell. By now, Merrigan had taken Cicely home, and Tabitha had disappeared to look out old clothes for Delphine, since she was shorter than Blue and slighter than Merrigan. So Blue towed Delphine to her father's study, a quiet room overlooking the street and lined with books. Delphine had never seen so many books. A great many of them were brown.

'Daddy,' said Blue, when he looked up, 'I have someone for you to meet. This is Delphine. She's going to be staying with us for a few nights. It's a bit of a story – may we tell you?'

Mr Camberwell – Kenneth, he insisted – was a dream of a man, warm and sympathetic like his daughter. *Perfect people in their perfect home*, thought Delphine. He looked like Blue too, tall and slim, with a proud nose and thick golden hair waving back from a high brow. His eyes were sparkling grey where Blue's were dreamy brown, but otherwise she was a right chip off the old block. He ushered them in and sat them down, apologising for the uncomfortable chairs, and Delphine listened to her own story being told by Blue.

'Good God!' said Kenneth, looking disturbed. 'Appalling. Simply appalling. I'm so very sorry, and of course you must stay with us. I wouldn't hear of anything else. Be at home, Delphine, and rest assured that we will do whatever we can to help you. Most, most troubling. Life can throw the most terrible things in our path, but it's astonishing what we can survive. "Healing is a matter of time, but it is sometimes also a matter of opportunity." Hippocrates, you know. Let us be your opportunity, my dear.'

Delphine wondered what this elegant patriarch, with his lovely home and his gracious family, had experienced that made him talk like that. The war, she assumed. With men these days it was almost always the war. She nodded and thanked him, wishing she could say so much more but afraid to try.

It was hot and airless in the study and tiredness overwhelmed her again. Blue noticed and pulled her to her feet. 'Thank you, Daddy. You're a gem. I *might* just forgive you for the other thing because you've been such a trooper with Delphine.'

*What other thing?* wondered Delphine.

'Ah,' said Kenneth standing up and embracing his daughter. 'I really do feel like the most ghastly oaf, Blue, darling. I'd take it back if I could. But sadly, er, another letter came for you this morning.'

He picked up a letter from his desk. Blue's wide mouth compressed into a straight line and Delphine saw her shoulders rise and fall.

'Spare me your wrath, oh daughter of mine,' he pleaded, only half in jest.

'Oh, Daddy. I know I can't stay mad at you forever. Only . . .'

'Only another day or so?' he suggested.

'Maybe a week . . .' She smiled, and led Delphine from the study, tucking the letter into her dress pocket.

She showed Delphine to a spare room, beautifully made up and quiet and clean. This was all Delphine had time to notice before she fell into the deep, dreamless sleep she craved.

# Chapter Eleven

Blue was so upset by Delphine's story that she hurried out to see Elf, who lived in what they called the Cottage, at the bottom of the garden. Really it was more of a cabin, built of logs. It long pre-dated the Camberwell family, so they didn't know who had built it or why. As girls, Merrigan and Blue had played Cowboys and Indians there with Tabitha and, when he was old enough, Foster, who had been regularly tied up and tortured. They would all drag tired feet homeward at the end of a long day's scalping and rain dancing, covered in cobwebs.

When Elf came to live with them, Audra had swept, dusted and scoured. She'd even sewn curtains and a decorated bedspread, though needlework wasn't one of her natural talents and there had been many pricked fingers and unladylike exclamations.

It was entirely unchanged since the day Elf had arrived. Merrigan and Blue, then aged fifteen and eleven, had watched arm in arm, wondering who this strange man was and why he was to live in their garden.

'Girls, this is my dear old friend, Miles Elphwick,' said Audra. 'Miles, meet Merrigan and Ishbel. We call her Blue.' And of course, he immediately became Elf.

It was like having a second father. He was a year or two older than Kenneth, and whereas Kenneth was outgoing and mercurial, Elf liked to daydream and reflect, like Blue. Back then, they didn't know why he was there, but they came to understand that the first year of the war had been bad for him – very bad. Now he was as much a part of Ryan's Castle as any of them. It felt as though he'd been there forever. 'Moss could grow on him!' Merrigan sometimes said, and it was true that Elf rarely left the Cottage and even less frequently ventured down Richmond Hill. Blue couldn't imagine life without him.

Elf was one of those new and mysterious creatures – a psychoanalyst. Well, they weren't *totally* new, of course, but not everyone had one in the garden. He had even studied with the great Carl Jung in Switzerland for a time. Elf thought a great deal about the collective unconscious and life after death and other transpersonal matters.

He was Blue's best listening ear when she was unhappy. In the time after Audra died, only Elf could comfort her. Merrigan and her father were wrapped in their own, deeply personal griefs. Other people meant well, but said things like 'She's gone to a better place', or 'Time heals all wounds', and even, memorably, in the case of one whiskered friend of her father's, 'Tally-ho, old chap.' ('I shouldn't have believed it if I hadn't heard it myself, darling,' Merrigan often marvelled when she recalled those days.)

Today the heat of the last days had built to a crescendo. The sky had thickened into blotting paper, darkening to the colour of a bruised eye. Blue could feel thunder, though it hadn't come yet. She rapped on Elf's door and went in without waiting for an answer.

'Blue, darling!' he cried, looking up from his work and taking off his glasses. As usual, a pile of books sat crooked at his side, a second tower of books teetered on the floor next to him and the desk was spread with papers. He rarely saw patients these days, but pursued his studies voraciously.

Blue hugged him. 'Call me something else.' She gave a little laugh. 'I seem to be everyone's darling lately.'

Elf smiled his crinkly smile which made his eyes narrow and rummaged in the cupboard for a plate and some chocolate biscuits. 'Ishbel, my young friend,' he amended, handing her the plate and moving to the couch, clutching two biscuits. 'Better?'

'Better.' Blue adopted her usual position, sitting mermaid-style on the red rug on the floor, and took a bite. Elf did likewise, scattering crumbs over his moss-green pullover of indeterminate fashion origin.

Blue took three letters out of her jacket pocket and brandished them at him. 'Three!' she said. 'Received over the course of a week. I thought all the nonsense would have died away by now, but I see I was being far too optimistic. I still cannot *believe* my father could be so imbecilic.'

Elf shook his head. 'If it's any consolation, neither does he. But none of us can turn the clock back, nor deny our more foolish selves.'

'It's such an *intrusion*.' She sighed. 'I've come to dread the sound of the postman. It sends me into spirals of thought. Should I reply firmly and explain? Or will it all end sooner if I don't enter into it in any way? Then I think of the poor men waiting and waiting and never hearing anything, and I feel I *must* write. Then I feel angry – why should I have to waste my time writing replies? I never asked them to write in the first place! How I am to make progress with my writing if I have to keep stopping every five minutes to write love letters? Or non-love letters, in fact.'

'Are you really not interested at *all*, Blue? Three letters, and none of them *remotely* tempting? You are of age, after all.'

Blue tried to slay him with a glance, but she wasn't very good at evil looks. 'Absolutely *not*!' she huffed. 'Men would be a distraction now. Goodness, I'm only twenty-one. There's aeons for all that. And writing is so . . .'

She trailed off. It was difficult to explain quite how much it meant to her. Since she had first discovered that capturing thoughts and images, words and ideas, gave her hope, could seemingly heal her of any distress, it had become a compulsion to sift through the world and make sense of it, finding ways to transcend the sadness and celebrate the goodness.

'How *is* your writing going?'

Blue had always valued Elf's support, especially since Merrigan was dubious about her dreams. It wasn't that she doubted Blue's ability, but she didn't think her sister should shut herself away 'and moon about in bowers and such' as she put it.

'It's no *life*!' she would insist. 'You become so obsessed, Blue, when you're writing. We might all disappear for six months and you wouldn't know anything about it! What about making your way in the world? What about starting a family of your own? Commas and paragraphs can't keep you warm at night.'

Blue felt differently. Many of her happiest hours had been spent reading in bed. But all she said was, 'If you all disappeared for six months it would make a gem of a story! Where would you all go – and why?' Merrigan had sulked.

'Slow, frustrating, daunting,' she answered Elf. Her face broke into a wide smile. 'And utterly magical! Oh, Elf, it's the most exciting thing in the world. I can't marry yet, I just can't! I know I can't stay in Ryan's Castle forever, but I just want to get somewhere first! Perhaps when I have a published article or two under my belt, and the first draft of a dreadful novel piled up in the corner of my room, perhaps then I'll have enough momentum to think about other things. But I'm not there yet.'

'Well, perhaps there's something in that,' mused Elf. 'Sometimes it's easier to concentrate on one thing at a time.'

'Although, if I'm perfectly honest, Merrigan does have a

point,' Blue conceded. I do disappear from real life when I'm writing. Is there something wrong with me?'

Elf looked around at his desk, his books and papers. 'I think you're asking the wrong person. For me, this *is* life, this realm of thought and ideas. But we both know that I'm not here for any enviable reason. Oh, *I'm* content, but you wouldn't be. You're young and beautiful. You wouldn't be happy if you lived like this now.'

'I know.' Blue sighed. 'I do know. But sometimes I long for total retreat. Imagine never having to waste time talking or eating or brushing your hair . . . But it would be impractical, I suppose.'

Elf nodded. 'And Merrigan would have something to say about it.'

Just as he said it, the storm broke at last. Thunder crashed and a sudden, sharp downpour of rain curtained the windows.

Blue laughed. 'Yes, that would basically be Merrigan's reaction!'

Elf chuckled. 'Have you written today?'

Blue sighed. 'No. Something's happened. Something utterly tragic, in point of fact, Elf. I was at the river with Merry and Tab. My plan was to go out early, see the girls, then come home and work. *But . . .*'

She told Delphine's story for the second time, but whereas with her father she had been as brief as possible for Delphine's sake, now she could open her heart.

'Elf, why do people *do* such things? I despair sometimes, I really do. I mean, there was the war, and so many people damaged or dead. Haven't we learned *anything*? For a man to hit his own *wife*? And there's worse than hitting, I'm certain of it. She didn't say much – she struggles to say anything at all – but I can see it in her face that she's been to hell.'

'The poor woman. What do you mean she struggles to say anything? Is she shy?'

'More than shy. She looks as if she would disappear off the face of the earth if she could. She has quite a stammer, but that's the least of it really . . . It's more as if her thoughts keep sliding away out of her grasp. It's almost as if she's swimming in and out of consciousness, though she didn't faint or anything.'

'Dissociation. When someone's been under a huge amount of strain, for a long time, they can detach, as a way to survive.'

Blue nodded. 'I remember when Mother died. I could be in a room but not take in one jot of the conversation. As if only my body were there.'

'That's it. Perhaps with time and kindness your new friend will come back to herself, and then she might find it easier to communicate.'

'I hope you're right. I can't bear it, Elf, sometimes I really can't bear the world and all the cruelty in it. And yet, look! Wondrous!' She nodded at the navy-purple sky beyond the window, the press of trees and rain about the cabin and the occasional shiver of lightning that darted through the garden.

Beauty always fortified her. She got up to boil the kettle, lighting the temperamental stove with an expertise borne of much practice. 'Go back to your work, Elf. I'll sit here and read until it eases off a bit.'

She made tea for them both, with more biscuits, and sat in her usual spot, the rain hissing down close by. She tried reading one of Elf's obscure, esoteric tomes, but after a few pages it made her head spin, so, sheepishly, she pulled the letters from her pocket.

# Chapter Twelve

Darling Blue,

You know, I never really thought of it before – you and I. But now that I have, what a match! I know your father said to write anonymously, but I don't think I've got the patience for that. Besides, we've known each other too long for me to say anything much at all without giving it away.

He also said to capture your imagination. Well, I can say flat out that I don't know where to start with that. I'm not romantic, if romance is those quirky little gestures and deeds that speak a secret language. I can't think of them – they don't come to me. I don't read books or admire paintings or shed a tear over the string section. I like my life. I like people and the things that happen. I like the world. I prefer it to a flight of fancy. So I'm not really writing in the way your father suggested at all. I don't want to capture your imagination. I don't want to be chosen for you by Ken.

Don't know why I'm writing at all, come to that. I could just call round and sit down with you and chat. Or take you out on the river, if

*I thought we'd survive the heat! But there's something, after all, about the idea of writing. Perhaps it's cowardice. Perhaps it seems easier to receive a polite note of refusal than to see the look of incredulity on your face when an old friend seems to take leave of his senses, and hear you say, 'Dorian, don't be a fool! We're friends, that's all.' It's not just cowardice though. It's private, this writing things down. Makes me better able to say what I want to than when I talk. Oddly compelling, this idea of your father's.*

*We've always had a good time together, you and I, and we've never had a falling-out. I'm always pleased to see you. I really don't know why I didn't think of this before. I'm not much good at the apple sauce — telling a girl her eyes are like stars and all that (yours are, but I bet you could think of a dozen better ways to describe them, and I bet every other goof writing to you is saying the same thing).*

*Let's dud up and go out dancing, Blue. Let's drink champagne and get a little fizzy, but not drunk. Let's dance with each other and only each other and pretend there's no one else in the room. Let's go outside afterwards and stagger around in the moonlight. Let's go on a date, give it a try. But only if you want to. And if you don't, I hope we can carry on being friends. You can't blame a chap for trying.*

*Love, and a cheeky kiss,*
*Dorian*

*My dear Miss Camberwell,*

*I hope this letter finds you well and content in your castle! I am a stranger to you, but I saw Miss Forrester's lavish account of your party in the newspaper and it made me smile. Reading her words, one might imagine you quite the fairy-tale damsel, sighing in a tower and clasping your hands as you dream of true love. Then one looks at your picture (very lovely, if I may say) and suspects the case is quite different.*

*I imagine you to be a thoroughly modern woman, though with an old-fashioned soul, perhaps. I imagine you to live and love every day to the best of your ability and to have interests and ambitions beyond those of husband and family – though perhaps including those. I imagine you had a somewhat complex reaction to your father's announcement! (Did he forewarn you? Miss Forrester says you looked as surprised as anyone.)*

*But why should I, a total stranger, imagine you at all? I must admit, I'm intrigued. Yes, I'm a romantic, and a bachelor of thirty-two who hopes one day to find his heart's partner. A picture of a beautiful young lady, therefore, was bound to catch my eye. And the story! Hard to imagine such a thing happening in this day and age, and I admit it causes me no little discomfort. You are not your father's chattel, to be competed for and won in that way. Yet I find myself picking up a pen, even though we have never met and I cannot imagine why a lady such as yourself could possibly wish to spend her valuable time reading the rambling letters of strangers. Odd, when one finds oneself acting against one's proper judgement.*

*An out-of-character impulse, to write this letter. Yet if we only ever acted in character, what a narrow range our lives would span. I am content to be a fool, if foolishness might open up an unexpected avenue. And if not, nothing is lost, except your time in reading this, for which I hope you will forgive me.*

*Capture your imagination? How could I hope to? The imagination is perhaps the most precious faculty we possess; as subtle as the colours of the sea and as personal as a thumbprint. Yours will not fire in precisely the same way as mine, nor mine as your father's, nor that of my small nephew. Nor, may I add, as that of the young lady bringing me my third cup of coffee as I sit in the Silver Spoon and write this. Her face expresses disapproval of fellows who take up her table space to write letters in her cafe. Nevertheless, this is a pleasant way to pass the morning.*

*I hope I have not intruded. I hope you are as blessed as you look and as happy as you are beautiful. I have no expectation whatsoever that you might wish to write back. Nevertheless, it seems rude to impose a letter upon you without giving any sort of return address, so that you may have at least the opportunity to tell me not to write again. I do not live in Richmond. I am merely staying nearby for the next two months or so on business, so if you did wish to reach me you could always leave a note at the Pheasant in Barnes.*

*With very sincere warm wishes,*
*L. W.*

*Darling Blue,*

*Golly, you're swell. Oh Lord. I've gone right in there . . .*

But Blue couldn't bear to reread poor Foster's letter. So eager. So awkward! Too painful.

She wanted to believe Tab, that his feverish words were the product of libido and a passing fancy, but she knew Foster and he wasn't that boy. Or perhaps she was naive and all boys were that boy.

'If you would consent to write back to me . . . I'd be the happiest boy that ever lived . . .'

Had she done the right thing, asking her father to speak to him? Her thinking had been that if he took back his words, it would somehow nullify them and all the harm they had done. But hadn't it gone further than that already? Foster had written to *her*. He had told her something that she couldn't forget. And she felt terrible.

'Please write back, darling . . .'

Perhaps she should. Nothing too serious. Nothing intense and guilt-ridden. Just a few words to put him straight – kindly. Or should she leave it to her father? Oh Lord, she just didn't know. There was no etiquette guide for a situation like this! It was – in typical Kenneth Camberwell style – unprecedented.

As for the others . . . she couldn't believe they'd made her smile. Her pride wouldn't let her admit it, after the fuss she had made, but she was only human, after all. She couldn't help feeling flattered – and curious. The mysterious L.W., who professed to find her so intriguing, had her a little intrigued in return! And as for Dorian! Well, for heaven's sake . . . She'd never entertained the idea either. And she shouldn't now. She really, really shouldn't . . .

# Chapter Thirteen

Avis was out shopping, so when the doorbell jangled, Midge ran to answer it. It was Clemmie Foxton, Tabitha and Foster's mother.

'What a lovely surprise!' exclaimed Midge, and she meant it. She found gruff Mr Foxton rather off-puttingly old-fashioned at times. She could easily understand how Foster had come to droop in his shadow, like a young sapling. Anthony expected a great deal from both his children, and so far Tabitha had done nothing but kick up her heels, while Foster had yet to grow into whatever it was that he would become. It was easy to imagine storm clouds gathering there. Clemmie, on the other hand, was feminine and fun. She was pretty, and had further endeared herself to Midge by being one of the only local women *not* to flirt with Kenneth at every opportunity.

'Won't you come in? Avis is out at the moment, but if you have time I can make us some tea.'

'Thank you, Midge, I will.' Clemmie entered with her gracious smile and took the proffered seat in the drawing room, with its view of the long and lovely lawn. Meanwhile, Midge ran around the kitchen preparing a tray.

'I've even found cake!' she announced as she rejoined her neighbour.

Clemmie beamed. 'That's not hard in Ryan's Castle,' she observed. 'Your Avis is a treasure. Mrs Porter does a wonderful Sunday roast, but she disapproves of sweet treats.'

'Let me cut you some lemon sponge,' offered Midge, and Clemmie came to sit opposite her.

'I hope you don't mind me calling unannounced,' said Clemmie. 'I was just passing on my way home from my Ladies' Circle luncheon and . . . well . . .' She looked troubled suddenly.

'Are you all right, Clemmie?' asked Midge.

'It's Foster. I suppose I just wanted to talk to someone I thought might be sympathetic. I thought of you. Tabitha hasn't . . . said anything to you about him, has she?'

Midge was surprised, and somewhat gratified. She and Clemmie had never been on confidential terms. She poured the tea and sat back. 'No, she hasn't. But I suppose she'd be more likely to talk to Merry or Blue than to me. What's wrong?' Was this about that dratted letter? Did Clemmie even *know* about that? Midge didn't want to betray anyone's secrets.

'He's seemed very down lately, to me. Anthony says I'm imagining things and not to fuss.'

Oh, how Midge hoped it wasn't the letter. 'It's a difficult age.'

'Yes. Anthony doesn't have much patience with Foster's . . .

sensitivities. But I'm his mother and I just have a feeling some-thing's wrong.'

'An affair of the heart? That sort of thing?'

Clemmie looked surprised. 'Oh! I hadn't even thought of that. He still seems so young to me. It's something at school, Midge, I'm sure of it.'

*Not the letter then!* thought Midge with relief. 'The pressure of work? He only has a year before university, doesn't he?'

'That's right. And I'm sure it doesn't help – Anthony expects great things, after all. But then, Foster's always been bright, so I don't think that's it.' Clemmie tugged on one curl – a gesture Midge had often seen Tabitha make. 'Might I tell you what I think, even though I have no proof whatsoever?'

'Of course.'

'Foster's always loved his music, as you know. He was always fiddling away around the house. He used to talk about his music teacher *all* the time – how talented he is, how inspiring. Now he doesn't mention him at all and the violin playing's stopped. I asked him about it and he said that Mr Mathews doesn't feel he has any real talent. And all the spirit seems to have gone out of him since then. I think this fellow has killed his joy for music. I even wonder sometimes if he's . . . *bullying* him. But Anthony says it's all nonsense and that it's a first-class school with only the very best masters. And of course he doesn't think music's important. He says it should only ever be a hobby, though I'm not sure that's how Foster felt about it.'

'Heavens! I'm so sorry, Clemmie. It's all news to me, I'm afraid – I can't shed any light. Is there anything I can do?'

'Thank you, you're a dear. No, I think for now I must just keep an eye on him. I can't go about casting aspersions on well-qualified teachers when I might be completely mistaken. And will you keep it to yourself, please? Anthony keeps telling me to let the matter drop. He loves Foster, but I think he feels it's a criticism of *him*, of the school he chose, when I keep saying something's wrong.'

'I understand.' Midge raised the teapot questioningly but Clemmie shook her head. 'You will let me know, won't you, if I can help at all?'

Clemmie nodded and finished off her cake. 'Goodness, that was delicious. Yes, I will. And thanks, Midge, it's nice to be able to tell someone what's been on my mind.'

The clock struck three. Clemmie gulped down the last of her tea. 'I hadn't realised it was so late. Must dash. Heavens,' she added, taking a last look around her as she got to her feet. 'Ryan's Castle is just wonderful, isn't it? Such a beautiful room, this. I've always loved it.'

Now was not the time to tell Clemmie that it was soon to be changed forever. Midge showed her out then went to clear the tea things. Was she doing the right thing? Everyone loved Ryan's Castle just as it was. Everyone!

Midge had lost no time once she decided to decorate. She'd gone to Kenneth (politesse only, for he always gave her carte blanche over the household and his chequebook) and outlined her plans. She'd spent feverish hours poring over *Country Life* and jotting notes. She looked out the leather portfolio that had been a gift from Merrigan and Lawrence; she'd never had occasion to use it before. It was good to have a reason now. It made her feel purposeful, sophisticated.

She'd always admired the younger generation. Blue with her writing ambitions; Tabitha with her outrageous behaviour. When she was their age she'd never have dared! And she had wondered, sometimes, what it would be like to have a goal of her own, something to work towards with all her heart. Is that what music had meant to Foster? Had this teacher killed a secret dream, perhaps? She hoped it was nothing worse. It was painful to think of the dear boy being bullied. She would have to keep an eye on him when she saw him, though he hadn't been round for ages.

Her portfolio was bulging. The scope of such a grand over-haul made her head spin, but at least while she was preoccupied with logistics, her mind was prevented from straying to dark places. She set aside several sheets of ideas and lists and took out a magazine. She would work on only a few rooms at a time, she decided, so that peace could always be found somewhere. She would start with three.

The kitchen was one. Although spacious and gleaming, it was positively antiquated. But it was the twenties! Midge wanted toasters, kettles, an electric oven! Kenneth's bedroom was another. He could sleep in his dressing room while it was underway. Or he could sleep with her.

And the drawing room, this lovely drawing room, was the third. She would have it painted a deep, earthy green. With all that lovely light blooming through the French windows, it could easily take the darker colour. And if it needed further brightening, she could introduce trims and accents in the cream and yellow that were all the rage now. As she leafed through the pages of her magazine, the most wonderful feeling arose inside her, a mixture of excitement and peace. She would order new armchairs. She would move the piano to the opposite wall. And she would move Audra's portrait. To another room. One they didn't use so often.

# Chapter Fourteen

'I say, Blue!' declaimed her brother-in-law, striding into the sitting room. 'Is it just me or has the old girl gone completely off her rocker?'

'Shh!' hissed Blue, looking up from her work. She pointed to the sofa, where Delphine was curled up like a dormouse. She had come to sit with Blue and read, while Blue wrote, but within half an hour the book had slid to the floor like a fainting debutante. Blue wasn't surprised. Delphine fell asleep at the drop of a hat! Lawrence clapped a theatrical hand to his mouth and waved a silent apology.

The 'couple of days' Delphine had agreed to stay had lengthened into nearly a week. And the sleeping was the reason; she had done little else since she arrived. No plans could be made with a girl who was asleep. Looking at her now, Blue thought she looked like someone under a spell, so small and frail-looking, eyes fast closed. One cheek was pressed into a cushion and the other, with the pink mark, was hidden by long, wavy hair very like Blue's own, except dark.

'Another one!' Merrigan had sighed, disdainful of any head that was a fashion-free zone. Delphine had looked tearful – she was yet to grow used to, and therefore dismissive of, Merrigan's opinions.

'Is that her?' whispered Lawrence, stage-tiptoeing over to Blue. 'The lost girl?'

'The very deliberately lost girl. Exhausted, poor thing.'

'Bad business, very bad.' Lawrence bent to kiss Blue.

She grinned up at her brother-in-law. He was tall and boyishly handsome, with straight, shiny hair the exact same shade of nut-brown as Merrigan's. They did say people tended to marry partners who looked like them. Lawrence was very dapper, with a sharp side parting in his hair and a brown moustache neatly trimmed into a precise semicircle on his upper lip. Personally, Blue didn't favour a moustache, but then she didn't have to live with him.

'So what's my sister done now?'

'Eh? Oh, not *that* old girl, the other old girl.'

Blue waited for further clarification.

'Midge,' Lawrence explained, looking rather awed. 'She's gone rather potty on this decorating lark, hasn't she?'

'Oh, has she?' Blue was surprised. She'd been so preoccupied with Delphine and the love letters and a short story she was trying to write that Midge's project had rather faded into the background. 'What's up?'

'Well,' said Lawrence, pulling out a chair next to Blue, 'she wants all the new appliances in the kitchen – electric toaster, electric oven, electric kettle. Yes, I can see what you're thinking – she's entitled to want what she wants – but hear me out, old girl. She even wants a *refrigerator*!'

Blue frowned. She didn't think much about kitchen appliances.

'They're not safe,' Lawrence explained. 'It's not a question of taste. They leak gas! It's a compression gas, which works because . . . Oh, never mind.' He got back to the point when he saw Blue's eyes glaze over. 'It's poisonous, basically. And they explode. It happens regularly.'

'Well, that doesn't sound good,' admitted Blue.

'No, and your pa agreed. And golly, did she give him a piece of her mind! Started on about how this is *her* project and *her* decision. Then *he* said he'd happily applaud any decision she made that didn't involve the likely deaths of all his household. Then *she* said he was exaggerating the danger, so *I* said . . .'

He paused when Delphine gave a little moan, but all she did was shuffle about a bit and settle down again.

'So *I*,' he resumed in a quieter voice, 'told her that old Ken's on the right track and that there really have been a number of explosions.'

'And?'

'And she absolutely *rioted*!'

'Define riot.'

'Threw the book at me. Literally, the book that was on the

kitchen table at the time. Quite hard.' He rubbed his cheek, looking rather lost. Now Blue came to look at him, it did look a bit red. 'Then she ran out of the room.'

Blue knitted her brows. 'How queer. How really very strange. Perhaps she's taken on too much. It might be quite debilitating, I suppose, dismantling a home, all the pressure for everyone to like it afterwards.'

'Well, it hasn't debilitated her overarm,' said Lawrence with feeling. 'Have a word, Blue, I don't want to fear missiles every time I come to visit.'

'Fair enough,' murmured Blue, eyes already straying to her last paragraph. Did it read better with or without the rhetorical question at the end?

'And another thing!' Lawrence jolted her from her thoughts, tapping her on the arm. 'Merry swears she's obsessed with that bible of hers.'

'Bible?' Blue hadn't seen any increase in Midge's devotions lately.

'Yes! *Creating a Super Home*, or whatever it's called, by that Harriet Orpington-Whistle. She carries it with her everywhere, Merry says, pores over it night and day. Quotes from it like billy-o, as if old Orps is a cross between a professor and *God*!'

Blue *had* heard Midge mentioning someone called Harriet quite often. She'd assumed Midge had met a new friend.

'Curious,' she agreed. 'She's obviously gone overboard. I'll talk to her, don't worry. Now, anything else I can do for you, or can I get back to my story?'

'Well, I wanted to meet your new house guest. How's about I just take a seat over there and relax till she wakes? I won't disturb you.'

Blue raised an eyebrow. Lawrence by his very nature was a disturbance; it would be like having a puppy in the room. Then again, she didn't want to send him away. So she settled back to her story; at least he wouldn't chew her slippers.

# Chapter Fifteen

An hour later, Delphine awoke. A satiny ribbon of air from the open window slid over her. She was perpetually disoriented these days, waking up in all sorts of places – on sofas, chairs, in the garden . . . She sat up, feeling heavy and languid. Blue was sitting at the table, scowling at the wall. In an armchair behind her a strange man was asleep, head thrown back, snoring softly.

Blue saw that Delphine was awake and beckoned her past him.

'Merrigan's husband,' she explained. 'Came to meet you. Let's go into the garden, I've been sitting there long enough.'

'D . . . did you get v . . . very much done?'

'Five lines.'

Outside, the air was hot as bathwater. Delphine adored the garden at Ryan's Castle. The lawn, at present yellow-green and slightly crispy, was scattered with petals and twigs from an array of trees and shrubs that crowded round the edges. Offering privacy and comfort to the family, the foliage also housed any number of birds. Delphine loved to lie in the shade and listen to the hundreds of songs that created a sparkling web of sound that hung between the garden and the rest of the world.

They plopped themselves on the ground under the cherry tree. Blue seemed lost in thought and they sat without speaking for a while. The silence was comfortable, but eventually Delphine decided to break it. She took a breath, marshalled her words and then, very slowly, formed her question without stammering.

'Are you thinking about your story?'

Blue smiled at her. 'That and about a dozen other things. Do you find that everything that's on your mind tumbles about in your head like butterflies, all at the same time?'

Delphine thought about it. 'N . . . no. Not me. One th . . . thing at a time, usually.' Survival, usually. Doing the tasks that Foley had set her so that when he came home he wouldn't have a reason to be angry. Not that he needed one, but she sure as eggs didn't want to increase the chances. Also, she'd decided that if you had nothing to think about that made you happy, it was probably better not to think. Although, she reflected now, if you didn't think, and you didn't communicate, what were you? She had turned into a hedgehog, rolled into a ball, waiting for danger to pass. She would have liked to tell Blue all this. She would try.

'My husband k . . . kept me busy and I didn't want him to be angry. So I c . . . concentrated . . . Got into the habit.'

'That makes sense.' Blue rolled onto her side to look at Delphine. 'I know I've said it before, but I'm so sorry, Delphine, for all you've gone through.'

'Thank you.'

'Do you think you'll be all right? Recover? Find a way to be happy? You know we'll do anything we can to help, don't you?'

'I appreciate it m . . . more than I c . . . can say.' Delphine took a deep breath. 'I w . . . wish my w . . . words would come back. I hate not being able to t . . . t . . .' She thumped the ground in frustration. '*Talk.*'

'When did they go away?'

'Since F . . . F . . . Foley. He s . . . said everything I s . . . said was stupid. And he sh . . . sh . . . shouted all the time. He was so loud and I got quieter and quieter. And now I've lost me voice, is the thing of it. Not my *voice*,' she explained, pressing her hand to her throat. 'But . . .' She sighed. How to explain?

'Not your literal voice, but your ability to speak out and express yourself?' suggested Blue.

Delphine nodded. *Exactly.*

'I had a thought about that, you know. I don't know if this sounds silly, but I wondered whether writing things down might help? It might not. I think writing helps everything because I love it – but it's not for everyone. Merrigan would rather stick her hand in a fire. But if that connection between what you're thinking and what you can say has been severed, maybe writing could bring it back. I had a letter recently from a . . . friend.' Blue blushed and Delphine wondered what the story was there. 'He said that writing was a private thing. He said it makes him better able to say what he wants to than when he talks. It made me think of you.'

Delphine considered it. She hadn't been much of a scholar at school. But she'd had other things on her mind back then. And the thought of writing anything down at Foley's, where he might find it, was worse than speaking! But here there was silence and privacy. She had seen Blue's contentment when she was absorbed in her notebook. Even when she wasn't writing, but tapping the pen on the page or against her teeth, Delphine envied her that complete immersion. To imagine herself writing in a notebook was to imagine a woman totally different from the Delphine who had cowered from her father, from the Delphine who had married Foley, believing him to be a different kind of man and finding out in the worst of ways that he wasn't. A Delphine who could think and write and perhaps take part in things again could not be threatened by Foley.

She nodded. 'I'd like to try. It's a good idea.'

'Oh, good!' Blue looked so pleased. 'I'll fish out a pen and a book for you, if you like. I've heaps.'

'Th . . . thank you f . . . for thinking of me. Wh . . . what else were you thinking about?'

'So many things. What to do with my life. How to finish my story. Whether my sister's right and I should be thinking about getting married. And Lawrence was just telling me that

Midge is obsessed with her decorating. I was wondering why. I think it might be to do with the time of year.'

Delphine gave her a questioning glance. So many preoccupations! Blue reminded her of a swan, gliding and graceful and so lovely to look at. But just as a swan had those funny black feet paddling away under the surface, so Blue's head had some sort of engine that seemed not to stop. She hadn't known Blue was wondering about marriage. And why should this time of year disturb Midge? That was the question she started with.

Blue screwed up her eyes, as if in pain. 'Still really hard to talk about it,' she said. Short sentences, no embroidery. Just what Delphine did when talking was too hard.

'Oh, don't tell me!' she blurted. 'I'm s . . . so s . . . sorry I asked.'

'No, I'd like to tell you, if you can bear another sad story. You have enough of your own.'

'Tell me.'

'My mother died just after the war,' said Blue. Delphine had of course gathered that Midge was Kenneth's second wife, but she knew nothing more.

'It was horribly ironic. Daddy came home – what a blessing! – and then Mother died. It was the Spanish flu.'

Delphine nodded. She had known people who had died in the pandemic too – though no one as close as her mother, thank God. Half a million British people had lost their lives.

It felt as though the country, being dealt a second hefty blow right after the war, might be out for the count.

'There's nothing to say about that that you can't imagine. She was the life and soul of this family. We all loved her so . . .' Her eyes filled with tears and Delphine could see her breathing, waiting to regain control of herself. 'Anyway. Two years later, Daddy met Midge, and, well, some people were shocked that he married again so quickly. We were only glad he married at all. We were frightened for him. *Anyone* who could anchor him, we would have welcomed. But it wasn't just anyone, it was Midge, who is wonderful, and loves us . . . We're so lucky. It hasn't always been easy for her though. Daddy didn't mean to be cruel, but he's never stopped loving Mother and sometimes it seemed that his heart wasn't fully with Midge, and she'd given him hers so *completely* . . . But then things got better! We've become a family, you know?'

'I can see.'

'And then . . . Midge got pregnant.'

Delphine's eyes widened, then her heart sank. 'Oh. Did she lose it?'

Blue shook her head, digging her teeth into her bottom lip. 'No, the baby was born,' she said softly. 'Percy, our little brother. He was adorable. For Merrigan and me, having a little brother after all those years was such a joy. We doted on him – Daddy too, of course. His first son! It was like renewal, like spring coming after a long, hard winter. You can't imagine . . .'

Delphine could imagine. It was how she felt now, here.

'One day, when Percy was about six months, Midge took him for a day out. Daddy was away, and Midge always hated that. He's rather handsome, isn't he, and women are always crowding around. Merrigan and I were in Bath for a few days, visiting some old friends. Midge was invited but she was rather overwhelmed back then. Having a baby, not sleeping, all the paraphernalia every time you went somewhere and all that . . . She'd get very flustered, and she used to cry a lot, which isn't really her.'

Delphine nodded. Midge was certainly the epitome of composure, so elegant and mannerly. But then having a baby could dismantle the most mettlesome of women; she had seen it.

'She found it embarrassing, and it was easier to cope in her own environment, with Avis to help. So she stayed behind and got really bored. Being in the house all the time was driving her mad, so she decided to take a day trip – one that wouldn't be too long to cope with.'

Delphine listened with a horrible feeling of doom. In her mind's eye she could see little Percy, cherubic and delightful, with Kenneth's fetching smile and Midge's mild eyes.

Blue was silent for a while, remembering. Then she rubbed her hands over her face and began again.

'It took her ages to get going. She found his socks and he threw them off again, she forgot his bottle and went back for it . . . So she didn't reach Esher until lunchtime. She went to a sandwich shop – she didn't like taking him to cafes, because when he cried he did make the most fearful roar. It was a hot day so she found a park . . .'

Blue hesitated. Her voice had grown smaller and smaller and Delphine could see that the sequence of events was well worn, the phrases mechanical. She imagined that Midge must have told the story a hundred times, that Blue must have lived it in her imagination a thousand more.

'She sat under a tree so that Percy would be in the shade,' Blue continued with a sigh, 'and because he was asleep she started to read a book. Then *she* fell asleep. She said she was absolutely worn out from the odyssey of getting a baby to Esher.'

Blue looked at Delphine. 'I can understand it, can't you? I mean, sitting in the sunshine is so relaxing. And mothers are often tired beyond tolerance, so they say. I mean, she couldn't *help* falling asleep. But I don't believe she's ever forgiven herself.'

'Of course she couldn't help it,' said Delphine, clasping Blue's wrist. 'L . . . look at me now. A d . . . dormouse. It's hard to f . . . fight it when you're so tired you can hardly breathe. And when she woke?'

'Percy was gone.'

'Oh, Blue. I'm so sorry.'

'I still can't . . . I mean, it was three years ago now and we don't know . . . Is he still *alive*? We don't know. He could be out there somewhere, happy and healthy, we hope. Or he could be dead. Snuffed out before he properly began. Or – and this is the worst possibility – is he alive but suffering? I'd wish for anything but that. You hear of such unspeakable things.'

'And someone definitely took him? He d . . . didn't wander off? No, he was too s . . . small.'

'The police asked all around but no one had seen a crawling baby. No . . . no *body* was ever found. And then they found his baby basket stuffed into a bin near the station. It seems most likely someone took him, ditched the basket and caught the train somewhere. It's hard not to imagine a monster. A kidnapper. A baby thief. All those horrible words. But if it was just someone who was desperate to be a mother, someone blinded by longing, confused into doing the wrong thing . . . We feel the loss of him like a tear through our very souls, but at least in that scenario he'd be happy. He'd know no different.'

'H . . . how have you all c . . . coped all these y . . . years? Your poor family.'

Blue shook her head, her face the picture of desolation. 'Can you imagine if he were here now, Delphine? Running around the garden, chasing butterflies, tripping over, having to be set on his feet again? I keep picturing what it would be like if he were still with us. Would he like trains and buses? Would he be artistic or sporty? I keep imagining him here, because it's where he belongs. That's the way it *should* be. But it's not the reality. And we don't know what the reality *is*.'

Delphine looked around the garden. For a minute, she could see it, the picture Blue had painted. 'How did your father take the n . . . news? W . . . was there a b . . . big search?'

'Yes. It was in all the papers for a while. Whoever snatched him was either very lucky or they had a good plan and were just on the lookout for the right opportunity. My father was grief-stricken. Can you imagine? Losing my mother and then his son. And Midge . . . well, to say she was distraught doesn't even begin to describe it. For weeks she just locked herself away, couldn't look at any of us, said she could never forgive herself. In the end she came out of it, but she's been a shade or two paler ever since, I swear. It was about this time, three years ago, so maybe that's why Midge is a little crazy. Maybe that's why she threw a book at Lawrence.'

'Maybe,' said Delphine. 'I'm am . . . am . . . amazed she seems as calm as she does.'

'Life goes on, *you* know that. It's one more blow to absorb, one more loss. But we still have so much. We still have each other, the four of us – and Lawrence and Cicely now. And we're prosperous, when so many are without homes, without decent food . . . It's a hard world, and we have our portion of difficulty just like everyone else. I don't think it can be any other way.'

Delphine didn't know what to say. She could feel it all: Midge's panic on waking up to find her baby gone, the sick duty of telling her husband and stepdaughters, the disorientation and fear and hope. Most of all, she could feel Blue's struggle to make sense of a world so beautiful and so horrible in equal measure that it confounded understanding. She lifted Blue's wrist, which she was still clutching, and kissed her hand before setting it down again.

Delphine gazed up at the dark blue sky. Two swallows swooped in euphoric circles and the sunlight was so bright she could see the texture of her own eyelashes. Blue had asked her earlier whether she might recover, find a way to go on after Foley. With some astonishment, she realised now that if this family could go on, after all they had lost, then yes, she thought she could too. She hadn't been sure before.

# Part Two

## Autumn

*A time to take bulls by horns*

# Chapter Sixteen

Dear Foster,

*My father is an ass. He should never have made that announcement! Please stop writing me these heartbreaking letters. I can't bear that you should be hurt. You're one of my oldest and dearest friends. I know Daddy's explained to you that I never asked him to make that speech. Foster, I don't want to get married! Not to you and not to anyone. Please don't take this personally, and please remember that you're young. I don't say this to make light of what you're feeling, but you have time, so much time, ahead of you to find someone to love. Many girls to love, before you settle down! You are a bright, kind young man with a wonderful future ahead of you. I do love you, but only as a friend. I want to be your friend always. But nothing more. And if you really care about me, please accept what I say, put this aside and find a pretty girl your own age whom you can ask to dance at the next party you go to! Promise me, dear, no more pining!*

*Your sincere friend,*
*Blue Camberwell*

It had to be said. Kenneth had tackled Foster, as promised, offering abject apologies for any hopes raised. However, Foster had written three more times, each letter more desolate than the last, begging Blue to reply and leave her note in the hollow in the apple tree. She had been determined not to be drawn into this ridiculous charade. She wanted to be a *writer*, for heaven's sake, not a wife! She would talk to Foster herself, she decided, the next time she saw him. But he hadn't visited, and when Blue went to see Tabitha, he was nowhere in evidence. Even his insouciant sister had started to admit it might be more than a passing crush. His latest letter made Blue's stomach knot like a bag of snakes.

> *I love you, Blue. It's hopeless. Without you, there's no North Star. I walk around outside myself and can't concentrate on anything, not my family or my studies, not even my music. These things used to matter. Now they're only ashes.*

Blue tucked the letter into an envelope, wrote 'Foster Foxton' on the outside and took it into the garden. Since Foster wasn't coming to the house any more, how would he find the letter in the apple tree? Yet in every letter he had been very specific in his request. She hoped she had been firm but kind. She hoped it would work. With the letter deposited, she felt a load lift from her shoulders.

Hot, weighty summer days had slid like toffee into September, and suddenly Blue could breathe again. The air was clear and cool in early morning – so delicious that it pulled her from her bed before anyone else was about and lured her to the riverside, where her boots crackled on the first fallen leaves. The days still blossomed into summery warmth as the sun grew stronger, but for these private early walks she could draw her favourite knitted cardigan (detested by Merrigan) about her to protect her from the chill as she walked and wrote. Her thoughts bobbed in reverie while swans glided in and out of the riverside mist.

Autumn had always been Blue's favourite season – the burnished colours, the sharp light, the amber air. Blackberries bowing the bushes and the scurry and splash of birds preparing for winter. Autumn made it easy to accept the inevitability of change. Old things falling away, disintegrating. So be it. New things just around the corner, hiding like excited children, longing for you to find them and play.

Blue was writing more than ever. Having romance thrust upon her made her all the more determined that she would have the career she wanted. She had finally completed two humorous pieces commenting on different aspects of Richmond life, which she hoped might suit a local newspaper. She'd written to Juno Forrester to ask if she would be willing to take a look at them before Blue sent them to an editor. It was a shame Virginia Woolf had moved out of Richmond the previous year, otherwise Blue would have taken the liberty of calling with a manuscript and begging the writer to cast a glance. She'd often daydreamed of doing so but had always been too shy. Now, she was no longer shy; she was ready to reach out, take risks. This time of year gave Blue a ferocious energy. It was a time to take bulls by horns.

To wit, she'd also written back to L. W. at the Pheasant, and to Dorian, with whom she had then gone dancing, just as he'd suggested. Blue had known Dorian for years. He was disconcertingly good-looking, she'd always thought, like a moving picture star or a model for cigarettes. He had dark hair, blue eyes, chiselled features and a smile that proved electricity was a phenomenon not confined to telegraph wires and light bulbs.

Despite, or perhaps because of, his good looks, Blue had never thought of him in that way. She had always thought it must be exhausting to be the consort of such a man, and Dorian was not one to handle his blessings graciously; he was vain and assured, bestowing attention on women as if he were sharing sweets among children. However, he was saved from being unbearable by a sunny personality and a vast enthusiasm for high jinks of all sorts. He and Blue had become friends, of sorts, over the long years; not intimate, but cordial. They met at the same parties and outings and there was always laughter between them.

His letter had astonished her. To be sought out in that way by Foster, who was like a little brother to her, and then by Dorian, who was like a charming but distant cousin, was bewildering. She liked Dorian. Admired him, even. But it had never occurred to her that there might be common ground between them. His letter had hinted at hidden depths, however, and she was impressed by its eloquence. The thought of having that delicious, fun-loving Adonis all to herself for one evening was too appealing to turn down. Therefore, with a certain reluctance to enter into the epistolary courtship her father had conjured for her, she said yes and told no one.

It had been a surprisingly wonderful evening. They danced all night and drank champagne under the stars and talked. They didn't have a great deal in common, but the conversation was no less enjoyable for that. A boat trip had followed a week later, on the first of the cooler days. And yesterday they had taken a lunchtime stroll.

So far, to Blue's relief, no one had cottoned on. Perhaps Merrigan had simply given up on her sister. Midge was still distracted. Her father was out and about often enough that he didn't notice his daughter's every coming or going. And Delphine, who was still staying with them, didn't know the Richmond scene well enough to raise eyebrows at the mention of Dorian's name. So far, Blue had been able to do whatever it was she was doing in private. Was it courting? She would have denied it vehemently if asked, but a small part of her acknowledged that it was at the least something very *like* courting.

Dorian was a gentleman and made no demands; there was no rush to define or decide anything. This left Blue free to write to L. W. without guilt. There were things in his letter that interested her. Things that played on her mind after reading them and led her to take the letter out again and digest them more fully. Things that yes, though she hated to admit it, had tickled her imagination. She'd be damned if she'd tell her father *that*!

*A total stranger . . . A romantic . . . A bachelor.*

'The imagination is perhaps the most precious faculty we possess,' he'd written. 'As subtle as the colours of the sea and as personal as a thumbprint.'

Blue couldn't have agreed more. And his empathic powers did him credit. He had exactly summed up her position with regard to her father's grand gesture:

'I cannot imagine why a lady such as yourself could possibly wish to spend her valuable time reading the rambling letters of strangers.'

And his good wishes at the end were graceful, she thought.

'I hope you are as blessed as you look and as happy as you are beautiful.'

He'd told her next to nothing of himself, she noticed. And of course, he could be ugly. Very ugly. But, she reasoned, his letter had been an opening gesture only. He hadn't expected that she would take an interest, so it stood to reason that he would keep things brief. And so, despite the fact that she objected to everything about this whole blasted letter-writing challenge, despite the fact that she knew nothing about him whatsoever, she wrote back and asked what she wanted to know. There was no point cutting off her nose to spite her face.

# Chapter Seventeen

Midge wanted a decorative toaster with a Celtic knot design on the lid. She had seen one advertised in *The Times* and thought it extremely elegant.

It had become a bone of contention between her and Kenneth, but only a small bone – a metacarpal, at most. He teased her gently about it from time to time. He was doing so now, in the kitchen, which was gradually being reinvented with walls of smoky pink and trim of lemon and gleaming black accents everywhere. Midge was most delighted with the glass cupboard handles; little things were so important.

The family were gathered to help Avis make a chocolate rum cake for Delphine's birthday. Their help largely consisted of stealing ingredients and consuming them with relish.

'But here's the thing, darling. None of us is remotely Celtic! We don't have a Celtic bone between us. But if my darling wife wishes for a Celtic toaster then a Celtic toaster she shall have, and I shall eat toast from it with all the Celtic vigour I can muster. I shall even wear a fur cloak and helmet if you like, Midge, darling.'

'Isn't that Vikings, Daddy?' queried Merrigan, picking up chocolate shavings and eating them, one by one, with close attention.

'I think the Celts as well,' said Blue. 'I mean, they needed to keep warm too.'

'Never met a girl yet who didn't like a fur cloak!' grinned Kenneth.

'As if you had one!' exclaimed Merrigan. 'I can't think of anyone less rugged than you, Daddy. If you led a Viking raid, you'd do it in a panama hat.'

'Well, I think you're all being very silly,' Midge put in suddenly, her face looking rather hot and her eyes suspiciously bright. Of course, it might just have been the heat from the oven.

'Well, yes, we are,' agreed Kenneth. 'That's what we do.'

'But must we do it *all* the time? Some things are serious, you know.'

'Like toasters?'

'Yes!' shouted Midge, slamming down a tin of glacé cherries and striding out of the room. 'Like toasters.'

Kenneth, Avis, Merrigan and Blue looked at each other.

Midge escaped, heart hammering. She'd blown her top again. How frightfully embarrassing. She fled to her room. It had a small alcove, which might have served as a dressing room for another woman, but which Midge had converted into a workroom, with a table for her sewing machine and shelves for her work baskets and bolts of fabric. It was a little rainbow corner all her own, cheerful and workaday in the midst of the turn-of-the-century elegance that marked the rest of the house – a style that was all Audra.

Midge had always sewn. When she was younger, she'd had to. They couldn't afford much, and her skill with a needle had allowed her to squeeze new life from old dresses and coats and even, for special occasions, to create something altogether new. She'd come to love it and turned out to be very good at it, so she and her mother were always better turned out than they might have been. This was part of the reason Margaret Fawcett had been considered a second-tier invitee by the same circles that welcomed Kenneth. She might not be exciting, but she would never be a disgrace.

Now, as Kenneth's wife, she could afford the sorts of materials that she'd only dreamed of before. As well as silks and chiffons and the finest of trims, there were all the modern developments like zips and press studs, which made getting dressed easy (*and undressed*, Tabitha often exulted with a wicked wink) and sewing even more fun. Now, she made clothes for the sheer pleasure of it, taking unadulterated pride in her ability. And she *loved* having the girls to sew for. Their squeals of delight when she presented them with something new were one of her greatest joys. When they remarked covetously upon something in a magazine, she would listen. While they discussed what they would change, what colour they would prefer, she took mental notes, stole the picture if she could, then hid herself away until the garment was made. Midge had never considered herself imaginative, but this was her small way of turning dreams into threads and seams for her girls. She sewed love into every stitch.

For a long time, she had thought that sewing wouldn't really feel like sewing without the rise and fall of her foot on the treadle and the rattle of the flywheel as she worked. But then Kenneth had given her a compact electric Singer for her birthday last year and she had been seduced. She still kept her old one in a place of honour in her workroom, but now she used the new one more often than not. It was whizzy and friendly. Whenever she sat here at her table, everything seemed to make sense for a while.

She was currently making a skirt for Blue. It would be on the long side of fashionable, in a midnight blue cotton. Merrigan would hate it, but Blue lived and died in those skirts, loose and practical, comfortable for swinging round Richmond with her leather satchel full of notebooks. Even this simple task absorbed Midge, so that her breathing steadied without her being aware of it and she sank into a more peaceful place. All too soon the skirt was finished and Midge sat back and stretched, the satisfaction of a job well done sliding all too soon into the uncomfortable memory of her outburst in the kitchen. She knew she was unsettling them all.

Poor Avis had become very worried when Midge started talking about all the new devices she planned to buy.

'Am I going to be out of a job, Mrs C?' she'd asked. 'Only, if I'm to go, it'll take some adjusting. I love this family, if it's not impertinent to say.'

'Out of a job?' It had never even occurred to Midge. 'Heavens, Avis, we'd be sunk without you. That's the last thing any of us would want. Why would you think that?'

'Well, if you're going to get something to heat the water and something to toast the bread and a fancy new oven . . . Well, there'll be a lot less work, won't there?'

'Oh,' said Midge, 'but we still need someone to *work* the kettle and the toaster and the oven, dear Avis, and prepare the food. A house this size always generates work. There'll be plenty for you to do, *always*.'

She'd been careful since then to consult Avis, rather than simply announce her plans, but it had made her realise how wrapped up in her own little world she'd become. Midge herself couldn't have truly explained why she was so nervy and raw. She'd started the redecoration with high hopes and the best of intentions, but now it had taken on a life of its own. Somehow it felt imperative to reinvent Ryan's Castle, the timeless house that everybody loved.

The house often held a dreamlike air, especially in the early mornings, as if it were reluctant to wake up, as if the past were a golden glow it wouldn't shake off. Was it clinging to the good old days when the family was intact and everything was the way it was meant to be? And was she, Midge, secretly trying to obliterate every trace of Audra, to stamp her mark on the place in a way she couldn't quite feel proud of? She sank her head into her hands and sighed. Jealousy was a terrible thing.

So was guilt. In the heat of high summer, her project had felt like the only available breath of fresh air – the only hope of *life*, even. She hated August and its insistent skies, its annual reminder of that appalling day. Perhaps *that* was what she was trying to obliterate, rather than Kenneth's first marriage. Little Percy gone. All her fault.

Even now she woke at night, thinking she could hear him wail. In reality, when he'd cried at night it had made her teeth grind. Midge had always been someone who needed her sleep, and she used to feel that it was impossible to go on like that. But now she would give anything to have him back. No matter how worn down and irrational and parchment-faced she grew, she would welcome those late-night screeches because it would mean that vile day had never happened. No amount of redecorating could bring Percy back.

Should she stop now, at three rooms transformed, and leave the rest of the poor house alone? But if she did that, the new rooms would stick out like sore thumbs, incongruous reminders of a flight of fancy not entirely grounded in sanity. Visitors would come and they would wonder. Should she just put everything back the way it was? That seemed equally ludicrous – and shockingly wasteful. She shook her head. The only way now was forward. Perhaps it was just the imbalance between old and new in the house that was so unsettling. Perhaps when it was all done, it would match her original vision and she would feel comfortable again.

It would be cohesive and fresh and Kenneth would marvel. It would be fashionable in a whole new way and Juno Forrester would write about it. Midge could invite her round for an exclusive early viewing. She could even write to Harriet Orpington-Whistle, enclosing photographs and explaining what an inspiration she had been. Harriet might feature Ryan's Castle in a book, or in a piece for a magazine. She might even come and visit, offer Midge an apprenticeship. Imagine starting a career at her age! Imagine Midge Camberwell being a modern woman, after all!

Thank God for autumn, here not a moment too soon, cooling the blood, soothing and whispering of transformation. Midge slid into a happier daydream, reassured. Pressing on was the only way. She wondered how Kenneth would feel about a mock-Regency balcony over the porch. Painted in peppermint green.

# Chapter Eighteen

～～～

Delphine had been banished from the kitchen. She didn't take offence; it had come up in conversation just recently that she would be twenty-eight tomorrow and now the scent of sweet baking came wafting up the stairs. She smiled. When was the last time she'd had a birthday cake? Years ago. Not long before she left her job at the children's home to marry Foley. The girls had made her an apple cake and teased Delphine about her wedding night.

Delphine shuddered and something of her old horror shook her again. But it was over. No point dwelling on what couldn't be undone.

Now that she wasn't sleeping quite so much, there were idle minutes when the memories crept in. Delphine had never had idle moments before. She'd started work at fifteen, working in a florist in Whitechapel. Then she'd done some domestic cleaning for a while. Then the job at the orphanage – or the home, as they liked to call it – had fallen into her lap. She had loved working there best of all. She would still be there, no doubt, if she hadn't met Foley. Then she'd married and been busy all day, every day, keeping house and running errands for her husband. 'The best job in the world!' the ladies' magazines called marriage. It hadn't been for Delphine.

She took the stairs two at a time and went to her room. *Keep busy, don't think . . .*

Except she had nothing to do. Her eyes fell on the notebook and pen that Blue had given her. So far, she'd only tried using them once. There was something spectacularly intimidating about the sight of a blank page. It wasn't as though Delphine wasn't used to intimidation, but when she'd picked up the pen and opened the notebook, it had been a confrontation that felt almost violent.

Taking up the pen, she had been little Delphine Painter again, struggling to concentrate in class, fighting to ignore the whispers and giggles about her weird face mark. Little Delphine Painter, trying to do her homework in the evenings after helping her ma with the chores, working by the meagre light of an oil lamp, hurrying to stuff her books away when she heard her father coming in. Little Delphine Painter, tormented at home and distracted in school, trying her best in tests but never getting the marks she dreamed of. 'Stupid Delphine,' the children called her, and though the teachers scolded them, she could tell from their faces that they didn't disagree.

When she'd opened the notebook, that expanse of creamy page had become a canvas for every unkind thing Foley had ever said about her – and *that* could fill a book! 'Stupid. Hunchback. Freak show. Useless. Mangy dog. Hideous. Only good for one thing and not much good at that . . .'

She'd slammed the notebook shut pretty sharpish. But Blue had intended it as a vehicle for Delphine to rediscover *her* voice, not to listen to Foley's. Was he to claim even this small part of her as his own? Should she try again?

Delphine left her bedroom door ajar. One thing she loved about this house was the way privacy was respected. No one here was going to barge in, demanding anything of her. They had given her a small guest room at the end of the landing. It had an old-fashioned four-poster bed, and a switch that operated an electric light within a shade of multi-coloured glass. There was a gilt-framed mirror on one wall, and she stood before this now. As though facing an attacker, she looked up to meet her own eyes in the glass.

Big, blue, beaten-looking eyes. 'Cringing,' Foley had said. 'Pathetic.' But pretty, perhaps, with a different expression. Blue had described her eyes as beautiful. Framed by very black eyelashes, it was a striking contrast.

'Such a pretty girl,' a different voice sighed in her mind. Her mother's. Even after her father had taken the iron to her face. Although 'Poor Pretty' became a more frequent lament after that.

She turned her face to the left. All she could see was that mark: a pink triangle covering her cheek, the apex a smaller smudge, far less obvious, just about her eyebrow. Her eye had escaped unscathed – eyelid smooth, vision perfect. She remembered her father coming at her with the iron in one hand, the other raised as if to strike her. That was the hand she'd watched, ducked away from, never dreaming even *he* would use the other. She turned to the right. Smooth, white skin, high cheekbone, diminutive chin. Esther used to call her Snow White. That was when they were very small.

She looked straight into the mirror. *Mirror, mirror on the wall. Who am I, now?*

It was a long time since she'd looked at herself. She never liked to see the mark, of course, and she'd never thought herself lovely, even without it. There'd never been the chance for even a healthy vanity to grow within her. Since Foley, she'd come to hate her face, not only for its visible imperfections, but because it was the face that identified her as *her*: stupid, useless, only good for . . .

No! Those were the opinions of one man. And her father. Two men, then. She'd always assumed there must be something wrong with her to have attracted all that. It was time to think again. She looked into the mirror and gazed into her own eyes until she began to find a measure of acceptance. She saw a girl who hadn't been handed a very lucky deck of cards. No one would have put money on her shining in life. She'd been beaten and bullied and dissuaded from doing anything to better herself. Her young girl's dreams had been torn to shreds. Yet even so, she had gone on to find a good job, make friends. She looked steadily at her reflection, remembering how she had gone to work every day through the war, solving problems and keeping things running smoothly. At the home, there had been the children, poor motherless souls, to remind her that lots of people weren't lucky.

Then had come Foley, tormented by the war, so he claimed. Foley had a body honed by soldiering and his job in the docks. Not unattractive, if you liked that strong-featured, foxy look. Delphine didn't think she was in any position to like or dislike anyone who took an interest in her. There was her first clue, perhaps, as to where it had all gone wrong.

She'd been hurt. Far too many times. The pain was writ on her face just as clearly as her father's iron-burn. But she was still here. She had escaped, however imperfectly. And fate had somehow brought her to a better place. Her biggest fear was that Richmond, like the children's home, would be only a temporary reprieve from the disaster that was her life. What if Foley found her? What if someone else came along who would hurt her, and she still didn't have the wisdom to see it coming and make a different choice?

She kept looking as the fear rose within her and her skinny chest rose and fell. She mustn't let that happen. She needed to understand. Perhaps she could talk to the man the others called Elf. He was trained in that sort of thing. Of course, she couldn't pay him, but he seemed very kind. Perhaps he would be willing to talk to her, just once. But for that, it would really help if she could speak properly. Otherwise it would take all day!

She turned from the mirror at last and looked at the notebook and pen on the small table. Both very beautiful, as any possessions of Blue's were bound to be. A brown leather notebook and a pink fountain pen. Hers, now. She approached them as if they were a snorting bull. She sat at the table and picked up the pen. *Stupid Delphine! Three out of ten! You'll never learn!* She stood up again hastily.

Blue didn't often write at a table. More often she'd sit on the lawn with her spine against a tree and her knees steeply bent. Or she'd be curled mermaid-style in an armchair, taking one slug of cocoa to every few words written. Delphine picked up the notebook and pen and sat in her window seat. It had become a favourite spot already. It was cushioned and comfortable and she loved watching the weather change over the garden. She opened the notebook. Stroked the page, as if making friends with a nervy horse. Took a deep breath.

'I am Delphine Painter. Rightly, I should say Foley. That is my name since I married. But I reject that man as my husband. I reject his claim on me and I reject everything he has said about me. Here is what I know.'

She waited a long time, tapping the pen against her teeth, staring into the garden. Its yellow-green hues were melting into gold and bronze. Perhaps she knew nothing at all.

She took another breath and started a new line. 'Here is what

I know,' she wrote again. 'I like strawberries. My sister, Esther, is my best friend, even though I ain't seen her for three years. I am safe here in Richmond with my new friends. I miss my mother. I miss my sister. I miss my old job and the friends I had there. I am looking at a garden and it is beautiful.'

She paused. It wasn't much. But it was something. A whole paragraph of something! She turned back to her page. Already it felt like a friend.

# Chapter Nineteen

When the letter came, the world exploded into bright lights and possibilities. Blue hurried to the Cottage, squirrels whisking urgently about their pre-hibernation business, the garden turning nutty and rich. The scent of woodsmoke from the Larrabys' garden next door rose in lilac-grey coils, drawing Blue to a standstill of bliss. Soon it would be the Camberwells' autumn party, a small gathering for family and closest friends. They would build a bonfire and play records and dance on the lawn. If it was possible to be in love with a season, autumn was Blue's one and only.

She found Elf having his mid-afternoon snooze and laughed as he sputtered awake, books sliding from his tummy to the floor.

'Tea?' he invited when he had righted himself, but Blue shook her head. She brandished a tin of cocoa at him with one hand, then drew the other from behind her back like a magician at a children's party to reveal a tin of Slade's Gaiety.

'Oh, you angel.' He beamed, getting up and setting milk to boil. 'I'm in need of sweets. What brings you here, Blue?'

Blue leaned against the door frame as Elf bustled around. 'I haven't seen you for a few days. And now . . . there's this!' She pulled the letter from her pocket.

'Another one?' sympathised Elf. 'Not Foster again, surely? Oh, Blue. Is it driving you to distraction?'

'It's not that. And no, I haven't heard anything else from Foster. My note's gone from the apple tree, by the way – I don't know how he's done it. I hope it's done the trick. But this is something else! Did I tell you I wrote to Juno Forrester and asked if she'd look at some of my stuff?'

Elf nodded, pouring milk with great concentration. 'You did. Has she said yes?'

'Yes! But even *that's* not it!'

'Well, hurry along, Ishbel, dear,' he chivvied, carrying the mugs to the sitting room so they could take their habitual seats. 'I'm all agog!'

'The point *is*,' said Blue, pulling the lid off the sweet tin, with its brightly coloured Pierrot design, 'that she said yes, and I sent them, and now she's written back to say she loves them!'

'Blue! Oh, my dear girl, that is *wonderful* news. Writing's a precarious game, I know, and nothing's assured in that world. A published journalist commending you! That must give you hope. What did she say?'

Blue grinned. Elf understood. She felt so fragile about her writing, so wishy-washy and unformed. She spent part of nearly every day wondering if she were simply deluded for thinking she could do it. She handed the letter to Elf so that he could read it for himself.

She watched as his gaze travelled the lines. 'A fine turn of phrase and a lively sense of style,' he read aloud, nodding approval. And a moment later, 'Intelligent without being turgid, fun without being specious.' He looked over his glasses at Blue. 'I must say, Miss Forrester's gone up a long way in my regard.'

'Read on!' Blue commanded.

'For one so inexperienced, your work shows great promise. I should say you could pursue a career in the journalistic arts, perhaps even the literary, if you work hard, and if my humble opinion counts for anything.'

Blue stamped her feet on the rug in glee, then hugged her knees tightly. 'Good old Juno! Elf! *Perhaps even the literary!* Does that mean she thinks I could write a novel?'

'I assume so. Perhaps you could meet and ask her? Oh! What's this?' His eyebrows lifted with interest. Blue knew he'd reached the last paragraph, which she'd committed to memory by this stage.

'I took the liberty of showing your pieces to our editor, Gordon Whiskett. Mr Whiskett wonders if you would do him the honour of calling on him in the office at your convenience. Between us, though, "at your convenience" is merely a figure of speech. The truth is, he's almost never here. So I peeked at his diary and he's in the office on the afternoon of Thursday next, if that should suit.'

Elf folded the letter and gave it back to Blue.

'Well!' he said. 'What do you think he wants?'

'I don't know. But I *have* thought . . .'

'I *did* wonder . . .' said Elf at the same time. 'Pardon me, my dear, you first.'

'No, you say it.'

'No, you say it!'

Knowing from experience that they could go on like this all day, Blue said it. 'Do you think he might want me to write something for the paper?'

'That's exactly what I thought. Blue, imagine! A commission, perhaps!'

'I don't want to get my hopes up,' said Blue carefully. 'He might just be interested to meet a young person who's so interested in writing.'

'No doubt he's very civic-minded. But if he's as busy as Miss Forrester describes, I don't see that he'd have the time. He must have something in mind.'

'I hope you're right! Oh, I hope you're right.'

He beamed at her. 'Darling Blue. Today the *Richmond Gazette*, tomorrow *The Times*!'

# Chapter Twenty

'Another letter for you, Miss Blue,' said Avis the following morning. Blue could tell that she was trying hard to be discreet about the sudden flurry of correspondence, but her dark eyes were sparkling with curiosity and her fingers twitched as though longing to rip it open. Merrigan, Lawrence and Cicely were visiting for breakfast.

'Who's that from?' asked Merrigan at once. 'A beau?'

Her father, next to her, raised an eyebrow. '"How far away the stars seem, and how far is our first kiss, and ah, how old my heart."'

'No,' said Blue, snatching the letter. 'There's no need for Yeats, Daddy.'

Merrigan looked sceptical. 'I don't see why you should hide it from *me*! You know I wholeheartedly approve of you having a bit of love interest in your life.'

'Well, it's *not* a beau, just an old friend. I'll read it later. How are you getting on at work, Lawrence?'

Merrigan groaned. Lawrence was an architect – the single

most frustrating profession in the 1920s. There were few people with the money to build, and with a scarcity of materials since the war, the projects had been few and far between these last few years – and most of those had been funded by Kenneth, who badly wanted to make a difference. Unfortunately, no one personal fortune was going to solve the problems of the nation.

Lawrence shrugged. 'Looking up, I think, since this latest housing act. At least they're channelling money in the right direction. Then maybe I can get out on site again and bring real homes to fruition instead of sitting in my office building houses from matchsticks.'

When the visitors eventually left, Blue decided to try to write something about all this. Three years ago, Lawrence had, at her request, taken her to see one of the 'overcrowded districts'. It had been the most upsetting thing she had ever seen. Three separate families might live in a single tenement, sharing just one toilet between them all. Lawrence explained that a water tap might serve four families or more. Blue talked to several children and wanted to cry. One adorable moppet of about three, with a head of blond curls, had contracted an infection from living in such close quarters with so many older brothers and sisters all bringing home germs from school. They couldn't afford a doctor. The infection had left him deaf.

Blue had emptied her purse on the spot to them, but felt guilty as she did so. They would still be here after that money ran out, and she was going home. She was withdrawn and tearful for weeks after that and Lawrence vowed he would never take her again.

If Mr Whiskett offered her work, how would she fare? Journalism wouldn't be just sitting in Ryan's Castle spinning words. She would have to go out to research things – maybe difficult things. She *wanted* to think that she would do whatever it took, but how did you ever know until you were in the position?

But doing so could make a difference! And that would be worth the heartache, surely. Imagine if she could write *and* be paid for it *and* help people! Thanks to Lawrence, she had insider knowledge about the improvements that were happening now. So it needn't be an *entirely* depressing article. Blue was so excited that she wrote and wrote for over an hour before she remembered the letter. A reply from L. W. at last!

Why 'at last'? She caught and questioned herself sharply. It had only been a week since she'd written. What on earth was she expecting? Impatient, she shook open the page. A small photograph fell out. She paused, laid it face down on the table and read the letter first.

*My dear Miss Camberwell,*

*What a joy to receive your letter! I really had no expectation whatsoever that you would write. You have made me very happy.*

*I am glad to hear that your writing ambitions are progressing apace and that your family and friends have enjoyed this towering summer.*

# Darling Blue

*I confess, I am an autumn man myself and yearly await with keen anticipation the coming of the burnished season. I wonder which is your favourite. For myself, nothing can mar the beauty of that diamond light, the shivers of early morning, the fireside colours . . . Nothing, that is, but the absence of a sympathetic companion to lean on my arm as our feet scruffle through the leaf drifts, to point in delight at the flit of a robin or a cornucopia of shining blackberries.*

*But I must stop! It might transpire that you are a true blue summer girl, or that spring commands your loyalty, or that you are a dyed-in-the-wool winteran! And then you will either cease our brief correspondence immediately, appalled by the wrongness of my preference, or write back pouring scorn upon my choice. But no, you are too kind to do that, I know that already from the tone of your letter.*

*You asked me several things and I shall endeavour to satisfy your kind interest. I believe I mentioned, I am unmarried. My first sweetheart, Clara Billings, broke my heart at the age of eight. My romantic adventures subsequently have been uninspiring and few. I work as a designer of hats. I do not make hats for royalty or anything of that colour. I merely make workaday hats for ordinary folk, but I take pleasure and pride in doing so. I supply the family store and between us we run a good, solid ship. I am currently staying in Sheen because I have a series of meetings in the area with designers, suppliers and buyers. This arrangement is more convenient than travelling each time to and from my home, which is in St Albans. And I confess, sometimes I am glad of the variety. I grow lonely at home, with no one to welcome me at the end of a day and no one with whom to eat poached eggs of a morning.*

*I have only one sibling, a brother, Graham. He is married with a small son, Amory, who is destructive and delightful in equal measure. Amory, should you be unaware, means famous ruler. Let no one say my brother is not imbued with a healthy grandiosity!*

*I do not suppose that the details of my life are so fascinating that you must wish for more, so I shall stop at those basic facts. But I am happy to tell you anything else you might wish to know, in as much detail as you can tolerate. I confess, I realise I am already looking forward to your letter – but you must not feel any pressure to reply unless you should wish to. Finally, Miss Camberwell, I enclose a small picture of myself – I thought it only fair that you should see my face, since I have seen yours in the broadsheet and I would like us to be on equal footing. I hope it is not an imposition.*

*Yours in gratitude for a delightful letter. I wish you well.*

*Yours truly,*
*Latchley Winterson*

Blue read the letter a second time. A hat designer. St Albans. Latchley Winterson! A deliciously romantic name. An open, enthusiastic, yet humble manner. And a fellow lover of autumn! She took up the photograph and squeezed her eyes shut. *Don't be ugly, don't be ugly,* she thought wildly, then opened them.

He wasn't ugly. He wasn't handsome either – not Dorian Fields handsome, but then few men were. He looked slightly older than his age – a mature thirty-two then, not a Peter Pan.

Would they look strange side by side? She didn't think so. He couldn't be mistaken for her father. His clothing appeared smart, yet unpretentious. He seemed to have hair of a medium shade and light eyes – blue or grey? Hazel or green? She rued black and white photography in that moment. He had a square chin and a steady expression. He was not smiling, but there was a hint of a smile about the corners of his mouth and she thought that he looked like somebody you might want to talk to. A smile curled Blue's own lips. And she wasn't entirely sure why.

# Chapter Twenty-one

'Overwhelmed!' gasped a small headline in the classified section of the *Richmond Gazette*.

> Advertisement entitled '*Live-In Situation – Capable Girl Wanted*', withdrawn, as the first advertisement brought an overwhelming response. Yours truly.

Delphine smiled, turning the page. From that overwhelming response, *she* was the capable girl who had been chosen. She would be leaving Ryan's Castle at the end of the week, although the Camberwells would probably let her stay here forever. She *wished* she could stay here forever! But her pride would not permit it. She must make her own way, and she would be staying in Richmond, only moving down the hill and along a bit. She would be able to pursue her friendships with Blue and Merrigan; friendships that still seemed to her improbable and wonderful. She would be making her own money again and living close to that dappled gold and green river. She could hardly believe her luck.

She would never forget her first sight of the river that day, nor the sudden explosion of motion that had catapulted her into it, nor the sludgy green waters closing over her head. Sprawling on dry land, gasping like a landed fish, she could never have imagined that she had found her new home. But the Fates must have decreed it from the moment she woke up on the District in Richmond. Why else her illogical tarrying? Why else would she have been rescued by the kindest family on earth?

And a further miracle: when she'd seen the advertisement in the paper, she hadn't known to whom she was applying. It gave only a box number at the newspaper office and the initials P. G. This had turned out to be Paul Greenbow, none other than the kindly dairyman whose horse had knocked her into the water in the first place. Life was guiding her; she could see it plainly. Chucking her into rivers where necessary.

It transpired that Paul and his wife lived in a cottage on Old Palace Lane, next door to Paul's parents, Fanny and Stephen. They were getting on, their health fading rapidly, but Stephen had been a tobacconist before his retirement so they had a small nest egg that allowed them to employ someone to help. Paul hadn't fancied spending his life in a shop, so he did the deliveries for the local milk company in the mornings, then helped out at the dairy the rest of the day. Delphine was to live with his parents, caring for the house, shopping for food and running errands, leaving them to enjoy life with whatever vigour remained to them. She might also, from time to time, help out next door, as Paul's wife, Sylvia, had just given birth to twins. Overwhelmed indeed!

When she saw the advertisement, the whole family, including Merrigan, Avis, Elf and even Tabitha, had gathered around the kitchen table to discuss what she should do. At last Delphine could stay awake long enough to hold a sensible conversation! Day after day of feeling safe, of long days on the lawn, of sleep, sleep and more blessed sleep, had brought her back to herself. She formed the habit of writing in her notebook every morning; by starting her days in her own company she got to know herself again. And she slowly started to find her voice again, albeit on paper first.

It felt odd to be the subject of a family conference. Even though times were changing, it wasn't every family of their standing who would show more than dutiful kindness towards someone like her. But the Camberwells seemed to have no concept of 'someone like her'. She was just Delphine. She was part of them now.

'As much as I really don't want to lose you,' said Midge. 'What are the merits of you staying here versus getting as far away as possible from your beast of a husband? I would love to have you nearby. But would it be better for *you* to go to Betty? Would you be *safer* there?'

Kenneth nodded. 'I agree. Safety must be tantamount. Although it did occur to me that you don't really *know* anyone in Sussex. A childhood friendship lapsed more than fifteen years ago might not turn out to be strongest of bonds. It might not prove much of a solution at all. I *was* turning over another idea, which is that I would happily give you the money to start a new life anywhere you choose. You could go even further, if you like.'

Delphine cried out in protest – it would feel like banishment – but Kenneth held his hand up.

'I've already rejected it. It would do you no good to be cut off altogether. To start anew among strangers isn't easy. I don't see how Foley could ever find you in some arbitrarily chosen spot *or* in Sussex, but if he *should*, at least here you have us. You have protection.'

'True,' said Blue. 'Surely there's safety in numbers, in community.'

Delphine nodded. 'Richmond might not be f . . . far, but there's worlds and worlds in London, one right next to the other. F . . . for the most part, people don't even know the other ones exist. They don't care.' It was true. In parts of London, the post-war slums were still devastating whole areas, yet here in Richmond, chestnut trees waved their leafy, lime-green heads and willows dreamed by the river. Wherever you were, it was easy to stay in ignorance, of worse things *and* of better things, unless you made the effort of imagination and enquiry.

'And I don't think F . . . F . . . Foley would ever dream I could be accepted s . . . somewhere like this,' added Delphine. 'He doesn't have a high enough opinion of m . . . me.'

'Vile man,' spat Tabitha, striking a match with some force, as if wishing the whole situation up in flames. She rose and opened a window through which to smoke.

'Foley has no contacts in this area?' Kenneth queried. 'No cause to come here, for work or any other reason?'

Delphine told him no, none.

'Very well.' Kenneth nodded. 'I'm satisfied that this is the best place for you, that we're not just biased because we want you nearby.' His words made Delphine feel warm inside. 'But, my dear, I must ask you one thing. It need not change your plans, but I must ask it.'

He stood up and took a drag of Tabitha's cigarette. 'Might we not go after him?' he asked. 'I feel deeply unhappy that a man like that should get off scot-free with what he's done, and that you should have to live with the knowledge that – heaven forbid – your paths might yet cross. You would have our full backing and I for one would feel much happier if that bounder were behind bars.'

'And left there to rot,' added Midge with feeling.

Delphine's throat tightened. She couldn't say a word.

'And another thing,' said Merrigan. 'You're *married* to him. What if you meet someone? Like this, he'll always be like a leash around your neck. One day you may want to divorce him. Wouldn't it be better to have a police report on file now?'

Delphine wanted to cry. The peace of mind she had mustered so far had come about from *not* thinking about Foley.

From just accepting that it had happened, it was over and that she could start anew. As for being free, that was irrelevant. Who would ever want her? More to the point, whom could *she* ever want? She could never bear to be intimate with a man after what Foley had done. Her speech was improving fast, but any extreme emotion chased it away again, and the thought of Foley did it more surely than anything.

'No, p . . . p . . . please,' she begged. 'I c . . . can't see him. I can't think about it. I d . . . don't want to. I can't!'

Kenneth looked unhappy. 'We certainly shan't *make* you do it, dear, so put your mind at rest on that score, but hear me out, if you will . . .'

He began to argue in favour of reporting Foley, trying for a prosecution. But all Delphine heard was a dull rushing like a powerful wind. The very idea of returning to Whitechapel, of explaining to official people how it was to live with Foley, was appalling. To appear in court, perhaps, with Foley there, knowing she was a snail without a shell before him . . . The conversation around her sounded like the wireless when you were trying to tune in and not quite hitting the station. Tinny worms of sound borne away on waves of static before you could catch them. The roaring intensified; the fear mounted inside her . . .

And the next thing she knew, she was being picked off the floor by Elf, and Blue was murmuring soothing words and stroking her hair. Delphine looked around, blinking.

'You passed out for a moment,' said Merrigan, taking her

hand across the table. 'Daddy, it's too soon for her. You're absolutely right in everything you say, but she can't take it now.'

'I shan't say another word,' said Kenneth. 'I'm sorry, Delphine. We shan't pursue it. We shall just support you and keep you safe. How's that?'

Delphine nodded gratefully. Tabitha brought her a glass of water, which she gulped, and offered her a cigarette, which she refused. The world shifted again and settled back on its axis.

'Then how do we manage this?' asked Kenneth. 'We don't want to create a life of undue fear and subterfuge, but some measures must be taken.' And a new discussion began.

No one in Richmond knew her real name besides the Camberwells, Tabitha and Elf. That was an easy thing to change, since she didn't want to keep Foley's anyway. They rejected the obvious choice of reverting to her maiden name and settled on Brown as a pleasantly anonymous alternative.

It had been as Delphine Brown that she attended her interview and secured the post. And so she would be known henceforth in Richmond.

Delphine could see that living under an assumed name, always tied through marriage to a brute, always living under the shadow of perhaps seeing him again one day, must look like an imperfect and shabby sort of freedom to the Camberwells. But living under a shadow was better than living with a terrible daily reality. And it was far more than she had ever dreamed she could have.

# Chapter Twenty-two

Midge was getting ready for bed when she heard a tap at her door – Kenneth, she knew at once.

'Come in, darling!' she called, her heart pounding. Sometimes he called on her late in the evening just to talk over the events of the day. That was lovely. But she hoped it wasn't just that.

She heard the door being nudged open and pushed across the cream carpet. She was sitting in front of the mirror. She had just taken her hair down and was about to unfasten her pearl necklace, but she stopped, her hands hovering at her neck. Kenneth liked pearls. She fluffed at her hair instead. Loose, it softened her narrow features. Then, as if it were simply a part of her bedtime routine, she puffed a little scent onto her wrists and collarbones, instead of slathering her face in cold cream.

'My dear,' said Kenneth. She turned on her stool to face him. He was holding two small glasses of port. He smiled down at her and kissed her forehead. She hated that. Kisses on foreheads were for children.

'Not for me. You know I'm not keen,' she demurred when he held a glass out to her. She instantly regretted it when he set down both glasses and turned away. *Would it* kill *you to share a little late-night spirit with your husband?*'

Kenneth sat on her bed. 'Delphine leaves us in a couple of days,' he said.

'Yes,' said Midge, going to sit beside him. 'Do you think she'll be all right?'

He took her hands. 'That she'll be content in her post I have no doubt. The Greenbows are good sorts, and Delphine is so grateful they could probably keep her in a cellar and she'd count herself lucky.'

Midge smiled. 'I don't think they'll do that, darling. But you're quite right.'

'Have we done the right thing, Midge? Will she be safe? What if that dog hunts her down? I wish I knew more about him, about the way he operates. But one doesn't like to ask . . .'

Midge smoothed a thick lock of gold off his face and ran her fingers through his hair to push it all back. It was all she could do not to seize it in her fist and hold on tight; his hair was one of his many beauties. But she didn't. He was troubled and this was one of the countless reasons she loved him. For all his faults and insensitivities, he was a kind man. He cared deeply about others.

'I know you, Kenneth. I know you're turning it over and over in your mind, looking for alternative courses of action . . .'

'It seems too easy,' he said, with a pleading expression. 'I want to do right by her.'

'And you are. You have. We can't force her to do anything. And I honestly can't think of a better alternative, apart from going after that awful man as you suggested. But as you've seen yourself, she is *not* strong enough! If it's any consolation to you, she's pretty confident she left no trace.'

'How do you know?'

'Blue told me. They've talked about it. Apparently, Delphine didn't pack a thing beforehand, so he couldn't have a clue what she was planning. She didn't take a suitcase, nothing to arouse suspicion. She told her neighbour she was off to Covent Garden and agreed to call in when she got back. To all intents and purposes she was just off to do some errands. Her blasted husband wouldn't have noticed anything amiss until he got home that evening – by which time Delphine was already here with us.' Midge nodded with some satisfaction. 'So you see, darling, even if he started hunting right away, however would he find her? She didn't even end up where she *planned* to, which is fortuitous! Even if the ticket seller *did* remember her among all the hundreds of customers that day, she was supposed to be going to Victoria. He'd go looking there – and find nothing.'

Kenneth squeezed her hand. 'That does ease my mind. You're right: she's a grown woman. It's not for me to presume what's best for her. Especially as I can't even begin to imagine what she's been through.' He grimaced. 'I thought I'd seen enough that was gruesome and foul during the war. But lo and behold, cruelty lurks not only on the battlefield but in ordinary homes. Her own *husband*! How does a woman go on after treatment like that?'

Midge shook her head. 'I truly can't fathom, my dear. My husband is a good and kind man.' She hesitated, then added softly, 'And a desirable one.' He looked at her enquiringly and she nodded. 'I've never known anything but goodness at your hands, Kenneth, and as you know, there was no one before you. I've never known a bad man, thank God. Only ever you.'

*But sometimes indifference can hurt just as much as cruelty*, hissed a slippery, unworthy voice in her head. She was shocked at herself. As if the things that hurt her – the thoughtless comments, the admiration of other women, the constant reminders that she was second best – could *possibly* be compared to Delphine's experience.

*He is a good man*, she told the snake-voice sternly, *and ours is a good marriage.*

*Oh yes, a fine marriage*, it sneered. *Is that why he ignored you at that breakfast party to talk and talk with Roberta Grady? And the others? And when you made some small comment about it later, he looked at you in charming disbelief and said, 'Well, you are a grown-up, darling. I shouldn't have to babysit you.'*

It had hurt. He knew she was a shy woman, that she felt out of her depth in her new social milieu. When a woman like Roberta was around, brassy and big and thrusting herself between them at every opportunity, Midge shrank. And Kenneth was too in love with attention to remember Midge.

*Kenneth would never cheat on me. He's too honourable.*

*There are a million small ways to betray someone without that.*

'Enough!' cried Midge. Kenneth looked startled.

'Sorry, darling.' She laughed, gathering herself. 'I was just imagining . . . that marriage . . . and I don't care to. Such a lovely young woman. But she's here now, and safe.'

'Yes, you're right. Thank you, my dear wife. What a comfort you are to me.'

*Only a comfort? Nothing else?* Hiss, hiss.

'I must let you get to bed.' He kissed her forehead again and stood to go.

'Oh, wait, darling. Why don't we have that port, after all? Talk about happier things?'

He looked surprised, and Midge hurried over to the dressing table to pick up the glasses. Her satin dressing gown slipped open and she saw his eyes graze her narrow, lace-edged night-gown. She kissed him, lightly, on the lips, and saw under-standing dawn in his eyes. *Finally.*

'Perhaps I might stay awhile, wife.' He grinned, bending to kiss her properly this time.

*Wife*, thought Midge as she kissed him back. *I'm his wife. He's my husband. He's mine, he's mine, he's mine.*

# Chapter Twenty-three

Early one mist-hung, glowing morning, Blue tapped on Delphine's door to go to the river. She squinted at Blue for a bleary moment, hair straggling across her face, then she remembered.

'With you in a jiff, Blue,' she said, sitting up and feeling the shiver in the air.

'I'll let you get dressed,' said Blue. 'Meet me in the hall.'

The previous night, they'd been talking about Delphine's growing fondness for writing in her notebook, and Blue vowed there was nothing quite like writing on a bench early on an autumn morning – Delphine must try it. These were precious and private times for Blue, Delphine knew, so she felt very honoured by the invitation. But Blue was ecstatic that her suggestion had proved helpful to Delphine *and* that it was bringing her happiness, too. Delphine was convinced that her writing and Blue's were poles apart in terms of ambition and accomplishment, but the love of it was something they had in common. It set the seal on an already burgeoning friendship.

All the Camberwells (and Delphine included Tabitha in that

grouping) were kind and funny and wonderful. They all took
care of her – clothes, safety, shelter – but Blue was the one
who thought about her stammer and what might help, who
lent her books to inspire her, who included her in her own
personal loves, like this walk.

Blue was right. The riverside was heavenly at that time of
day, that time of year. Great ropes of bright berries looped
through the hedges, and the water was green and still, wearing
a chiffon of mist as pale as mistletoe. Blue looked subdued, but
Delphine wouldn't ask her about it right away. Blue would tell
her in her own time – if she wanted to tell her at all.

So she pursued her own thoughts, hoping, very much, that
they would still see each other often once she moved to the
Greenbows' at the end of the week. She had no doubts about
her course of action. She'd already been at Ryan's Castle over
a month – a far cry from the 'few days' they had first agreed.
It was blissful, but Delphine had always been independent.
When you were poor, your pride was all you had. Foley
had taken that from her too, for a while, but he wasn't here
now. She wouldn't linger on and become a burden on these
good people.

They walked in companionable silence for a while, their soft
footfalls and the occasional outraged cries of swans and geese
marking their progress along the path from bridge to bridge.

'Here,' said Blue after a while, and they sat on a bench and
took out their notebooks and wrote for a while, still in silence,

still with the good feeling growing deeper between them. But for once Delphine was writing more than Blue. Blue was gazing into space, and the look on her face wasn't contented reverie but one of sadness.

At last Delphine nudged her in the ribs. 'Oi, missus,' she said, 'what's on your mind?' Blue was much more cultured than she was, better educated and with far bigger ideas about life; Delphine often felt like a child trailing after her in wonder through her magical world. But Blue was so gentle that Delphine felt safe to be herself, to tease and ask questions and offer opinions. And Delphine was older, after all. She had lived more in other ways, so they seemed to meet in the middle and feel just right together.

Blue sighed and nudged her back. 'Don't mind me. It's just the same old saga, worrying me senseless.'

'The newspaper saga, or the letters?'

'Both, in fact!' She rummaged in her satchel and drew out a folded copy of the *Gazette* and a white envelope. She handed them both to Delphine. The paper was folded back to a page where a picture of Blue and a picture of a handsome man Delphine didn't know were separated by only a few lines of text.

Readers will surely remember the extravagant announcement by Richmond's very own Kenneth Camberwell at his daughter's coming-of-age in August. The man who could capture her heart in a letter would win her hand, we were told. Over the weeks, the *Gazette* has endeavoured to follow the story of the romantic fate of this Richmond belle. However, there has been very little to report until recently. Read on!

Richmond's darling, Blue Camberwell, has been seen several times lately in the company of the debonair Dorian Fields, son of Tristan Fields, financier and all-round top banana.

'Just friends,' was the only comment blushing Blue has ever given. But last night, wearing yellow ochre satin, she attended Violet Larraby's birthday bash on the arm of delicious Dorian and the two looked very cosy. Have two old friends been brought to a realisation of love by a lavish toast? Who knows? When this roving reporter enquired, delicious Dorian responded with a wink.

'Gawd,' said Delphine. She knew how much Blue hated seeing herself in the papers, and how she lived in hope that they would lose interest in her story. Privately Delphine thought it would be a while until they did, and Tabitha said the same.

'He's a pretty one, I'll grant you,' she commented. 'You could see that face on a packet of ciggies, couldn't you?'

Blue nodded. 'He's very beautiful,' she agreed. 'But it's not – we're not . . . Oh, the papers make it feel so . . . inescapable. That I'll marry *someone*, I mean. Daddy would *never* hold me to what he said, of course, but I know he really wants to see me settled. It would make him so happy. It's worked out so well for Merrigan, and he loves having a son-in-law and a grandchild. He's a patriarch, my papa. But I can't force it. I *won't* rush into anything. And then there's this . . .' She took a letter from the envelope and handed it to Delphine.

*Darling Blue,*

*I know you told me not to write again, but I have to. I don't mean to make you uncomfortable, but I can see it so clearly, you and me. I'll do anything, Blue, anything to make you happy. I'm a good person and the world is full of cruelty. We can shelter each other from that. When I think of you with someone else, someone who might hurt you, I feel frantic. And when I think of myself with someone else, just as you said . . . I can't! I can't, Blue, I can't give up on you, on us. Please reconsider. Please let me take you out. Dinner? A concert? A walk in the park? Whatever you like. Write me a note and leave it in the apple tree, and I will oblige.*

*Yours with true and abiding affection,*
*Foster*

'Gawd,' said Delphine again. She was shocked to see Blue's eyes shimmer.

'He's such a dear,' said Blue in a voice thick with tears, 'but he's frightening me now. What's he talking about? Sheltering each other and a world full of cruelty? He doesn't sound like the Foster I've always known and loved.'

Delphine tipped her head, considering. 'He's certainly smitten with you. And you definitely, definitely don't . . . couldn't?'

'Definitely! Golly, Delphine, it would be like kissing my little brother. I've *never* thought of him that way. And I never will. But I care about him! And I've tried everything I can think of to make him understand. Where's this come from? There was never a mention of it before, and I know Daddy made that speech, but surely that didn't *make* him fall in love with me?'

'Can't have done. Doesn't work like that. Well, I don't know much about romance, Blue, but sure as eggs you can't fall in love because someone wants you to. There's a funny feeling to that letter, isn't there, as if something's . . . wrong somehow? But you can't be clouded by what Foster wants, or what your father wants, or any of it. You know what *you* want, don't you?'

Blue nodded. 'To work on my writing. To follow up this chance that Juno's given me, wherever it might lead. To see Dorian, or whoever I want, if it suits me, and not rush into anything.'

'Well then. I know too much about being pushed into things you don't want to do. Don't worry about your father. He might want all those things for you, but he loves you. He'll understand. I wish my father had been a tenth as kind.

And Foster . . . I don't know. Can't you get Tabitha to have a word or something?'

Blue squinted, considering. 'Maybe,' she murmured. 'I'll think about it. Thank you. I feel better for talking to you. He makes it sound so simple – a straightforward matter of not withholding my affection! He makes me feel so cruel!'

Delphine snorted. 'That's the last thing you are. He's just lost his way. Meanwhile, you have your life to live! You've got your interview at the paper tomorrow. You need something good to happen, something just for you.'

The thought of anyone making Blue feel this way made Delphine indignant. She had little patience for men and the various different ways that they exerted pressure to get what they wanted. And that talk about Blue being with someone who might hurt her – that made Delphine shiver. What did Foster Foxton, son of one of Richmond's best families, young, sheltered and spoiled, know of such things?

# Chapter Twenty-four

Thursday came bearing Blue's appointment with Gordon Whiskett on gusty winds and beams of mercurial sunshine. 'Should I take an umbrella?' groused Blue. 'I really don't want to take an umbrella.'

'Take an umbrella!' said Merrigan, looking up from her newspaper. 'I do not understand your preposterous aversion to the things. It's a perfectly reasonable, practical invention.'

Blue curled her lip. 'Reasonable, practical. Two words that spell death to the soul!'

Merrigan rolled her eyes. 'There's nothing wrong with being practical. You can trot out of here all unencumbered and romantic, but if it rains on your way down the hill, you'll turn up at your interview like a drowned rat and drip all over his desk. That's not romantic; that's stupid.' Then she looked at Blue properly. 'You're nervous,' she relented, closing the paper. She got up and gave her sister a hug. 'It's all right, darling, you're going to be wonderful. You'll be devastatingly impressive, wet or dry. And it'll be the start of something. You'll see.'

Blue squeezed her sister and took a deep breath. 'Thank you, Merry. You're right, I am nervous. I'd better take a blasted umbrella.'

'Tell you what. I'll walk with you. I'll carry the umbrella, hold it over you if it rains, deposit you at the doors of the *Gazette*, then retire discreetly. If you get soaked on the way home, who cares?'

Blue laughed. Was that the definition of family love? Humouring the other person's quite unreasonable foibles? 'Thank you. You're the best sister.'

'Of course I am. There should be an award. Come on, stop dithering about or you'll be late. Wait, not like that.'

She had persuaded Blue into wearing one of the cloche hats that, she maintained, could not fail to give a woman an air of sophistication and mystique. Blue complained that they blocked her vision. As such, she did a very half-hearted job of wearing them. Merrigan rammed it forward and pulled it down fetchingly.

'Now look!' she commanded. And she was right. The style perfectly suited Blue's face. Her wide mouth and dainty chin looked a picture underneath the curved lines of the cloche. Merrigan pulled one blonde strand of hair forward to complete the look. 'Perfection,' she said. 'Divine with that smart grey suit.' And off they went.

The office was a red-brick building of indeterminate age, somewhere near the station. For a moment, Merrigan's flippant manner departed and Blue could see genuine excitement sparkling in her dark brown eyes. 'Good luck and enjoy, clever sister,' she said fervently. 'I know I want other things for you as well as writing, but it doesn't mean I don't admire and support you. Whatever opportunities are in store, take them!'

Blue watched her go, then went inside. *Enjoy*, she told herself. *Take opportunities.*

A receptionist with the shiniest lipstick Blue had ever seen greeted her. For a moment, Blue thought she had walked into the office of a Hollywood studio, not a local newspaper.

'Cherry,' said the receptionist, noticing Blue's gaze. 'Aren't these new flavoured lipsticks the cat's whiskers? I'm Sheila. Welcome to the *Gazette*.'

Sheila showed her to a large room on the first floor with seven or eight desks dotted across the space. 'Over there,' she said, nodding towards a door with a glass panel at the far end of the room. 'Just knock and go straight in.'

Blue felt self-conscious as she walked across the floor. Men were sitting at the desks, clutching the handsets of telephones, frowning over copy or leafing dully through large reference books. They were dressed, for the most part, in shirts, ties and waistcoats and they all stopped to watch her progress with varying shades of interest. There was no sign of Juno.

*Gosh*, thought Blue. *What must it be like to come here to work every day? To be the only woman?*

When she was halfway across the room, a voice rang out.

'Got lost, have we, darling? The department store's down the street. No silk stockings here, I'm afraid.'

She was so surprised that she spun on her heel and lost her balance, bumping into a tall plant in a pot, which rocked sideways and knocked into a nearby desk. 'Oh dear,' the same voice drawled. 'Not a very promising start.'

*Start to what?* wondered Blue, composing herself. She wouldn't squander her attention on an asinine blister. She had an editor to meet.

Gordon Whiskett was about fifty and fraying at the edges. He was bald, with a few strands of grey hair slicked back from his forehead in straight lines, giving the rather odd effect of a grey and pink striped head. He wore eyeglasses and had his sleeves rolled right up, as if he were doing something very physical, like delivering a calf. In fact, he was consulting a thesaurus. He looked up when Blue came in.

'Miss Camberwell,' he said at once, getting up to shake her hand. 'Thank you for coming in.'

'I was happy to come, Mr Whiskett. I'm delighted you wanted to see me.'

'Good, good. Call me Gordon. At the *Gazette* we're all far too rushed to be formal.'

Blue smiled. 'All right, Gordon. And I'm Ishbel.'

'Yes, I know. Now, I'm due at a riot in half an hour so I must be brief.'

Blue raised her eyebrows. She hadn't imagined a riot was a

thing one made an appointment for; the word implied spontaneity.

'This piece you sent Juno, about school funding . . .' He scrabbled around in a haystack of papers. Blue spotted the distinctive letterhead of Ryan's Castle and handed it to him. 'Ah, thank you. Well, it's excellent, that's all.'

'That's all?' He'd invited her here just to tell her that?

'Yes. I mean, usually there's some spare fluff here, a poor simile there. That's where I come in. But here, nothing to say. A thoroughly professional piece of writing.'

Blue's heart started doing the kickadoo. 'Thank you. I can't tell you how much your good opinion means to me. I've always wanted to write and I've—'

'Yes, well, you're on the right track. Now, Griggs is off.'

'Griggs?'

'Yes. It's his leg, you know, since the war. Been playing up something rotten for a good while now. He's struggled; we've accommodated him. First-class writer, Griggs.'

'Oh,' said Blue. 'Jolly good.'

'He had a fall two weeks ago. Doctors and so forth . . . The latest page in the issue is that he won't be able to get about properly for six months. Normally I'd recruit and it would be too bad for Griggs. But his writing's sharp, you know?'

'I see.'

'So I had the idea to hold his job open. Can't pay him, of

course, but at least the job's there for him to come back to. Better than nothing. Best I can do.'

'I should think that's very kind.'

'Yes. Good. So do you want it?'

'Pardon me?'

'Do you want the shot? Full-time staff writer for six months – or however long it is. Of course, it's unlikely there'll be a position for you at the end of it. If Griggs wants it, it's his, and I imagine the others are pretty much here for life. But it'll be experience – might help you get a spot on another paper. Can't argue with that.'

Indeed she couldn't! Blue smiled broadly. Was this really happening? Any doubts she may have had about the daily realities of being a journalist vanished in an instant. She wanted this.

'May I just check, Mr . . . Gordon? You're offering me a job, on a temporary basis? Here at the office? You want me to come in every day and go out on assignments and write articles and . . . and . . . so forth.'

'Exactly so. Start on Monday, if you'd be so kind. Nine sharp. Juno'll show you the ropes.'

'Er, wonderful! Yes! I'd love to. Thanks awfully.'

'Now, I'd better get on. You can see yourself out?'

'Of course. I'll be here on Monday. You can count on me, Gordon.'

'Splendid. Now, my keys . . .'

'Here,' said Blue, picking them off the windowsill. 'Goodbye.'

She paused at his door, wondering whether she should mention the untoward comment from the sarky reporter, then decided against it. Gordon was her boss, not her protector. If she was to become a working woman, she would need to fight her own battles – though so far it had only been one stupid remark. Less a battle than a skirmish, really.

As she walked through the office, she beamed at everyone. A couple of the men smiled back and a couple muttered friendly good mornings, which heartened her further. Then she collided with a man in the doorway; he was hurrying and ran into her with quite a bump.

'I'm very sorry, miss!' he exclaimed.

At once the same sharp voice behind her called, 'Oh, what joy to have a clumsy mumsy in the office. I do think every paper should get one.'

Blue turned to see a man of about twenty-five, handsome in a generic sort of way, with dark-framed spectacles, leaning back in his chair and sneering. It was the only word for his expression, thought Blue, automatically scrolling through synonyms in her head.

'I'm not a mumsy,' she said clearly. 'My sister has a child. I do not. I should remember if I had. Is checking facts not the done thing on this paper?'

'Jolly well done, miss,' chuckled the man she had bumped into, who accompanied her into the hall and shut the door behind them. He had light brown hair, wildly untidy, and dark brown eyes. *Not generically handsome*, Blue noted. *In fact, not handsome at all. Not cultured-sounding, like his colleague in there, nor half so smartly dressed.* She liked him at once.

'Am I right in supposing that you're Miss Camberwell?' he asked with a friendly smile.

'Yes indeed.' She held out her gloved hand. 'Ishbel.'

He shook her hand. 'Barnaby Tanner. Staff reporter. Been here a year or so. Sorry I rammed you. You're not hurt, I hope?'

'Not at all. Nice to meet you, Mr Tanner. And your friend in there? Is he always like that?'

'Pretty much, yes. At least when there's women around. He doesn't think they belong here, you see. Thinks they're taking jobs that men need now they're back from war with families to support.'

'I see. And you, Mr Tanner? Is that what you think?'

He laughed. 'Wait till you've known me a few weeks and then ask me that. I've five sisters. Four of them work. Proud as punch of 'em, I am. I'm what Cauderlie in there – that's your nemesis, Robert Cauderlie – calls a progressive. So be it, say I. Barney Tanner, progressive, at your service.'

Blue smiled. 'Mr Whiskett's asked me to start work here on Monday. To cover someone called Greggs or Jeggs . . .'

'Jimmy Griggs. Yes, terrible what happened to him. We all knew, you see, that Whisky was going to ask you. Cauderlie's been simmering about it. Didn't help, mind, that Gordon showed your article round the office and said that's how it should be done. Cauderlie doesn't like anyone being better than him.'

'Oh dear. Perhaps that wasn't the most tactful thing he could've done.'

'He's got the tact of a biscuit, old Whisky, but we're all used to him. Cauderlie won't bother you though. He's all bark and no bite . . . A lot of bark, in fairness. He won't put you off taking the job, will he?'

'Certainly not! This opportunity for me . . . Well, I can't tell you how happy I am to have it, Mr Tanner.'

He grinned – an utterly disarming grin. 'I'm pleased to hear it. Now let me walk you down.'

'No, please, I've detained you long enough.'

'Rubbish. Eight men in there and not a gent among 'em, leaving a lady to walk out alone.' He offered his arm and Blue took it, enjoying his old-fashioned manners. At the doorway they said goodbye.

'Thank you for the welcome, Mr Tanner.'

Blue waved to Sheila, then left the offices of the *Richmond Gazette* with a spring in her step, a new job and the beginning of at least one new friendship. Not bad for a fifteen-minute visit.

When Blue arrived home, the first person she saw was Merrigan, putting on her hat and gloves in the hall. 'That was quick! Didn't it go as you'd hoped?'

'It went *better*!' Blue grinned and told her the news.

'My darling sister! My word, a real job! A working woman, doing what you love. Oh, Blue! I'm so pleased for you, so proud. I'm already on pins to read a piece in the paper and see your initials at the bottom – B. C.'

'I. C.,' Blue corrected her. 'I'll go by Ishbel in the office, and for my writing. More professional. Blue's for home.'

'Quite right. Yes, that's the ticket. Blue, darling, I have to go. I promised Lawrence I'd be home before him for once, but let's meet up tomorrow and you can tell me everything. I'm taking Delphine to the hairdresser's at eleven. After that?'

'Delphine to the . . .? Anyway, yes, fine. Toodle-pip.'

No one was home and Blue was frustrated, bursting to tell the world. She ran out to the Cottage.

'Darling Elf, the very utterly best of news!' she cried as she burst in.

'You're going to write a piece for the *Gazette*!' he exulted, leaping to his feet. 'Tell me all!'

'Even better than that. Elf, I've got a job! It's only for six months, but afterwards . . . Well, with experience like that, who knows? I'll learn so much! Why, Elf, whatever's wrong?'

Her happy, tumbling monologue trickled to a halt when she saw him turn away. She watched him remove his spectacles, rubbing the bridge of his nose as though he had a great discomfort there.

'Elf, darling? Are you ill?'

He gave her a worried smile. 'No, not ill, just . . . well, shocked! Do you mean to say you're planning to go out all day, every day, to work in an office?'

Blue's concern turned to bafflement. 'Well, yes!'

'But have you thought this through? I mean, how much time did this Whiskett chap give you to think it over?'

'Well, none. But I didn't ask for any.'

'You don't mean to say you said yes on the spot?'

Blue faltered. She obviously wasn't explaining it right. 'Elf, it's a *writing* job! A *paid* writing job! For six months. It's a hundred times more than I was expecting. Why wouldn't I say yes? Why are you looking as though I'm going to prison?'

Elf sat heavily on the sofa. 'I'm sorry if I'm raining on your parade, but this all seems rather sudden. One minute you're hoping to get a commission, the next minute you're a full-time reporter? You know your upbringing's been rather sheltered. You're such a . . . a *lady*! How can you just start traipsing over London with those, those *news hounds*, getting up to who knows what? I'm not sure this is appropriate at all!'

'You don't think I can do it?' asked Blue in a small voice.

'It's not that I don't think you can do it, exactly. The writing, well, I know you can do *that*. But is it the sort of environment where a girl like you can flourish? You're a sensitive soul, Blue! I've seen you moved to tears countless times by the grim realities of this world. You'll see a whole lot more of them in that job, I promise.'

It was extraordinary. He was voicing all her own worst fears about herself. Yet hearing them laid out bare like that had an unexpected effect. It gave her a new determination that they shouldn't be true.

'They'll expect you to grow hard-bitten and thick-skinned like *them*,' Elf added bitterly.

'How many reporters do *you* know?' asked Blue in growing outrage. It seemed a sweeping generalisation to her. 'You *knew* I wanted this.'

'I thought you were going to accept commissions, grow your reputation as a writer of skill and discernment. I thought you were going to stay *here* to work on your literary ambitions. I thought you wanted to write a novel!'

'I do! But that's not easy, Elf. I need experience . . .'

'Not this kind of experience – it's irrelevant!'

'*All* kinds of experience!' Blue insisted.

She looked around this peaceful refuge, adapted for Elf by her mother ten years ago and unchanged since. She thought of the strange and lovely fact of having him living at the bottom of the garden – and the fact that he hardly ever left. He was a soldier who'd been broken by the war; he was an analyst who didn't see patients any more. He was scared, she realised suddenly. Of living a life beyond Ryan's Castle, of change, and now he was scared that she would fail too. Maybe she would. Perhaps if one of them admitted it, it might make everything right. He'd always said the truth was a great magic.

'I'm scared, Elf,' she confessed. 'It will be different for me, and challenging and rough. I don't know how I'll hold up.'

He looked at her imploringly. 'Then don't do it,' he said. 'It's not too late to write and say you've reconsidered. If you're scared, don't do it.'

Elf was her great font of wisdom. This was the first time he had ever said something that felt entirely wrong to her. But perhaps that was what growing up was – recognising bad advice, even when it was given to you by the people you loved the most. That was *his* way, she realised – to let fear steer him away from things. It wasn't hers. She would have to run the gauntlet and if she failed, she failed. At least she would have tried.

# Chapter Twenty-five

When Delphine Foley had left Whitechapel in sweltering August, she didn't have much to lose. Nevertheless, she'd lost what little she had in the mighty Thames. Now autumn offered a new beginning. The old feelings of fear and self-loathing had retreated into the cool, deep shadows and the honeyed light brought fresh emotions to the foreground: hope, gratitude and a sense of possibility. Delphine Brown left Ryan's Castle on a day bursting with promise. This time she had a suitcase containing several of Tabitha's cast-offs, lovely things all. And she wasn't alone: Blue and Midge accompanied her, even though it was a ten-minute walk and she was a woman starting work, not a child starting school.

The Greenbows, both the senior and junior branches, were so good-natured and easy that she knew she would be comfortable there. They invited the Camberwell ladies in for a pot of tea and they all – employers, employee and wealthy up-the-hill folk – sat round a table together. Blue invited them all to the Camberwells' autumn garden party.

'Come,' echoed Midge. 'Our paths don't cross often enough. We'd love to have you.'

'And come and see us soon, Delphine!' urged Blue, when they said goodbye. 'As soon as you can. We shall miss you.'

'She'll come on Sunday,' said Mrs Greenbow the younger, juggling babies. 'We're all going to visit my parents. Delphine can have a day off.'

Delphine had to laugh. Sunday was the day after tomorrow. Parties and days off before she'd properly begun? What kind of job was this?

With the Camberwells gone, she turned to some light duties – washing dishes, making beds and some dusting. Then Fanny suggested she unpack and settle in. 'This is your new home, after all. We'll call you if we need you, dear.'

She had a tiny room at the front of the house, overlooking the street that led to the river. The first thing Delphine did was to move her small table to just in front of the window and lay her notebook and pen upon it. She could sit here all day, she felt, and watch the folk traipse up and down. Between house and street was a small, neat front garden, and she longed to watch the seasons change among its branches and blooms. Already she had spotted a robin bouncing from tree to wall and back again, and the fantastical branches of a magnolia tree in the garden.

She laid out her very few possessions on a shelf, beside a small oval mirror that swung in a teak stand. A comb, lipstick, mascara and a small pot of cold cream, all given to her by Blue. Essentials, so Blue insisted. She peered into the mirror and ran the comb through her hair. It only took a moment. The previous day, Merrigan had taken her to have her hair bobbed. Although Delphine had cottoned on to Merrigan's mission to bob the world, she could see it would be more practical when she started work. Plus, there was nothing like a new hairstyle to make a girl feel different. Delphine Foley had long, weighty hair like pondweed. Delphine Brown was a modern girl, a working woman. *She* had a bob!

'You'll have to wash your neck now you've had your hair cropped,' Tabitha had teased her yesterday.

Delphine clutched her neck in horror. Was it dirty?

'She's *joking*!' Merrigan told her. 'It's not even her joke, it's what *I* said to *her* when she bobbed hers.'

'It's not even *your* joke, you got it from a magazine!' retorted Tabitha. Delphine didn't care whose joke it was, so long as she hadn't disgraced herself with a dirty neck.

# Chapter Twenty-six

Things had been going too smoothly, decided Blue on Sunday afternoon, picnicking in Richmond Park with Merrigan, Tab and Delphine. It was one of those perfect September days — drifts of copper leaves settling into the long grasses, the air bright and clear. Her mind had been put at ease once again about Foster. Tabitha had had a word with him and assured Blue he'd give up his courtship. Blue had been so relieved, and so happy about her job at the paper, that she'd confided in the girls about Dorian and L. W. She was regretting it.

'What kind of a name is *Latchley*?' demanded Merrigan. 'He sounds like a Deep South plantation owner! He sounds as though he should be puffing on a cigar and pacing on a veranda!'

'He's not pacing on a veranda.'

'He *could* be! How do you know? You've never met him! He could tell you anything at all and it might not be true.'

'That,' said Blue, 'is rather the point.'

'What do you mean? Oh no. You're not going to meet

him, are you? For heaven's sake, Blue! Have you lost your mind? Is it addled from squinting over too many semicolons and commas?'

'I can't believe you've been seeing *Dorian*!' marvelled Tabitha. 'I mean, he's rather spiffy, Blue, you must admit. Do you think it could be something?'

'Never mind *Dorian*!' wailed Merrigan. 'My sister's about to go and meet a complete stranger, an utter cad, and he'll lure her into all sorts of improper adventures and exploit her and leave her broken-hearted.'

'Well,' said Blue, nibbling a stalk of grass, 'you did tell me to get out more.'

Tabitha snickered.

'Oh, *you*!' Merrigan whacked her sister's thigh. 'Be serious, Blue.'

'I *am*! Merrigan, you were the one who told me I should be thinking about love, looking for a husband. I wanted nothing to do with it. Even though you weren't impressed with Daddy's wild scheme, you *did* say – I cite the evening of August eighteenth – that if it only got me *thinking* about men, there would be a silver lining'.

'I was there, Your Honour, I can testify!' grinned Tabitha, raising her hand.

'You're always there,' growled Merrigan. 'Anyone would think you didn't have a home of your own.'

'And now that someone's actually done what Daddy said,

and captured my imagination — or piqued it anyway — you're acting as if the sky's fallen in. There's no pleasing you!'

'But, Blue. What kind of a man writes to a complete stranger?'

'Well, there *was* an invitation. Issued by our *father*!'

'What I mean is . . . what kind of unmarried man of thirty-two writes to a much younger woman he's never so much as set eyes on?'

'An unmarried man who'd like not to be?' suggested Tabitha.

'Anyway,' said Blue, heartily sick of the subject. 'The correspondence has been a welcome distraction, but it can't just go on and on. In his last letter he suggested we meet . . .'

'I'll bet he did,' fumed Merrigan.

'And I'm inclined to agree. I haven't written back yet. I'm not rushing into anything. And I'm still seeing Dorian. You can hardly accuse me of putting all my eggs in one basket. I just want to *investigate* the situation. He might not be what he seems, in which case why waste time writing more letters? Or he might be perfectly lovely, but just not the chap for me. Again, better to know now. I could meet him during the day in a public place. I could even ask someone to go along and sit nearby — Tab or Delphine, maybe. But not you, Merrigan. We can meet, and talk, and then I'll know. Something.'

Merrigan gave a weighty sigh. 'It sounds hideous to me. What do you think, Delphine?'

'I think she should meet him.'

Merrigan sat up. 'Truly? I thought you of all people would caution against that.'

'No,' said Delphine softly. 'Because you never know. F . . . F . . . Foley and I met in the usual way, courted. And look what happened. Lookin' back, there were all sorts of little things that might've warned me, but I didn't see them for what they were at the time. I don't see how this is any more or less risky than meetin' someone any other way.'

'I think you're right,' said Tabitha. 'Merry, people meet at dinner parties, at bus stops, all sorts of so-called acceptable ways. Some marriages turn out to be marvellous; some an unmitigated disaster! Who knows, maybe writing to strangers then deciding to meet up could be the courtship method of choice in decades to come!'

'Oh, don't be ridiculous!' snorted Merrigan.

'Did you say you have a picture, Blue?' asked Delphine, a gleam of intrigue in her eye.

Blue smiled. 'I do,' she said. 'But I don't suppose anyone wants to see it.'

Shrieks of outrage followed and she laughed and found the photograph. She passed it to Delphine first.

'He *looks* all right,' she said. 'I mean, he looks like he's got all his fingers and toes, as Ma would say.'

Tabitha's manners ran out and she grabbed the picture. She wrinkled her nose. 'Oh, Blue. Really?'

'What do you mean?' asked Blue indignantly.

'Well. He's all right, I suppose. But *Blue*! Do you really think you could go for him over a likely chap like Dorian?'

'I don't know! Dorian's . . . Well, we have a ball together. But I don't know if he *suits* me.'

'This chap looks as if he'd suit a farm in the Outer Hebrides! I wouldn't want him designing *my* hats!'

'Oh, *Tab*. He's not unfashionable. He's just not the height of glitz like Dorian. I don't think fashion sense is the first attribute of a good husband.'

'It can't *hurt*,' suggested Tabitha.

'Oh, for heaven's sake!' cried Merrigan. 'Let me see.' She snatched the picture and pored over it. Handed it back to Blue.

'Well?'

'Well,' said Merrigan, looking exasperated. 'I never heard of such a thing.'

# Chapter Twenty-seven

All the way back to Old Palace Lane, Delphine pondered their conversation and hoped her advice to Blue had been sound. Though she doubted it would make much difference. Blue was gentle but she was determined. If meeting Latchley Winterson was what she wanted to do, then meet him she would.

Inevitably it made Delphine think back to when she had met Foley. It was early in 1919 and she had a day off from work. Ma had forgotten carrots, so Delphine went to the market to get some. There she saw Peggy, the old lady who lived at the end of their road, and as they strolled round the market together they had bumped into Foley, who was very charming and offered to carry Peggy's bag. He was a friend of her grandson's cousin or something – at any rate, he knew Peggy a bit.

He saw Delphine and Peggy home and, to Delphine's unspeakable astonishment, asked if she would have a drink in the Smith's with him the following evening. Men – and women, too – often looked at Delphine with sympathy, sometimes with distaste. But no one had ever looked at her as Foley did, with a big smile, as if she were a pie at Christmas. She couldn't fathom why he would. So she asked him in the Smith's, and he said she looked sweet and kind.

'Really nice women are in short supply,' he said. Afterwards, she realised that was the observation of a man who didn't think much of women. At the time she took it as a compliment; she didn't get many.

They courted for six months and she enjoyed his company. Or perhaps she enjoyed *having* company. She loved her mother, but of course it wasn't the same, and now that Esther was married, home was even quieter. Any rate, Foley was confident and talked to her about his experiences of the war, the places he'd seen and his opinions on the world, of which there were many. He was quite gentlemanly, and not unattractive, and all in all Delphine couldn't quite believe her luck. Didn't her physical imperfections bother him, she asked him once, timidly. Not at all, he said. The other bits of her were pretty enough, and after what he'd seen at war he wasn't queasy.

Delphine laughed in disbelief as she hurried down the steps to the river. She'd never thought of it before, but she suddenly realised just how low her opinion of herself had been. How could she have taken 'not as bad as an atrocity of war' as any sort of a compliment? It wasn't so much that she held a higher view of herself now; it was just that after being with the kindly Camberwells, and even reading L. W.'s letter to Blue, she could see what a shocking thing that had been for him to say. It was just that she'd felt so ugly, it seemed credible, at least. It persuaded her.

She'd been so busy thinking *she* wasn't good enough that there was no room for doubt of any other kind, like whether he was what he seemed to be, or whether he could make her happy. The one or two flashes of temper that he showed, he apologised for, explaining them away as after-effects of the war. And this persuaded her too. If he was damaged as well, it made them more of a pair. It meant she had more to offer. She wasn't a beauty, but she could offer comfort and understanding.

They married in haste and Delphine was repenting still. But she'd got away from him at last and now there was a new life. The contrast was so vast, it hurt her head sometimes.

It came upon her in the evenings, mostly. When she cooked dinner for the family, she remembered cooking dinner for Foley, one eye on the clock, terrified lest something go wrong. Even when it didn't, there was no guarantee she was safe. Watching Foley's tense, critical face, chewing and chewing, she could hardly manage a morsel herself. When the Greenbows sat down to dinner, Delphine ate with them – they insisted. When she stood to clear the table, they detained her. 'Stay,' they said. 'Relax. Have another biscuit.'

Night-time had been the worst, with Foley. But when the Greenbows went to bed, Delphine would stand at her window with the lights off, watching as foxes with eyes like lamps slid by, or courting couples swayed in the shadows on their way to the river. Her most fervent wish was that this precious happiness, butterfly-soft, might last.

# Chapter Twenty-eight

Blue had no time to think about meeting L. W. once she started at the newspaper. She presented herself on Monday morning, and the first thing she saw as she pulled open the office door was Robert Cauderlie's supercilious face.

'Good *morning*, Lady Ishbel.' He smirked as he took a hat and coat from a stand beside the door. 'Or should I call you *darling Blue*?'

Her jaw dropped but she pulled herself together quickly. 'Good morning, Mr Cauderlie,' she said with a terse nod. Informal the environment might be, but she couldn't bring herself to call that man Robert. For some reason it hadn't struck her before that she would now be working at the newspaper that was following her personal life so avidly. How would *that* work? And how unfortunate that Cauderlie had already made the connection.

Fortunately, he was heading out and she had the morning to acclimatise without his caustic presence. Juno was a great help – showing her where everything was, explaining the filing system, introducing her to her fellow reporters.

'You made it, kid,' she said with a quick, fierce smile. 'You're talented. I'm happy for you, happy I could help.'

Blue squeezed her hand but Juno shook her head. 'None of that around here. No girly-girly, as Cauderlie would call it. We're here to work!' But she gave Blue a wink.

Blue had more time to take in her surroundings than she'd had on her previous visit: the mismatched furniture, the round ceiling lights, the typewriters, the telephones on stands with holders for notepads attached – she quickly came to learn that the pencils were always missing. Similarly, the desks were always covered in paper and no one ever put the reference books back on the shelves. Blue had a desk of scratched mahogany next to Juno's, which was of cheap black lacquer.

'You'll be sharing with Will Slee,' Juno explained, 'but the two of you are highly unlikely to be here at the same time. And if that should happen, there's always something you can do anywhere – some reading or phone calls or whatever.' The desk had a tall aspidistra beside it and a window nearby, through which Blue could glimpse the street, the buildings opposite and the tops of buses.

Barnaby Tanner was there for an hour or so, then he had to rush out to cover a meeting of the Twickenham Piscatorials. 'Nothing like roach and gudgeon to make you feel you're at the cutting edge of journalism,' he said with a wink as he left. 'You'll see.'

But roach and gudgeon were not on Blue's menu that week.

Nor were the discontented rumblings of underpaid brewery workers in Ealing, nor the housing crisis, nor the closing of the Exposition Internationale des Arts Décoratifs in Paris on the twenty-fifth of October. Nor was the hullabaloo caused by one particular gang of 'Bright Young Things' in Twickenham when they held a party at which champagne was the compulsory drink and anyone caught drinking anything else was forced to shed an item of clothing. No. Anything of national significance, anything that invited social commentary, slid past Blue to land on other desks, to be written and published under other initials. Blue covered fashion and gossip.

At first she thought it was because she was new. She quite understood that she should cut her teeth on the less important stories, so she raced off to the Richmond Ladies' Crochet Group tea and Sally Varney's engagement party with a swift pen and a light spirit. She dashed off her accounts with vigour and was proud of herself for mustering such enthusiasm for such slight matter. After all, she was covering Jimmy Griggs. She doubted *he* would have been sent to write a critical appraisal of the new rayon dresses. At least the simple assignments allowed her to use her energy to adjust to a working week.

She received a mixed reception at work. Juno gave a great show of solidarity and made much of having another woman in the news office. Barnaby was as friendly and wry as he had been on their first meeting. Cauderlie continued to be vile and the other men ranged from disinterested to welcoming.

One of them, Spencer Clayton, was a little *too* welcoming. Blue quickly learned to keep out of the reach of his plump hands. Sometimes she found herself longing for long lunches with Merrigan, or her rambling talks with Elf in the enchanted setting of the Cottage. Weren't humans contrary, she reflected. She had wanted this so much – still did – but it was hard to leave the nest. Nevertheless, she was here to work and further her career. One tea dance at a time.

And there were new comforts to brighten the working day. On Thursday, she finished work to find Delphine standing in reception, succumbing to Sheila's insistent request that she try on a strawberry lipstick. Flavoured lipsticks were to Sheila as bobbed hair was to Merrigan. Delphine greeted her with a wide strawberry smile.

'Thought I'd surprise you,' she said. 'I've got an hour. Fancy a cuppa?'

Blue's heart filled because the gesture was so welcome and thoughtful. 'I can't think of anything nicer,' she beamed, linking her arm through Delphine's.

On Friday afternoon, she found herself leaving the office at the same time as Barnaby, and he fell into step beside her. He had a perpetually rumpled air, she had noticed, and his thick thatch of straw-coloured hair stuck up every which way, but it didn't detract from his lovely friendly manner.

'You live on the hill, don't you?' he asked.

'Yes. And you?'

'Acton. Are you going home now?'

'Yes. Well, I have to call into the cobblers to pick up something for my sister first.'

'Shall I walk with you? I'm meeting a friend in the Roebuck so I'm heading up that way. Or would you rather be alone to clear your head after a week at the *Gazette*?'

'I'd enjoy the company. You don't mind about the cobbler? I'll only be two minutes.'

'Not at all. I'm early anyway.'

So they collected Merrigan's shoes and walked slowly up the hill. Blue told him about her week's work.

'And you're bored,' Barnaby surmised.

'Deathly,' she admitted. 'It's not that I'm arrogant. I know a newcomer can't expect to waltz in and snag all the best stories. But . . . the Richmond Dental Institute Annual Boules Night and Raffle?'

Barnaby laughed. 'Your face!' he explained. 'Though it's no laughing matter, really. I hate to say this and disillusion you, but I don't think it's because you're new.'

'Oh?'

'I think it's because you're a woman . . . and, well, quite nicely brought up, and . . .'

'And?'

'Well, sorry to say so, but you're rather attractive, I. C. And that combination doesn't exactly shout "hard-nosed journalist" to the establishment.'

'The establishment being Gordon? But he hired me!'

'Oh, Gordon won't care about any of that. It's good writing *he* likes. But he *represents* the establishment, when all is said and done. People like Cauderlie and those like him in more influential positions. And he has staff morale to think about. About half the men in the office are thrilled, you know, to have you there. Before the war, it was only really agriculture or service where men and women routinely worked together, wasn't it? So from half of us, it's a jolly hurrah for the woman in the workplace. *And*, before you, Spencer only had Juno to squeeze, and she'd knock a man out for less. He's yet to learn that you won't put up with it either, so he's living in a happy little dream where the two of you might end up kissing in the lobby after everyone else has gone home.'

Blue shuddered. 'And the other half?'

'You already know.'

'I'm a pretty, useless, upper-class doll they have to tolerate.'

'Taking a job that rightly belongs to a man, in the pursuit of pocket money. "While the man of the trench looks on – bitter, hopeless, desperate",' said Barnaby. 'I'm quoting there, by the way, from an article on this very topic. It might be the 1920s, Ishbel, but you're still a phenomenon.'

Blue sighed. 'It's true, though, that I don't need the money, isn't it? Sometimes I wonder if I should feel guilty.'

Barnaby cocked a scornful eyebrow. 'You don't feel guilty, but you think you should? What's the point of that? I suppose you mean that your father can afford to keep you? But then we could say the same for Cauderlie! No one expects a *man* to live off his family money. If I'm not mistaken, you want to do something with your writing, don't you?' Despite his affability and lack of polish, Barnaby's dark eyes were quick and shrewd, Blue noticed. He talked rapidly and passionately.

'I do. I *need* to write. It's how I make sense of things. It's who I am, really. And I want to be able to make my own living doing something that's true to me. Not something vapid like filing receipts or selling dresses.'

'I hate selling dresses too.'

Blue laughed. 'You're very wry.'

'If you last a month at the *Gazette* you will be too. Oh, it's not a bad place or anything. But the *nonsense*, sometimes! Anyway, you have just as much a right to be there as anyone. More, if you take your career so seriously that you're prepared to learn your craft with boules-playing dentists! The same can't be said for some of 'em. Spencer, Roger . . . they just drifted into it during the war – they couldn't serve – and never drifted out again. In Roger's case, it keeps him out of the pub during the day and he knows he needs that. Work is *always* about more than just the pay cheque. Besides, what if – heaven forbid – your father lost all his money? By finding a way to be independent, you'll always be prepared for a rainy day.'

Blue looked at him, pleased. 'Thank you, Barnaby. You've

just put into words, very succinctly, all the things I've been thinking. Your sisters have taught you well.'

He grinned. 'Nah, I taught them. Taught them everything I know!'

'I'd love to hear about them sometime. But I'm home; this is me.'

'Have a lovely evening, Ishbel.'

'Enjoy your drink. See you Monday.'

Blue felt lighter that evening. It wasn't a good situation, to know that women still faced so much hostility in the workplace, that the work she was given would be dictated by her sex, that so many people still thought women didn't have the right to the same fulfilment and self-sufficiency as men. And it wasn't as though men did such a fine job of taking care of women, she thought hotly. Just look at Delphine and Foley! But there was a welcome relief in naming the undercurrents she sensed and struggled against, but couldn't quite acknowledge, because no one else did. Barnaby Tanner was frank and unsentimental and that helped Blue to see her situation clearly.

On Monday, she hardly saw him, as he was out all morning and she was out all afternoon. But spotting him on the street in between, she hailed him warmly.

'Must dash,' he said. 'Red-hot notes burning a hole in my notebook. But I had a thought last night, about what you can do.'

'Why, thank you, Barnaby.'

'Oh, it just infuriates me, these hypocrites setting their shoulders against progress. How's the workload? I bet you're already dashing off these social pieces without too much struggle?'

'Yes, you're right. Not that I haven't learned anything. The first few came in for some heavy editing from Gordon. He really made me think about the point of them. But now I've got the hang of it, I think.'

'Course you have. Well then, in your spare time, write other things. Use the newspaper resources to check your facts and do your research. Keep putting the finished copy on Whisky's desk. As long as you're still getting the work he sets you done, he can't complain. And I bet sooner or later you'll hit on something that'll spark his interest and he'll print it. And Bob's your auntie, you'll have broken out of your box. If nothing else, it'll stop you going stark staring mad with boredom.'

It made sense. It was a way forward. Otherwise, six months would come to an end, Jimmy Griggs would come back and Blue's portfolio would contain nothing but fluff. 'I'll do it,' she said. 'It's a marvellous idea. Thanks, Barnaby.'

He tipped his hat and entered the office at a run. Blue set off thoughtfully towards Kew, and the christening of the great-granddaughter of Lady Somebody or Other. Gordon had given her a list of eight illustrious names sure to be there and told her to make a close account of what they wore.

# Chapter Twenty-nine

Time passed. Delphine was growing used to her new position and getting to know the area. She stopped jumping at shadows, and people in the shops and post office came quickly to recognise the Greenbows' new 'girl'. When you could greet three or four passers-by by name on any given outing, you started to feel part of the community, she reflected, smiling to herself as she went about her errands.

The Greenbows, all four, were a delight. Paul and Sylvia were busy, happy and grateful that Delphine was there to help out. Stephen and Fanny had, between them, every kind of ailment in a medical compendium. They regularly fell, fainted, took to their bed and needed a doctor. But in between times they lived life with relish.

Fanny's particular love was the theatre and she attended every production staged within a reachable radius. Sometimes Delphine accompanied her. She was awed by the pretty, Victorian theatre tucked away on Little Green. She also enjoyed the gusto of amateur productions in community halls. Her favourite was a school play in which a young relative of Sylvia's was playing Peaseblossom in an abridged version of *A Midsummer Night's Dream*. Puck's wings fell off twice, Mustardseed forgot where she was and hitched up her skirt to have a good scratch and the entire script was delivered in high piping voices that paid scant attention to sense or punctuation. But the atmosphere of parental pride and infectious excitement pulled at Delphine's heartstrings. She wished, more than anything, that this had been her childhood – hers and Esther's.

Delphine hadn't been married long when Esther had twigged that something was awry. Not realising quite how bad it was, she tried talking to Foley, mistaking him for a reasonable human being. After she'd left, he took it out on Delphine and threatened to strike Esther too if she ever broached it again. A couple of years went by with Esther gritting her teeth for Delphine's sake, but eventually it became easier not to see each other at all, and Foley liked it that way.

It was a rich life that was springing up around Delphine now. Once a week, sometimes twice, she met Blue after work. By the time Blue finished up, Delphine would have done her day's chores and prepared the evening meal, giving her a brief interlude before she needed to go back to cook it. They would consume a hasty cuppa together in a nearby tea room if it was open, or in the tiny 'kitchen' at Blue's office if not. Once or twice Juno or Sheila joined them, but mostly these visits were opportunities for Blue and Delphine to rattle through a hasty heart-to-heart, a sharing of the private things they would only tell each other.

The evenings were drawing in and at night she lay huddled beneath her blankets, reading books borrowed from Blue and thinking about the good things that were happening. She met neighbours, watched swans, bought her first small possessions to decorate her room. She was planning her outfit for the Camberwells' autumn party. She was reading, writing, visiting the theatre. The whole world was opening up for her, and she wanted to tell Ma and Esther. She wanted to share it with them. She kept reminding herself that she was free of Foley and had her own life again, that it would have to be enough.

But it wasn't enough.

She saw now that the Camberwells were right: this was a half life. She didn't believe anything could be done to better it, but perhaps she should at least listen to what Kenneth had to say about it. Nothing more.

So on her next free evening, the Camberwells and Delphine gathered in the recently completed drawing room, with its new green walls and smell of fresh paint. The kitchen was at a stage of its reincarnation that rendered it unusable, so Avis had gone to visit her aunt for a few days. As soon as one room was finished, Midge got to work on another. She had designs for at least six more drawn up in advance.

'I'm so pleased you've agreed to talk about this, my dear,'

Kenneth said to Delphine, pouring her a snifter of sherry. 'And that you feel better able to do so. You look well, I must say.'

He went to stand before the fireplace and clasped his hands behind his back. Above him was the new painting by Laura Knight, about which Elf got very excited. Midge, Merrigan and Blue were draped over various sofas and chaises longues, wearing serious faces. Delphine was sitting near the window, concentrating; she could already feel her mind tugging, threatening to take her away. *There's no need to be afraid*, she told herself. *We're only going to talk.*

'So, my dear,' said Kenneth. 'Where would you like to start?'

'I d . . . d . . . d . . .' said Delphine, then stopped. It didn't augur well, she felt, that even the thought of *talking* about Foley could take her words away. They'd come back so easily over the past few weeks that she'd almost forgotten how stubborn they could be. She took a deep breath. *You don't have to do anything you don't want to. It's only a conversation.*

'I don't think I'm ready to *do* anything,' she said, looking around imploringly. 'Honestly, I don't think I'll ever be. I just w . . . wanted to hear what you thought. But I don't want you to think this means I plan to go after F . . . F . . . Foley.'

'We're not here to talk you into anything,' said Midge. 'We all understand how difficult this is, and how personal.'

The girls nodded. Delphine felt choked with relief. 'Thank you. Only, I keep thinking about the things you said. That he shouldn't get away with it. That I'm not free. I miss my ma.

And my sister. But I'm af . . . afraid to send word to them. Yesterday I saw a houseboat. All brightly painted it was, with a little chimney puffing smoke and children playing on the deck. And I wanted to tell Esther. But I can't. So I want to hear what you wanted to tell me. But I don't think it will make any difference because F . . . Foley . . . he's . . . he's . . .' She shrugged in frustration.

'Never mind him for a minute,' suggested Midge, rising like a cobra to survey the new mahogany drinks cart.

'Gin and it, darling?' offered Kenneth. 'A scotch and soda?'

'Just a tonic water, thank you, darling.' She turned back to Delphine. 'The first thing to say is that if you want to make contact with your family without leaving a trail of breadcrumbs for that man, there will be a way to do it and we can talk about that. But I know Kenneth has a few things he'd like to say.'

'It's never easy, of course,' he agreed, handing his wife a glass. 'Our culture has always encouraged us to keep such problems within the family. You know what people are like. No one wants to face up to an unpleasant truth if there's any way to turn a blind eye. But times *are* changing.'

He paused, marshalling his thoughts, then continued. 'Time was that the authorities turned a blind eye – wives were husbands' property, to be dealt with as they saw fit. You've heard the phrase "the unwritten law"?'

Delphine hadn't.

'It's the idea that a man has the right to chastise an errant wife. Beating her after finding her with another man, for example.'

'Unwritten lunacy, rather,' growled Merrigan, echoing Delphine's thoughts.

'Quite. But there's the point. A judge in a recent case called it something similar. I forget the phrase – unwritten folly or something of the sort. And he made short work of it as a defence argument, I can tell you! I read the case with great interest. But it's not all good news. Since the war, the progress seems to have been reversed again.'

'Wh . . . why should that be?'

'Yes, Daddy, why? I would have thought it would be the other way around.' Blue frowned. 'So much has changed for the better, for women.'

'You may have hit on the very reason, Blue. So some chaps think anyway. Human nature being what it is, any liberating effects that the war has provided for women are making some people uncomfortable.'

'Women taking jobs meant for men and all that . . .' murmured Blue, thinking of Robert Cauderlie's scornful face.

'Precisely. A build-up of resentment against women and all their new freedoms.' Kenneth sighed. 'I've read some shocking things. So you see, Delphine, I do understand what you would be up against and I'll always be honest with you about the way things stand. That said, there *is* cause for hope. This judge the other day, for example. In his closing remarks he talked some real sense about men and women and how they should treat each other. I was very impressed. And then there's the concept of shell shock . . .'

'Couldn't that just be seen as another excuse?' asked Merrigan, scowling. 'Another reason to let men off the hook?'

'Well, potentially. But from what I've read it doesn't seem to be going that way. For years, women have been described as hysterical at the drop of a hat, while there's been no recognition that men have any sort of emotional life at all. Now people are asking questions. Women aren't just property, and men aren't just autocrats defending that property. The new ideas seem to be forcing people to look more closely for the truth of things.

'Now, I wouldn't suggest, Delphine, that you risk your safety on the strength of *any* of this. But there are intelligent people out there, thinking the right sort of thoughts – and acting on them in court. I wanted you to know that. The real issue, if you ever *did* decide to take action, is that you didn't report anything at the time. That's not a criticism. I more than understand that you couldn't. But it means that from now on, there'll be little or no evidence. I did wonder . . . well, our family doctor, Dr Harcourt, is very discreet. If you *did* wish to have something on file, we could ask him to conduct an examination. It would be entirely confidential, of course. There may still be evidence of – pardon me – old injuries which he could note. Again, completely up to you, old girl.

'And now I'll shut up! I have no wish to pry or dictate,

Delphine, but you're our friend now, and I didn't wish this to be the elephant in the room. I didn't want him to have that power either.'

'I understand,' said Delphine soberly. 'Y . . . you're very kind. The doctor . . . I don't know. What would he . . .? I mean . . .?'

'Perhaps we could talk at another time about exactly what it would entail?' suggested Midge. 'Just you and I, as two married women.'

Delphine nodded.

'Just don't leave it too long, if you *are* thinking of it,' urged Kenneth. Delphine knew that, despite her reluctance, he was still daydreaming of bringing Foley to justice. She rather loved him for it.

'We'll chat later,' said Midge, nodding at Delphine. 'But what about your mother? Your sister? What can we do about them, Kenneth?'

Delphine sighed. What had she done to deserve friends like these? 'F . . . Foley always s . . . said I was too stupid to run away. Perhaps he was right, after all, because I didn't even get to Victoria and I only ended up here by accident. Only it's turned into ever such a happy accident. I'm so lucky I met you.'

'Yes. Foley,' said Kenneth, stepping towards her, then catching himself, as if he didn't want to seem too eager. 'Delphine, I wanted to ask you what kind of man he is. Oh, I don't mean cruel. That much is evident. But is he clever or stupid?

Hot-tempered or cold? Is he a little crazy, perhaps? Could *he* use shell shock as an argument? I just want to . . .' He gritted his teeth and Delphine saw how much he hated the very thought of Foley. 'It might help to feel I understood the man a little.'

Delphine didn't want to think about him or talk about him, but it was part of why she was here. 'I d . . . don't know if he's crazy. In the beginning, before we were married, he blamed his temper on the war. He'd seen terrible things, of course. He was a prisoner of war in Holzminden for a while. Sometimes his temper was hot. Explosive. And the rest of the time he could be so cold. Cut me with a look, you know? As time went on, I realised there was a method to it, the way he treated me. I felt like . . . he'd done it before. But he'd never tell me that, of course. So does that mean he was mad? Or just a horrible man? I don't know. And clever? Yes, Foley's clever. He's the cleverest person I know.'

# Chapter Thirty

The Camberwells' autumn party was held later than usual so that the dining room could be finished and the guests fed. The kitchen was still a work in progress, but no one would see it, and at least it was functional again.

Blue stood in the garden hugging herself before the bonfire. The two-week delay gave the party a slightly different atmosphere. Usually it had the brightly coloured, brilliantly lit atmosphere that October always wore. Now it was the first of November and it was darker, more chill and brooding. Blue rather liked it. It felt more mysterious, more *pagan*, somehow.

She already wore a sweater over her long indigo dress. Properly speaking, she should be waiting inside for the guests. She should greet them all – prettily attired, jewellery twinkling – before making the necessary concessions to the weather and going outside. But she couldn't resist the lure of the flames. Their burning heart held her mesmerised, and if the wind was whipping her hair out of place or if the fire was scattering her cheeks with tiny smuts, it was a small price to pay for the magic.

Besides, it was a casual, intimate affair. There would be no flannel about the party in the paper, no Juno. They were becoming friends at work, and Blue had to remember to be very careful when it came to mentioning her out-of-work plans. Juno was charged with following up every lead and every new development with regard to Blue's romantic progress. Well, of course she was – she was the only other female there and Blue couldn't write about herself! Much as Juno sympathised with Blue's dislike of being the star of a gossip column, it was her job and she would do it. Besides, she was fascinated.

'I can't help it,' she apologised. 'I'm a journalist, I'm a woman, and I have no love life of my own. I like and respect you, but my nosiness will continue.'

It had been easy to keep it quiet, since the *Gazette* was currently full of the forthcoming Remembrance Day celebrations – Blue should know, she had written a piece about it. The services of about seventy ladies had been secured to sell the poppies, which were made locally in Petersham. There was much debate in the paper about the music that should be played in the parade. Some wanted traditional brass, others pleaded for woodwind or strings for a bit of variety – 'Provided that there is a fitting flavour of the martial embodied in the programme!' they conceded. It was the nearest Blue had come to polemic.

Their next-door neighbours from either side, the Larrabys and the Waldegraves, were coming, as well as Delphine and the Greenbows, and the Foxtons, of course. Even Foster was coming, apparently. Blue was so glad. She hadn't set eyes on him for three months, and she hoped fervently that this meant that he was over her.

And Dorian was coming. The thought made Blue's heart leap with a flame of its own. So tall and handsome. So cheerful and charming. So warm and wanton with his kisses. She still didn't know what she thought about the two of them; she couldn't envisage becoming Mrs Fields. She still wanted to meet L. W. But the thought of Dorian lit up her days. Home was intense, with Midge growing ever more fraught and fretful. The office was full of trials and challenges. Then there was Dorian. He just made her laugh.

Despite her deadlines, she had dreamed several times over the past week of dancing round this very fire with him, of being pulled away into the trees, into his arms. He was heady company, like champagne. Was it lust, then, she wondered? But she liked him, too. Love and all its associated conundrums, she decided, were complicated.

Suddenly he was at her side. Dorian, early? He was Mr Fashionably Late. She'd imagined having time alone with her family first, and only later, when he rolled in from some adventure, becoming grown-up Blue. Heart-racing Blue. Kissing Blue. But instead he was the first to arrive. Evidently, he wanted to impress.

He kissed her and slid a proprietorial arm around her shoulders. She hadn't expected that. Then the Greenbows joined them at the fire and Blue played the hostess while Dorian played the host, which confounded her a little more. But she liked that he was so gracious and jolly with them.

'Where's Delphine?' she asked.

'Talking to Midge inside,' Fanny told her. Then she proceeded to give a full and frank description of the play they had seen the previous night. Stephen's eyes shone in the firelight as he relived the evening with his wife, and Paul and Sylvia listened in amusement. Fanny liked to talk *at length* about the theatre. Blue liked to listen; she enjoyed Fanny's passion. When Dorian detached himself abruptly from her side to go indoors, she noticed both how cold that side of her body felt without him and the brief flicker of hurt in Fanny's eyes when he strode off mid-sentence.

The dusk deepened. Delphine appeared and Blue welcomed her with a warm embrace. Elf ambled up from the Cottage and struck up a debate with Mr Larraby about Freud. The neighbours had wafted in at some point in the proceedings, blown on the autumn breeze.

Dorian returned, drew Blue just a little way off and bent his head to hers, telling her the latest gossip. Other conversations shimmered behind her, but it was hard to tear her eyes from Dorian. Then Tabitha burst into the garden. She struck a dramatic pose in the doorway, making everyone laugh and murmur, 'Oh, *Tab*!'

Then, taking in the scene at a glance, Tabitha bounded over to Blue. 'Foster's here,' she whispered, then turned to Dorian.

'Hello, Dorian. *My*, you look handsome,' she purred, giving Blue the chance to slip away from Dorian's hand, which had been lying magnet-like on her arm. Somehow Blue didn't want the first thing Foster saw when he arrived to be her and Dorian looking *quite* so together.

She joined her father and Midge in greeting Mr and Mrs Foxton. Anthony Foxton leaned on a cane, due to an old war wound, and was in a flurry of indignation about the world of banking. Glamorous Clemmie Foxton rolled her eyes at Midge and patted her husband's arm in a 'there, there' sort of way.

Foster lurked behind them like a timid whippet, even though Ryan's Castle was essentially his second home. Midge greeted him warmly and told him that there were plenty of devilled eggs and profiteroles – his two favourite things. He smiled and thanked her, and Blue kissed his cheek; she was determined to get things back to their right order.

'I've missed you, Floss,' she said frankly. 'I'm so glad you're here. Come and stand at the fire with me and tell me things. Tell me about school and your music. I've started working at the paper, you know.'

He swallowed and cleared his throat. 'Tab did tell us,' he croaked. 'You're awfully clever, Blue.' He followed her to the bonfire and in the ruddy light she saw that he'd lost weight – and he'd been rather a skinny boy to start with. His collar was a hoop about his neck. Beneath his eyes the skin looked thin as mist. It gave Blue rather a fright.

'Not an awful lot to tell really, old girl. I've rather given up the old fiddle as a bad job. Turns out I wasn't especially talented after all. Jolly lucky I didn't play at your party, what? Father says I need to work in the law or something of that description anyway, so I'm studying like billy-o – complex chap, the law, you know?'

'But are you happy with that? I mean, there's nothing wrong with studying hard, if it's what you *want* to do.'

He shrugged. 'It's the least of my worries.'

She swallowed. Was this about her? Should she ask? 'What do you mean?'

'Oh, nothing. There've been one or two things lately . . . Blue, are *you* all right?'

Blue was surprised. She'd been so busy worrying about him that she couldn't imagine why he might worry about her. 'Me? Never better! Only that I'm worried about you . . . Why on earth do you ask?'

He shuffled from foot to foot. The flames threw pink lights on his face, but they somehow only served to show how pale he was. 'There's a chap . . . Well, something happened at school and . . . It's just that . . .' He shook his head in frustration. 'Never mind. It's boring talk. Not for a party. Just as long as you're happy.'

'Foster, dear, are you all right?' she asked in a low voice. 'I haven't seen you for so long, and I'm so sorry, you know, about the letters. I want us to be friends, just as we've always been. You are over all that now, aren't you?'

After all, the question couldn't be ignored, not with his cadaverous face before her in the firelight. She watched him cast about for an answer, scuffing the lawn with his shiny black shoe. Horrors. She shouldn't have brought it up.

He lifted his head, his eyes a little lost, as if he had a lot he wanted to say and didn't know where to start. Finally he said, 'Blue, I . . .'

But Dorian was beside them, having slipped Tabitha's charming net. 'Hello, Foxy, old chap!' he greeted Foster, pumping his hand. Next to his bright vigour, Foxton seemed to pale a shade or two more. 'Jolly nice to see you. When are you off to college then, this year or next? Lord, you'll be grown up before we know it.'

Foster didn't seem able to muster an answer, but Dorian rolled on. 'Suppose it'll be time for me to settle down soon, though it'll be a sad loss for the ladies! I say, Foxy, if you need any tips on that score, look me up. More than happy to share the fruits of experience, don't you know. What say you, Blue? Make an honest man of me?' So saying, he flung his arm around her again and kissed her nose.

Blue wanted to sink into the lawn and become mulch and leaf and slug. She wanted the fire to roll over her and crisp her to non-existence. She dared not look at Foster, who started to cough, then the cough turned into choking and Dorian whacked him on the back. And he was *still* talking! 'Oh, didn't you know, old chap? Yes, Blue and I have rather decided to give it a whirl. All since that potty wheeze of her old man's, you know. I wrote her a letter – can't say it'd ever occurred to me before, but I thought, well, why not? So watch this space. I'm not saying your sister needs to buy a hat or anything, not quite yet, but we do make rather a fine-looking couple, if I do say so myself.'

Foster looked betrayed. It was the only word. No gentle synonym would do. Blue roused herself and put her hands firmly on Dorian's chest. 'Dorian, go and talk to someone else, won't you? Look, there's my sister. Go and talk to Merrigan. Please.'

Looking slightly wounded and not a little confused, Dorian tipped a non-existent hat to Foster and sauntered off. She would have to make it up to him later, but for now her concern was Foster. 'I'm sorry,' she said again, wondering if she would ever come to the end of the apologies she felt she owed him. 'He doesn't know. He didn't mean to be . . . And we're not . . . Oh Lord. Floss, it's not *that*. I mean, he's a good age for me and he's . . . But it's not serious. Not at all. He's just being flippant.'

'Blue, it's all right,' said Foster, cutting through her torrent of words. 'You don't owe me any explanation. You're a grown woman and you can see who you like. Dorian's very handsome and very exciting, anyone can see that. All us boys look up to him. Of course he was going to get the best girl in town, Blue. You mustn't feel bad.'

Blue felt uncomfortable. Was that how it worked? That

the best man won the best girl? And what did 'best' mean anyway? Was he the handsome to her pretty? The panache to her sparkle? And *had* he 'got' her?

'Thank you, Foster. You're very gracious. I meant what I said: I want us still to be friends, just as we've always been. Can we?'

'Of course, Blue,' he said quietly. 'Of course.'

So she started telling him about life at the paper, believing him because she needed to.

# Chapter Thirty-one

It was almost midnight. Feeling the goosebumps on her arms, Midge went inside to check the fire in the drawing room for those who preferred to huddle indoors. This was traditionally her responsibility, while Kenneth tended to the bonfire. At the moment, everyone was outside.

Midge paused at the threshold and looked out at the little crowd, allowing herself a moment of satisfaction. The evening had gone smoothly and people had enjoyed themselves. She'd been anxious; it was the first time anyone aside from Tabitha and Delphine had seen the new rooms. If they'd disapproved, if they'd thought the new look tasteless or de trop, she would have taken it to heart. Ryan's Castle was a bit of an institution, and overhauling it was an act so daring she could scarcely believe she'd undertaken it.

But everyone had been extremely complimentary; Clemmie Foxton and Blanche Larraby in particular. Clemmie's taste was exemplary and Blanche was a traditionalist by nature, so if she'd won their approval she must have done something right.

It was lovely having Delphine and the Greenbows there. She was glad they had come. Strange, seeing Blue with a beau, but not a bad thing, certainly. Kenneth was delighted. He longed to see his younger daughter happy and for him that meant marriage. Dorian was certainly charming company. Did he suit Blue? Midge wasn't sure. He was a good match, on the surface of things, but Blue was a soulful young woman. Dorian seemed more the sort who took life as it came. Of course, that *could* be a good thing for Blue, but somehow Midge couldn't imagine her spending a lifetime with someone she couldn't have deep heart-to-hearts with about the things that were important to her.

Eyes roving idly over the little gathering, Midge could see her handsome husband deep in conversation with the other men, and the Greenbow ladies chatting to Merrigan. Tabitha was talking to her brother, and Foster's face struck Midge like a hammer blow. He didn't appear to be paying any attention to Tab, gazing like a frozen man into the 'orchard', as the Camberwells called the cluster of five fruit trees in the centre of the lawn. She followed his gaze and saw Dorian and Blue locked in an embrace. She felt relieved when, after a moment, she saw Blue pull away and return to the party, Dorian closely in tow. But Foster still looked like a boy under a spell. Midge experienced a moment of dread; it wasn't a good thing to adore one person to that extent. She knew that better than anyone.

She remembered what Clemmie had confided in her. They hadn't had a chance to talk in private tonight, and in any case, this was the first time Midge had seen Foster since Blue's birthday. Was someone at school being unkind to him? Did he miss his music? Or *was* it only Blue?

A wind as grey as a cobweb swept in, tossing leaves and grit into the room. Midge shivered. Autumn was passing on. Change was relentless. She stoked the fire to a roaring blaze.

# Part Three

~~~~~~~~

# Winter

*The leaves going, the light going,*
*everything all about death*

# Chapter Thirty-two

'Winter is coming in,' wrote Delphine in her notebook. 'Never liked it myself, but maybe it'll be different this year. I've always thought the only people who like winter are those who don't have to worry about keeping warm, who can think about things like presents and parties. Well . . . am I one of those now??

'It might be a better winter, but it still won't be a good one. I don't know as there can be such a thing. Winter is dark and wet and cold and everything harder because of it – the leaves going, the light going, everything all about death.'

She snapped her book shut and looked out of the window. Incredible to think she could feel glum with all her new-found good fortune. But she'd been feeling melancholy since submitting to Dr Harcourt's examination the previous week. Midge had been wonderful – gone with her, bought her tea afterwards – but it had still been a horrible experience. In fairness, the doctor had been very gentle and sensitive, just as the Camberwells had promised, but it brought it all back – such dark memories – when the whole point of the exercise was to know that she'd done all she could and put it behind her.

The season was getting to her, and she still missed her family. Despite hours of discussion with the Camberwells, she couldn't decide what to do. She daren't write to them; the thought of written evidence of her new life existing, even for the briefest time, was paralysing. Obviously she would never go back there. They'd chewed over the possibility of someone else going to see her mother, but a Camberwell would stick out in that neighbourhood like a sore thumb, and it was a lot to ask of them. Delphine's fear translated itself into a sort of lethargy. She kept trying to tell herself it was better for everyone if she stayed lost. Perhaps the price you paid for comfort, safety and a measure of peace was that it gave you time for wistfulness and regret.

The magnolia branches in the garden were bare; dark, snaking shapes. A light rain fell and the footsteps in the street were hurried; they carried that faint note of discomfort, of wanting to reach somewhere warm and dry.

She wanted to go somewhere herself, she decided. Ryan's Castle. It was her day off, and it was the weekend, so Blue might be at home. She would go visiting and tell Blue how she hated winter and no doubt Blue would open her wide brown eyes in shock and tell her at least ten good reasons to *love* winter – and Delphine was more than happy to be persuaded.

She clipped through the rainy streets, avoiding the river

today because there was nothing drearier than the sight and sound of rain falling on water. As she passed the haberdasher's she remembered that she had taken a shilling from Merrigan last week to buy some ribbons for Cicely's fast-growing wisps of chestnut hair. Merrigan's in-laws were staying, leaving her little time for the usual errands. So she ducked inside and, finding the counter unmanned, browsed for a little while among the bright colours. She laid out the white and pale pink ribbons that Merrigan had specified, and because she'd also requested 'a colour or two', Delphine chose emerald green and scarlet. She'd never had a ribbon, growing up. Her mother used to tie her hair back with the cotton belt of an old apron that had been discarded when it caught fire.

She gave a smart ding to the bell on the counter, and Mary, the daughter of the family, hurried through the doorway from the back.

'Sorry to keep you! How can I . . .?' Then she saw Delphine and gave a little scream.

'Mary? Are you all right?' Delphine was used to startled responses when people first saw her, but she and Mary had already met several times. People around here were used to her now.

Mary held her hand over her mouth, as if a second scream might escape otherwise. Her eyes were big and round.

'Mary! What's wrong?'

'Sorry, miss, I'm sorry.' Mary lowered her hand at last and

gripped the side of the counter, unable to take her eyes off Delphine. 'It's only that . . . Well, miss, you're supposed to be dead!'

Delphine stormed up the hill clutching the copy of the *News of the World* that she had wrested from Mary. She kept her head down, afraid to look about her for the first time in a long while. She hammered on the door of Ryan's Castle, praying someone would be home. The door opened.

'Oh, thank goodness!' she said, then stopped when she saw Avis's face. 'You've seen it too, then.'

'Come in, Miss Delphine,' said Avis, closing the door after her. Delphine felt as if she'd reached a real castle, fortified and defended against the outside world.

'Go and wait in the kitchen,' said Avis. 'Water's boiling. I'll let them know you're here.'

Delphine did as she was told, passing several doors that stood ajar, emitting paint fumes and glimpses of ladders. The kitchen was taking shape. The new design seemed to be settling comfortably on the old structures, and the contentious toaster with its Celtic knot sat proudly on one work surface. Daringly modern framed prints of ladies in diaphanous dresses and cats with cunning whiskers graced the walls. On the table was a cup of coffee and a newspaper spread open at the page Delphine didn't want to look at ever again.

She sat at the table and buried her head in her hands.

'Delphine!' Blue, Kenneth and Elf burst in a few minutes later. Blue kissed her. 'Sorry, darling,' she explained. 'Most of the rooms are . . . well. So we went to have tea with Elf.'

'Midge is visiting her mother,' said Kenneth. 'But tell us what's happened and we'll fill her in later. Avis said something about a newspaper?'

Delphine nodded and pulled Avis's paper round to show them.

'Oh noooooo,' moaned Blue, seeing the detailed artist's sketch of Delphine. With the iron mark drawn exactly, the big eyes and small features, it was unmistakeably her. The only difference was that in the picture, Delphine had long hair.

The headline read, 'Delphine Foley. Missing since August. Now tragically presumed dead.'

'Good heavens,' said Elf, pulling a stool up to the table and settling on it. Blue and her father crowded behind him, and they read the article in silence.

Delphine unpicked the damp folds of the paper she'd brought with her and opened it to the page in question. Avis came and read it over her shoulder. Delphine digested what she had skimmed through in the haberdasher's. Cicely's ribbons, she remembered now, were still on the counter.

The article recounted how two ladies' handbags had washed up from the Thames near Greenwich and been discovered by Al Black, the landlord of the Chime and Chalk. Black took the bags to the police. After extensive investigation they were identified as belonging to Delphine, beloved wife of George Foley, who had left home one August morning and never returned.

> She said she'd drop by at noon,' said Muriel Thackeray, neighbour. 'I had a nice bit of plum cake with her name on it, but I never saw her again.'
>
> 'We were very close,' said Foley, 38. 'I've been breaking my heart all these months and now my worst fears are confirmed. Her mother and sister are beside themselves with grief and so am I. She was the best wife a man could have asked for. I'll never forget her.

According to the article, a small memorial service would be held the following Thursday, at St Joseph's in Aldgate.

'Oh Lord,' said Blue, at last.

Kenneth looked at Delphine soberly. 'That's about the worst luck we could have had, save Foley turning up in Richmond. You'll have to answer a lot of questions now.'

'What on earth can we say?' asked Blue.

'I suggest staying as close to the truth as possible, whilst remaining vague,' suggested Elf. 'Perhaps something along the lines of being estranged from your family. Say you've cleared up the mistake about your death but you wish to remain here in anonymity. It might prompt a bit of speculation for a while, but I'm sure it'll die down.'

'What about your poor mother?' wondered Blue. 'We'll *have*

to get word to her now, won't we, Delphine? We can't have her thinking you're *dead*, for goodness' sake! This has forced our hand, hasn't it, Daddy?'

'I rather think it has,' mused Kenneth. 'And Elf, you may be right. I'm sure we can handle it diplomatically and wait for it to blow over. But the worst of it, in my view, is that if someone who knows Delphine is here in Richmond should chance to be in conversation with someone who knows Foley . . . then what they might intend as a reassuring remark could be incendiary.'

'That's not the worst of it,' said Delphine.

'Then what on earth is?' asked Blue.

'The worst of it is that Foley won't ever stop looking for me. You read what he said. "I'll never forget her."'

'Goodness,' said Elf. 'I thought he was only playing the grieving widower.'

'That's because you don't know him. That's why there's an illustration. With this mark' – she rubbed her face – 'there's no mistaking me. I can't even claim it's my twin or anything. He's got my bags. He'll know I left. This is his way of saying to me, "I know what you've done. And I won't give up." And all under the disguise of caring about me. I told you he was clever.'

# Chapter Thirty-three

In the end it was Midge who went to Aldgate. She wore old clothes and did nothing fashionable with her hair or make-up. As she got on the District, she had the oddest feeling that she was Margaret Fawcett again, that her wedding and her life as Kenneth's wife had all been a dream.

Kenneth had wanted to make the trip, of course. He didn't like the idea of his wife undertaking it. But Midge argued that a visit from a strange woman might sit better with Anne Painter than a visit from a strange man. Besides, she'd added quietly, she too was a mother who'd lost a child.

She didn't read on the tube. She was lost in thought as she rocked gently, allowing the clickety-clack of the movement along the tracks to sink into the background of her mind. She thought about Delphine and how this must be for her. She thought about Blue, who was tackling her new job with impressive tenacity, but whom Midge missed now that she was out of the house so much of the time. She thought about Kenneth, and Percy, because she always did. And most of all she thought how lovely it was to be out of the house. The redecorating was giving her cabin fever, if she were honest.

Although, of all the places she could have been going, there were few she'd be as reluctant to visit as East London. In fact, apart from Esher, there was nowhere worse. She couldn't bear reminders of that fateful day when life had turned upon a sixpence. But today was no pleasure trip; she had an important task to carry out and she must keep her wits about her.

In the busy November streets, Midge Camberwell might stand out. But Margaret Fawcett was nondescript – always had been. She'd committed Delphine's directions to memory and made her way along the main road to the Smith's Arms, where she turned left. She passed Gadsby's Pie House, and the almshouses, with their weary-looking trickle of comers and goers. At a tea house that advertised 'CHOPS, STEAKS, HADDOCKS, BLOATERS' in black capitals painted onto whitewashed bricks, she turned right. Two women in battered black straw bonnets laden with an unfeasible weight of glass cherries laughed wildly as they gulped jellied eels from white teacups. A small boy in a bowler hat was tap-dancing on a wall.

She might hope she looked like Margaret Fawcett today, but she *felt* like Midge Camberwell. She couldn't help deploring the lack of space, the lack of greenery. Omnibuses crowded along the thoroughfare – three abreast, even. She thought of Richmond Hill, of the river and the park. She had grown used to a fine life.

When she reached the greengrocer's, she turned into a street of terraced houses and black lamps. At number seven, she knocked on the door. *Please be in*, she willed Anne Painter. She'd come at a time when Delphine *thought* her mother was likely to be home, but of course, one never knew.

The door opened promptly. Midge saw a short woman, slight like her daughter, peering out as though nothing good could come through that door.

'Mrs Painter,' Midge said, as kindly as she could. 'I'm sorry to disturb you, but I have something rather important to discuss. Might I ask, are you alone?' That was the important thing to ascertain first, they had all agreed. Heaven forbid Foley should have come a calling and hear her mention Delphine. Another reason for Midge to come instead of Kenneth. A man couldn't turn up on a strange woman's doorstep and ask if they were alone without sounding very dicey indeed!

There was a long moment of suspicion; Midge saw the other woman's eyes dart all around.

'What's that matter to you?'

'Only that what I have to say is rather delicate in nature. You might prefer to keep it private. Nothing's wrong, I promise.' Midge held her gaze, trying to transmit motherly energies, a sympathetic manner. She'd never been very good with all that unspoken, otherworldly stuff; Blue was the girl for that. But maybe it worked, because Anne Painter relented and held the door open.

'Yes, I am. You'd better come in.'

'Thank you.' Midge stepped into a house so narrow it felt as though the houses on either side were squeezing it with all their might. They entered a dingy front room with thick window nets that choked any light that threatened to shine in. She was rather glad of the privacy they afforded. She looked around and listened. She could hear thuds and laughter through the wall, but this house, indeed, felt empty. She wasn't offered a seat, so she began.

'Mrs Painter, my name is Margaret Camberwell and I'm a friend of your daughter's.'

'Oh lawks, not Esther too. Is she all right?'

'No, not Esther. Delphine. Mrs Painter, she's asked me to come and see you.'

At once it was though a lamp had been lit inside Anne Painter. She seized Midge's hands and her eyes grew bright. 'Delphine? She's alive then? Is she all right?'

'Very much so. She's well and happy and safe. Only she misses you and her sister dreadfully . . .'

'I knew it!' exulted Delphine's mother. 'I *knew* it. Oh, Mrs . . . What did you say your name was? Will you take a cup of tea with me? Please. And take a seat, and tell me everything!'

'Certainly, yes. It's Mrs Camberwell. But you must call me Midge. As Delphine does.'

She perched on a hairy green sofa which sank several inches lower than she'd bargained for.

'Oh! I'm so glad you've come, missus!' Anne's voice floated from an unseen kitchen. 'I was hoping and hoping she'd run away. I miss her so bad – though we didn't see that much of her those last few months. And then they found her bags and . . . well . . . I started to wonder.'

After a while she reappeared with a tray and a teapot. She was so flustered she kept spilling the milk, and the teacups slid off the saucers. In the end Midge said, 'Please, sit,' and poured for the both of them.

'So,' said Anne, sitting opposite her on a ladder-back chair with a dark red seat. Midge was again struck by her resemblance to Delphine.

'You look alike.' She smiled, and Anne softened further.

'I'm sorry, missus, I'm all over the place. I just can't believe . . . This ain't some sort of prank, is it? Oh Gawd, Foley. Don't ever let him know where she is, will you?'

'Emphatically not! That's why I wanted to make sure you were alone. Before I go, we must think of a story in case anyone asks you who your visitor was. Delphine was of the opinion that a stranger on this street might be noticed and remarked upon.'

'She's right there.' Anne nodded. 'Yes, we'll do that. So, missus, where is she?'

'Please, call me Midge, and I'll call you Anne, if I may. Delphine lives in Richmond now.'

'Richmond? That's west, ain't it? And oh, not very far!

That's good – to know she's just the other side of this big ants' nest.' She waved a hand at the street outside the window and the whole city beyond that.

'Twelve miles away, that's all,' said Midge. 'And she thinks of you every day.' She recounted the story of Delphine's accidental arrival in Richmond and the way in which she had crossed paths with the Camberwells. She described her current situation and her bobbed hair and how fond everyone was of her. She described the river and the Greenbows' house and finally reached the day when they'd seen the piece in the *News of the World*.

'That decided us,' she explained. 'We'd been talking about getting word to you for so long, but because of the risks, you know, time kept sliding by. Then we saw there was to be a memorial service, for heaven's sake. We had to tell you in person and I was elected as the least conspicuous member of the family.'

'I won't tell a soul,' Anne vowed. 'You can be sure of that. Apart from Esther, of course. That's all right, ain't it? Del would want that. That man made her life a living hell and not one of us could do a damn thing about it. Excuse me, missus. Midge. He cut her off from Esther, even threatened Esther one night when she told him to ease off our Del. So Del told her to stay away for her own good in the end. He was even cutting her off from me at the end. I hadn't seen her for months when he came round here like a fury, demanding to search the house. I hadn't a clue she'd even been planning anything! And good for her. It was the only way.'

'Delphine would love it if you came to visit her one day. Is there any chance you could, do you think? He isn't following you or anything?'

Anne sighed heavily. 'I don't think so. I wondered at first. And he did show up a couple more times. I heard he was asking around. But that's the upside of a street like this. Everyone knew I was beside meself. Everyone knew I hadn't a clue. It all spread like wildfire. Oh, I'd love to see her.'

'You could take precautions. Make a false start to your journey, just in case.'

'Yes, yes! I could go in rush hour, go in the wrong direction, disappear in the crowds . . . When should I come, Midge?'

'It might be as well to wait a while, don't you think? Go through with that ghastly memorial service so as not to arouse suspicion, let any furore from the newspaper article die down?'

'But before Christmas?' Anne shone with a bright hope. 'Do you think that's long enough? I'd love to see her for Christmas.'

Midge drained the last of her tea. 'I should think that's just long enough. And that might be a time you could reasonably be expected to take a trip, don't you think? After losing your daughter, you wouldn't want to stay here alone for the whole of the festive season, would you?'

'I wouldn't.' Anne grinned. 'Proper heartbroke, I'd be. All them memories here. I'd have to go and visit my cousin in Chorleywood, wouldn't I, rightly speaking.'

'Rightly speaking,' agreed Midge, setting her cup down.

'Anne, if you'd like to come for more than a day, you'd be most welcome to stay with us. Delphine has become, as I said, very dear to us. She's a close friend to my stepdaughters. Anything we can do to facilitate her happiness will be our pleasure. So make the arrangements that you see fit. Now, I'd rather not write down our address for obvious reasons, but will you remember it? It's not difficult.'

'Course I will. And Midge? That service on Thursday? I promise you, no one looking at me will guess anything but that our Del's gone and I don't know how to go on. I'll proper play the grieving ma.' She grinned at Midge with relish.

Midge left soon after that. Anne would put it about that Midge was from a church she used to go to many years ago; that she'd seen the article and come to pay her condolences.

'Goodbye, Vivienne, thank you for calling. Sorry I didn't recognise you at first, after all these years. God bless you,' Anne called after her as she left.

Midge smiled. It turned out that Anne was quite the thespian!

She didn't linger, however. Being in the house where Delphine had been brought up and suffered so grievously at the hands of her father had brought her history alive in a whole new way. She kept a weather eye about her as she went, fancying dark shapes on every corner, but despite her sharp outlook she saw no wiry, foxy-faced men and no one gave her a second glance.

# Chapter Thirty-four

It was December before Blue finally managed to meet L. W. Her writing was keeping her fully occupied, especially since she was researching and writing longer pieces in any spare moment. On the sixteenth of November, a pilot called Alan Cobham had left London to fly to South Africa – a flight of 8000 miles. And had Blue been asked to write about it? She had not. *Cauderlie* wrote the paragraph for the *Gazette*, and *he* didn't even believe Cobham would make it! So Blue worked harder than ever; tea parties were *not* her fate. She was completely steeped in words; in ideas and how to frame them in words. Sometimes she felt she did nothing but write. In the office, in the evenings, even when she attended a function or inspected a new line of shoes, she was mentally drafting what she would write about it later. And in her spare moments, she wrote to L. W.

Her letters necessarily grew shorter, while his grew longer.

*My dear Miss Camberwell,*

*How very pleased I am that we continue to communicate, all these weeks after my initial lunatic impulse to contact you. Our correspondence brings me much delight. I particularly enjoyed your description of your family's autumn party, of the bonfire and the sparks dancing on a black November night.*

*I'm aware that I indulge myself somewhat in penning these letters. My well-worn work routine and solitary, peaceful evenings are conducive to writing lengthy missives and I'm aware you do not have the same luxury of time. Perhaps I am living vicariously through you — just a little! I had not thought that I had become a stick-in-the-mud, but how exciting I find your tales of venturing out into the workplace — a new environment, a meaningful challenge, a chance to learn. Perhaps my routines have become too well polished after all.*

*I like my life, Miss Camberwell, but there has been little in it to excite me of late. Really, just our growing friendship, if so I may presume. How good it is to know someone who can provide a truly sympathetic listening ear (or in our case, perhaps I should say reading eye!). Today I passed a field in which four muddy horses stood nose to tail, like an equine daisy chain. It made me smile and I immediately thought of you. Am I right in thinking such a sight would please you also? Such moments are gifts, but those gifts are vastly inflated when shared. I hope you will do me the indulgence of allowing me to continue to share them with you.*

*Your work is new and demanding and keeps you busy by day.*

*Your supplementary articles fill your evenings. You live with family and are surrounded by friends. I am surprised you have time to write to me at all, though I am very appreciative that you do. Please do not feel under any obligation to write back at similar length. I would hate to cause you any pressure due to my enthusiastic epistolary habits! I hope they merely serve to divert you when you come to the end of your long day and to assure you that you have a friend thinking of you with warm regard.*

*That said, if you do have time to answer any or all of the following, I am extremely keen to hear: firstly, how does your plan to escape the curse of the gossip column progress? Secondly, when and how might you put your rather obnoxious colleague in his place once and for all? Should I send a marksman to eliminate him? And thirdly, is your kitchen yet complete?*

*In finishing, I enclose a piece I found in one of my sister-in-law's magazines about ladies in the workplace. It seems to me to make good sense and even includes a paragraph about a journalist, so I thought it may catch your interest and perhaps even provide some inspiration.*

*Wishing you well, as ever, I remain full of admiration for your zest and ambition,*

*Latchley Winterson*

Blue was touched by his consideration and encouragement. She loved unfolding his pages and seeing how much thought he'd put into writing to her. Despite the delay, she still wanted to meet him. Blue believed that if you felt the same way about something for more than a month, you should act on it. So, whilst December was a busy time, she recognised that there would probably never be a quiet time. She would set her extra-curricular endeavours aside until the new year in order to enjoy the social side of advent.

She still thought of him as L. W. It was just that Latchley was a bit of a mouthful and L. W. was how she had thought of him first. Also, she had started thinking of *everyone* as their initials since she started working at the *Gazette*. Juno was J. F., Barnaby was B. T., Will was W. S. Only Cauderlie remained distinct. *Vile man*, was how she thought of him!

They met on a rainy evening in the dining room of the Amberley Hotel. He was already waiting for her when she hurried in and plunged her umbrella into the umbrella stand, heartily glad to be rid of it. A waiter spirited her wet coat away; L. W. waited politely until she was ready. She threw a quick glance at her reflection in the glass – she would have to do! Then he came to greet her, smiling as he said, 'Miss Camberwell. So very pleased to make your acquaintance at last.'

Blue was wearing a buttercup-yellow silk dress with a dropped waist and a draped neckline. Otherwise it was plain; the lovely glowing fabric and her slim figure could speak for themselves. She wore a violet headband – a bold choice with the yellow. Beneath it, her hair looked the colour of butter and her eyes darker than ever.

Blue had absolutely forbidden her sister to spy on her in the Amberley. 'You'll probably turn him to stone with a glance,' she scolded. 'I won't be able to relax with you frowning across the room at us.'

'You hadn't mentioned him for so long I was hoping you'd abandoned the whole idea,' Merrigan grumbled.

So Tabitha had taken on the task and would be arriving later with a date of her own. 'No need for *him* to know what we're up to, darling,' she said firmly. 'All *he* needs to know is that he's lucky enough to be taking me out for dinner.'

Blue was glad she had a short while without the distraction of Tabitha; they'd decided that if L. W. *were* a screaming lunatic intent upon chopping Blue into small pieces, he probably wouldn't do it in the first half hour at the Amberley. Indeed, he showed no such inclination as he guided her to a table near a window, pulled out her chair and asked whether the location was too draughty. When they were seated opposite each other and another waiter had brought cocktails, she let out a long breath and smiled. Here he was at last. Now she could see the things that hadn't been evident in the photograph.

His hair was dark blond, or light brown, depending on the fall of the light. His eyes were blue, but not the brilliant gemstone colour of Dorian's. They were a gentle shade, like an old coat of which Blue was fond. That curl at the corners of his mouth was ever present and his manner was diffident, but not so much as to make her feel she must work hard to put him at ease.

They enquired after each other's journeys. They ordered dinner and discovered they had completely opposite preferences in food. Then they fell silent for a minute; Blue was overcome with the oddness of the situation.

'Curious, isn't it?' he said, smiling as though he longed to break the barrier that bobbed between them. 'We've corresponded so much that all the usual first-meeting conversations are redundant! I came here tonight feeling as though I were meeting a good friend. But in reality, we don't know each other at all. Whatever ideas of you I've held must drop away now so that I can come to know the real Ishbel Camberwell.'

'Cocktails might help!' quipped Blue, tipping her glass at him. 'You're quite right. We're in the very strange process of turning from imaginary friends into real human beings. For instance, I had no idea that you liked oysters. What a terrible, terrible disappointment.'

He laughed. 'I'm afraid the disappointments may only just begin there! Wait until you find out my secret passion for cold chocolate milk, or that I don't understand a note of jazz. I'm not very sophisticated, I'm afraid.'

Blue tutted, eyes sparkling. 'I do nothing but scribble away in every spare moment,' she countered. 'My best dresses are covered in ink. I'm practically a recluse, my days are fuelled by biscuits and coffee and my right hand has become a claw from all the time it spends gripping a pen.'

'There's a reason the phrase "mad as a hatter" was coined.

You know mercury was once used in the production of felt? Well, I love the smell of felt. Sniff it all the time.'

'I won't use an umbrella. Except tonight.'

He sat back and surveyed her with bright eyes. 'Are we trying to frighten each other off?'

Blue looked at him flirtatiously. 'Nothing like lowered expectations to make an evening run smoothly. Are you frightened, Mr Winterson?'

'Scared to death,' he admitted. 'But here's to facing our fears and overcoming them.' He raised his glass.

The evening slid on. Tabitha arrived, dressed in emerald green sequins, obligatory date on her arm. 'Why, Blue, *darling*!' she cooed. 'I didn't know *you'd* be here tonight. How delicious to see you. You know Charlie, don't you?'

'It's lovely to see you both,' said Blue, standing up to kiss them. 'May I introduce my friend Mr Latchley Winterson? Latchley, I've told you about my friend Tabitha Foxton. And this is Charlie Larkin.'

They shook hands all round and Tabitha eyed Latchley like a leopard assessing a grazing antelope. Blue wondered what conclusions she was drawing.

'Divine to see you, Blue. Pleased to meet you, Mr Winterson. We'll leave you to your dinner. Charlie's simply longing to buy me champagne, aren't you, Charlie, darling?'

'Tally-ho,' agreed Charlie vaguely. They retreated to the

other side of the room, far away enough that Blue could forget they were there. *Bless Tab*, she thought.

'She's exactly as you described her,' said Latchley. 'Honestly, coming to Richmond to meet you, I feel as though I'm stepping into a story and meeting the characters. I've read your letters so avidly these last months. It's all taken on rather a vivid aspect in my mind.'

'I'm sure we're not nearly so interesting in person,' said Blue. 'But yes, Tab is larger than life, it's true.'

Over dinner they talked about everything: their families, dreams and foibles. Latchley talked a lot about his brother and nephew and about his wish to have children of his own. He talked about designing hats and made it sound fascinating. But most of all it was the little things that gave Blue a sense of pleasure in his company. There were so many things they both loved: walking, roasting chestnuts at Christmas, going to the picture house, collecting books. It felt like talking to someone from her own family, but he wasn't family, he was an attractive stranger.

Blue grew a little giddy from the candlelight and the cocktails and L. W.'s undisguised admiration. When he asked if he could see her again, she said of course. She didn't stop to think about Dorian or Merrigan or any of the people who might have something to say about it. He was her friend – and who knew, one day he might be more.

They said goodnight in the lobby of the Amberley. 'Can

I walk you home, Ishbel?' he asked. 'It's cold and dark and I wouldn't feel like a gentleman if I didn't.'

'Not at all,' said Blue. 'We're close to the station here and my house is completely out of your way. I do this walk all the time. Please, start your way home. You have a much longer journey than I do.'

So he left her reluctantly with a kiss on the cheek and a promise that they would meet again. Wanting to savour her evening, Blue took the long route home, past the theatre, where something had just finished; crowds poured onto Richmond Green, chattering about their evening. *How lovely*, thought Blue. *Maybe I'll see something with L. W. soon.* Then she meandered along the river, listening to the calls of unseen birds, and back up the stone steps by the bridge to the hill, hazy with happiness.

But in the warm, softly lit hall of Ryan's Castle, she was met with some shocking news. Foster Foxton had tried to kill himself.

# Chapter Thirty-five

Kenneth drove Blue to the hospital. She in her yellow silk joined Tabitha in her green sequins and the two of them clung together while they waited for news. Tabitha's parents were there too. Blue had a horrible fear that they might not want her there, given that she could be seen as the reason for all the trouble, but she wouldn't leave Tab – or Foster – until she knew all would be well. Besides, she hardly saw them. Anthony couldn't stop pacing, despite his limp, up and down the corridors as they waited for further news. Clemmie clung to his arm and paced with him.

It was Clemmie who had rung with the news. With a mother's instinct, she had known to fear the worst, even though the situation wasn't quite as cut and dried as it had seemed at first. Apparently, sensible, timid Foster had gone to the birthday party of one of his chums, where he'd drunk the best part of a bottle of rum and quite a bit of whisky too. He'd been rushed to hospital and was currently being treated for alcohol poisoning. No one was *quite* certain if he had done it on purpose.

But Blue, like Clemmie, had a dreadful sinking feeling. Even if it hadn't been a deliberate attempt, he had simply stopped caring enough; either way it was desperate. She wasn't the only one who felt guilty. Tabitha blamed herself, because Foster had overheard her telling their mother *why* she was going to the Amberley – Blue was having dinner with a man she hadn't met, a man she only knew by letter. She'd thought Foster had already left for the party.

His mother felt guilty too, because mothers always do. 'I should have said something, done something,' Clemmie murmured as she passed. 'I *knew* something was wrong.'

Foster's friend Andrew Barton was also at the hospital. He had been at the party too. 'I should have stopped him,' he slurred, tottering a little as he walked back and forth across the corridor, 'but I'd had one or two myself and I . . . I didn't notice. And then I did everything *wrong*. Oh God, if he dies, I'll have *killed* him!'

'There, there, old chap,' said Kenneth hastily, seeing Tabitha's stricken face. 'He's not going to die, and you were trying to help, we all know that. Come with me for a turn about the corridors.' And he ushered him away.

'It's true, though,' whispered Tabitha. 'He did all the things that the doctor's just told us you shouldn't. He gave him coffee, which apparently is a brute after alcohol because they both dry you out. He walked him around for ages, but Floss was too drunk and kept falling over so he's covered in cuts and bruises.

And *then*, when Floss didn't sober up, he left him to sleep it off. The doctor said the alcohol keeps absorbing into your system even while you sleep. Imagine, he was effectively getting more and more drunk while he lay there! It doesn't bear thinking about. He doesn't usually drink much. The poor goose must have lost his mind for a while!'

'How did he get here?' asked Blue in a small voice.

'He had a seizure. I know, it's horrifying. But a bloody good thing, as it turns out, because one of the other chaps noticed at last and called his father, who turned up quick smart. He rushed Foster here then called the folks. Good man.'

'And what can they do for him?'

'They've put a tube in to help him breathe and he's on a drip to replace water and sugar and so on. They seem to think there's a good chance he can recover. But it's not certain. Oh, Blue, I wish I hadn't laughed so at his letters to you now. You kept telling me it was no laughing matter . . .' Her beautiful face was a picture of remorse. 'I'm so *cross* with him! But he's my baby brother, and I love him.'

Tabitha gazed at Blue, shivering, her bright green eyes swimming with deep currents like the sea. Blue thought she knew what Tabitha was seeing: memory after memory of Foster as a boy. She could see it too. The four of them running around the lawn of Ryan's Castle, screaming like savages. Foster's bony knees pumping up and down, elbows working like pistons, as he tried to escape from his older sister and her friends. Foster shimmying up the trees and falling out. Foster being gagged and tied up, but wriggling free, his skinny body lithe as an eel. He'd been the baby, borne the brunt of every practical joke, and yet in every way that mattered, he had seemed indestructible. Whatever they inflicted on him, in the guise of cowboys, Knights of the Round Table or the Sheriff of Nottingham's men, he would bounce back, laughing. Blue prayed it would be so now.

'I'm sorry, Tab,' she whispered. 'I feel dreadful, if this is anything to do with me.'

'Oh, Blue, so do I! I was so impatient with him when I spoke to him the other day. Told him to stop making a pest of himself to you and jolly well buck up. Hardly the sympathetic sister, was I? Only I had no *idea* . . . If he pulls through, I'm going to take him more seriously and really try to understand him. I swear it.'

By two in the morning, Kenneth was bent upon taking Blue home. 'I know you want to stay, but your being here doesn't increase Foster's chances and you need to sleep.'

They were arguing it out when the press arrived, in the form of Barnaby Tanner, looking rumpled in a flat cap and a capacious raincoat.

'Ishbel!' he exclaimed. 'What on earth are you doing here?'

'Barnaby! My friend is . . . unwell. What are you doing here?'

'New assignment about a party run wild – a real blow. Lot

of rich schoolboys drinking everything they could get their hands on. One fell out of a window – only a ground-floor window, but still. One got into such a state he thought he was Stanley Baldwin and ran around in the street accosting passers-by for their vote. And one young lad rushed here close to death, I understand.'

'Yes, but Barnaby, that's not a story, that's my friend.'

'Please, Barnaby, please!' cried Tabitha, who had never met him before. She threw herself at him and clutched his lapels in a desperate manner. 'Please don't print his name in your paper! He's my brother. He's never done *anything* like this before. He wants to go to university. My parents are beside themselves. *Please*, Barnaby, dearest!'

Barnaby looked down in amazement at Tabitha glittering in her green sequins. She looked, thought Blue, just as a woodland fairy might if they'd bobbed their hair. She'd adopted such a posture of supplication and tragedy that she couldn't fail to stir any man to chivalry. Mascara ran down her cheeks and her red lipstick was faded from her anxious chewing on her lips.

Barnaby set her gently down on a nearby seat. 'I'll be discreet,' he promised. 'Any friend of Ishbel's . . . A bad business, then?' He looked to Blue for confirmation.

'The worst.' She nodded. Then she stopped, realising that for all she thought of him as a friend, Barnaby was in fact a colleague and they hadn't known each other very long. If he'd been sent to cover this story, it was in his own best interests to do so –

thoroughly. Barnaby took his job seriously, both the craft of it and the salary. Cauderlie, she supposed, wouldn't hesitate to lay out the grisly details. Barnaby might hesitate, but could they really ask him to miss out a whole chunk of the story?

'I know it's a lot to ask,' she said in a low voice, 'but he's a childhood friend. This is Tabitha, his sister, and like a sister to me. He's a lovely boy, a good boy. He's had some . . . disappointments lately and he's at that age where he takes things hard. He misjudged things tonight and now . . . If we lose him, for all of us, it would be . . .' Blue started crying. It had been a long night. The swoop from floating euphoria to this had been nauseating. The possibility that her refusal had made Foster drink that much, that she could be in any way responsible for the fact that he might *die*, was appalling.

Barnaby stepped forward and held out an arm. Blue walked into its arc and cried on his shoulder for just a moment before composing herself. 'Gracious,' she said, rubbing her eyes dry with the back of her hand. 'How unprofessional of me. How dreadful.'

'You're not at work now,' he said tersely, and sat down beside Tabitha. He took out his notebook. For a moment Blue thought he might start asking questions, but instead he read over his notes silently. Then he put the notebook away. 'I've got enough,' he said. 'The Stanley Baldwin thing alone will keep Gordon happy. I don't need to write about your brother,' he added to Tabitha.

'Oh, thank you, you're an *angel*! Blue, won't you introduce your friend? I've made a complete ass of myself clutching at him and wailing, and he's being so very kind.'

'Of course; I'm sorry. Tab, this is Barnaby Tanner, a colleague from the *Gazette*. He's been most helpful and welcoming to me. Barnaby, Miss Tabitha Foxton.'

They shook hands then he stood up. 'Blue?' he asked, with a small smile.

'Long story. It's what all my friends and family call me. I thought my real name would be more professional for work.'

He nodded. 'Tell me the story sometime. Meanwhile look after yourself. And your young friend. I hope he makes it.' And he was gone.

'Will he really keep it out of the papers?' asked Tabitha, looking after him fearfully. 'Isn't that your job, you reporter types, to tell the full and factual?'

Blue shrugged. 'I write about cream teas,' she said.

'But Barnaby, he seems a decent sort.'

'I think he is, Tab, I think so.'

After many entreaties to the Foxtons to call him at any time with news, or if they needed anything at all, Kenneth finally persuaded Blue to go home. All traces of her evening with L. W. seemed to have vanished, except for the yellow dress. When she caught sight of herself in the mirror, it reminded her that before the hospital there had been a hotel and laughter and dinner. She pulled off the dress but didn't go to bed; instead she donned old clothes and sat in her bedroom, staring into space until the sun came up and the phone rang with the news that Foster had pulled through. Then Blue cried as she hadn't since Percy had vanished.

# Chapter Thirty-six

Midge tramped the woods at the edge of Richmond Park, gathering armloads of holly and ivy with which to deck the halls. It was cold, and silvering mist had swallowed the horizons. Here in the woods it collected in gauzy pools amongst the green-black foliage and writhed like fairy spells. Midge wore trousers and gumboots and only wished she'd remembered her gloves. Her hands were red and torn.

Strange to be preparing for Christmas again, already. The years seemed to pass by more quickly since Percy's loss, as if an accelerated life were her punishment. Strange that he'd only been with them for one Christmas, yet he defined it, still. This year he would have been old enough to have favourite foods, look forward to presents, run around filling the air with joyful squeals. The girls would have spoiled him rotten and Kenneth would have taken him on manly errands, like collecting the turkey or the tree. All these absences hung about her like paper chains. Where oh where was Percy now?

Blue usually accompanied Midge on this seasonal mission,

but this year she was at work. Midge might have waited for the weekend, but she was restless today and thought the fresh air might do her some good.

That nasty episode with young Foster had shaken her to the core, as it had all of them. Midge realised she was the latest in a long line of people to feel guilty. She'd seen his face at their party; she had known that something was very wrong. And she knew better than anyone the terrible things a person could do under extreme emotional pressure. Should she have said something? But to whom? It wasn't as though his family could have held him any closer – he was their bright star, their pride and joy. Blue couldn't do anything about the fact that she was a source of torture to him just by existing; she hadn't led him on or been unkind in any way. And how could Midge, a middle-aged married woman, have helped Foster, a lovelorn young man on the cusp of life, to see things in a clearer light? It was unlikely that anything she might have said would have helped, but still she wished she'd tried. One more thing to feel guilty about.

She found herself sitting on a log and surveying the wood. Dark undergrowth, white mist, red berries – a fairy-tale palette. She remembered Delphine saying that her sister used to call her Snow White. Although Delphine's problem was not a wicked stepmother but a vicious husband. Midge hated the word stepmother. Not that she was a wicked one – far from it. The least of her sins lay there.

*Red can be employed to great effect as an accent, but should never be the main feature*. She inwardly quoted Harriet Orpington-Whistle as she gazed at the holly berries. Really, without all that she was learning and the new environment she was creating, she would hardly know what to do with herself.

She'd been so ungrateful, when she fell pregnant. Now, looking back, she could hardly believe it. It had been a particularly difficult time with Kenneth. She never doubted his technical loyalty to her because he was, after all, an honourable man. But to a woman in love, that was only the visible stitching. The entire network of seams and knots and lining that held the whole thing together – *that* was emotional. She had often found him gazing at the portrait of Audra with a haunted expression. Once she'd even found him asleep in his study, holding a photograph of Audra, the marks of tears clear on his face in the light of the lamp above his chair.

But Audra was one thing. Midge had never really expected to win his heart from her. What made everything worse for a time was the way he looked at other women when they went out. It was around the time when, if he were still a single widower, he would be starting to reawaken. A beautiful woman would turn his head once in a while. He would find himself bursting into unexpected laughter at witty conversation and remember with relief what it felt like to admire and be admired. One day, gradually, he would find himself ready to love again – and so he did, except with one inconvenient addendum: he had already acquired a wife along the way.

When Midge saw him with Christie Dawson-Hobbs, she knew he had married far, far too soon. As far as she knew, Kenneth and Christie never spent time alone together. But at parties, at dinners, it was obvious to Midge – and, she suspected, to a great many others – that there was a special sympathy between the two of them. Christie was young, beautiful and accomplished. She was as blonde as Audra had been dark, but with a similar air of frank enthusiasm and gracious manners. She was a lovely girl, always polite to Midge – until Kenneth entered the room, and then she quite simply forgot everyone and everything else. Midge couldn't blame her for that. And her heart ached, that the man she loved so desperately should find himself yearning for a woman who was neither of his wives.

Midge never doubted that, if not for her, he would have married Christie. But Midge hadn't asked *him*! She'd even asked him once, bravely, if he wasn't rushing himself a bit. But he poured rebuttal all over her. He loved her, he swore it. He couldn't go on through these thorny days without her at his side; he quite simply wouldn't make it. Well, if it was a question of saving his life!

She didn't fool herself that it would be some romantic dream. But she had hoped that what would grow between them would become beautiful in its own way. She'd never reckoned on someone else, someone other than Audra, coming along and making her feel insecure all over again.

Christie was petite where Midge was gangly; her features

were generous and pert, while Midge's were sketchy and narrow. Her golden hair made Midge's look like faded straw and her natural air of assurance shone an unmerciful light on all Midge's faux pas and uncertainties. And then Midge was pregnant.

For about five minutes, she had thought that this would solve everything, that she and Kenneth would now be bound together in the glow of a unique bond that would send Christie into shadow. But it wasn't like that. Kenneth was thrilled about the news, and very solicitous of Midge. He took the best care of her. But as they continued to go out and about, seeing Christie and the other lovely women of the neighbourhood made everything worse for Midge. They continued to be their radiant selves while her body bloated and blew. Her moods escalated and her careful self-control was attacked. Pregnancy, for Midge, had been nine long months of humiliation. Kenneth saw her being sick, bursting into great hiccupping, red-faced sobs, begging him in the bedroom – for pregnancy had done nothing to quench that particular flame. He saw Christie fox-trot and dazzle, always poised and perfect. It was agony.

Then, when Percy was born, Midge felt inadequate all over again. Kenneth doted on him. The girls adored him. Midge mostly felt cross and tired and scared. Her place in the Camberwell family was stronger than ever – many women might have put themselves in this position on purpose – but her place in his heart felt as tenuous as ever. If she was only valued as Percy's mother, that wasn't worth much at all.

Now Percy was gone, and Christie Dawson-Hobbs had married a young aristocrat and moved to the pleasingly distant county of Cheshire, and another Christmas was rolling round. Midge kept trying to understand what had happened to her. Had God punished her for not loving Percy enough? Or should she take comfort in the fact that any rival for Kenneth's affections – Audra, Christie – had been removed, one way or another, leaving Kenneth and Midge and the girls to live their lives in peace at Ryan's Castle. Maybe it was meant to be that way after all.

She sighed and got to her feet. The huge pile of greenery she'd gathered was a foolish amount for one person to carry. For a moment she considered leaving half of it here, in a neat pile, and coming back for it with Kenneth tonight, or perhaps with a wheelbarrow. But she craved the physical difficulty of the task. She wanted to struggle with simple things, make life hard for herself. So she piled it all up and spread her arms wide to receive this burden of trailing fronds and prickling leaves. It blocked her vision and tangled around her feet and she staggered all the way home like that, like the woods of Dunsinane, dropping bits here and there and looking just as eccentric as if she did have a wheelbarrow on the streets of Richmond.

'Hello, Midge!' called out a neighbour here and there. And Midge hulloed back in a cheery voice, even though she couldn't see who they were through the forest she carried.

# Chapter Thirty-seven

Dashing Dorian may have competition for the affections of Beautiful Blue of Ryan's Castle, our sources inform us! The young lady was spotted leaving Richmond Theatre last night on the arm of an attractive stranger, whose name she refuses to divulge. The performance was a tale of Wildean intrigue, and certainly the plot of Blue's romantic fate thickens, unhindered by her literary ambitions and considerable talent. Like Mrs Cheveley in the play, Blue is 'a genius in the daytime and a beauty at night'! Perhaps when summer comes, her father, local philanthropist, reformer and monumental crush-magnet Kenneth Camberwell, will indeed be announcing *An Ideal Husband*!

'Sorry, Blue, it had to be done,' said Juno.

Blue sighed. 'It could've been worse. Thanks for saying I'm talented.' She was starting to look forward to a bit of family time over Christmas. It was claustrophobic at times to work at the paper that was following her personal life with such commitment.

The *Richmond Gazette* Christmas party started as a desultory trickle from office to public house as one by one they finished their day's tasks. Blue had never actually visited a pub before and felt rather a louche thrill as she and Juno put on their hats to leave together. She was glad of Juno's company. Walking into such a place alone, she felt, was rather risqué. Juno was scornful of such considerations, but then she was as boiled as an egg, so Merrigan always said.

When they arrived in the Schooner, only Gordon, Cauderlie and Spencer were there before them. Blue's heart sank. Cauderlie wasn't palatable in any dose. And five people didn't give a girl sufficient scope to evade grabby Spencer if necessary. She hoped the others would get here soon.

'Ladies, let me buy you a drink,' said Gordon. 'What would you like?'

Juno ordered a half of Old Snifty, a brackish-looking stout that the men were drinking in pints. The smell didn't appeal to Blue. She didn't think she could order a gin and it or a glass of champagne in this context though, so she asked for a tonic water.

'My, you really *are* a lady, aren't you?' Cauderlie smirked.

Blue shrugged, seeing nothing wrong with that. Gordon went to the bar and Spencer leaned over to welcome them with a damp kiss each. 'Festive cheer and all that! Don't need to stand on ceremony today, do we, girls?' He puffed, looking rather pink in the face. Blue wondered how many pints into the Old Snifty he was. Cauderlie grinned and Juno slapped Spencer's arm – hard.

'Lord, what a bore,' she complained. 'Stuck in the pub with the man with the hands and a relic from two centuries ago. We should've stayed in the office a while longer, Blue.'

'You probably should,' agreed Cauderlie. 'Those columns about pearls and stockings don't write themselves, dears.'

Juno ignored him. 'You're working on something interesting though, aren't you, Spencer?'

Spencer nodded. 'Human interest piece,' he said. 'The terrible things men do when their hearts are pierced by the old unrequited.'

Blue winced. This wasn't about Foster, was it? Had Gordon got wind that there was more to the story than Barnaby had written? Or *had* Barnaby said something?

'Always amazes me,' said Cauderlie.

'I'm sure,' parried Juno. 'Can't imagine you giving two hoots about any woman. Please, don't ever marry.' She took her drink from Gordon with a smile.

'Anyway,' continued Spencer, 'it's something I've been looking into. You know, quite a few returning servicemen, jilted by wives or girlfriends, chose suicide as a way out of their disappointment.' Blue sipped her tonic, feeling nervous. 'There's one chap who took a rather novel approach! He developed a habit of stealing coats and ripping them up after his girlfriend gave him the old heave-ho. Imagine! So I've started looking into the crazy things men do for love.'

Blue shivered. 'I think I'd find that terribly depressing,' she murmured.

'Yes,' said Cauderlie, 'I expect you would. Suffering and the realities of life among the ordinary people – it's probably all a bit much for the girl who has suitors scrabbling over themselves to win her heart with a letter. I'm going to write the next piece about you. Juno can't be everywhere at once.'

'Oh! You're *that* Camberwell!' exclaimed Spencer, the penny dropping several weeks after the rest of his colleagues'. 'Well, well. I hadn't put it together.'

Cauderlie rolled his eyes.

Blue scowled. They knew how she hated the paper's continued interest in her story but, Gordon had sighed, news was news. Only Cauderlie thought it was wonderful that serious-minded I. C., earnest apprentice reporter, and beautiful Blue, Richmond's darling, were one and the same. For the most part, he scorned the society pieces; when they were about Blue, he wanted to cover them. So far Juno had fielded the assignments and gone easy on her. But still it worried Blue that Foster could so easily see the stories about her. It was one thing minding being painted as a heartbreaker on her own account; it was worse to think that Foster might see her that way.

Ever since his narrow escape, she'd wanted to speak to him,

but couldn't decide if it was wise. She didn't want to seek reassurance at his expense. But she'd already lost one little brother. There hadn't been anything she could do to bring Percy back, but perhaps there was something she could say that might help Foster. As the others grew more excitable on the Old Snifty, she grew more withdrawn.

When Will and Roger arrived, they talked with Blue about their plans for Christmas and that made the time pass pleasantly enough. Then Sheila appeared and they discussed the wonders of waterproof mascara and eyelash curlers for a while. Blue decided she would just stay until Barnaby arrived so that she could wish him well for Christmas. An hour passed and everyone had arrived but him. The pub was full and Blue was squashed against a wall, hardly able to hear the conversation around her. And she was still thinking about Foster. Suddenly she was on her feet and saying her goodbyes.

'Poor little rich girl,' scoffed Cauderlie. 'Wants pin money to spend on frocks. But doesn't fit in at the coal face when all's said and done. Back to her castle she'll go and breathe the rarefied air and have a scented bath.'

Blue just turned away, hugged everyone else and hurried out of the fug and the crush into the cold early evening. She stood on the road and breathed long drafts of clear air – the rarefied air! Normally, she thought, she did a pretty good job of fighting her corner when it came to Cauderlie. But since Foster, she felt so unsure of everything. So *unentitled*. What right did she have to enjoy her life when he was so unhappy because of her? What right to pursue love and romance when she had broken his heart? She'd thought she was starting to grow up and take a more realistic view of the world, but really, sometimes reality was just *unbearable*!

She *did* want to get back to her refuge, take comfort in her home and family, her pretty room, her writing and her books. Did that make her wrong, somehow? Or did it just make her sane? But she wouldn't go just yet. Halfway up the hill, she turned left, before she could change her mind, onto The Vineyard, where the Foxtons lived. She knocked the door sharply and stood shivering on their top step in the cold wind.

Their manservant opened the door. Blue was a frequent and long-time visitor to the house, so he ushered her at once into the warm hallway. 'Are you here for Miss Tabitha?'

'Could I speak to Mr or Mrs if they're at home?' asked Blue, still shivering even though she wasn't cold any more. She was afraid of being persona non grata here; afraid that they might think she was culpable. Deep down, she feared that she somehow *was*.

'They're both in the library, miss. I'll show you through.'

'Blue!' exclaimed Clemmie, looking up from the *Gazette*. She was sitting opposite her husband, their chairs arranged either side of a roaring fire, looking the picture of marital idyll. 'Are you looking for Tab?' Was it Blue's imagination or did they both look slightly uncomfortable?

'No, I've come to see you. Sorry to drop in unannounced, but I wasn't sure . . . Well, I was passing . . .' Blue pulled herself together. For goodness' sake! If she was doing this, she was doing it. 'Might I sit down a moment? I won't keep you long.'

'Of course, my dear.' Anthony got awkwardly to his feet. It always took his leg a while to adjust to changes between sitting and standing. He gestured to his seat, pulling up a small library stool and settling on it.

It was only as Blue sat down that she saw the title of the large book he'd been reading, laid face down on the table: *A Study of Endogenous and Reactive Depressions*.

'Caught in the act!' Anthony admitted. 'We're boning up a bit. Trying to understand, don't you know?' His attempt at cheer fell short.

'That's what I wanted to talk to you about,' said Blue. 'I wanted to say, firstly, that I'm so sorry for what Foster's going through, and all of you. I know how worried you must be.'

'Thank you, Blue,' said Clemmie.

'And also, I wanted to say, well, that I'm sorry. You know, I mean, because . . . Oh Lord. Well, I know this might be because of me, and I can't bear to think that, but if there's anything I could have done differently that might have been easier for him . . .'

'No, Blue,' Anthony interrupted, and patted her arm. 'We don't hold you responsible. We've known you all your life. You're not a girl to trifle with a man's feelings. And for heaven's sake, you're a grown woman, you've come of age, you're ready to marry. If you wanted to marry Foster tomorrow we'd hardly be happy, would we? We want all sorts of things for him before he takes a step like that.'

'Of course.' Blue was relieved. She hadn't thought of it like that, but of course it was true. She was as unsuitable for Foster as he was for her. It seemed everyone could see it but him.

'I *am* angry, Blue,' Clemmie admitted, 'but not with you. With whom? I don't know. I tried to be angry with your father for a while because he made that silly announcement, but no one else's son is trying to kill himself over it. I didn't even know he'd written to you until Tabitha told us after that awful night at the hospital. I've been angry at Foster, for acting so irrationally and putting us through this. I've *definitely* been angry at that Mathews fellow . . .'

'Darling,' said Anthony. 'We've been through this.'

'What Mathews fellow?' asked Blue.

'Foster's music teacher,' Anthony explained. 'Old girl's got a bee in her bonnet that he's tormenting the boy or some such. Bloody first-class school though.'

'Anthony won't even countenance that Foster's being bullied. Thinks a Foxton man must be above all that. But I'm telling you, Blue, I don't think this is *just* about you. About six months before your party, I noticed a change in him. He sort of wilted, like a carnation.

'It's his age!' countered Anthony in the tone of one who had said it often before. 'Facing up to manhood and all it means. A chap puts away childish pleasures, starts to think about making his way in the world.'

'No,' said Clemmie. 'That's not it. I think something or someone has been making him very unhappy, Blue. But he won't tell *me* – I'm his mother.'

'Oh, Clemmie.' Blue didn't know what to say. She could feel the older woman's pain coming off her in waves. 'Would you like me to talk to him? I'd be happy to, if you think it might help. In fact, I'd like to. I might be the last person he wants to see, but I want him to know how much I care, even if it's not in the way that he would like.'

'I appreciate your offer, Blue. I know it can't be easy for you either. But he's not at all robust at the moment. Perhaps we should wait until he's on more of an even keel,' said Clemmie, 'and then ask him how he feels about it.'

Blue nodded. 'That sounds sensible. More so than us trying to puzzle out what he wants. Just as long as he's safe . . .' She started to cry, overwhelmed.

Clemmie reached across the table and took her hand. 'Time is a great healer, dear. You know that better than anyone. It seems impossible now, but in time, we hope, he'll be back on track, and we'll look back on all this and shake our heads in wonder. That's what I pray for.'

'I'll pray for it too,' sniffled Blue, utterly exhausted. She was glad, now, that she didn't have to face Foster tonight.

# Chapter Thirty-eight

As winter wore on, Delphine started to relax a little. At first she hadn't felt she ever would or could. She jumped at every noise and saw Foley in every passing male of a certain height and age. And oh, she felt conspicuous – as if she'd been hung with a large banner saying, 'This is the woman in the *News of the World*'.

Quite a few people had asked her about the article. Several times in shops, murmuring women had fallen to a hush and stared at her with wondering eyes. She did as she and the Camberwells had decided, answering questions as directly as she could without going into any detail.

At first it was hard. Her stammer was back and it took a long time to get her simple explanation out. But that proved not to be a bad thing, acting as a deterrent to further questions. The Camberwells did their bit to quell the fire; Delphine knew that each of them had had a discreet word in appropriate ears. Eventually, people seemed to accept that a bad situation lay behind her and had been dealt with. The curiosity fell away sooner than Delphine could have hoped, in public at least, and Delphine's glowing brand seemed to fade. Although the unsafe feeling lingered, life continued as it had been before the article.

Now it was nearly Christmas. And Delphine, despite the imperfections of her life, felt something like excitement for the first time. During her childhood, any Christmas cheer had been snuffed out by her father. Ma had tried, giving the girls a threadbare stocking each, so they could rise on Christmas morning to small wonders like an orange, a sweet, a penny. She had stopped the tradition when her husband pulled the stockings down before they could unpack them and threw the contents out of the window into the snow. They were forbidden to fetch them, and during the day saw their treats being picked up by other children or trampled by horses.

With Foley, of course, Christmas was nothing more than the torture of having him at home for an extra day. Worst of all was the time that he was in the pub – not because she missed him, but because anticipating the state he'd come home in was worse than anything else.

A Richmond Christmas was entirely different, Delphine was learning. And it wasn't just the Camberwells who made much of it and showed her the true meaning of celebration. The Greenbows, too, were endlessly engaged in secret whispering and giggles, breaking apart when other members of the clan came into a room, a conspiracy that smacked of childlike glee and loving plans. On Delphine's last visit to Ryan's Castle, she'd been astonished to find every room lavishly draped in greenery. Holly, ivy, fir and mistletoe lay in deep drifts like green snow and scented the air deliciously, bringing the shiver of the woods into the house. Midge had gathered it all, apparently. Delphine thought she must have stripped the whole park!

She'd been invited to celebrate Christmas with both the Greenbows and the Camberwells, and it was easily settled that she would spend Christmas on the hill. She would see plenty of the Greenbows in the days beforehand and it seemed more fitting to holiday with people who were purely friends than with friends who were also her employers.

She knew that she mustn't let the shadow and the threat of Foley ruin all her days. As the weeks passed, safely, without him, that became clearer and clearer. Each day was a gift. But she also knew she must never, ever, let down her guard and forget that he was out there. They were difficult imperatives to reconcile. It was like having a cold, dark column of memory planted in one side of her mind. She must never stray too far from that column, never wander out of reach, but she mustn't keep bumping into it either. It was hellish, really. But still, she managed to find pleasures, small and large, in every day. And every day she prayed. She hadn't done so since she was a small girl, and she didn't give any thought now to the form or foundation of her faith; her prayers were spontaneous uprisings. A prayer for protection each morning when she walked out of the front door; a prayer of thanks when she slipped beneath the warm covers at night.

And now there was only a week until Christmas and it was her day off. Blue's, too, so they would meet for lunch and altogether be two Richmond ladies living life to the full. It seemed extraordinary to Delphine.

Delphine had already bought presents for all the Greenbows. She'd bought a book for Fanny: *The Enchanted April* by Elizabeth von Arnim. She'd bought Sylvia a box of her favourite fruit jellies, dressed in a beautiful purple bow. Delphine had never bought such luxuries as books and boxes of sweets before. For Stephen she had bought handkerchiefs. She'd never bought gifts for a man either, and this was her first experience of how difficult it was. She'd assumed that she was simply shockingly uninspired, but Blue assured her that no, men were stinkers when it came to gifts. For Paul, she had bought some good tobacco, which Sylvia swore would delight him more than anything.

Strange to be choosing Christmas presents for families not her own. She comforted herself by imagining what she would buy for Ma and Esther if she had any way to give them gifts. A pretty pin for Esther, a scarf for Ma . . . Or if she were rich, all manner of feminine luxuries: hand cream and perfume and jewellery. She sighed. Maybe one day.

She was meeting Blue at the bridge, so she walked along the river, then climbed the stone steps to wait on the Richmond side of the bridge that spanned the Thames to Twickenham. As always, she marvelled at the view, the jade-green ribbon curving out of sight and fluttering with activity, both human and avian. It was a bright, clear day, which made Delphine feel she couldn't keep feuding so fiercely with winter any more. It had its charms. Like wrapping up in a warm old coat of Tab's and getting out and about in the sharp, shining day. She loved that coat. It was purple and lined with navy silk, with a stylish belt to tie around her middle. To Delphine it was outrageous luxury, but Tabitha had pooh-poohed her.

'It's an old thing, darling,' she said. 'My new one suits me *so* much better.'

As Delphine watched a heron swooping from tree to river and back again, she heard a low voice behind her. A voice she hadn't heard for a long, long time.

'Delphine,' it said. 'Del!'

She could have sworn she felt her blood slow and still. The other noises receded and all she could hear was that low voice.

'Del?'

She turned her head slowly and saw not Blue but two hatted figures, looking shabby and worn in old black coats.

For a moment she thought her voice was going to fail her. 'Ma,' she said in a voice full of emotion. 'Esther. Is it truly you? Are you really, really here?'

They both nodded, bobbing their black hats up and down, waiting for her to believe the evidence of her eyes.

'Oh, Ma!' she breathed, a great joyous bubble welling up inside her. 'Oh, *Ma*!' She threw her arms around her mother.

Anne, who had learned the hard way not to indulge in physical affection, hugged her right back, in the middle of the street.

Then Esther wanted a turn. 'Oi,' she said, prising them apart and gluing herself to Delphine. 'Big sis,' she muttered. 'I'm here. We got two whole days!'

'Oh, *how*?' asked Delphine, pulling back. 'Have you really? Was it Blue, did she arrange it?'

'It was Midge,' said Anne. 'Well, all of 'em, really. Midge told you she came to see me? Well, she said to come, after a safe while. Said we could stay with them. Course, we didn't want to take the liberty. Esther took out all her savings so we could stay in a room one night. We agreed we wouldn't send word – best leave no clues for Foley, you understand? We went to their place first, so they could tell us where to find you, and course, once we got there they won't hear of us bookin' in nowhere. So we're up at the house.'

'And lo an' behold,' added Esther excitedly, 'they tell us we've only gone and arrived on your day off. If that's not good timin' I don't know what is. Blue said she was meeting you, so they sent us instead, for a surprise!'

'Oh.' Delphine swiped at her eyes with the back of her hand. 'They're so kind. Endlessly kind.'

Anne nodded. 'They said you'd want to take us around, show us all the places you go, like. Then we're to go back up the house for dinner.'

Delphine nodded, the reality sinking in and the possibilities dawning. 'Oh, Ma!' she said again. 'Oh, Esther! This is ever such a lovely place. You'll love it. We've really got a whole afternoon, just the three of us, to enjoy? When did we ever do such a thing? Well, first I want to show you the river, and we'll go past where I live. And then we'll take tea and cake in this little place I know, and we'll talk and you'll tell me everything . . .' She trailed off when she saw them staring at her. 'What?'

'Delphine, love, your *speech*!' her mother said. 'No trace of a stammer, every word's coming out clear.'

'I've never heard you talk so much!' marvelled Esther. 'Look at you, all full of plans – and full of beans at that. And so smart! You look *rich*, Del. And beautiful.'

Delphine laughed, and realised that was something she hadn't done in a long time, even with the improvement in her spirits and circumstances. 'Esther, you talk as much rubbish as you ever did.' She giggled. 'I do *not* look beautiful, as you very well know. And I'm not rich. I'm earning a modest wage as a domestic. But Tabitha – she's a friend of the Camberwells – she's small too, so when I first arrived she gave me some of her old clothes. And then, when winter came, she gave me this coat. Ain't it lovely? I never thought I'd have a coat like this. She's got a new one, green to match her eyes, so I got this. I think purple's my favourite colour.'

Her mother squeezed her arm. 'Listen to you, chatterbox, with your fine friends and your favourite colours. Talk while you take us around, will you? This is a special day, the most special *ever*, let's not waste a single second.'

It *was* the most special day ever. Delphine felt like a girl in a storybook. The realities of her life had been nothing like this. Yet here she was in her favourite place with her mother and sister and with nothing for them to do all day but enjoy themselves. Best of all, even Ma seemed different here. Delphine had last seen her six months ago and had been struck, as always, by how defeated she seemed. The harsh experiences of her own life, her inability to bestow any advantages on her daughters and, latterly, Delphine's spectacular suffering had snuffed Ma out like a candle. Even if Delphine did manage to visit for an hour, Anne wouldn't leave the house for a turn about the market; she wouldn't even settle in for a proper heart-to-heart over a pot of tea. Instead, Anne asked fretful questions over and over again. 'Where's it all goin' to end, Del?' or 'Why didn't I show you a better way?' or 'What if he kills you? What then?' And Delphine had no answers.

But today, in Richmond, Anne had a gleam in her eye and looked about her with keen interest for once. Perhaps such a complete change of setting allowed a new outlook. Or perhaps it was just relief that Delphine wasn't dead, after all.

She towed them around Richmond, showing them the river, the theatre and the green, then noticed Ma was looking tired, scuffing her feet a little as she walked. So she took them to a tea room and ordered tea and cake for three.

'Well, I never,' said Ma, looking in wonderment at the white tablecloths, the gleaming wooden dressers, floral-print china and the uniformed waitresses with their neatly coiled hair.

Esther grinned and then her eyes grew round. 'Oh! I nearly forgot. Mr Camberwell, he said to give you this.' She rummaged in her bag and drew out a square white envelope. 'He said it's your Christmas card from them lot but you're to open it now.'

Delphine was curious to know why a Christmas card should be opened a full week before Christmas. When she opened it she understood. Inside was a ten-pound note. The message scrawled in the card read: 'Merry Christmas to our new and dear friend. We thought your gift might be more useful before Christmas than after. Love and best wishes, the Camberwell family.'

Delphine would have bet any money – well, ten pounds anyway – that this was not the gift they'd planned. She felt pretty sure this was a hastily contrived excuse to give her money with which to spoil her family. She wasn't sure she should accept such largesse, but she knew that she would. She grinned.

'Must be a cracker of a card,' observed Esther.

'It is,' said Delphine, sliding it into her bag without showing them. If she did, she knew what they'd be like. *Oh no, you keep it, it's yours, we're all right, we don't need a thing* . . . Delphine had other ideas.

# Chapter Thirty-nine

Blue sighed and tidied her desk a bit, shuffling some papers together. She still had a piece to finish before she could go home and enjoy Christmas. She'd worked hard and fast all day and now her impetus was gone.

Blue adored Christmas. Audra had always made it magical. Blue remembered snowmen in the garden, treasure hunts around the house on Christmas Eve and fairy tales around a roaring fire. She remembered being kissed by her father under the mistletoe, on the top of her blonde head. She remembered rolling marzipan for the cake, sitting in a kitchen that smelled like gingerbread while her mother and Avis created culinary miracles.

For a while, the magic seemed to have died along with Audra. The two Christmases afterwards had been dreadful. And the first Christmas with Midge had been tentative at best, everyone subdued and being terribly polite, going through the motions. Blue had wondered if Christmas would be spoiled forever.

But by the following Christmas, Midge had found her feet at Ryan's Castle. She'd spent a lot of time encouraging the girls to talk about their childhood Christmases and relive their happy memories. It was healing for them, and they realised when the next December rolled round that Midge had gleaned ideas. She couldn't have re-created an Audra Christmas, nor did she try, but she did capture the spirit of Christmas in her own way.

Midge's Christmases were more elegant, more grown-up. But then the girls were growing up too. They grew to love the new Christmases, which included drinks parties for the neighbours and, instead of the Christmas Eve treasure hunt, a family walk in the park, whatever the weather, then home for hot chocolate with a dash of brandy in it. Audra's decorations had been whimsical: lots of coloured glass and funny little Christmas dolls; odd but beautiful things in unexpected places, like a lilac feather boa along the mantelpiece or a silver chest, filled to the brim with sweets, on the hall table. Nowadays the house was decorated in traditional greenery, with simple lights and gold ribbons. But whenever there was snow, Midge always made a snowman – or -lady – while the others were out, and always dressed him or her in something hilarious. Blue and Merrigan loved coming home to find an icy visitor wearing Kenneth's cricket blazer, or an old dressing gown. One year they encountered a snow-woman wearing Blue's sequinned headband, Merrigan's long string of blue beads and Midge's satin evening gloves! She looked extremely flirtatious. It was a running joke, and it kept the memory of Audra alive too. You had to hand it to Midge, reflected Blue. It hadn't been easy for her, stepping into Audra's shoes. But when it came to the girls, she was as generous and gracious as could possibly be. She had never tried to downplay their relationship with their mother, nor to replace her. Blue and Merrigan both loved her for that.

Blue sighed again, her eyes falling to the page before her. So far, she'd written her title. And that was it. It was to be a write-up of the Hatley-Gardners' Christmas party, to which Blue had been sent on behalf of the paper. She had also been invited as a guest.

'Conflict of interest,' Cauderlie had tutted, as though it were a court case or a decision of parliament. As though *he* didn't have a conflict of interest when he'd written a spiteful little piece the week before, insinuating that letters galore were still pouring into the Camberwell household as a result of Kenneth's speech.

*Stupid man*, thought Blue, rueing that she was struggling to write, today of all days. Her mind kept drifting ahead to home, and Christmas with her family. She wanted to help Midge with the Christmas tasks; she was worried about her. She seemed always to be worrying about someone these days, she realised. If it wasn't Delphine it was Foster, and if it wasn't Foster it was Midge. Would she ever again be able to relax and know that everyone in her world was fine?

'Tricky, isn't it?' said a voice in her ear. She jumped and

turned to see Cauderlie looking over her shoulder. She realised she was still staring at a blank page, chewing a thumbnail, her pen dripping ink all over the desk.

'I mean,' he continued, 'you have to think of things to say, and in what order to say them. You have to be able to form letters and spell words and *everything*! It's a lot for a lady's little brain, isn't it? Well, I'm sure you'll only be a few more hours. *I'm* going home to start my Christmas. Bad luck, Blue.'

She scowled. *Boorish*, thought Blue. *Unmannerly, barbaric, ungracious . . . Swinish!* Christmas was wasted on the likes of him. 'Off you run then,' she said. 'There are hundreds of women out there for you to insult, don't waste your gifts on me. Try to make some children cry, too. And don't call me Blue.' It had been a dark day when he started using her nickname.

Cauderlie bowed and left. Blue looked around, dazed. Was she the last person here? The desks were all empty and beyond her desk lamp the office was black. She got to her feet and gazed out of the window. The dark streets were busy and scattered with lights. People were hurrying to and fro. Out there, somewhere, was her family. She really didn't want to be here, writing about Penelope Hatley-Gardner's new pearls.

'Ishbel, you've done nothing but sigh for the last three quarters of an hour!' said an amused voice from the shadows. Blue jumped again. Why must all her colleagues keep *lurking*?

'Who's there? Where are you?' she demanded crossly.

'Sorry, it's me,' said Barnaby, walking into the light of her desk lamp. 'Not that I'm monitoring your progress or anything, but . . .' He glanced at her desk. 'You haven't written a word!'

'I've written a title,' she snapped.

He raised his eyebrows. 'Not a very good one.'

'Thanks! What are you doing here anyway? Why were you sitting in the dark?'

'I'll show you.' He beckoned her towards what the *Gazette* staff loosely termed the 'kitchen' – a separate but very small space. So small that calling it a room would have given it delusions of grandeur. In this space there was a table, a Swan kettle with a built-in heating element – to quench the endless appetite of journalists for tea and coffee – and a shelf, which held such riches as biscuits, cups and the odd forgotten sandwich turning mouldy. Its small window framed a quite charming view of the rooftops of Richmond, the station and the railway lines snaking off to Waterloo and beyond. Although there was no light in the kitchen, a street lamp outside the window shone enough light that you could just about see. Barnaby had dragged in a stool, and Blue saw a notepad and pen on the table.

She understood. It was cosy and secret to sit in the dark, and the shapes of the roofs, the winding tracks, made an evocative view. Nothing like a corner of this sort to engender creativity, she well knew; she'd spent long hours tucked away in window seats, corner seats, landing alcoves and the like. The notepad was covered in writing.

'May I?' she asked hesitantly, knowing instinctively that this was no newspaper article and knowing how writers felt about such things. He gestured assent.

She began to read a description of a man looking for work, walking the streets, growing ever more despondent. She turned the page and encountered a different character: a woman tending a garden in Kent. She looked at him. 'A novel?'

He nodded.

'You don't type it?'

'Can't. The typewriter's for journalism; pen and paper for fiction. Don't ask me why, but that's how it is.'

'How lovely,' said Blue. 'I mean all this – your hideaway, the view, the light, the novel. Do you have much yet?'

'Forty pages so far, most of them poor.'

'Reads pretty well to me,' she muttered, returning to the woman in Kent who was picking apples now.

'That's one of the good pages.' He grinned.

'I admire you. I've written a couple of short stories – found them dashed hard, as a matter of fact. I've always wanted to write a novel. Planned to start this year in fact, but then I got this job and there's nothing left of me after that.'

He smiled. 'There's never a good time to write a novel, that's what I've learned. So maybe you ought to start, even if it's only five lines a week. Those lines will add up.'

Blue felt a tingle inside her. 'You're right. Of course you are. I'd forgotten, almost, about that particular dream. Life's just sort of . . . taken over. But seeing this makes me want to try. What's it about?'

He looked at his wristwatch. 'Ishbel, don't you want to go home tonight?'

'More than anything. It's Christmas and I miss my family. If the plum pudding overcooks or the special candles don't arrive, my stepmother may have gone completely potty by the time I get there. But I have to finish this piece first.'

'The one you haven't started yet?'

'The one I haven't started yet.'

'How long is it to be, anyway?'

'Five hundred words.'

'Oh, come on, that's about ten minutes' work for you. Look, how about I sit and write another execrable line or two while you do your thing? Set to, old girl, as Gordon would say, then we'll leave together. You'll *have* to make it snappy if I'm waiting for you, or I'll be late home and it'll be all your fault.'

Blue rolled her eyes, but she did need an incentive, it was true. 'Very well. I appreciate the added pressure. Perch in your strange kitchen-haven and I'll let you know when I'm finished.'

Somehow, knowing she had company helped. So did the thought that she would write a novel! She would begin it over Christmas. The excitement of it filled her with new focus. All that was standing between her and the delicious terror of beginning a new literary endeavour was this short piece about the party – and *that* she could write standing on her head!

Soon it was done. She put it on Gordon's desk, along with a slim file containing four articles she'd worked on over the last two months and a Christmas card.

'Happy Christmas, boss,' she'd written. 'Please read the file. Not really *Gazette* material, I know, but hopefully they show what I can do and you might know someone who can help. At the very least, let me have one decent story a week! Festive cheer to you and your family. I. C.'

'Walk you home?' Barnaby asked when they stepped outside into the freezing night.

'It's completely out of your way,' she protested. 'I do this walk all the time.' If she had a shilling for every time she said that, she thought, remembering her last two lovely evenings with L. W., she'd have a nice little sideline.

'I'd like to. In fact, would you like a quick drink in the Roebuck before we go our separate ways? We missed each other at the party, after all.'

Blue wrinkled her nose. 'That's true, we did. It rather put me off pubs, I confess, although it *would* be nice to have a holiday drink.'

'Good. I think you'll find this one rather different,' he said. 'And if you don't like it, it's a coffee house next time.'

'Deal.'

They set off at a brisk pace and peeled off to the right when they reached Terrace Gardens to walk above the meadows.

'Isn't it glorious?' sighed Blue. 'I live here, for heaven's sake, but I never get tired of it.'

He looked at her. 'You appreciate your life; it's a lovely quality. It's beautiful, yes.'

'Tell me about where you live, your family. You mentioned five sisters! What are their names?'

'Ella, Daphne, Grace, Mavis and Polly.' Blue could tell by the way his voice softened when he said her name that Polly was his favourite. 'I've got two brothers too, Lewis and Philip. Ella's the most independent of us. She lives in a room in a house with six other girls who all work at the same typing firm. Lewis is married, so he and his wife and son live just down the street. Daphne and Grace moved in with them to give us all a bit more space. We're a close family. It's just as well.'

'Goodness,' said Blue, reflecting on a family with eight children. 'And how old are you, Barnaby?'

'I'm twenty-six. But before you think I'm one of those fellows who just wants to live with his ma forever so she'll do his washing, let me put you straight. We're poor, Ishbel, very poor. We *were* even poorer, but now that we're all working, all except Polly anyway, we can save. I won't lie to you, it's quite horrible living in such close quarters. I mean, it's how we were brought up, but we were kids then. Now we're adults, we all find it hard in different ways. But if we all went and got our own accommodation, we wouldn't have nothing left over at the end of the month. Anything. And it's not as though we're awash with housing options these days, are we? So we make something positive out of the situation. Maybe in a few years' time there'll be houses to buy, and we'll have saved enough to buy one. One each, maybe!' He laughed. 'That's my plan anyway.'

'I'm impressed,' said Blue. 'I can see it might not be easy. But having a goal and seeing a way forward, even if it's not a quick one, must help.'

'Yes. It's something to hold on to.'

They reached the Roebuck, which Blue knew to be a six-teenth-century inn perched high on the hill, and Barnaby held open the door for her. She found herself inside an atmospheric room with windows and nooks cosy with candles, and a ceiling with thick wooden beams. It was altogether charming. Blue felt as if she'd stepped inside the pages of some novel of high adventure. Instead of the jostling crowds of the Schooner, there were four or five small groups dotted around talking quietly. And instead of grabby Spencer and vile Cauderlie, she was with Barnaby. Blue relaxed at once and accepted when he offered to buy her a pint of 'best mild' even though she'd never tried such a thing.

He seated her in a quiet nook and went off to the bar. Blue looked around and felt rather thrilled. She was about a minute's walk from Ryan's Castle, yet she had never been in here. There were rakish legends about its past – of highwaymen robbing the gentlefolk of Richmond, of pirates rowing up the Thames to stash their oceanic booty here under the care of a sympathetic and utterly corrupt landlord. Blue could easily imagine treasures still hidden here, forgotten for hundreds of years. A silver platter lodged in the roof, perhaps, ornate with engravings of grapes and frolicking hares; a bag of coin in the crevice of a wall; a ruby necklace slipped under the floorboards. Surreptitiously, she started nudging at one rather uneven floorboard with the toe of her shoe.

Barnaby, returning with their drinks, looked at her curiously but didn't ask.

'What's the difference between mild and best mild?' asked Blue, inspecting her frothy glass with interest.

'A penny a pint,' quipped Barnaby, tipping his head towards the drinks list written in chalk on a slate over the bar.

Blue felt terrible. He'd spent a whole extra penny on her when he was living with about four hundred relatives. She wasn't sure her palate deserved it; the best mild tasted funny to her – though not unpleasant.

'So tell me more,' she prompted. 'Where did you go to school? Pardon me, Barnaby, if this comes out wrong . . . I don't mean to sound condescending. It's just that you write like someone very well educated, but I don't imagine your parents had the money to send you to college, from what you've told me.'

'You're right. They didn't. *And* it's hard to make the most of school when you're always hungry, and you haven't slept because your little brother's been kicking you in the shins in bed all night. So I didn't do too well there. But I knew children who came to school with black eyes, filthy clothes – kids who couldn't even read. That wasn't us. Ma and Pa always encouraged us. And when school was behind us and we were all trying out different jobs, wondering what on earth to make of ourselves, I learned very quickly what I didn't like. I knew I couldn't sit at a desk all day counting and tallying. I knew I wasn't going to work on the docks or in a factory. I did labour for a while, but I was so bored. The best thing about that job was the camaraderie, but you don't go to work for the conversation – or so my boss told me when he fired me.'

'Oh dear,' giggled Blue.

'Exactly. I served in the war just for the last year and when it ended I was more determined than ever to make the most of life. So it came down to this: I liked books and words, I liked talking to people and seeing new things, and I liked writing down what I'd seen. It was easy to see how all that would pull together into a career, but not so easy to *get* that career! My grammar wasn't good, my speech wasn't good. Lord, my *writing* wasn't good! I mean, I could hardly spell. So I taught myself. I went back to one of those stuffy desk jobs for a while, just because the other men there spoke differently from me and I wanted to listen to them. I joined the library and read books galore, and I found a grammar reader too. I'm a bit of a hybrid, really, Ishbel. It comes and goes with me, the proper way to speak. I'm not trying to lose my accent, I just like to get things *right*. I found a book on etiquette too, but I thought most of that was poncey nonsense. But I like *manners*. I like treating people right. So that's what I aim to do.'

'That's admirable,' said Blue. 'To know who you are and be proud of it; to know what you want and to work towards it. I should say that makes for a life well lived.'

'Strikes me I could say the same of you.'

'I'm not sure.' Blue took another sip of her best mild. It was growing on her. 'It's not that I'm not proud of who I am – my family are wonderful. My father's my hero, really. But sometimes I wonder if I deserve it, you know, all that privilege. *Am* I doing the best I can with it? Especially now that I'm "out in the world" as Cauderlie would say. There are times I feel that he's right, that I'm precious and spoiled. I *do* struggle with life – certain aspects of it, anyway.'

'*Everyone* struggles with life,' said Barnaby.

Blue grimaced. 'Really? Sometimes I feel surrounded by strong, sure people who just take life as it comes at them without thought or question. But I'm not made like that.'

'But who made the world what it is? Thinkers. Einstein, Freud, Aristotle, Thoreau – I bet *they* struggled! They couldn't have made the contributions they did otherwise. From where I'm sitting, you're doing all right. You appreciate your lovely life. You're breaking out of the castle. You have a dream. Writing's a tough field for anyone, and even tougher for a woman.

You know that but you don't let it stop you. The only place *you're* going wrong is giving a second thought to what Cauderlie says. Any conversation that cites Cauderlie is a conversation you shouldn't be having.'

'Thank you.' Blue smiled. 'I appreciate that. Sometimes that's what I think too. Sometimes it isn't.'

'If we never doubted ourselves,' said Barnaby slowly, 'we wouldn't learn and we wouldn't grow. Doubt is the bedrock of real strength, I think, so long as we don't let it take us over.'

'So young, yet so wise!' Blue was surprised. 'You're something of a philosopher, aren't you, Mr Tanner?'

'Don't tell anyone.'

'Your secret's safe with me.'

'I struggle, too – all the time. Is it all right to improve myself, to want more than the hand my childhood dealt me? Is it a betrayal in some way? Have I bitten off more than I can chew with my job, my ambitions? But every crisis of confidence is a chance to come back stronger than ever. If you never stopped and wondered, success wouldn't really mean anything, would it?'

'Perhaps not,' mused Blue. She'd always thought of her fears and doubts as something that meant she was slightly defective, not really cut out for the world. But perhaps they were the opposite. She'd like to believe that.

'How is your young friend? The one at the hospital. I know he pulled through – I checked – but I wondered, after something like that . . . ?'

Blue looked down. Everything inside her still went dark when she thought of Foster. She'd received a card from his mother yesterday, saying that Foster was very touched that she'd called but wasn't quite ready for visitors yet. 'Let's leave it until the new year,' Clemmie had written. 'I think we all need a quiet Christmas. At any rate, he's doing well and looks forward to seeing you.'

Blue wondered how much of this was Clemmie being diplomatic. But half of her was relieved she didn't have to face Foster for a little while. How much could she tell Barnaby? It felt absurd and dramatic to confide that a young man had come close to death because of his feelings for her.

'I believe he's doing well enough. Spending Christmas at home with his parents.'

He seemed to sense her reticence. 'Well, that's the main thing!' he said heartily, raising his glass and touching it to hers. 'Health and happiness for old friends and new.'

They left after the one drink and parted company outside Ryan's Castle. 'Goodnight, Ishbel,' said Barnaby. 'Have a merry Christmas.'

'The same to you and your family. And please, call me Blue.'

# Chapter Forty

It was the best Christmas Delphine had ever had. From that extraordinary day that Ma and Esther had materialised beside her on Richmond Bridge, it felt like one delight leading into another. Over tea and cake, they had talked and talked; in the case of Esther and Delphine, they were catching up on the larger part of three years. Of course, they knew about each other's lives from Ma, but it wasn't the same as *seeing* one another.

Esther looked just the same: slightly plump, with creamy skin that glistened when she grew warm, carroty hair, orange freckles and big blue eyes. Apart from her eyes, she looked nothing like Delphine. She hadn't had an easy time of it growing up, but Delphine had received the brunt of things from their father, and if her suffering had saved Esther from worse, then perhaps it had served some purpose. This might have been why Esther had always been the more ebullient sister – or maybe it was just her nature.

After that, they'd looked around the shops, Esther and Ma

oohing and aahing over the luxuries. Delphine paid close attention. Then, when it started to grow dark, Delphine sat the pair
of them in another tea room.

'Ma looks worn out,' she said. 'Have another sit, Ma, before
we walk up that hill.' Then she pretended she'd forgotten
something urgent and dashed off. When she returned, they
were disgruntled.

'You were ages!' said Esther. 'It's not like we see you every
day, you know!'

'We thought you'd fallen in the river again,' added Ma.

'No,' said Delphine, setting four parcels on the table. 'Open
them. They're for you.' She couldn't have waited to give them
their presents at dinner, or anything else with a sense of ceremony,
not for love nor money. She certainly couldn't have sent them
off with their gifts unopened, to be unwrapped at Christmas.

She'd bought a green hat for Esther – one she'd been wishing
she could buy her for weeks – and a warm sweater in pale blue
for her mother as well as lovely little sets of hand cream and
scented soap for each of them. She'd spent almost the whole ten
pounds and would have spent the same again if she had it, for
the heady tingle of generosity it gave her, comforting as sugar.

They were beside themselves. Esther's squeal when she saw
the hat earned them looks of surprise around the restaurant.
Her mother's eyes, which the sweater had been specially chosen
to match, filled with tears when she stroked the soft wool. 'It'll
be ever so warm, love,' she whispered.

When they returned to the Camberwells', they found that Midge had ordered a special dinner, which Avis had cooked to perfection. There were candles on the table of the newly painted dining room and the new, thick curtains were drawn against the dark night. The whole family, including Elf, had gathered.

Esther cooed over Cicely and Merrigan proudly introduced her: 'This is Cicely Audra Camberwell,' she said, and Midge looked sad. Delphine was aware that Midge always felt herself to be in Audra's shadow. She must feel it keenly that Kenneth had had two wonderful daughters with Audra, yet they had lost Percy. *Poor Midge*, thought Delphine, thanking her for the lovely meal for the hundredth time.

The following day, the Greenbows gave Delphine the morning off.

'But I just had a day off!' protested Delphine.

'Early Christmas present,' said Stephen. Delphine was growing very fond of early Christmas presents. She spent the morning at Ryan's Castle with her family and walked them to the train station before lunch.

'Best go now,' said Anne. 'It'll take a fair while to get home, the route we'll go.' Then Delphine remembered that they were still taking precautions to throw Foley off her trail. A cloud passed over their goodbye. Would they even be able to wear their new finery at home? she wondered suddenly. What if Foley should see that sweater, or that hat, and wonder? But the cloud passed swiftly; this had been the best time together they'd ever had. It had been just over twenty-four hours, but it made up for months.

Then Delphine was back at work and the last days of advent raced by until it was Christmas Eve. Paul walked her up the hill to Ryan's Castle in the evening; she'd missed the walk in the park but they saved the hot chocolate with brandy until she came.

The following morning, she came down to a light breakfast followed by a present-opening ceremony around a tall tree in the drawing room. Her suspicion that the 'early Christmas present' from the Camberwells had been no such thing was proved right when Blue, reading gift labels with a serious face, laid no fewer than four presents before Delphine. One from each Camberwell.

'You shouldn't, you shouldn't,' she kept saying, sounding like Ma.

'But we did!' said Blue gleefully.

Christmas Day passed in a bright, brilliant daze of pleasure and togetherness and Delphine fell into bed at midnight, her head dancing. The next morning, she drew her curtains on a frosty day sparkling with early sunlight and softened with wisps of mist. She dressed and went out to the garden.

The lawn underfoot was hard and knobbly, and the fruit trees glittered as though they'd been glazed with sugar. Everything looked as if it would snap at a touch and Delphine found herself walking lightly, holding her breath, in case the fragile vision trembled and vanished. A small robin bounced along an apple bough and, facing her square on, opened its little mouth and sang loudly.

Elf came crunching towards her from the direction of the Cottage. 'Your own personal carol service.' He smiled, stopping at a distance so as not to disturb the robin. They listened, motionless, until the little bird tired of that particular tree and flitted off.

'Morning,' Elf said, coming towards her.

'Morning. Weren't yesterday lovely?'

'Splendid. Where would we be without the Camberwells, eh? Would you like to come to the Cottage for a coffee? I expect they're all abed.'

'Yes, they are, but I just want to make the most of every moment. A coffee would be lovely, thanks.'

As they headed towards the little wooden cabin, Elf stopped and frowned.

'What is it?'

'Just thinking about young Foster, poor chap. I think I've found out how he got in and out to leave his letters in the apple tree. See here.'

At the edge of the garden, thick fir trees grew between the lawn and the street alongside. Behind the trees was a high brick wall. But Elf showed her a place where the bricks at the very end had crumbled away, leaving a space that a slim person could just squeeze through, into the piney mass – and from there it would be easy enough to slide between the branches into the garden.

Delphine shivered. She thought of poor Foster, seized with the romantic spirit, slipping in to leave notes for Blue in a picturesque spot, hoping against hope to capture her imagination. Look where it had landed him.

'That must be it.' She nodded. 'God bless him.'

'Come inside,' said Elf. 'You're cold.'

It was the first time that Delphine had visited Elf alone. They chatted about small things, her position at the Greenbows', his unruly appetite for mince pies. Delphine had wanted to talk to him for a while, but she didn't know if Boxing Day was quite the time. Then he asked how she had been since the newspaper account of her supposed death, giving her an opening.

'Better, now that Ma's been and we've all had such a lovely Christmas,' she said. 'There's been plenty to take me mind off it, that's for sure. But otherwise . . . I'm scared. Scared someone will tell him where I am, that I won't get to keep my life here. And questions, Elf, there's lots and lots of questions running around in my head.'

'What sort of questions?' he asked gently. 'Unless you'd rather not say.'

'No, I'd like to. If you don't mind. I just wondered . . . I mean, Foley weren't the first man to, you know, hit me and such. My

Pa did it too. And there was . . . there was worse than hitting.'
She lifted scared eyes to Elf, not wanting to have to say any more
about that, but he was nodding to show that he understood.
'Well . . . *why*? It shouldn't happen to anyone, I wouldn't wish
it on a soul, but I do know, from talking to people, that not
everyone goes through it. So what's the difference? Between us
as go through it and the other ones that don't? And Ma . . . Oh,
I love Ma. I'd do anything for her. But *she* chose a man like that.
Is that why I'm like I am? Because I'm like Ma?'

'These are good and natural questions,' said Elf. 'I'm sure
you can imagine there are no definite answers. But I'll tell you
what I think, if you like . . .'

They talked for ages. Delphine told stories she'd never told
anyone, and she cried; every few minutes, it seemed to her, she
was crying. But it felt good to talk about it. Listening to Elf
brought home to her that others did go through the same terrible
things. It didn't comfort her to think of them suffering too, but
it made her feel less alone, less marked out. He told her some of
the theories that existed about what motivated men, and sometimes women, to behave like that, and it made her feel better that
someone, somewhere out there, was paying attention, and cared.

They talked for so long that Blue came rapping at the door
in a light house dress with a long woolly scarf wound around
her neck. The hairs on her arms were standing up at the cold.

'Oh, there you are!' she said in relief when she saw Delphine.
'Hobnobbing with Elf, that's all right.'

'Sorry, Blue,' said Elf. 'My fault, I've been yammering away. You know what I'm like when I get company.'

'No, it's *my* fault,' Delphine argued. 'I've been plaguing him with questions about my life. I should be paying him for his time.'

'Don't be silly,' he scolded. 'If you were a client I would've conducted it all most differently, I assure you. It's been a very interesting discussion. If it's helped at all, I'm glad.'

'Oh, good,' said Blue, understanding. 'Good. Sorry I interrupted. I'll leave you to it.'

But it was time to finish that particular conversation. Delphine felt exhausted, as if she'd been doing a hard day's work, so she went back to the house with Blue, Elf promising to follow shortly.

'Did it help?' whispered Blue as they crossed the garden. The robin was back, like a little sentinel.

'It really did.' They paused among the fruit trees, even though it was cold. Delphine took off her coat and handed it to Blue; her sweater was warmer than Blue's dress.

'I told him all sorts of things about . . . F . . . Foley . . . Trying to figure it out, you know. How couldn't I tell what he was? And Ma – oh, at first she was all for him, on account of the steady job and the nice clean shirt and his good manners, but after the wedding . . . she saw it in me face. It'd happened to her, see, with me dad. Only he left her, and she was better off without him, no matter how poor. He were a mover-on, my dad. No such luck with Foley. He's dogged, is Foley. Elf says maybe I was acting out Ma's unfinished business or keeping some sort of, of *contract* with her, by going through the same things, by not being happier than she was. Do you think that can be true?'

'Perhaps,' said Blue, shrugging herself deeper into Delphine's coat. 'It makes sense to me. Parents are the most important people in a child's world, aren't they? That love goes so deep we never want to hurt them, and nothing hurts them like feeling they've let us down?'

'I never thought of it before,' mused Delphine. 'Only now that I have, I think it could be right. I remember so many times when I was little, not wanting Ma to feel bad. Telling her it was all right when Da pushed me over or something, because she looked so *upset*, and I couldn't bear it. Oh, once you start thinking about your life, about why you do the things you do, it can sort of take you over, can't it?'

Blue nodded. 'And after a point, thinking about it isn't so helpful. You still have to *live*, after all. You still have to get on with it, find happiness where you can. Sometimes it's easier said than done though.'

'People are complicated creatures,' said Delphine, starting to shiver.

'I couldn't agree more,' said Blue with feeling, handing her coat back. 'Let's go inside and get warm.'

# Chapter Forty-one

The note was penned in Dorian's flamboyant scrawl.

*Blue,*

*Supper before the party? Peach Tree at seven.*

*D*

During these precious few days of leisure, Blue hardly wanted to leave her family and home. Such wonderful days, every private moment spent scribbling her new novel. The very thought of it was like hugging a delicious secret. But before she went back to work, she agreed to see both L. W. and Dorian. She hadn't seen much of either chap lately.

Although shouldn't she be more enthusiastic, she wondered, pulling on a hat and hurrying out to meet Dorian for the Hatley-Gardners' New Year party. Was it wrong that, at heart, she'd rather stay in and eat toffee cake with her stepmother or curl up in a window seat with a good book?

But at least she *looked* the part. She was wearing a daring silver dress that Merrigan had given her for Christmas. Ah, Merrigan. It had a plunging neckline and a shimmer of beading. It was sleeveless and the bottom six inches were nothing but fringing, which dangled beneath the hem of her smart new coat (made by Midge and trimmed with silver-grey velvet). She wore her violet hat, plenty of black eye pencil and bright red lipstick.

Her heart might belong with hearth and home and bookshelf, but there was a side of Blue that loved looking beautiful and feeling decadent. And this was the side that thrived in Dorian's company. She hurried into the Peach Tree and found him in an armchair before a roaring log fire. His long legs were stretched out, his hat tipped down over his eyes, looking every inch the entitled gent about town. *Suave*, thought Blue, looking for the right word. *Indolent. Louche*. She smiled. *Gorgeous*.

'Dorian,' she said. He pushed his hat up with a finger and looked over. She took off her coat and walked towards him, watching his eyes widen as he took her in. She liked feeling desirable, womanly. A waiter materialised from nowhere to take her coat and hat, and Dorian leapt to his feet. He kissed her cheek then held her away from himself and laughed.

'Great Scott!' he declaimed, striking a fist over his heart area. 'You're a vision, Blue, a goddess! You look spectacular, darling.'

'Thank you, darling.' She laughed, falling into a kiss. 'You look rather special yourself.'

He wore a sharp, tailored suit in navy with a pinstripe jacket and wide lapels piped in scarlet. Under the jacket she glimpsed a dazzling white shirt and scarlet braces. His shirt was unbuttoned at the collar as if, once he knew the effect was dazzling, he couldn't quite bother to stretch to a necktie.

'We scrub up all right for a party,' he agreed. 'I thought we'd dine here,' he said, pointing at the low table and two armchairs before the fire. The dining room's jolly busy. Plus the fire's rather a marvel.'

'Lovely idea,' said Blue, seating herself in the low chair and wondering quite how to arrange herself. The fringes of her dress parted on either side of her knees, revealing a fairly eye-catching amount of leg. 'Stop it,' she said to Dorian, who was enjoying the view.

They ordered a thick tomato and cucumber soup and slow-roast brisket, hearty fare to fuel them through the party. After dinner, over port – 'A goblet!' said Blue in delight, swirling her bulbous glass – they talked about their Christmases. Dorian had been to every party going and had gossip about almost everyone they knew. Blue told him about the Christmas Eve walk and the joy of spending time with Delphine and her family, but felt her tales to be rather lacking in comparison. She didn't mention the novel.

Then it was time to go, and the rest of the night was a whirl. The Hatley-Gardners were lavish hosts, that was for certain. You had to be in the mood for one of their parties – and after a couple of hours' flirting with handsome Dorian, Blue was. She started off chatting to everyone she hadn't seen in a while, then as more and more champagne circulated, she stopped talking, kicked up her silver heels and danced. She danced with Dorian, danced with other people and, at one point, clambered onto a table and danced on that. It wasn't often that Blue let her hair down like this. Perhaps it was the dress!

The next day, Blue woke late to a sore head and the sensation of black bats' wings beating in her brain. She sat up and squinted at the thin winter light filtering through the curtains. As she climbed out of bed, everything swayed a little. Was it the champagne, or the very late night, or both? What time *had* she come home, anyway?

The day outside was not a cheering sight: grey skies, listless rain, not even a breeze to stir things. Desperate for coffee and food, she skulked downstairs.

'Ah!' cried Merrigan from behind the *Gazette*. 'Ritzy Blue! Welcome, and tell us all.'

Blue raised a painful eyebrow. Merrigan and Tabitha were huddled together at the breakfast table like a pair of mischievous witches, looking unfairly groomed and wide awake.

She gave an indistinct growl, meant to indicate that no conversation was permitted before coffee. She gulped down a cup, helped herself to eggs and bacon and got stuck in.

'*Ritzy?*' she asked at last, looking up from her plate.

'Ritzy Blue,' confirmed Tabitha. 'The Queen of the Hoofers.'

Merrigan waggled the paper at her and Blue groaned, holding out her hand. *Really, Juno?*

There was a photograph of Blue, wide smile and big eyes, dancing on the dining table at the Hatley-Gardners'. It was rather a flattering shot, she conceded blearily. Her fringes were flying.

'Ritzy Blue, The Queen of the Hoofers, kicks up a storm at a glittering party last night,' announced an excited headline.

'Oh nooo,' she groaned. Funny, she didn't remember seeing Juno there. She skimmed the article.

> The plot thickens! Despite a correspondence courtship involving at least five suitors, Blue Camberwell, otherwise known as *Gazette* reporter I. C., seems to have narrowed the field to two: hatmaker Latchley Winterson of St Albans and local playboy Dorian Fields. She attended the Hatley-Gardners' New Year party with dashing Dorian – the front runner for her affections in the opinion of this humble chronicler – but favoured a large number of young men with dances and smiles over the course of the night.

Blue gasped! How *could* Juno? Of course, it wouldn't be hard for anyone to piece together that 'darling Blue' and the *Gazette's* I. C. were one and the same, but Blue had always been grateful that Juno had never made the connection overtly. And how on earth had she found out who Latchley was? He wasn't the sort of fellow who'd want his name splashed all over the papers: he wasn't Dorian! And it made *her* sound like a . . . a . . . well! Blue scowled and read on. The piece ended by quoting the 1923 Vogue definition of a vamp:

> 'You propose to her by telephone and marry her by wire-
> less; she is not the person to set up house with but to
> take out to cocktails and dancing.' Take note, Dorian!

Then she noticed the initials at the bottom of the piece: R. C. Cauderlie! No wonder.

'So is it serious? With Dorian?' asked Tabitha, eyes agog.

'Serious?' demanded Blue. '*Us?*' She brandished the picture. She was dancing on a table. Dorian was in the background among a little group of onlookers, laughing uproariously.

'You've been seeing him for a few months now,' commented Merrigan. 'You could be.'

'I don't think this is . . . *that*.'

'What is it then?'

'Oh, need you *ask*, darling?' said Tabitha. 'Have you seen him? If *I* got my hands on him . . .'

'But it's not that either,' protested Blue. 'Not yet anyway. It's just . . . Oh!' She dropped her head in her hands. 'I don't *know*!'

It was almost a relief to don a smart day suit and choose a dusky pink lipstick instead of flapper red – *vamp* red, even! – to go and meet L. W. that afternoon. It felt more comfortable to walk to the station in sensible shoes and sit on the District and take out a book. L. W. had suggested meeting in Liberty's for afternoon tea. It felt more her. And yet, last night *had* been fun!

She met L. W. at four o'clock just inside the main entrance of Liberty's. He greeted her with a warm handshake. She liked the way he was so gentlemanly and unassuming. He was so different from Dorian, whose self-assurance and roguish charm meant he could break through barriers of convention with a kiss, a touch, a wink. But she liked that *too*! She was obviously a thoroughly uncertain woman.

'So!' he said, when they were sitting at a window table with London shimmering below, looking at her with undisguised delight. 'Tell me everything. Christmas, your work at the paper. I feel as if I haven't seen you for months! And did you say you were beginning to write a *novel*? Is there no end to your talents?'

*This is how it's supposed to be*, thought Blue, smiling and tucking into a dainty cucumber sandwich. *You have to feel comfortable, too, I'm sure of it.*

She launched into her stories and listened to his in turn. He recounted his nephew's antics on Christmas Day and described the special joy of festivities with family. 'I know *exactly* what you mean,' she murmured, munching through another sandwich. Poached salmon this time.

Then he talked about work. 'I've been feeling quite inspired to design lately. It's been some time since I thought about anything like that, but I sketched out a few ideas over Christmas. In fact, I took the liberty . . . I wondered if you might be willing to tell me what you think of them.'

'Of course!' said Blue, delighted. 'Let me see at once!'

'Oh good,' he said, fishing out a small sketchbook from his coat. 'They're ladies' hats, you see. In fact' – he blushed a little – 'you inspired them. Working on the production side of things as I do, one tends to get mired in expediency, and forget there was ever any magic in it.'

'What a lovely thing to say!' said Blue, turning the pages. 'Oh, these are lovely, L. W. – very unusual indeed. Bold. Chic. I like them.'

'What's that you called me? L. W.? You haven't forgotten my name?'

'Oh!' Blue laughed. 'Did I say that aloud? I was being absent-minded. It's how I think of you, that's all, because it's how you signed yourself in your first letter. It's sort of stuck. Do you mind? I can absolutely call you Latchley if you prefer me to use, you know, your actual *name*!'

'Heavens no, I rather like having a nickname bestowed upon me by a beautiful woman.'

'And I rather like being called beautiful by a lovely man.' She smiled.

There was a long moment when they smiled at each other rather self-consciously. Blue glanced away. A newspaper lay abandoned on the table next to them.

'Oh no!' said Blue, snatching it up as though by capturing one single copy she could contain the spread of reputation. 'What's that doing all the way over here in the middle of town?'

'Isn't that *your* paper?' asked L. W.

'Yes, but it's particularly out of favour with me today.'

'Why so?'

Blue hesitated. She didn't want to hide it from him. And she'd never promised not to date other men; it wasn't as if she and L. W. were . . . well, anything, really. They were just two people getting to know each other.

Reluctantly, she turned to the offending page. 'I went to a party with my friend Dorian last night. And this was in the paper today. That ghastly chap in the office wrote it. I'm so sorry. I haven't the slightest idea how he found out who you are. I feel terrible.'

Was it her imagination or did his eyes widen a little when he saw the picture? He seemed to take a long time reading.

'Aren't newspapers the actual pits?' asked Blue eventually, aiming for a light, world-weary tone. 'And that coming from someone who works on one. Such nonsense!'

He folded up the paper and returned it to her. 'So I'm notorious at last,' he quipped. 'So be it. You know, it's silly really, but sometimes I quite forget that you have a whole life, a real life, in Richmond, with friends and suitors and your family. Goodness, Ishbel, I don't think I'd be much use for squiring you to "ritzy" parties, you know. I should confess to that without delay.'

'Oh golly, I don't need you to be! What I mean is, I'm not bothered about parties. And please, call me Blue.'

'Might I stick with Ishbel? I like it very much – it's so pretty and winsome.'

'Oh!' said Blue. 'Of course. Thank you.' She wasn't sure why she was thanking him. For complimenting her name, she supposed. She could hardly object, when he'd agreed to her ridiculous habit of calling him by his initials. Only, if he was always going to call her Ishbel, she'd feel as though he were a work colleague. And . . . *winsome*?

'And Dorian? Not that you owe me any explanation.'

'I don't mind telling you anything you want to know. Dorian's a sweet. He's been a friend for years – we know the same people, go to the same parties. Though he goes to a lot more of them than I.'

'And are you . . .? No, never mind. I've no right to grill you.'

'If you're asking me if . . . if there's any romance between us, then I suppose there is a little. But I'm coming to suspect it's only skin-deep. He's good fun, but I don't think we want the same things for our future.'

'And might I ask . . .? Oh, I feel foolish. We've only met a handful of times.'

Blue's face flamed. This was excruciating. But everyone deserved honesty. 'You were going to ask me where you fit into this, weren't you?'

'Yes. If this too is skin-deep. But Ishbel, please don't feel you must answer that. Honestly, the pleasure of your company is an unexpected honour. You're young and beautiful. You're the Queen of the Hoofers, for heaven's sake!'

'Oh, I am *not*!' exclaimed Blue. 'I do like to let my hair down, so to speak. But I like to do it about once a year. And when I do, everyone makes a big fuss about it. But the rest of the time I'd far rather be walking and writing and all the things we've talked about. As for you, you're right, it's far too soon to think of the future or know very much at all. But I do know that I like you a great deal and I enjoy our meetings and your letters. And that's a full account of the current state of mind of Miss Ishbel Camberwell,' she concluded with a grin.

He looked rather pleased. 'All hope's not lost then! Jolly good. Gosh, you're very frank, aren't you?'

'I know it's not particularly fashionable,' said Blue, 'but I think it's the best way. People's feelings matter to me. I've learned we can't *always* avoid causing hurt, but I like to cause it as little as possible! I think honesty is a good start.'

'A good policy,' said L. W., nodding. 'A very good policy. You're an exceptional woman, Ishbel. Now, shall we have some cake?'

# Chapter Forty-two

With Christmas and the new year's festivities behind them, it was time for Midge to turn her attention back to the kitchen. It had proved the most contentious room of the house. She and Kenneth had argued about everything from the Celtic toaster to the refrigerator to the oven. Most recently and vehemently the oven.

'I don't want to have to go without a square meal whenever we have a blackout,' he said when she announced her intention to replace the old gas stove with an electric oven.

'How often do we have blackouts?' demanded Midge.

'They happen,' he insisted, 'from time to time. And we would go hungry. You can't cook over a candle, Midge, darling.'

'Then I'll get one of those new gas ovens,' said Midge. 'There's a sharp style featured in this month's *Country Living*.'

'But then, what's the point of changing it at all? We have a perfectly serviceable gas oven as it is.'

When Christmas approached, her grand designs had been suspended. But now she needed the distraction and purpose of the redecoration once again. She'd come to feel rather afraid of the kitchen, so she'd begun her new year's decorating with an inconsequential room, just to get back in the swing of it.

'Is it *worth* doing the second guest room?' wondered Kenneth, when she told him. Then he saw her expression and added, 'But whatever you think, darling, you know best.'

She was delighted with the results. She'd had the walls painted not fashionable cream or lemon but a stark, gleaming white. She'd furnished it with all the heavy mahogany furniture she'd moved from other rooms but that Kenneth wanted to keep. The light and the dark offset each other rather wonderfully. In other rooms she'd installed wall-mounted lights with upward-pointing covers – 'To create a diffuse, sophisticated light and uplifting ambience,' Harriet Orpington-Whistle advised. But here there were only lamps, with bowl-like shades of glass patterned in the new style, fresh from Paris, all bold shapes and striking outlines picked out in jewel-rich colours. She'd found a Chinese rug for the floor that was similarly bright. Midge was rather proud of it and daydreamed about sending a photograph to Harriet, who might write back applauding Midge's vision and offer her an apprenticeship. Then she would be a working woman, like Blue!

But when it came to the kitchen, she had no such confidence. It was the heart of the home, after all. A place where family foregathered, Avis's place of work, a place where their very sustenance was created. *Heaven forbid they miss a single meal*, snipped

Midge as she prowled around the empty kitchen, trying to recapture her former sense of excitement.

*Everything* Kenneth said these days irritated her. Only yesterday he'd teased her about 'her lover, Lutyens'. It was true that Sir Edwin Lutyens was her hero. It was also true that when Lawrence told her he'd once met the great man, Midge was positively green. Well, he'd designed the Cenotaph in Whitehall, for heaven's sake! *And* Queen Mary's Dolls' House, with its flushing toilet, miniature books and miniature works of art. But what was so unusual about admiring a great talent? As if *he* had anything to be jealous of. The very fact of him teasing her about it showed how smug and complacent he really was.

She heard voices in the hall and cocked her head, listening. Kenneth and Avis had arrived home at the same time, by the sound of it.

'Let me take those for you,' she heard him say. The sound of his voice, deep and refined, still made her shiver with delight. Avis clattered off somewhere and Kenneth came into the kitchen with a ton of groceries.

'Hello, darling!' he said, then noticed that she was standing still in the middle of the kitchen doing nothing at all. 'Oh no,' he said. 'It's time for that again, is it?'

'Well, you could be a little more supportive,' she snapped, knowing she was being unfair. But really, she couldn't help herself!

He set down the groceries and took her hands. 'Midge, let's

not fight. We've had a lovely Christmas. Thank you for putting your plans on hold. If you want an electric oven, we can have one. I won't even complain if there's a blackout.'

He kissed her and tears sprang unexpectedly to her eyes. He was so good. So good. But what she said was, 'Well, you've done nothing *but* complain so far.'

He pulled back a little, startled. 'No, darling, really. Everything you've chosen has turned out wonderfully. The house is marvellous.'

'You've changed your tune,' said Midge, carried by a wave. 'All it's been from the very beginning is you making fun of my ideas! When I wanted a Celtic toaster all you could say was, "Are any of us remotely Celtic?" And when I bought the Swan jelly moulds, you said, "Do we *eat* jelly?" And when I asked you what you thought about a tea urn you smirked and said, "Are we to bathe in tea?" Honestly, Kenneth! If I hear one more silly question from you, I shall scream!'

'Midge, darling! Whatever is the matter with you?'

So Midge screamed. She hadn't done it since she was a very little girl and she hadn't done it very much then; she'd always been the docile sort. But now she planted her two feet firmly apart, tipped her head back and screamed. The sound was shockingly loud and bounced around the kitchen. Kenneth's face was a picture. And somewhere during her diatribe the girls had arrived: Merrigan, Blue and Tabitha. They were standing in the kitchen doorway, their mouths open like baby birds.

'Not one word!' commanded Midge, cutting them off with a wave. 'No more questions from *anyone*. Always questions, questions, questions and never the right ones. Never a one that leads to anything important. So no, Kenneth, we are *not* Celtic. We *may* eat jelly and if I wish to bathe in tea, I shall do so. Excuse me, girls. Tabitha, don't you have a home of your own, for heaven's sake?'

She pushed past them, bent on escape or destruction, whichever came first, and saw her gumboots standing in the hall, neatly paired. She thrust her feet into them and wrenched her coat from the stand, which rocked violently and started to topple. *Let kingdoms fall!* thought Midge grimly. She was distantly aware of Merrigan leaping to catch it and Blue starting after her as she opened the front door.

'No, Blue, not even you. Not today.' And she fled from the house. She charged up the hill, scarcely noticing the torrential rain. She hastened past the Terrace Gardens, drenched and forlorn, then the Roebuck, fuggy and bustling, and into Richmond Park.

Fortunately for Midge, the park was empty, apart from a pair of unseasonal deer beneath a stand of oaks, bellowing mournfully. At least there were no neighbours to see Midge Camberwell, long grey coat flapping, belt trailing, stomping through the wet grass and sobbing. Oh, the relief and release of crying. She hadn't realised until this moment how much she'd been longing to do it. Buckling beneath the yoke of emotion, she stood on the edge of Conduit Wood, hung her head and wept. When she'd cried herself out, she felt desperately horrified. What had she *done*? What had she *said*? Oh, Tabitha! Oh, *Kenneth*!

A vivid reprise of the scene in the kitchen tortured her – as if she were watching it on screen in the picture house: Kenneth's face as he tried to make sense of her nonsensical tirade; the girls huddled in the doorway like a Greek chorus; the rocking coat stand and her own dramatic exit. And what had she said? That none of them ever asked the questions that really mattered? *Well, thank heavens!* The continuation of her life as she knew it depended on that.

Whatever was the matter with her? She hadn't felt very well over Christmas. There had been dizzy spells, times when the delicious foods hadn't tempted her and she'd felt unfairly fatigued at odd moments in the middle of the fun. What if it was something serious? Would they . . . would they miss her if she was gone? Or . . . Lord, she couldn't be pregnant again, could she? Not at her time of life, surely! Life couldn't be so cruel. Not after last time. Exhaustion from the decorating and all the difficult emotions, pent up over years, were a far more plausible diagnosis.

Sometimes she loathed being a respectable, middle-class English wife. Whatever was going on inside Midge, all that ever showed on the outside was tidy, calm and drab. How she wished she could be a feisty flamenco dancer or an Amazonian warrior, someone who could express rage, jealousy, passion and regret like paint on a canvas. In a fit of rejection of everything about herself, she threw herself to the ground, wanting to paint herself mud-dark, splashy and rich. She fell awkwardly, cracking her knee on a stone, and sat up after only a moment. What was she doing *now*? She was absolutely losing the thread.

This was extreme. She supposed other wives might shout and run from the house sometimes – she was certain most of them *wished* to – but who on earth ran to the park in the rain and flung themselves face down in the mud? But then, who else had done the terrible things that she'd done? She sat up and took a few deep breaths. At least no one had seen her. No one knew the worst of it. She got to her feet. It was a question of limiting the damage now. The rain was already washing the mud from her face and hands and hair. Her clothes were ruined, but she could just say she'd slipped.

She was frightened by how she seemed to split inside some-times, fleetingly becoming some other deranged person, unable to call on her usual resources. She would need to make this up to Kenneth somehow. It was hardly alluring behaviour, was it? And she couldn't *bear* to lose him. It was just that she was so tired of always needing to be on her best behaviour just to command a modest level of love and desire. If only she could know, *really* know, that he truly loved her, the way she loved him, all the demons would simmer down, she knew. Instead, the tepid regard he had for her was slipping away. The way she was behaving, it had to be.

# Chapter Forty-three

January wore on. *Possibly my least favourite month of all*, thought Blue as she trudged through the rain after work. Not that February had much more to recommend it, aside from being that much closer to spring. How these long nights and twilit days wore one down. How the lack of variation, day after day, sucked the spirit out of one.

She'd been back at work for two weeks. Only two months remained until Jimmy Griggs would return, if his recovery went to plan. Blue didn't feel ready to leave the *Gazette*. There were some things she wouldn't miss: the early mornings; the endless reporting of vapid pastimes and, of course, Robert Cauderlie. But other things, other people, she *would* miss – and, more than anything, the sense of purpose and identity it gave her. Well, she comforted herself, it wasn't the end of her life as a writer, it was only the end of her apprenticeship. Leaving would give her more time to work on submissions for other papers, and on her novel. Anyway, she could hardly begrudge a man his return to health and employment; she'd only ever been keeping the chair warm for Griggs.

Heavens, it was hard to keep one's spirits up beneath such a darkness of sky. Blue's mind was like a revolving door, presenting Midge, Foster, Delphine in endless rotation. Since Midge's outburst the other day, they'd all been walking on eggshells. She'd come home soaked and muddy, shivering like a greyhound. Avis had run her a hot bath and after a while Daddy went to see her. The next day Blue went to talk to her, but Midge said she was only tired after Christmas and all her hard work in the months before. She would take things a little easier for a while.

'And . . . is everything all right with you and Daddy?' Blue asked, wondering if she was venturing where she should fear to tread. 'You know, he really does love you, Midge.'

'Oh, darling. I love your father, and you and your sister, more than anyone or anything else in creation. Perhaps I love you all *too* much. The thought of losing you, any of you . . .'

'Don't worry, Midge. We're not going anywhere. We love you, too.'

Since Percy's disappearance the Camberwells did sometimes cling to each other with a particular desperation. Love could be terrifying, thought Blue. Quite terrifying. Well, she'd tried to reassure Midge, and there was nothing she could do for Delphine, since Foley remained blessedly, tormentingly absent. But Foster . . .

Two weeks into the working year and she hadn't heard a

word from Clemmie about visiting him. Despite their agreement, Blue somehow knew that Foster would never send for her. There had been no further dramas – thank God – but Tabitha said that Foster was sunk into a black mood which showed no signs of letting up. 'He's at home *all* the time, but I've never missed him more,' Tab sighed.

Blue had to talk to him. It might do more harm than good, and she wasn't looking forward to it in the slightest, but she had to do it, she just had to. And it should be soon. *What's wrong with now?* asked a voice in her head as she neared The Vineyard. She stopped still. 'Now?' she whispered. She didn't feel brave enough to do it now. Then again, she probably never would. She sighed. No time like the present and all that.

As she knocked on the Foxtons' door, Blue drew a shuddering breath. All those years of coming here to play, of standing on this very doorstep hand in hand with her sister, anticipating a royal welcome, knowing they were about to have the very best of times. And now this.

Tab and her parents were eating an early supper. Foster was nowhere in evidence. Blue explained why she had come and, seeing Clemmie and Anthony exchange worried glances, jumped in before they could concoct a definite no.

'I know what you're thinking,' she said, 'but I really feel it's the right thing to do. I can't explain it, but please trust me. I only have his best interests at heart. I think it'll help. I don't know how, I just think it will.'

'I think she's right, actually,' said Tab, to Blue's relief. 'We're all pussyfooting around him and that's not helping. Blue's the reason for all this, according to Foster. At least, that's his excuse. So let him confront it. Because we all know it can't possibly be just that.'

'It's difficult to know what to do for the best,' said Anthony, drawing his thick eyebrows together. 'What do you think, Clemmie?'

After a lengthy pause Clemmie replied. 'I agree with the girls actually, darling. Foster hasn't so much as laid eyes on Blue since November, and he's no better. The Camberwells are our closest friends! One way or another he has to learn to see Blue again; she's still in our lives.'

'And still his friend,' added Blue softly. Anthony nodded at last.

Blue felt weak with relief and trepidation. Tab squeezed her hand. 'Good luck, Blue,' she said.

Blue made her way to Foster's room and knocked softly on the closed door. A muffled voice said something that may or may not have been 'Leave me alone'. She went in.

The curtains were closed and the only light came from a small table lamp. Blue hadn't been in here since it had been a little boy's room, with teddy bears and framed pictures of gnomes and fairies. Now she supposed it must be different, but it was too dim to see very well. She squinted at a huddled shape in the bed and discerned Foster, reading in the weak light of the lamp.

'Floss?' she said into the gloom.

He shot up as if someone had poked him with a stick. 'Blue? What the devil? What on earth are you doing here?'

'I wanted to see you. And you never come round any more. So if Mohammed won't go to the mountain . . . I wanted to come sooner, Floss, but I was afraid of making things worse. I was waiting for you to send for me but then I started to think you never would. Is it all right, Floss? I really want to talk to you.'

Foster leapt out of bed, pulled a dressing gown over his pyjamas and switched on the overhead light. He ran a comb through his dishevelled hair and Blue looked around the room. The magical pictures had gone and the walls were rather bare, as if he'd been at a loss to know what to replace childhood with. One small rural landscape hung over his bed. A pair of bookshelves ran along opposite walls, crowded with books both vertical and horizontal.

'You couldn't run to another shelf?' asked Blue, eyeing the sagging supports.

'You know there's a shortage of building materials these days.' Foster's attempt at a joke was undermined by his nervous smile. He glanced down at his pyjamas. 'Well, this is a strange state in which to receive a visitor. Wouldn't you rather wait in the library while I dress and join you?'

Blue narrowed her eyes at him. 'But would you?'

'Probably not. Well then. May I offer you some tea?'

'Stop trying to get rid of me, Foster. Have a seat, and I shall do the same.'

'Jolly good,' said Foster in a resigned tone. 'Jolly good.' He perched on the edge of the bed and Blue removed a few shirts and cardigans from a chair for herself.

'Foster, I was so sorry to hear what's happened with you.' She'd promised herself she would stick to the point. 'It was crushing news. I've been worried sick. And I wanted to ask you . . . so many things. Oh, so many things, Floss, that I hardly know where to start.'

'Ask away then, old girl.'

For a moment Blue thought her nerve might fail her, then she remembered that she'd waited a long time for this conversation and this was her chance. 'Well, first of all, my dear friend, do you think you might do it again?'

'Gosh.' Foster's knobbly Adam's apple rose and fell, and Blue remembered noticing it on the night of her fateful birthday party. *Before* her father had ever said anything stupid. Foster had always been a nervous sort, she remembered suddenly, outside of the comfortable circle of their two families. 'You don't mince around, do you, Blue? Everyone else is tiptoeing about me, wringing their hands and speaking in whispers.'

'Well, it's rather hard to know how to be, if I'm honest,

Floss. We all love you so much, and it's been terribly . . . Well, *will* you?'

'I don't know.'

'Right.'

'Sorry, Blue, I know that's not what you want to hear, but I'm being honest. I never thought I would feel so . . . *uncaring* as I did that night. I don't *want* it to happen again, but sometimes these moods come over me . . .'

Blue looked down at her slender fingers, her right middle finger bumpy from long hours holding a pen. Her opal ring gleamed green and pink. Then she looked up at the golden-brown freckles splodged across Foster's pale cheekbones, his big eyes.

'Is it really about me? I mean, because I won't be your lady friend? Is that the reason?'

He didn't answer for a long time. Blue's thoughts were clamouring: *Please don't say yes. Please don't make me responsible for this. Can't you see how unfair it is, what it's doing to me?* But she bit them back.

'I thought it was, at first,' he said, 'but I was wrong.'

*Oh, thank God!*

'I don't fully understand it, Blue. I've tried and tried. When your father made that speech, and you stood there on the stairs in your shimmering blue gown, with your golden hair, well, you looked like an angel, Blue. And I thought . . . I simply thought . . . you should be *mine*. Because no one else could love

or admire you as much as I do and because I've known you forever. I do know how it sounds, Blue. It's just how I felt in that
moment. Maybe it was madness, or the champagne turning my
head.' He gave a bitter laugh. 'Or maybe it was those damned
chimes of midnight. But suddenly I was convinced that *you*
were the answer.'

'The answer to what, dear?'

Foster sighed. 'I don't know, Blue. To everything that was
wrong, I suppose.'

'And what *was* wrong?'

He was silent for a long moment. Blue remembered what
Clemmie had said about an unkind teacher and that Foster
wouldn't talk to her about any of it. If only he would confide
in her, if only he could learn that a trouble shared really was a
trouble halved. That was how she'd been brought up, but Foster's father was more of the stiff upper lip school. She waited.

'Don't you just find it all so terribly hard?' said Foster at
last, without looking at her. 'Life, I mean. Being who we are.
Hoping people will . . . be kind.'

Blue frowned. She remembered one of his letters to her:
'I'm a good person and the world is full of cruelty . . . When
I think of you with someone else, someone who might hurt
you, I feel frantic.'

'Who's unkind, Floss?' she asked, as gently as she could
manage. But he only shook his head, eyes brimming, lips compressed, as though at all costs he must stop his secrets escaping.

'It doesn't matter, Blue,' he said with a valiant attempt at a smile. It wobbled spectacularly. Blue bit her lip.

'Foster,' she said firmly. 'Don't you understand? I care about you. We all do. So far you've told me you might attempt to hurt yourself again, that there's something very wrong and that you need people to be kind. Well, give me the chance to be. Tell me what's wrong. What are you afraid of?'

He stared at her as though she were a ghost or an intruder. The question had obviously hit a mark.

'What are you afraid of?' she asked again.

And just when she thought he was never going to answer her, he spoke. 'Of losing your good opinion, Blue, of losing *everyone's* good opinion. Ma and Pa have such high hopes for me. I'm the golden boy, aren't I? I mean, there's Tab, yes, but she's a girl. And for all it's 1926 now, and the old parents are liberal as they go, it's not the same, not in this house. *I'm* the one who has to go to university – Cambridge, if they have their way. Forge a glittering career. Make an excellent match. They expect things of Tab, too, but she just shrugs them off. And she's so funny and gorgeous she gets away with it. But if *I* let them down, they'll be devastated.'

'Why would you let them down? Don't you want those things? It's all right if you don't, you know. I know your father can be stern, but he loves you, he'd understand.'

'No, he *wouldn't*.'

'Why?'

But the stubborn silence was back. Blue felt like crying. Then, on an impulse, she asked, 'Is it because of Mr Mathews? Your music teacher?'

And Foster looked as if he'd been struck by an arrow. *Clemmie was right!* thought Blue.

'What do you know about that?' he asked, looking horrified.

'Very little. Only that he was important to you and he's hurt you.'

'*Hurt* me? Mr Mathews? Oh no! No, that's not it at all!'

'Oh! Well, good, I'm glad. So what *is* it? Floss, can't you see, I'm not going to go away. You may as well just tell me. I'm sorry to hound you, but you need a friend and I can't be one if I don't know what's going on!'

'We kissed,' he blurted out.

For a moment, Blue thought she'd misheard. 'I beg your pardon?'

He looked away and she realised she hadn't misheard at all. And now he thought she was condemning him, just as he'd feared. She grabbed his hand. 'Sorry, Floss, you just took me by surprise, that's all. Your mother's convinced he's bullying you, you see, so I wasn't expecting that. Right. So you kissed. And?'

His face was a study of confusion, hope and pain. 'What do you mean, *and*? Aren't you disgusted? Don't you hate me now?'

'Of course not! I *told* you, I'm your friend. So what happened? What's *going* to happen? Golly!'

Now she understood his torment, his reticence. If Foster

was . . . one of *those* chaps, he wouldn't have an easy life ahead of him. A life in the shadows, a life either of lies or behaviour that might get him thrown in jail. And his parents . . . Yes, he was right, they would be devastated. They wouldn't stop loving him, she sincerely hoped, but it wasn't what they'd want for their son.

'So are you . . . that is, you like men, then?' She hoped she sounded neutral, unruffled.

He sank his head in his hands and groaned. 'Oh, Blue, I'm not even sure it's that! I'm confused. Horrified, actually, that it happened. But it did.'

'And he didn't . . . *make* you?'

'No! He was as shocked as I. I mean, he's a master! Even if I were a girl, he couldn't . . . I think he's that way though, and he apologised so profusely he almost cried. And I . . . Well, when he started teaching us I just *adored* him. He's so funny and smart and inspiring, Blue. And *talented*! My goodness. I started to stay in during the lunch break to play for him and he coached me – in his spare time – because he thought I had real talent too. It was the happiest I've ever been.'

'It sounds wonderful. Exciting. But you told your mother he said you weren't any good?'

'Yes, well, I had to tell her something. I used to come home every day and rave on and on about him. When it happened, it shook me to the core, and I stopped. Stayed away from him. Couldn't bring myself to mention him in case somehow she read my mind. So that's what I told her, just so I wouldn't have to talk about him any more. And then I had to pretend I was off the violin to make her believe it. I miss playing. But then, it reminds me of him, so it's easier not to.'

'I see. And do you . . . love him?'

He spread his hands wide. 'I don't know! I admire him. I loved his company. I wanted to be his friend. And when we kissed, it felt like a natural part of all that. But that would make me a . . . a . . .'

'And if you are? I know it wouldn't be easy, Floss. Believe me, I know. But it would still be better to admit it than to run from it. Admit it to yourself, at least, and a few people you know you could trust, and find a way from there.'

He reached forward and clung to her for a minute. 'Oh, Blue,' he murmured into her hair. 'Thank you. Thank you so much. You don't know what that means to me. To know that you still care for me, that you think others might too.'

'Of course I do. Of course they would. I can't pretend I know a great deal about it. None of my other friends are that way – that I know of!' Blue added with a grin. Though possibly nothing would surprise her after this. 'But I know there *are* people like that – you're not at all the only one – and I know that some people hate what they can't understand. But not everyone. It would be all right, Foster.'

He nodded. Took a deep breath. 'I don't even know that I *am*,' he said, and he was all different now – no longer a frightened child afraid of being found out, but a young man trying to work out his place in the world. 'I've never felt like that about another man and I really did feel like that about you, Blue. I had a *towering* crush. But you weren't the reason I did what I did, why it all felt so unbearable, nor why I pursued you so hard. This was why. I always knew, really, that you wouldn't love me like that. But can you see why it became so important to me, why I couldn't let it go?'

'Absolutely. Yes, I understand that. So are there . . . Sorry, Floss, I really don't know much about this, are there people who like men *and* women, do you think?'

He shrugged. 'I don't know much more than you! Maybe there are, and I'm one of them. Or maybe Mr Mathews was a once-in-a-lifetime thing and I'll grow up and get married and be happy. Or maybe *you* were the exception and I'll have that difficult life where I have to pretend . . .'

'But you'll never know. You'll never know any of that, will you, if you end it now. Foster, please, *please* say you won't try again. That no matter how hard life is, you'll stick with it, make it the best you can.'

'I think . . . maybe I can, now, Blue. I do want to find out the answers, find out who I am. I didn't before; I was too disgusted and afraid. But if you can accept me no matter what, then I can try to do the same, can't I?'

'I should jolly well think so. Oh, Floss. You can tell Tab, you know. I can understand why you wouldn't want to tell your parents, but Tab could help you. She's the most worldly of all of us! At any rate, she wouldn't judge and she'd want to know. Merry, too, though of course I won't tell a soul. That's for you to do.'

He nodded. 'Perhaps you're right about Tab. I'll think about it, Blue, I promise. And Blue, you won't tell Dorian, will you? Please.'

'Not a soul,' she repeated. 'I promise. And Floss? Start playing the fiddle again, won't you? It's part of you. Just because you're struggling with this, you can't cut yourself off from that.'

'I'd love to. I miss it. I can lose myself in my music; I feel more *me* in it than anywhere else in life.'

'That's exactly how I feel about my writing.'

'But Pa would have something to say. He thinks everything's just tip-top, that I've given it up to concentrate on my studies, that I'm going to go into the law. I'd much rather concentrate on music, but he'd never agree to that, would he?'

'Foster, I'm sure your father would agree if you told him you wanted to fly to the moon at this stage. You nearly *died*! I know he has some fixed ideas, but he doesn't want to lose you.'

Foster rubbed his eyes. He looked exhausted, but his eyes were clear at last and there was an air of relief about him as tangible as clean sheets. 'Oh, Blue, I'm glad you came. Talking to you has helped! I didn't think it could.'

Relief blew through Blue like a southerly wind. 'I'm so glad, dear. I just want you to be happy. I'm so relieved you aren't being bullied, as your mother thought.'

A cloud passed over his face again. 'Well . . .'

'What? Oh, Floss, no. Who? Why? Because of this?'

'One of the boys guessed. Didn't actually see the kiss, but walked in afterwards when we were . . . emotional. And now . . . Well, never mind. It's not bullying, exactly, just unkind comments. But maybe they'll stop.'

'Who is it? Can I do anything? Do you want me to speak to someone?'

'Lord, no! It'd be poking a nest of snakes with a stick. Really, Blue, I can handle it. I'll let you know if it gets worse.'

'All right. Yes, do that. Floss, I'm so sorry for all of it. I hate that you felt so alone.'

'I should've told you before. Blue?'

'Mmm?'

'Do you think you'll marry Dorian?'

She laughed. 'No.'

Foster gave a little smile. 'Good,' he said. 'Because he's really not good enough for you.'

# Chapter Forty-four

Delphine was sitting in the drawing room of Ryan's Castle one dark night in January. The drapes were open and the garden was a tall rectangle of shining black behind the glass, an occasionally shifting mass of bush and tree. It was a little eerie to see it like that; the familiar English garden grown other-worldly.

Kenneth and Midge had gone out for dinner, just the two of them, and Blue was curled up on the sofa opposite, alternately reading and staring into the fire. It was clear that something was preoccupying her, but when Delphine asked, Blue had only said, 'It's someone else's business so I can't talk to you about it. But oh, I wish I could.' Delphine was touched; she'd never really had a friend like Blue. Esther, of course, was dearer to her than her own heart, but their relationship had always been dictated by what was *not* said. What was unspeakable, in fact. Whereas she and Blue could and did talk about anything.

'Do you think I'm winsome?' asked Blue, looking up from her book.

Delphine grinned. 'Blue, you're lovely, but I'm not that way, mind . . .'

Blue rolled her eyes. 'I just mean, if you were describing me to someone, would you use the word *winsome*?'

'I've never used that word in me life. So I doubt it. You're the one who's good with words, Blue. Would *you* use it?'

'I wouldn't have. But then, are we really the best judges of ourselves?'

'Why? Who called you winsome? It's not a bad word, is it?'

'No, it's not. L. W. said it. *Dorian* calls me fabulous and stunning and irresistible . . .'

'You're not quibbling about them words, are you?' Delphine teased.

Blue blushed. 'No, you're right. I'm not. But you know, I never really *expect* Dorian to say things that seem right and true. He exaggerates everything. But L. W.'s more . . . well rounded, I suppose. I expect him to be more *accurate*. But he finds me winsome, I think.'

Delphine shrugged. 'Could be worse.'

'Mmm.' Blue nodded and returned to her book. A moment later, she spoke again. 'Do you think people should . . . save sex for marriage, Delphine?'

'Lawd,' said Delphine. 'Never thought about it, to be honest. It's not like I had men queuing up for me, if you know what I mean. Why? Are you considering?'

Blue blushed again. 'I suppose I am, rather.'

Delphine thought for a minute. 'Dorian?'

Blue's rosy colour deepened and she nodded. 'He's rather . . . well, he's very . . .'

'I can see that he is,' agreed Delphine. 'He's so lively and lovely to look at. What do Merrigan and Tabitha say about it?'

'Oh, I haven't talked to *them*! I'd only get an earful. Tab would say, "Do it immediately!" and she'd go on about how God made men like him for a reason. My sister would scold me for even thinking about it and tell me how happy she is that she waited for Lawrence, for the right man.'

'And what do you think?'

'There's my problem – I agree with both of them! They both make perfect sense.'

'Well, do you have to decide? I mean, couldn't you just wait and see if it gets any clearer? He's not trying to *make* you, or anything?'

'Lord, no, nothing like that. They're perfect gents, both of them. It's just that the more time I spend with them, all I seem to do with L. W. is talk, and all I do with Dorian is dance and laugh and flirt. He does have that effect on me. He makes me feel so daring and delicious. Yet if I were put on the spot and asked which of them I see as being a more likely long-term prospect, I wouldn't choose him! So what does *that* say about me?'

'You know, personally, I think I agree with Tab. Only because I know how very not-special it can be between a husband and wife. Then again, not many people think like that. What would your husband think, if you told him, if you married someone else?'

Blue fell silent again and stared into the fire. Delphine could see she was contemplating deeply, so she took up her own book. She was grappling with the muscular prose of D. H. Lawrence and, twenty-five pages in, hadn't yet decided whether she liked it or not.

The room was completely hushed when Blue broke the silence again. 'I say, what the devil?' she exclaimed loudly. 'Hey there!'

Startled, Delphine looked up to see a face on the other side of the glass, looking in at them. In the darkness it seemed to float spectrally. She screamed and they both leapt to their feet, remembering that Kenneth wasn't at home. The figure in the garden vanished. It didn't flash away in a panic of discovery, however. It took a last good look at them both, then sauntered into the shadows to dissolve into the night.

Blue darted from the room. Delphine couldn't move. She heard Blue dash to the front of the house and then the back, checking that the doors were locked. Avis came running.

'What's wrong, Miss Blue? What's 'appened?' she cried, flour drifting from her wringing hands to the rug below. She'd been making pastry.

'There was a man!' explained Blue. 'A man in the garden. The house is locked, but for heaven's sake! However did he get in?'

'And it weren't Mr Elf?' worried Avis.

'No, not Elf. Oh, how horrible. Some robber, I suppose, come to see what's worth stealing. Did he climb over the wall, do you suppose? Don't worry, Delph, we're quite safe. And Daddy will be home soon.'

But Delphine felt as if her feet were caught in quicksand. Any moment now she would be sucked in, over her head.

'Delphine?' Blue was shaking her arm. Delphine was aware of her pretty, worried face swimming somewhere close to her own, but she was drifting away now, out of reach.

'Avis, will you be a darling and pour a brandy? I can't let her go, she looks as if she might faint.'

Delphine heard Avis clinking the decanter on the drinks table.

'Delphine!' Concern was making Blue sound stern. 'What's wrong? Tell me at once!'

Delphine turned her head slowly to look at Blue. But when she opened her mouth, nothing came out. Avis came and thrust the brandy into her shaking hand. 'Drink a drop, miss. And take a breath or two.'

Delphine did as she was told and at last she could answer. 'It w . . . w . . . wasn't a b . . . b . . . burglar.' She saw Blue's look of understanding and horror at Delphine's imperfect words. 'It was F . . . F . . . F . . .'

'Foley,' whispered Blue. 'Here. But how?'

# Chapter Forty-five

The next day Midge visited the Greenbows to beg a few days off for Delphine. It wasn't that she didn't *want* to go back to work – she was just too petrified to leave Ryan's Castle even for a moment. She'd always thought of it as a real castle, impenetrable. Now the doors were kept locked even during the day and the French doors remained bolted. In January, that was no hardship. It was in the summer that the house was always thrown open to the garden breezes and birdsong. Would Foley still be at large then?

The Greenbows agreed readily. Tabitha offered to help Fanny with anything urgent in Delphine's absence, and the thought of Tab doing household chores was the only thing that brought a smile to anyone's lips that week.

Kenneth rose to the occasion, heading out at first light to talk to a local police officer whom he knew from his war days, and then across to the East End. He returned hours later, very little the wiser. He'd even gone to the docks, where he learned that Foley had completed his Friday night shift as always and

333

hadn't been seen since. The neighbours hadn't seen him for a few days either. Now it was Wednesday. He could be any-where.

The following day, Kenneth took Delphine to speak to the Richmond Constabulary, represented by the enormous, moustachioed person of Police Inspector Bernard Cromley. His manner was brusque, as though any leanings towards sympathy were regularly doused in a never-ending quest for justice. He wasn't elegantly spoken like Kenneth – his accent was more like Delphine's own – but he was crisp of thought and swift of tongue, and shared Kenneth's confidence about what he thought and his ability to express it. He embodied all of Delphine's fears about the law: officious, unemotional and intolerant of fools. Delphine was sure he only suffered her because of whatever comradeship he shared with Kenneth.

'If he gets the job done, that will be worth more to us than a thousand niceties,' Kenneth told her, sounding rather brisk himself. 'I should have hardened my heart a long time ago, Delphine, my dear. I should have *made* you speak to the police. It's done you no favours that your dratted husband has been left at large all this time.'

As mortified as Delphine felt beneath Cromley's sharp, assessing eyes as she stumbled to answer his rapid-fire questions, as shocking and personal and threadbare a history as she had to tell, she could not argue any more. For it was not only she who was in danger now. She had brought this threat into their midst. So she endured the meeting, which seemed to go on forever, and then a second one when Cromley came to the house with further questions. The man was a *fountain* of questions. Both times she wept blazing tears afterwards. Worst of all, Cromley told them that he didn't hold out much hope for a satisfactory solution. The attacks on Delphine had all been so long ago. Dr Harcourt's report had been put into Cromley's hands and a grim expression did flit, briefly, across his craggy face. But it was so long after the fact.

'As for this recent business, looking through a window ain't a crime, Mr C,' he said, sounding disappointed that Foley hadn't attacked anyone or vandalised any property.

'But trespassing with intent to intimidate surely is?' demanded Kenneth, outraged.

'Trespassin', yes, sir, but intent to intimidate? Beggin' pardon, Mr C, that's speculation, that is. In the eyes of the law, you understand me – it ain't that *I* don't believe you. And, if he don't want to be found, he won't be, from what the young lady's told us.' He sighed. Delphine agreed with that, at least.

Delphine had formed the habit of ending every day with her notebook and fountain pen. Even when it was late, even when she was ever so tired, she found that twenty minutes scribbling down her impressions and memories of the day ushered her into a better night's sleep than she would otherwise have. But since seeing Foley in the garden, she couldn't do it any more. Knowing he was near made her self-conscious, as though whatever permission had been granted her in Richmond to be herself had been removed. She didn't deserve happiness. She wasn't allowed peace.

Now each night she hurried to bed, undressed with frantic speed and dived under the covers like a child afraid of the dark. Foolish. It wasn't as though he could break in here. Kenneth was religious about checking all the doors and windows at night. 'Securing the perimeter,' he called it.

But even knowing that Foley was biding his time, remembering that only nights ago they had laid eyes on each other, was enough to freeze her. It was as if the life she'd led over the last few months had never really been. On dry days, Midge urged her to walk about the garden, but Delphine found it unsettling to be in the space where she had last seen Foley, even though the gap in the wall had been blocked up now, and she only endured these dolls' house circuits.

'I should have mentioned it sooner,' Elf wailed. 'I feel terrible! I meant to. I absolutely meant to. I even pointed it out to Delphine. But it was Christmas and there was so much happening and I forgot.'

'Don't worry, old man,' said Kenneth. 'He only got into the garden. Frankly that's the least of our worries. It's the fact that he's here at all that bothers me. If there hadn't been the gap in the wall, she might have seen him on the street or elsewhere, and we'd be in this exact situation or worse.'

Delphine hardly knew what to hope for now. She was certain

that whatever reprieve she'd been granted was over. But what on earth would happen? He was too clever to be caught, and he would never give up. She could hardly stay here forever, never leaving the house. Although, Elf did it. Perhaps Ryan's Castle could become her refuge too. But how would she ever repay the Camberwells if she couldn't draw a wage any more? And how could she resume her duties never knowing when he might appear again? For appear he would, she knew that. What could her life be, now, other than waiting?

# Chapter Forty-six

Amongst the horror of it all, Blue still went to work. Since Kenneth was busy sorting things out with Delphine, Elf winkled himself from the Cottage every morning to walk her to work, much to everyone's astonishment.

'At the end of the day, you must telephone for me to come and meet you,' he insisted. 'I won't have you walking around by yourself in the dark with that man out there.'

As for the rest of the day, when Blue walked from appointment to appointment and back to the office in between, there wasn't much they could do about that. Elf was all for her finishing her job before time.

'It's only a matter of weeks until that Griggs fellow comes back. Surely they can manage just for that short time?'

Kenneth wanted to have a word with Gordon and ask that Blue have an escort, or simply stay in the office and type copy for the others, but Blue would have none of it.

'I'm not a *typist*!' she railed. 'And the other reporters don't have an influential father, or the luxury of being able to lose six weeks' wages. Out in the real world, if I wasn't "darling Blue", I'd have to keep going, no matter what. And so I shall.'

Blue cursed silently as she waved Elf goodbye and entered the office each morning. *Why now?* It was weeks after Anne and Esther's visit. *Months* after Delphine's arrival. How had he found her? Had someone said something to him after the newspaper article? Had he followed Anne and Esther, and simply waited for opportunity in the weeks that followed?

It seemed especially unfair that Foley had reappeared just as things were beginning to look up for everyone else. She'd seen Foster just once since their long conversation and he still seemed reflective and subdued, but the torment was gone from him. He'd confided in Tabitha too, while Blue was there, so Blue knew he had love and support at home.

Tab had given them both a fright when she said she found the idea of men loving men upsetting. She waited just a beat before clarifying, 'Because it means there are fewer for me, darlings!' She grinned and wrapped her arms tight around her brother. 'Don't worry about a thing, Foster. I'm in your corner.'

Things seemed much cosier between her father and Midge again too. They were going on weekly dates and Midge had started to glow. Blue had just been starting to relax about her loved ones – and now this!

'Blue's got a new sweetheart,' smirked Cauderlie one morning, turning from the window where he'd watched Elf saying goodbye to Blue. 'I wouldn't have pegged you as a girl in need of a father figure. But they do say it's better to be an old man's darling than a young man's slave.'

'Oh, shut up, Cauderlie!' Blue was all out of witty retorts and clever comebacks. The situation was simply too fraught for any of that. 'You're an absolute *fool*.'

She chucked her coat, scarf and hat at the coat stand. All three missed the hooks and landed on the floor with a depressive *flump*. Juno silently picked them all up. Blue sank into her chair and scowled at her diary. She wore a forbidding barrier of self-absorption and anger and no one said much to her all day.

'Lovers' tiff, for certain,' whispered Cauderlie as she left the building for a Richmond Ladies' Circle luncheon.

'Women do have other concerns besides their lovers, you know,' said Juno. 'It could be anything. Absolutely anything at all.'

'And it's none of our business,' Gordon reminded them, passing through, his trilby dark with rain and dripping from the brim. 'As long as Ishbel gets her work done, it's no concern of ours. If she wanted to tell us what's happening, she would.'

'I hope so,' murmured Barnaby. 'But I'm not so sure.'

It was when five o'clock came and the dark had drawn in that Blue felt the worst. There was still work to be done and the blue shadows felt oppressive. She longed for spring and sunlight and freedom. That evening, when she filed her final copy, she stood to leave, then remembered her promise to Elf and reached for the telephone.

'Blue, may I ask you something?' Barnaby appeared beside her.

'Oh, sorry, Barney. I borrowed your thesaurus, didn't I? Here, I've finished with it.'

'Oh, thanks, but I'd forgotten about that. I just wondered if you wanted to talk about anything. Are you all right?'

'I'm fine,' said Blue, then hesitated. 'Well, I'm *not*, clearly,' she admitted. She groaned and sunk her face in her hands. 'Is it that obvious?' she asked through her fingers.

'Screamingly.'

'Night, chaps,' said Sam, one of her colleagues, as he switched off the light and headed for the door.

'Night, Sam,' said Blue without looking up. 'Yes, Barney, I would like to talk. Do you by any chance have time for a trip to the Roebuck?'

'Certainly.'

'And . . . would you be willing to walk me home afterwards? I'm not allowed to be out alone after dark, you see.'

Barnaby raised his eyebrows. 'Of course. Nothing simpler. Are you ready?'

'Just one thing first.' Blue telephoned home. 'Midge, darling, please will you tell Elf not to come and get me. I'm going for a drink with a work friend and he's going to walk me home afterwards. So no one need worry. Yes, Barnaby, that's it. Yes, he does. Yes, all right then. I won't be late. Toodle-pip, darling.'

'Do I have a reputation in your household as being the friend you drink with?' wondered Barnaby. 'I'm not sure how I feel about that.'

'Don't worry, they don't think you a bad influence,' Blue assured him, straightening her desk. 'I've got Juno for that. She's a demon on the gin.'

Soon they were seated in the same window table in the Roebuck and Blue started to talk. Once she started she found she couldn't stop. Not only did she tell him about Foley's appearance and the state of high alert that had reigned ever since, about Delphine's return to her shadow-like self and Elf's insistence on following her everywhere, but she also told him about Midge's uncharacteristic explosion, how worried she'd been about Foster and her fear that her rejection had caused his troubles – though she stopped short of telling him the full story, obviously. She described her own growing claustrophobia caused by the short days, the lack of independence and her growing sense of things coming to an end.

'My job, the way things are at home, my innocence, even.' She laughed, just stopping short of telling him about Latchley and Dorian, an act of discretion for which she knew she'd thank herself later.

When she finished pouring her heart out, Barnaby nodded and waited a while before answering, not in a way that suggested he was stunned from all the information she had showered on him, but in a way that suggested he was considering.

'You're on a cusp,' he said at last. 'Several, in fact. No wonder you're fraught; you've plenty to be fraught *about*. Hang it, Blue, I'm worried. This Foley character's a bad'un. Look, I know your father's got it covered, but just so you know, I'll keep an eye on you too. And I'll keep my eyes and ears open. I'm no policeman, but I'll talk to people, you know? See if I can find anything out.'

'Thanks, Barnaby. That's awfully kind of you. This isn't your problem though. I believe the fellow's a real wild card; I don't want anyone else getting hurt.'

Barnaby blew a scornful puff of air at the idea. 'He may be vicious, but I'm as tough as he is. It wasn't pretty where I grew up, and I survived. Don't worry about me, Blue. We need to sort it out. You can't live like this.'

Blue liked the 'we'. Of course, her family stood together over the Foley issue – it wasn't as though she had to deal with it alone, but with the rest of it, with Midge and work and Foster, she'd felt very alone there for a while. She'd mentioned to Dorian that Foster was having some troubles a while back, though she'd stopped short of discussing the suicide attempt, knowing that Foster wouldn't like it. And now she certainly wouldn't tell him more, after Foster had so specifically asked her to keep it from him. But it was good to have someone outside the family to talk to. Barnaby was a good person to have in your corner, she thought suddenly.

# Chapter Forty-seven

As January sighed its way into February, there was only one silver lining for Midge in the clouds that beset their life. Things were better between her and Kenneth, and that made everything bearable.

They'd returned home from a lovely dinner to the shocking news that Foley had been loitering in the garden of their home. And everything had changed. It was clear that he hadn't given up on Delphine at all. She was in danger – perhaps they all were. It wasn't a state of affairs anyone would have wished for, but it did put things into perspective, rather. Midge was suddenly able to do what had felt impossible for months; she stopped fretting about her projects and concerns and let them all drop, for now. Her family were more important.

Kenneth was like a man possessed, determined to find Foley and bring him to justice. But as the days passed and built themselves into a week, then a fortnight, it was clear that Foley had gone to ground again. Kenneth was like a beast in a zoo as his efforts came to naught. He turned to Midge to talk through his frustration, and for physical solace too. Midge found it easy to forget her petty resentments and fears when it was clear that he needed her so much. She found herself falling in love with him all over again, her brave, caring husband, so sure of right and wrong, willing to go to any length for a friend.

So even though Elf was escorting Blue to and from work, and even though Delphine was still staying with them, frightened as a prisoner in a tower, Midge found that she could breathe properly for the first time in so long. She looked after everyone. She cheered their spirits as best she could. She told them all that they would get through this strange time. And there was scarcely a day that passed without Kenneth telling her that he didn't know what he'd do without her.

She would stop worrying, she decided. The past was gone. It wasn't lurking in the garden, like Delphine's past. Everyone had made mistakes, everyone had things they wished they had done differently. It didn't bar one from happiness, or forbid one from getting on with life. God had put her here in this family for a reason, and with the way she'd been carrying on it would have been Midge and only Midge who messed everything up if she wasn't careful. From now on, she was going to accept her blessings and rejoice in them. As Elf had pointed out, there was only ever one way that one could go at any given time, and that was forward.

# Chapter Forty-eight

L. W. had gone to Nottingham for a felt convention, and then to see some prospective clients, so Blue didn't see him for three weeks. But he wrote regularly and his letters buoyed her through the dark blue days of February. When she came home from work to find a letter propped on the hall table, it was a treat to curl up with some tea and biscuits and read his news. You had to hand it to the man, he wrote a good letter.

She was still very confused about love. She'd always imagined, when she was young, that she would simply grow up, fall in love and settle down. But so far she seemed plagued with either feast or famine. The last couple of years, no one had caught her fancy. Now it seemed she was turning into Tabitha. She enjoyed her time with Dorian; she enjoyed her time with L. W. She couldn't really choose between them. Of course, she did realise there were other men in the world – she didn't *have* to marry either of them – but really, they were both appealing in their different ways. What was the matter with her? Why was she so . . . *indifferent*? She'd always thought of herself as a romantic, but maybe she was more of a good-time girl after all.

She thought back to her birthday party. It felt so long ago now and so much had happened – *years'* worth of things. Although she had dismissed her father's challenge as sheer nonsense, when she sat like this, with the rain pattering out its fretful dirge on the window panes, the fire leaping in the grate and L. W.'s letters for companionship, she couldn't help but remember it.

'Writers are a rare breed,' Kenneth had said that night. 'The hopeful suitor wishing to captivate such a woman must set out to capture not only her heart, but also her *imagination* . . . The bond your words can forge . . . You have the turning of the seasons . . . Whoever can win Blue's heart through a letter can have her hand in marriage.'

Blue snorted. Spectacular balderdash. And yet, the seasons *were* turning, and L. W. *was* wooing her, by letter, just as her father had proposed. She remembered Foster talking about that night, saying that he'd been struck by madness or champagne . . . or 'those damned chimes of midnight'. Perhaps there was something in it after all. She loved reading and rereading L. W.'s letters. He was intelligent and sensitive and he wanted to live a lovely life. Although he didn't put pressure on her, she felt that he'd like to do so with her. He had a good business, a nice family, from the sound of it, and she liked him very much. He was nice-looking too. Had Kenneth cast a spell after all?

Dorian was adorable. But there were just too many little things that were different, and not complementary, fortifying differences, but simply annoying ones. He found things funny that she did not, and vice versa. She worked hard at her writing because she wanted to; he loved that he was rich enough not to have to work at all. He was perfectly happy that Blue worked at the paper, but he didn't understand why she did. And she couldn't understand why he didn't do more with his fortune to help the people who had so much less. She had gingerly asked him about that one day and he nodded, smiling.

'Your pa's a real old-fashioned philanthropist,' he'd agreed. 'That's what you've grown up with. He's like someone out of Dickens, what? Dispensing largesse and helping the common man and all that. All very admirable.' Then he challenged her to a game of whist.

The things they had in common were superficial, she thought: their background, the people they knew and so on. Then there were things they *appeared* to have in common but which proved not to be so on closer inspection. They both loved clothes, for example. But for Dorian it truly was a case of 'clothes maketh the man', whereas Blue only got excited about them on special occasions; the rest of the time she simply thought of them as something that allowed you to go about your life without causing scandal.

So, as the seasons turned, Dorian was not the front runner for her hand, as Cauderlie had supposed in the *Gazette*. Even so, she still found him madly attractive. She admitted to herself at last that she wanted to act on it. If she didn't grab this experience now, she never would know how it felt to breathe him in while they lay in each other's arms, to have his long, elegant legs tangled in hers. It was the fact that she didn't see a future with him that made it so urgent. The romantic part of her dreamed, still, of true love and saving herself for the man she would marry. The part of her that lit up at Dorian's attention like a tree at Christmas just wanted what it wanted.

So after one of their dinners in Richmond, she found herself accepting his invitation to go back to his flat for a nightcap. She enjoyed those dinners as much as she enjoyed reading L. W.'s letters, but in a different way. Dorian made her feel like a beacon of desire.

He lived with his older brother, Harrison, in an apartment owned by their parents, near the river. Harrison was away visiting cousins, so Blue knew when she agreed to the nightcap that they would be alone. She could tell it was on Dorian's mind too as they sat in his opulent, if untidy, lounge, swirling brandy around fat glass bowls on stems; she could see it in the way he looked at her. He had the sort of charisma that made gazing at him almost a physical act in itself. You could almost *feel* him, just by letting your eyes linger on his mouth, by imagining. Blue sighed.

He hadn't lit the fire, though the flat was warm enough. But firelight was always nice, thought Blue, nervously. It put a gilded light on everything. But Dorian wasn't really minded that way – his gifts were social rather than aesthetic or emotional. She swallowed her brandy in a gulp.

'Top-up, Blue?'

She held her glass out. Conversation. That would ease things, if the brandy didn't.

'So. Tell me more news, Dorian. You've been out and about lots this week. Oh, you told me about Sally kissing Adam Erlington. Anything else?'

'I think I've told you all the latest. Oh, I saw Tabitha yesterday, with her brother. He looks like the walking dead these days, doesn't he?'

'Really? Foster was out with Tab? That's good. What time was it? How were they?'

'Oh, just about lunchtime. Not out in the evening or anything like that. I'm afraid it'll be a long time before that boy's ready for a party. Long time till he'll be *invited* to one, looking like that. Not exactly a barrel of laughs, is he?'

'*Dorian!*'

'Oh, sorry, Blue. I forget he's your little friend.'

'Well, yes, but also . . . Well, you know he's had some struggles lately. I'm so happy to hear he's out and about, it's a big step for him. You've made my night!'

He grinned! 'Well, that *was* my intention, but I must admit I had other methods in mind.'

And suddenly Blue wanted to kiss him, just for being the

bearer of good news, and for being so irrepressible. So she did. She got up and went and sat on his lap and kissed him. It was wonderful. Wonderful to be pressed so close to him. Lovely to be in that special position where she could hold him and be held.

'Blue,' he murmured. 'What a girl you are. What a devilish treat of a girl.'

She pulled back, laughing. 'You're not so bad yourself, Fields. So tell me more about Tab and Foster. How did they look? Worried or happy?'

'Lord, I'm not the fellow to ask about that. I mean, Tab looked luscious, as always. Green coat, claret dress, black shoes. A million dollars.'

'Oh, you're hopeless.' Blue twined her fingers through his, enjoying the strength of his slender hands. She remembered Tab describing Dorian as 'a specimen of physical perfection'. Oh, he *was*.

'But Foster,' he went on, making an effort for her, 'was wearing this dreadful knitted pullover – yellow and green stripes. I mean, there's no sense in that. If he wants to cheer himself up, surely he should try to look a bit better.'

'*Dorian*,' she chided.

'Yes, well, poor chap and all that. But I'm not sure he's quite cut out for our world, is he? I was talking to Carlton James at the club the other day, told him what you'd said – that he was all down in the mouth and whatnot – and Carlton said he'd heard that Foster made a disgrace of himself at some party a while back, got rushed to hospital! Jolly poor show.'

'You talked to *Carlton* about Foster?'

'Why not?'

'Well, because it's a bit private, I suppose. I only told you Foster was having a hard time because we're . . . well, friends.'

'A bit more than that, darling,' he whispered, running his fingers down the inside of her arm.

'Yes, but you know what I mean. We're close. We spend time together, we tell each other things. I trusted you.' She was *so* glad it wasn't she who'd told him about the hospital. And that she hadn't told him the rest.

'Blue, darling. A chap gets annihilated at a party and ends up in the hospital, people are going to talk about it. Nothing you can do about that.'

'I suppose you're right. But still, you know how worried I've been about him.'

Blue sat back and looked into his gleaming, rich blue eyes with their sooty eyelashes. He looked slightly puzzled, as though he *didn't* know how worried she'd been, as though he couldn't understand why he *wouldn't* talk about it with Carlton James, the most indiscreet man in Surrey. Suddenly Blue wished she hadn't talked to Dorian about it at all.

'There's a difference between confiding in someone you trust, and gossip for gossip's sake,' she elaborated, feeling like a stern headmistress. 'I always thought Carlton was rather in the second category.'

'Oh, Carlton's a decent chap! Do you know he once smoked five cigarettes in one go, all sticking out of his mouth – he looked like a scarecrow! And once he turned up to Lucy Trent's party in a dress. I'll never forget that.'

Blue smiled, but these glowing recommendations did little to reassure her that Carlton would have discussed Foster in a respectful and sensitive way.

'Oh well, never mind,' she said, climbing off his lap. She remembered suddenly that Barnaby could have had a front-page story about Foster that night at the hospital, but he hadn't said a word to anyone.

'Exactly, never mind,' said Dorian, coming and wrapping his arms around her from behind. He pressed himself against her and she was flooded with warmth, but the room was cold. At least, it *looked* cold with only the electric light, and Blue rather felt the moment had passed. She couldn't exactly say why. She felt uneasy somehow, as though the carpet had shifted beneath her, just a little. And she wanted this experience, if it were to come, to match the promise of their sparkling flirtation.

She unwrapped his hands from her waist and turned to give him a quick, placatory hug. 'Actually, Dorian, darling, I realise I'm terribly tired. Would you mind frightfully if I go home now? It's all been rather a strain lately. And it's very late.'

'Oh no!' His face fell like that of a little boy being denied chocolate cake. 'I wish I hadn't mentioned the fellow. Come on, Blue, shake it off. Have another brandy and forget all about it. Stay for just another hour or so.'

'It would be lovely, Dorian, but I really must go. Will you walk me?'

His face fell further. 'Truly? Oh, Blue darling, I don't fancy going out now. Jolly tired myself, as a matter of fact, and that wind is rather beastly. You're a modern girl! You've always said you're used to walking everywhere alone. Would it be terribly rotten of me to sit this one out?'

'Oh! Of course. Absolutely. Well, thanks for a lovely evening. I'll see you soon.'

'Sunday lunch with the Brierleys, if not before. Good night, darling.'

They kissed again and Blue walked downstairs. His voice floated after her: 'Simply adore that dress, darling.'

She opened the front door. That nasty, whistling wind shot in and she peered into the dark night. It wasn't that she minded the walk, or the wind, or being alone. In fact, she would much rather *not* be with Dorian at the moment; she thought she might be rather annoyed at him. It was just that she had promised her father – *promised* him – that she would absolutely not, under any circumstances, walk anywhere alone after dark while the Foley situation was unresolved. And Dorian *knew* that.

There couldn't be any danger, she told herself, or Dorian

wouldn't let her go alone. She squinted into the shadows. It was only a ten-minute walk to Ryan's Castle, and actually she longed for a solitary walk through the bracing night to shake off this new discomfort. She stepped outside and breathed in a sharp draft of air. Was it her imagination or did she smell, behind the wind and the February damp, a hint of spring? Oh, it would be fine.

But no. She'd promised. She was mortified that Dorian was content to make love to her but not to do whatever it took to keep her safe. Pride made her want to leave. But if she let her pride make this decision, her father would kill her if Foley didn't. She stumped up the stairs and knocked on the door.

'Blue!' Dorian grinned, opening the door, halfway out of his shirt and braces. 'You came to your senses. Come back here where you belong.' He pulled her into his arms.

'No, Dorian, that's not why I came back. I *can't* walk home alone, can I? It's not that I'm not willing, but I promised my father. You do remember about Foley, don't you?'

'Yes.' He sighed.

'Well, I'm really sorry, Dorian, but Daddy says it's not safe, so I either need you to walk me or I need to use your telephone to call home so someone can come and get me.'

He glanced at the clock on the mantel. It was half past one and she could only imagine what her father would say if she called him at this hour, explaining that Dorian wasn't willing to walk her home. No doubt Dorian was imagining exactly the same thing, for he buttoned up his shirt and slipped his braces back over his shoulders.

He picked up his jacket from the floor and his overcoat from a nearby chair then fished in his pockets for his keys, which he jangled. Suddenly Blue didn't feel like a beacon of desire. She felt like a nuisance.

'Come on then, old girl. Up the hill we go.'

# Part Four

—❧—

# Spring

*Sprigs and spurts and sudden extravagances*

# Chapter Forty-nine

March came in a flash of crocus and a flourish of daffodil and suddenly there was hope again. Bright, gusty winds chased away the clouds and when the rains did come they were sharp and glittering, like falling crystals – the sort of rain that made you laugh, not the sort that pinned you to the spot in despair. The evenings lifted and birds hopped back onto lawns and garden walls; dazed with sunlight, they started to sing again. And, despite every expectation to the contrary, Delphine went back to work.

It was as though, when winter finally lessened its grip, so did fear. When winter's shadows receded, so did the shadow cast by Foley. When the world felt joyous and bursting with hope, it was impossible not to feel hope within, in sprigs and spurts and sudden extravagances, as Blue put it – rather deliciously, Delphine thought. Over time, paranoia inevitably ceded to pragmatism. They had huddled together in Ryan's Castle like sheep beneath a hedge to wait out the rain. They couldn't go on like that forever.

Even so, Kenneth continued to insist on certain safety measures. Thus, Delphine had a slightly different timetable now. She only ran errands in town on Tuesday and Thursdays; the rest of the time she worked in the house. On her Richmond days, Merrigan would call for her in the morning, go about with her, and see her home again in the middle of the afternoon. It was nothing to her, she said; it was good to get out of the house and have some adult company. She saved her own errands for the same days and everything worked beautifully. On the rare days that Merrigan couldn't accompany her, Midge came instead. The days passed so pleasantly, in fact, that it was almost possible to forget there was a grim reason behind the new arrangement.

It was good to be back with the Greenbows. As much as Delphine loved Ryan's Castle, Old Palace Lane was where she found independence and purpose. Sitting with Stephen and Fanny in the evenings, talking of cabbages and kings, she felt as if she were with kindly grandparents rather than employers. She adored looking after the babies for poor, harassed Sylvia. Baby Max was an easy fellow, but Baby Oscar didn't sleep and could be only very cleverly persuaded to eat. Delphine loved babies and was happy to bring a smile of relief to Sylvia's poor face when she could snatch an hour's nap or go out for a walk by herself. Sylvia was as frazzled and tearful a mother as Merrigan was practical and calm. But then motherhood was a powerful and personal thing; no two people were the same.

Merrigan was pregnant again, to Lawrence's delight and

Kenneth's jubilation. 'Perhaps a grandson, this time,' he speculated. 'Although another little girl . . . We do make good girls in this family. Oh, which would I rather?'

Merrigan herself was unflappable, as ever. 'It'll be what it'll be, Daddy,' she reminded him, and went about her daily business with Cicely now starting to toddle at her side.

Life went on. New life was being created. Delphine had Fanny and Sylvia, Midge, Merrigan and Blue, with whom to talk over the large and small details of their lives. She was back in the land of the living, as Ma would have put it. Soon, she started writing in her journal again.

She devoted only a cursory paragraph to the lost time, as she thought of those past weeks.

'My "husband" took it upon himself to show up at R. C. and frighten the wits out of us. For a time I could not write, nor speak. Now I am back where I am needed and useful.'

That took up a whole page, just two small lines in the centre. Then she returned to her habit of writing before bed each evening: accounts of Oscar's eating patterns, conversations she'd enjoyed, the opening of magnolia flowers outside her window, sightings of thrush or lark.

One evening, she sat in a perfect, pearly dusk, knowing she really should put a light on and save her eyes, but reluctant to stir from the enchanted peace that had settled over her. Folk were traipsing back and forth to the river, her window was ajar and she was lulled by the song of blackbirds. The scents of woodsmoke, magnolia and cherry drifted in like fairy spells. She was happier than seemed possible, or advisable. The house was silent; Stephen and Fanny were visiting friends. But Paul and Sylvia were at home next door. It was pleasant to be alone, yet feel safe.

She idly watched a slim, sandy-haired young man toiling down the lane, carrying a heavy-looking bag and dragging one foot ever so slightly. He looked around him with a faintly disbelieving air, as though he'd arrived from another planet, and Delphine couldn't help but smile. He looked the way she'd felt when she first found herself in Richmond. Her indulgence turned to annoyance, however, when he opened the gate of this very cottage. His shoes tap-tapped up the garden path and she froze. A knock on the door. Now she was glad she hadn't put a light on. There was nothing to indicate that someone was home. She stood to the side of the window so she could watch him leave without being seen. But he knocked a second time.

Delphine scowled, biting her lip. She didn't like answering the door when she was alone. He didn't *look* dangerous; he looked perfectly fine. But then so many people who met Foley thought he was charming. You couldn't always tell. What if this young man was a crony of Foley's, sent to do his dirty work? Or a travelling salesman? It had been a perfect evening. She didn't want it disturbed.

'Oh, for heaven's sake! Take a hint, can'tcha?' she muttered as he knocked for a third time.

From her lurking point, Delphine saw him step away from

362

the door. He looked up at the house and all about. He drew an old-fashioned watch from his jacket and consulted it. Then he returned to his knocking. Delphine sighed. She would have to answer. What if he was a genuine caller? What if it was important? It was her job, really, to manage the house in the Greenbows' absence. She hurried downstairs and wrenched open the door before she could lose her nerve.

'*What?*' she demanded.

He looked startled. 'Er, pardon me. I'm looking for the Greenbows.'

'They're not here.' Delphine registered shabby clothing making an effort at respectability, his brave attempt at a smile, and started to suspect he wasn't a criminal or a salesman. Guilt made her words wobble a bit. 'Wh . . . what did you want with them? They're visiting f . . . friends.'

'Oh!' He looked as if he might cry. 'But they're expecting me. I'm Sid. Sidney Birch.'

She'd never heard of him. What on earth could she do? She didn't want to be alone in the house with a stranger, but it didn't seem right to send him away. As she dithered, he seemed to compose himself.

'Look, I'm sorry. You're obviously not expecting me and I don't want to put you out. I'll go and walk by the river for an hour or so. Do you think they'll be back then?'

'Yes, I should think so,' said Delphine with relief. 'Fanny gets so tired these days; they won't be late.'

'Oh! Is this Stephen and Fanny's house? I'm so sorry. It's Paul and Sylvia I'm looking for.'

Delphine could have kicked herself. Why hadn't she thought to check? 'They're just next door. That side.'

'Oh, thank you!' She could see he was relieved – a big smile lit up his face. 'Again, I'm very sorry to disturb you. Please give me best to Stephen and Fanny. I'll see them tomorrow, no doubt.'

'Yes. Of course. Mr Birch, you said?'

'Sidney Birch,' he agreed, holding his hand out. 'And you are?'

'Delphine. I work for the Greenbows.'

'Lovely to meet you, Delphine.'

Delphine doubted that. She watched him walk down the garden path then up the path next door with his limp and his heavy bag. The door flew open at once and Delphine heard Paul's delighted voice. 'Sid! You came! Can't tell you how pleased I am. Come in.' The door closed behind them and Sidney Birch was swallowed up by hospitality and welcome. *Bit of a contrast from me*, Delphine thought wryly. She closed the door and went back to her room. But it was nearly dark now; her peace was disturbed and the spell was broken. She jotted a couple more lines then threw her pen down, closed the window and went to bed.

# Chapter Fifty

Spring had taken up residence in the garden of Ryan's Castle. There was a day in the middle of March when Midge threw open the drawing-room doors for the first time that year and cold, fresh air edged with sunbeams came pouring in. Like a white satin dress trimmed with gold lace, Midge thought happily as she leaned against the door frame and listened to the lush music of the birds. Tall white narcissi bobbed under the apple tree and washes of golden daffs edged the kingdom. She smiled.

'Bye, darling,' said Kenneth, on his way to a meeting with Lawrence. A new housing initiative in Twickenham was under discussion and he'd promised to help with funding. Even society at large was stirring and moving towards something better, it seemed.

'Goodbye, dearest. I hope it goes well. I'll see you later.'

'And I'll look forward to it,' he murmured, nuzzling her neck for a moment and making her knees go weak. 'Dinner and an early night?'

She beamed. That was what they'd done last night. And they

had not gone straight to sleep. 'Absolutely,' she whispered. 'Excellent plan, darling.'

'It's a winning formula!' He grinned. 'Oh, and don't forget to close the doors when you leave the room, will you, Midge? Just in case.'

Midge hated to be reminded of Foley. It should be fine now; the gap in the wall had been repaired and the garden was as secure as it had ever been, but it was best to take precautions. She was just thoroughly glad to leave the winter behind.

Things were so much better now. Delphine looked happier again, Merrigan was pregnant and even Midge herself felt more relaxed. It was as if that dark time had been some sort of turning point for her marriage, as if she and Kenneth had both, in the privacy of their own minds, decided it was time to draw a line under old frustrations and embrace what they had. Kenneth was certainly more loving these days, and she had stuck by her resolve to forget the past and look to the future. Perhaps that was what had really made the difference.

She gulped down great drafts of sparkling air. Spring again! Summer to follow. Oh, the *luxury*. And what a relief to feel better! She'd been quite worried at one point. That exhaustion over Christmas and those unwell feelings had spoiled more than one festive function for her . . . And that day that she'd exploded in the kitchen, then run out to the park . . . Well, it was extraordinary to think of it now; she felt like a different woman entirely. But then, it was a funny business, being a woman.

Bea Standish, leading light in Richmond society, was quite outspoken about these things – when it was just women together, of course. Midge had been brought up never to speak of such things at all, but Bea scoffed at that. They all had monthly cycles, she said, and the more they kept it all hush-hush and secretive, the less they could help each other, or themselves. Bea talked quite frankly about the unbearable tension that mounted inside her for a week or more before her monthly bleed and confessed freely that during that time no one was safe from her tongue.

'I try not to go out in polite company,' she laughed. But Midge knew how it felt; she knew that feeling of being taken over, of becoming a stranger to yourself, yet at the same time feeling that this deepest, darkest part of you had been lurking there all along, awaiting an opportunity to voice its truth in blood-curdling yells. It was a great comfort to think that other women went through it too. Perhaps it was simply part of a natural biological process. Bea was a practical woman, a great follower of Dr Marie Stopes over issues like contraception and sexuality. Much of Midge's own knowledge was gleaned from Bea.

*So there we are*, decided Midge. *It's just nature. I just have to ride it out when it happens. Hide, if necessary!* She smiled to herself. And then her smile dropped. Except, it *hadn't* happened, not for ages. That day in the kitchen for example. That hadn't been linked to her cycle, had it? Her heart sank. Had she been pinning her reassurance on something that wasn't relevant to her after all? She would much rather believe she was affected by hormones than that she was infected with some dreadful defect of character that could strike at any time.

In fact, when *had* she last had a monthly? That awful day when she'd lost her temper had been . . . six weeks or so ago. But it had been a while before then, certainly. Suddenly, with a dart of pure, icy fear, she remembered standing in the park crying, worrying for a moment that she was pregnant. She'd dismissed it out of hand and hadn't thought of it since. She'd always been very careful in that department and there were so many other reasons to explain why she felt rotten. Except the fact was – she thought hard – her last monthly had been before Christmas. And now it was March! Oh God.

With growing horror, she mentally sifted through everything Bea had ever told her about a woman's processes. The garden, with its blooming, burgeoning evidence of rich and lovely life, mocked her. Midge felt as if she were standing in a dark, dreadful tunnel. Not pregnant, surely. Then a welcome thought struck her. Menopause! The monthlies became irregular then, didn't they? She was just late. Very late. Because of the menopause. Except . . . she was only forty-five. Well, it came early to some, didn't it?

She clutched the door frame, all her languid contentment gone. She would have to visit the doctor. But only for confirmation, she told herself fiercely. Because it *was* the menopause. It *was*.

# Chapter Fifty-one

Life was a funny old thing, thought Delphine more than once that March. A very funny old thing. Her blessings were now so many that she could feel herself expanding with happiness, billowing every which way like clouds. The Greenbows, the Camberwells, life in Richmond . . . And now Delphine had a new friend, Sidney Birch.

Yet somewhere in the back of her mind, like a heavy, repressive hand squashing her back down, was Foley. Never totally forgotten, never totally gone.

Sid was a young cousin of Sylvia's, come to stay indefinitely. When the family made proper introductions between them, she apologised for her hostile reception and he waved it away with a smile. Amongst the family she had grown to love, she felt safe and at ease and quickly saw that he was a gentle, even nervous, soul. To help him find his feet in the area, Delphine took him for long walks around town and far along the river, proud to show him the places she had grown to love in their spring splendour. As they walked, she learned something of his history.

Sid's father was Sylvia's uncle. Many years ago, he had moved to Essex, finding himself enamoured of a Pitsea girl, and there he made his life. Sidney was the youngest of their four children. Delphine gathered that Sid's father must be as different from Sylvia's branch of the family as could be imagined. He brought his children up hard, with a survival-of-the-fittest philosophy – and sensitive Sid hadn't thrived. His two older brothers and his sister, however, did just fine. They left school as soon as they could, found jobs, made money and married. Sid had wanted to learn. He wanted to make a difference in the world.

There was no question of college, of course, and when there was no more school to go to, his parents laid down the law. He found a job on the docks and he didn't mind the physical labour, though the lack of purpose demoralised him. That and being attacked on a regular basis by three of the workers who disliked the polite, slightly built newcomer. Sid preferred to read during his lunch break rather than gamble, he didn't join in with hollering at women on the rare occasions that one appeared and he wouldn't call the two black workers in their unit by hateful names.

At first, the sporadic beatings weren't so different from those he received at home from his father and brothers. 'Once or twice, even my mother,' he added, with a frown and a catch in his voice. 'Talk about the runt of the litter.'

Then two years ago he'd had to leave the docks when a load of timber had fallen on his foot. 'It's healed better than I ever thought it would.' He smiled. 'There was a time when I thought I'd be on a stick for the rest of me life. Me boss took me aside and said if it were up to him he'd keep me on, give me a job in the office. But he knew and I knew that I'd checked that load meself. Someone had loosened it and we all knew who it was. I was lucky it weren't worse. I'd only be in for more if he kept me on, so we both accepted how the land lay.'

Sid found a job doing accounts for a local pub, but his new boss wanted not so much an accountant as a book fiddler. Sid wasn't happy, and because he questioned everything, his new boss wasn't happy. The job was only part-time, so his parents weren't happy. Altogether, things were going from bad to worse.

'Then me sister got married. A big shindig, she wanted, not like me brothers who both got the job done quick, no nonsense. She was always my father's favourite so he laid on a big family party in the back room of a pub and invited *everyone*! And Paul and Sylvia came.

'I'd met them once or twice when I was small, but I couldn't really remember them. Anyway, I thought at once that they seemed really decent and we talked a lot that day. They said if I ever wanted to go and live with them I was welcome. But what could I contribute? How would I fit in? I didn't like my life but it was all I knew. And I knew that if I did go, it would be the end of relations with my own lot once and for all. Proud, they are, and much as they weren't thrilled to have me there, I knew they'd take it as a slight if I went off to be with a different branch of the family. So a year went by, and me and them wrote. Not many letters, but a few, and they kept repeating their offer.

'In the end I decided to do it. Things were bad. My job was illegal, my family weren't nice people, I was always wrong, always different, and I got tired of it. I had nothing to lose. When I told my father, he told me never to come home. Ma wouldn't speak to me at all. But for better or worse, that's what I did, and now I'm here.'

Now Delphine felt even worse about the poor welcome she'd given him. He'd broken with his family in the hopes of finding a kinder life and the first thing he'd encountered was her, scowling at the door! When she said as much, he smiled again, then he laughed, then Delphine started laughing too and soon they had to sit on a bench and wait for the fit to pass. She hadn't laughed like that in years.

As the days passed, something happened that Delphine would never, ever have imagined. She started to notice that Sid looked at her tenderly, affectionately. She used to think she could never feel safe with a man, but meeting Kenneth, Lawrence and Elf, then Paul and Stephen, had started to change all that. And she felt she just *knew* Sid. It wasn't only that he was part of the Greenbow family, related by marriage to Paul, who had pulled her out of the river; it was *him*. But of course, she was married.

She remembered Merrigan's words, soon after she arrived in Richmond: 'What if you meet someone? Like this, he'll always be like a leash around your neck. One day you may want to divorce him . . .' Delphine had believed that was the most preposterous and unlikely scenario imaginable, and the least of her worries. But Merrigan, as she liked to boast, was always right.

She made sure that Sid knew her situation so that he didn't develop any hopes in that direction himself. 'I'll never be free of him,' she spelled out one gentle balmy evening. 'He'll always be there in the background.'

'Let's just see what happens, shall we?' said Sid. 'Life's a funny old thing.'

# Chapter Fifty-two

⟨───∘∘∘───⟩

'Only a week to go,' sighed Blue, resting her head on folded arms, crushing the notes spread over her desk. Sometimes she felt she was the only person she knew *not* full of the joys of spring. Delphine was reclaiming her life – not to mention that rather divine Mr Birch who'd conveniently moved in right next door! Her father and Midge were like love's young dream. Merrigan was pregnant, and though to the untrained eye she had greeted the news like the confirmation of a hair appointment, Blue recognised the subtle ways her sister expressed joy. Even Foster was on the up, thank heavens. Elf was cheerful as Blue's job headed towards its close. But Blue was dreading it.

'If I was facing my last week in this place I'd be dancing on the tables about now,' said Juno from the next desk. 'Honestly, Blue, you're far too good for us. There's no doubt in my mind that you'll get work for one of the real papers, maybe even *The Times*. Whisky says so too. You've cut your teeth with us, now go and conquer the world, won't you?'

'Thanks, Juno. I'll try.'

Blue appreciated the compliments, but it was cold comfort at the moment. Finding work on another paper would be a solitary undertaking without a guaranteed outcome or timescale. Here at the *Gazette*, she knew where to be and what to write at any given hour of the day, and she was surrounded by people doing the same sort of work, which made them another sort of family. Oh, she would miss it badly. But then she was, as Juno liked to point out, a sentimental sort.

She reapplied herself to her piece on the opening of a new boutique on Duke Street but her attention kept drifting. At least home was a happier environment again. It was such a relief to see Midge looking more relaxed. One benefit of Blue's job coming to an end was that she'd be at home more; since beginning this job she'd talked to Midge less than she ever had. And she'd be able to take turns going to Richmond with Delphine, and help out when Merrigan's baby was born . . . Family was important to her and it would mean a lot to be able to be there for them. But, heaven help her, she needed more. Husband and children, well, those things would be great riches, she knew, if they ever came her way. But she would always have to write, always have to strive to find new truths and new ways to tell them.

'Blue! Blue!' Barnaby's voice roused her. 'You'd better get down the police station, quickly.'

She blinked at him. He was out of breath, as though he'd taken the stairs two at a time, and wearing a light coat that was dotted with rain.

'Why? What did I do?' she joked.

'Lord, don't tell me it's a crime against fashion,' drawled Cauderlie from somewhere behind her. He'd been particularly insufferable since covering the return of Alan Cobham from his epic South African flight. 'I always knew he'd do it,' he'd gloated, to Blue's intense annoyance.

'Nothing at all,' Barney reassured her. 'But I was just there about a story and I overheard . . .' He glanced at Cauderlie and lowered his voice. 'I overheard them telephoning your father. He's on his way there now. They've arrested a man and it's something to do with Delphine.'

# Chapter Fifty-three

Delphine had never been so happy to see Blue. Even though Sid had immediately put on his coat to walk her to the police station, it was deeply comforting to see Blue in the grim little waiting room when she arrived. She enfolded Delphine in a hug and led her to the desk, where Kenneth was leaning on the counter in muttered and urgent conversation with the constable.

'Hello, my dear,' he greeted Delphine. 'They've arrested somebody and they want you to confirm his identity if you can.'

'Is it Foley?'

Kenneth frowned. 'No one seems very clear, but I'm sure we'll find out soon enough. Hello there. Kenneth Camberwell.' Delphine remembered her manners and introduced Sid. The two men shook hands, and Delphine sat down. She could hardly believe that, after so long, she might find herself face-to-face with Foley again. It was terrifying. She couldn't let herself think beyond that to how wonderful it would be if there was some resolution.

After a few moments, during which they all tapped their

toes and drummed their fingers, Inspector Cromley himself appeared. To Delphine's surprise, he shook her hand before turning to Kenneth.

'Camberwell, I'm sorry, I think we've brought you here on a wild goose chase. Apologies to you too, Mrs Foley. We're holding a man in connection with a recent assault and my men had reason to think he was your husband. But I've just arrived and I don't think so. He doesn't fit your description and he's talking nonsense, frankly, though there's obviously some connection. Would you mind just taking a quick look? Then you can go home again.'

'Damn it,' cursed Kenneth, to Delphine's surprise. 'Sorry, Cromley, not your fault, of course. I just want to get that bounder behind bars. Delphine, how do you feel about identifying this fellow? I'll come with you, of course. Blue, you stay here with Mr Birch.'

'I'll take a look,' said Delphine, relieved and disappointed at once that it probably wasn't Foley. She was shaking from the prospect of seeing him, and the police station was not a cheerful place to be. She just wanted to be back in the sun and spring showers, back in her life – but it would be a real anticlimax if it *wasn't* Foley and nothing had changed.

Cromley led them along a corridor to a cell with a grille in the door. Through this, Delphine could see the man in question pacing up and down with a restless aggression that suggested he could and would wreak destruction without a second thought.

He was a hulking fellow, his face scarred and his arms tattooed. He looked like a cliché of a villain from a penny dreadful – and he was less menacing than Foley in every particular.

'It's not him,' she whispered.

'Ever seen him before?' asked Cromley.

Delphine shook her head. 'Never in my life.'

'Thought as much,' said Cromley, looking disappointed. 'Well, thanks for taking a look, and sorry again for the interruption.'

Just then the prisoner looked up. 'Ah, Mrs Foley!' he hailed her. 'Nice of you to visit. Your husband said you were a tender sort.'

Delphine froze. Kenneth instantly put his arm around her and led her away.

'You're *sure* you don't know him?' persisted Cromley, following.

'I'm certain,' she insisted. 'I'd remember a face like that, wouldn't I? But he knows me, don't he? He *is* something to do with Foley.'

'We'll get to the bottom of it,' Cromley promised. 'You're welcome to wait while I question him. Or you can go and I'll call you when I know something. It's up to you.'

Delphine looked at Kenneth. She didn't want to stay here a moment longer than necessary. On the other hand, she wanted to know whatever there was to know. She knew men like that, men who knew they could make other people afraid. And she wished she were braver, that she could have stared back boldly. She hated it all – the fear, the threat, the reminders of her whole sorry life before she came here.

'I think we should wait, if you can bear it,' Kenneth suggested. 'I'd like some answers, if there are any to be had. What do you say?'

Delphine nodded.

'Any idea how long it'll take, old chap?' Kenneth asked Cromley.

'Not really.' Cromley shrugged his beefy shoulders. In a fight between him and the prisoner, Delphine would have struggled to pick a winner. 'But I'm not planning on wasting more of my time than I need to on this lunatic.'

The little waiting room wasn't conducive to chatting. Blue sat by Delphine and held her hand. Kenneth asked if Sid needed to leave, but Sid wasn't going anywhere except the corner shop, where he bought several newspapers to distract them.

After half an hour, which felt like much longer, Cromley rejoined them. He pulled up a chair and told them what he'd learned.

'His name's John Gross. Mrs Foley, your husband hired him months ago to find you.'

'Oh.' Delphine's heart sank. 'Did he follow Ma and Esther here at Christmas?'

'No. He followed Mrs Camberwell back from her visit to your mother.'

'*Midge?*' said Kenneth in horror. 'That brute followed her?

But wait, that was ages ago! Are you telling us Foley knew where Delphine was for nearly *two months* before he appeared? Why?'

'Search me. Gross said Foley had men watching Mrs Foley's mother's place, *and* her sister's, for any unusual activity at all. Your wife, sir, was a stranger to the neighbourhood. Putting it bluntly, she was a beacon to Foley's man.'

Kenneth shook his head. 'We thought we'd been so careful. We had to let Mrs Painter know Delphine was alive, and we didn't want to risk putting anything in writing . . . Midge was so proud of herself.'

'If only you'd spoken to the police sooner,' said Cromley. 'We might have helped.'

'That's my fault,' said Delphine, remembering how Kenneth had urged and urged her to do just that. 'But I was too frightened. I regret it now.'

She braced herself for Cromley's scorn, but he only said, 'It's not uncommon in cases like yours. Well, Gross says that Foley's given up the whole thing as a bad job and gone abroad. I don't know what your feelings are, Mrs Foley, but I suspect that's a crock.'

Delphine nodded. 'I think so too. He'll never go abroad. And he'll never give up.' She glanced at Sid, who was gazing tactfully at his paper but clearly listening. She wondered what he was making of it all.

'Then we are as we were,' said Cromley soberly. 'We are as we were.'

# Chapter Fifty-four

───◦◦◦◦───

The following day was a Thursday. Merrigan was seeing the doctor that day, so Midge joined Delphine in Richmond, even though company was the last thing she wanted. She too had seen Dr Harcourt this week – and her worst nightmare was made real. She was pregnant. At the age of forty-five, despite all her precautions, and with all the traumas that motherhood had brought her last time – pregnant!

She wanted to howl and howl. Instead, they hurried through visits to the bank, post office and bakery, so that they could escape the nipping breezes in their favourite tea room. Carrying on with life, letting no one know what was going on beneath her surface, that was what Midge did. But it was getting harder, and soon it would be impossible.

The parallels and contrasts between her situation and Merrigan's were, Midge recognised, both sharp and painful. Both women were expecting a child. Both had loving husbands to take care of them. And both babies were due in the summer.

Merrigan's child would be born in July; Midge's would be an August baby, just like Blue.

Lawrence was the very picture of the proud father-to-be and Midge didn't know how she could possibly deny Kenneth the same joy. His wife and his daughter pregnant at the same time . . . New little Camberwells to come into the world and grow up to make it a better place . . .

'Midge, are you all right?' Across the white tablecloth, Delphine looked concerned. Her plate wore only a scattering of crumbs while Midge's chocolate cake was untouched.

'Miles away.' She smiled, picking up her fork. 'Sorry, my dear, I've a dozen things on my mind. Heavens, isn't this cake to die for?'

'Is it because that man followed you?' asked Delphine. 'You shouldn't feel bad. He was going to find me one way or the other, and it's thanks to you that Ma knew to stop worrying. I'll always be grateful.'

'Oh, bless you. It's kind of you to say, and yes, I did feel foolish at first. I thought I'd been so very clever . . . I suppose I'm not cut out to be a spy, after all. But never mind me. You have enough on your mind after that nasty business yesterday. I do feel cross that you had to go through that for nothing.'

'It weren't so bad. Blue and Kenneth were there. And Sid . . .'

Midge noticed the way that Delphine mentioned his name at every opportunity, and that when she did, a tiny smile played at the corners of her lips.

'I'd like to meet Sid,' she said. 'Kenneth liked him very much. And Blue says he's an attractive young man, too.'

Delphine blushed. 'Did she? I don't know. I suppose, maybe.'

Midge tried to buck up, but halfway through her cup of Earl Grey with lemon, the room swam and she clattered her cup onto the saucer. She grabbed the edge of the table and closed her eyes. To her relief, her head cleared in just a minute. She took a breath and smiled. But she wasn't fooling Delphine.

'Dear Midge,' said Delphine in a low voice. 'Why haven't you told anyone? You're having a baby, aren't you?'

'Heavens, no! Whatever gave you that idea?' said Midge brightly.

Delphine gave her a disbelieving look. 'Maybe you should see a doctor. I don't know why I didn't realise before. You weren't right at Christmas, and now I come to notice it, you have that look to your skin.'

'Oh, *skin*,' scoffed Midge, then added sharply, 'What look?'

'That glow, that light in your face. I don't know, I can't describe it. But I've seen it, so often. *Oh!* You and Merrigan will be expecting together – how wonderful! Isn't it? Oh, I'm sorry, it's none of my business, of course . . .'

'It's not that.' Midge squeezed Delphine's hand. She was such a dear girl and Midge didn't want to hurt her feelings, but she hadn't wanted to tell *anyone*. If it wasn't voiced, then it wasn't happening – that's what she told herself. But that was the height of foolishness. And if anyone had to guess, perhaps it was best it was Delphine, who understood that happy endings didn't always bring their promised joy.

'What's wrong?' asked Delphine softly.

Midge took a deep breath. How much could she say? Delphine was so much younger. Their experiences had been so different. And yet . . . 'I don't want it. I'm too far along not to keep it, but I wish I weren't,' she whispered. She braced herself for the look of shock and condemnation that must surely pass over Delphine's face, but saw only confusion.

'I see,' she said. 'Why?'

'I'm very old for this,' said Midge. 'It wasn't planned, I hadn't *hoped* for it, and I'm forty-five.'

'It's not that old,' said Delphine. 'I know women who've had babies even older, and you're healthy and you'll have the best of care. And it wouldn't be your first . . . Oh, is it because of Percy? I'm sorry, Midge, I can see it must be hard.'

'Partly, yes. But not only that. I didn't make a very good mother the first time really. Not just because I lost him. Before that, too. Some women aren't cut out for it, no matter what they tell us. I don't feel that it would . . . bring the joy that . . . that people expect it to.'

Again Delphine only nodded and Midge felt the absence of judgement like a cool breeze. 'Please don't tell anyone, dear. Although I'm a little way along, I've only just realised. I can't just move from having no inkling to celebrating and jubilating the way they'll expect me to. I just can't.'

'Of course I won't say anything. It's your baby. Your news. And I do understand, a little bit. I know it's an enormous change. And it brought you so much pain last time. But perhaps, when you've had time to get used to it, you'll feel happy. It's a new life, after all. All that possibility . . .' said Delphine – a little wistfully, Midge thought. Thanks to Foley, Delphine would most likely never have children, watch them grow, see what they would become. What a waste. What a shocking waste. And it made Midge feel even more guilty about her own feelings.

'If only you could give it to me,' added Delphine. 'Don't get me wrong, I'm glad I never had a child with Foley. You wouldn't want anyone to have a father like that. But I do love babies.' She grinned.

'That would be an excellent solution,' Midge agreed. 'But people can't just go around giving away their babies, can they?'

# Chapter Fifty-five

～っとっ～

Blue's last day at the *Gazette* saw her writing about the proposal to erect a statue of Aphrodite in the Terrace Gardens. There was a bequest for a piece of new statuary, but some of the more conservative council members felt that Aphrodite was not a respectable neighbour and had suggested a local war hero instead. Aphrodite's supporters had refused on aesthetic grounds. The debate had been at an impasse for so long that neutral parties were now suggesting a completely different idea: a statue of Porter, an Alsatian dog who had rescued a child from drowning.

'From Greek mythology to canine legend,' wrote Blue, 'we have come a long way from the original proposal. And agreement has still not been reached. What other solutions might be found? Might there be a feline feat worthy of commemoration? Is there a venerable goldfish in Richmond's history?'

She chuckled to herself and jumped at Gordon's impatient voice. 'Camberwell, aren't you finished with that piece yet? Don't choose your last day to become a laggard, for goodness' sake.'

Blue was surprised he would shout at her on her very last day. She still had plenty of time. 'But I . . .'

'Don't argue. I need it on my desk in five minutes.'

'Yes, boss, but why . . .?'

'Good.' Gordon slammed his door.

Blue raised her eyebrows and carried on. She didn't *want* to finish this piece, because then she'd have no reason to stay and she didn't want to go home early. Not today. Even so, she set to, penned her last lines for the *Gazette* and quietly wallowed in a moment of nostalgia. Then she crossed the office, remembering her interview, all those months ago. The office was fuller now than it had been that day. Unusually full, in fact. Everyone was here; no one out on assignment. What were the odds of that?

She knocked on Gordon's door and went in. 'Here it is,' she said. 'All finished. Oh!'

On his ever-untidy desk she spied two bottles of cheap champagne and a large yellow cake with icing smeared thickly over the top and escaping down the sides. It seemed to have been baked with more enthusiasm than skill and a little flag on a cocktail stick was stuck in the top. 'Farewell, Blue. We'll miss you,' it read.

'*Finally!*' Gordon exclaimed. 'She's finished, everyone!' he called to the office at large. 'Come on in! Free cake and bubbles!'

'That's never happened around here before,' said Juno, arriving wielding a silver cake slice. 'Cake, Blue? It's lemon. I made it last night.'

'Juno!' exclaimed Blue, touched. 'You *baked*?'

'I know, you never thought you'd see the day. Neither did my landlady. She kept coming into the kitchen and sniffing, didn't trust me not to burn the place down.'

'It's so kind of you.' Blue felt quite bewildered as she turned this way and that, her colleagues crowding into their boss's office all around her. They patted her on the arm or shook her hand: Barnaby, Will, Roger, Sam . . . all of them.

'Speech!' cried Roger when everyone had an inch of champagne in their glass.

'Well, yes.' Gordon stood up and cleared his throat. 'Quite. A few words. As you all know, this is the last day of our esteemed colleague, Ishbel. Griggs will rejoin us on Monday and decent chap though he is, no one can deny that Ishbel is easier on the eye.'

'Oh, for goodness' sake!' snorted Juno.

'That was a joke, Forrester. You remember those, I take it?'

'Barely. I've been working here too long.'

'I remember the day that Ishbel's name first caught my attention. She sent me an article about school funding that hit just the right note. I knew at once that she was a talented writer and I called her in. She's been putting up with us ever since, for mysterious reasons of her own, and I can only say that I'm sorry there are no vacancies for her, though I suspect she's destined for higher things anyway. Ishbel, I'd like to thank you for a job thoroughly well done. You're a first-class writer, professional and an all-round sport. I wish you every happiness and success. Don't be a stranger, as they say, and good luck!'

All around Blue, empty glasses were raised. 'Hear, hear,' everyone murmured.

'I should like to propose a toast,' he added. Juno hastened to pour another half inch of bubbly into everyone's glass.

'To Ishbel, known to us all as our very own I. C., also known as Blue. Your health and good fortune.'

'To Ishbel. To Blue.' The voices rang around the office and Blue was quite overwhelmed. She'd never stopped to consider how anyone else felt about her leaving, or that she might be valued other than as a means of getting copy on paper.

'Speech!' prompted Will. 'Say a few words, won't you, Camberwell?'

'Yes, of course. Well, firstly, Gordon, I'd like to thank you for this lovely send-off.'

'Most glamorous party you've ever seen, I bet,' said Cauderlie, but Blue just laughed.

'I never imagined you had this planned and I'm very, very touched. Juno, thank you for the lovely cake. Thank you all for coming and seeing me off. I'll miss you and the *Gazette* very much, and if there were a position here for me, you wouldn't be getting rid of me now. Thank you all for your warm welcome. Well, *most* of you anyway.' She gave Cauderlie a meaningful glance and everyone except Cauderlie laughed.

'I came here as a complete novice and I like to think I've

learned a thing or two since then about how all this works. I appreciate that opportunity more than I can say. I won't be idle over the coming months, but it won't be the same as working here, I'm quite certain of that. I wish the very best to you all and hope we can stay in touch . . .' Blue's eyes filled with tears and she had to stop. 'Good heavens,' she muttered, turning away. Juno put an arm around her. 'Cheers!' added Blue, lifting her glass.

There was a flurry of clinks as her colleagues touched their glass against hers.

'Now I'm afraid I have to go,' said Gordon, 'but whoever can spare the time, feel free to stay here and chat to Ishbel in her last hour or so. Enjoy your dri . . . Oh.' The champagne bottles were empty. 'I appear not to have catered sufficiently. Well, there's cake, anyway.'

'Fortunately for Blue,' said Juno, 'some of us have taken precautions.' She, Barnaby and, to Blue's surprise, Cauderlie, scooted over to their desks, each bringing out a bottle or two of wine.

'Much better! Jolly good, chaps!' said Roger, red-faced with delight.

'Good Lord,' said Blue. 'You *must* be excited to see the back of me, Cauderlie!'

He scowled. 'In all seriousness,' he said, looking deeply annoyed to be in this position, 'I have to say well done. Can't fault it. Cheers.'

By 'it', Blue presumed he meant the whole thing – the writing, the job, the way she'd battled through all his attempts to undermine her. But now wasn't the time to say anything about all that. She glanced at Will, who rolled his eyes and grinned.

She couldn't look at Juno at all – or Barnaby. If she did, she really would cry.

# Chapter Fifty-six

The search for the perfect words was the hardest thing. In fact, impossible! But then, how *could* there be perfect words for something as imperfect as this: human failings; the disappointments people meted out to each other; trust betrayed; incomprehensible actions . . . life.

Midge sat in her little sewing room, her best chance at privacy, and threw down her pen. How did Blue do it? Why would she want to make a living out of this devilish activity? Why would *anyone* want to do this every day?

She was perched on her sewing stool with a pad of writing paper, decorated with a seashell design, on her lap. It tortured her with its impenetrable blankness. So far she had written 'Kenneth, my darling'. And there she had stopped.

Should she address it to Kenneth *and* the girls? Should she write separate letters to all three of them? There was unlikely to be a guideline for *this* particular situation in any book of etiquette. Just the one letter, then. To Kenneth. He would read it, and his world would be rearranged. Somehow, eventually, he would find a way to tell Merrigan and Blue.

Oh! Midge couldn't bear to think of it. She had somehow superstitiously thought that if she ignored it, the pregnancy wouldn't be real. But it was. Unwelcome and problematical, but real. And the fact remained that there were things her family didn't know that made it impossible to carry on from here and play happy families, even though that was all she had ever wanted.

She bent forward to pick up the pen, feeling the tightening around her middle where her narrow waist was just a little fuller than before. *Baby*, she thought, fleetingly, then shook her head. Troublemaker, catalyst, that's what it was, coming to expose the truth, drive her out, make real what she had always feared: that she would be banished from Ryan's Castle ever after – an outcast.

The thought of a life with no Kenneth, no girls, no Tabitha forever calling in and Elf trudging up from the garden for dinner was unbearable. A cold, loveless, drear existence. The thought of them hating her was a living death. Yet so it must be. They weren't given to hate, any of them, but some things were unforgivable.

Her hand shook but she wrote a little more.

*Kenneth, my darling,*

*I don't know how to tell you this. When I do, you will find it impossible to believe that I love you, but I do—*

Heavens. How dreadfully dull and inadequate it was. When Blue wrote, she poured herself onto the page. Midge wouldn't be filling her empty days with novel-writing, that was for sure. She tried again . . .

'Midge, darling, where are you?'

It was Merrigan, clattering about in the lower part of the house. Cicely's squawks could also be heard.

'Merrigan?' Midge shot off her stool like a lit rocket. She stared about wildly, as though caught in some illicit act. She shoved her letter pad underneath a bolt of apricot georgette from which she had planned to make a dress for Merrigan. She would take all her materials with her and make everything she had ever planned and send them endless gifts . . . Though they wouldn't want anything from her. They'd burn them most probably, or, socially aware as they were, give them to the needy.

She emerged onto the landing, heart pattering, and saw Merrigan in the hall, stylish in bright red. She was a walking splash of joy on a bright spring day.

'Oh, there you are!' beamed Merrigan. 'I don't suppose you could possibly watch this creature for an hour or so, could you? I promised Winnie Stanforth I'd help her hang curtains this morning and the little goblin's being *particularly* fractious today, aren't you, Cicely Audra? We'll get it done far more quickly without certain troublemakers in tow.'

Midge hesitated. Today was the day. She had screwed up

her courage. But . . . perhaps she could have just one more day as a Camberwell.

'Of course, darling. Of course. Shall we pick some cherry blossom in the garden, Cicely?'

The child stuck her thumb in her mouth, stared at Midge with her big brown eyes and nodded.

'Angel!' exclaimed Merrigan.

'If you say so, darling. Do you want a cup of tea before you go?'

'I'd rather get going and have it done. I *was* wondering if you'd like to get a spot of lunch later, just the two of us. Or did you have big plans for this afternoon?'

'That sounds lovely,' said Midge softly. 'No, no big plans.'

# Chapter Fifty-seven

*Blue,*

*I hear from Ro that you're invited to her shindig, too. I shall escort you!*

*D*

'Darling Blue, it's absolutely splendid that your job's finished!' said Dorian. They were at Rowena Lowrie's engagement dinner. He was wearing a rather fetching indigo dinner jacket with a lavender cummerbund. Only Dorian could carry off black tie that wasn't black. It made his eyes magically blue.

'Is it? Why's that?' Blue snapped. She'd had about enough of that from Elf. It didn't *feel* splendid.

'Well, because you'll have more time, of course! A fellow can be jolly understanding about a girl's ambitions – support you all the way, you know that! But that doesn't mean he wouldn't like a little more time with a luscious lovely. I knew you were busy lately, so I've left you to it.'

*Really?* thought Blue. *I thought it was because you knew I wasn't very impressed with you the other night*. But she said something non-committal and promised herself she would think all this through when she was alone.

She did so the following day, a particularly quiet Sunday at Ryan's Castle.

For once there were no visitors. Lawrence was battling to persuade Merrigan to rest during her pregnancy; Tabitha was busy with Foster, who was playing a violin solo in a forthcoming school concert – that had to be a good sign! – and Delphine was spending the morning with Sid. Midge was locked up in her sewing room again, working on a surprise for someone, Blue assumed. Her father was taking the chance to catch up on his reading.

As for Blue, she was two weeks into her liberty – but it didn't feel the way liberty was supposed to. She'd imagined a great, bracing adventurousness, like standing on the prow of a galleon. Instead, it was a yawning sort of greyness.

In the absence of writing inspiration, Blue pondered her love life once again. The way Dorian had talked about Foster's plight had stayed with her. So had his annoyance at having to walk her home on a cold night when he'd wanted to stay in and do something quite different.

Everyone had faults, she knew that. Just look at her father! Kenneth could be insensitive and impetuous. He was a loose cannon; her last birthday was a case in point. But despite his shortcomings, he was a man of character: heroic in the war, tireless in his efforts to improve the world, kind, generous and supportive of his friends. On the surface, Blue realised, Dorian reminded her of him – goodness, what would Elf have to say about that? They were both charming, handsome and affluent. But whereas Kenneth cared deeply about worlds beyond his own, Dorian lolled in his privilege like a fellow in a hot bath.

Blue sighed. She was fond of Dorian; he was infectious as a cold. But she knew more clearly than ever that he was not a man she could build a life with. So what was the point of doing what they were doing? As for the *other thing*, her inclination had faded since that night in his apartment. She still found him terribly fetching, but it was like receiving a beautifully wrapped gift. Once you opened it and found there was nothing much inside, it was hard to feel quite so excited about it. Promise without substance. She didn't want to sleep with him any more, she realised. The moment had passed. Goodness.

She would talk to Dorian and explain that she wanted to go back to being just friends. Somehow she suspected that he wouldn't be devastated.

And so her thoughts turned to L. W. He was the one who made sense in her life. He was a man with character to match his pleasant exterior, and he was devoted to her, she could tell. He was patient, biding his time while she did whatever she needed to do to become ready for love. He'd been, throughout, the perfect gentleman. Almost *too* gentlemanly, really! It wasn't that they hadn't flirted *at all* – but then they kept subsiding back into politeness and sensible conversation. There was nothing wrong with that, but nevertheless, thought Blue impatiently, it had been months. It was high time for a kiss.

# Chapter Fifty-eight

April must be the sweetest month of all, Delphine decided, delirious with the scent of honeysuckle. The hedgerows were full of it, plumy bursts of cream, butter-yellow and magenta, their beauty heralded from several paces by that glorious smell. On Sundays, she and Sid had taken to walking further and further along the river. What had started out as a half-hour stroll here and there as the evenings grew longer evolved into a weekly fixture. At first they walked to St Margarets. Then they walked to Kew. Then to Mortlake, Putney, Barnes. One day they found themselves in Hammersmith, exclaimed over the time and caught a bus back before the Greenbows reported them missing.

Time was a fluid concept, Delphine had heard Kenneth say once. Remembering how slowly it had slithered, treacle-ish and foul, when Foley was pressing his body into hers, she had to agree. Then, five minutes was an eternity to be suffered. Since she came to Richmond, time had variously danced along, a minuet to be enjoyed, or obligingly suspended itself altogether. Now, with Sid, it was a sparkling stream, breathlessly swift, carrying her along so rapidly that she couldn't grasp anything solid.

From the beginning, Paul had been eager for Sid to settle in, decide for sure that Richmond was somewhere he wanted to stay. But now, Delphine knew, there was no question about it. Not only did he have no alternative but, like Delphine, he could hardly believe that he'd ended up somewhere so beautiful. And, of course, there was Delphine. She knew without him saying it that wherever she was, Sid would stay.

Sometimes she wondered about the wisdom of allowing their friendship to meander unchecked. After all, it was naive to act as though it were *only* friendship, yet there could never be anything more. Was it kind to either of them? Yet what alternative would be kinder? To live next door but hide away from him? To move away and give up her wonderful life? There was no solution that made sense.

Soon Sid found a position as under-gardener with a family in Hampton. He was one of a small team, so he could learn as he went along.

'I'm more of a pair of hands than a gardener,' he explained. 'I wheel barrow-loads of rocks around the grounds, I build walls and dig ditches. But I'm learning how to plant and grow and tend things. I love to be in the gardens every day.'

He continued to live on Old Palace Lane, rising early to go to work and coming back when the evening was at its richest.

Spring was a busy time for a gardener and his days lengthened with the light. Even so, he'd often call in to Stephen and Fanny's for his dinner and Delphine would sit and eat with him. Then, of course, there were Sundays and the long, longed-for walks.

One day they were walking back from Kew, their hands brushing together as they walked, their heads bent in conversation. And suddenly, as if it were the most inevitable thing in the world, he kissed her. Right in the middle of a sentence: she was saying something about *The Hound of the Baskervilles*. It wasn't a screen kiss, not all passion and bending over her with brooding eyes. He just leaned in and brushed her lips with his, then cupped her face with his hands for a moment, both sides, the scarred and the unblemished. She felt her heart spark and her whole body felt blissfully warm and light. She'd never felt that way at physical contact with a man before. In fact, she had never really been *kissed* before – not if kisses were this, sweet, an act of love.

'Sorry,' he said. 'I know we can't. I shouldn't. It's just . . .'

Delphine nodded. They walked on.

# Chapter Fifty-nine

Blue reread L. W.'s letters for the last time, then put them away in a drawer. It didn't feel gracious to dispose of them yet, but her hopes for romance were over.

They had dined together two nights ago. Still believing that it was time to try a kiss, she'd taken extra pains with her appearance and made her intentions pretty damn clear over the meal by leaning her chin on her hand and gazing at him dreamily. She'd agreed to him walking her home and at the threshold he had, at last, kissed her goodnight.

And she had felt *nothing*. For half a minute – maybe a whole one – she stood politely while he kissed her, and she had kissed him back a little, because she didn't want to be rude. She was quite astonished by how unmoved she was. It wasn't a bad kiss, she didn't think – not that she could write a manual or anything. It just didn't touch her, in any way.

*Heavens*, she'd thought as she'd waved him goodbye, closing the door behind her with some relief. *A lifetime of kisses like that would finish me off*. She could thank Dorian for that, at least: now she knew what kisses *could* do.

Such a shame. A lovely man. She would have to see him again to tell him how she felt – or rather, didn't feel – in person. That would be awkward. Or should she write? Perhaps she should have told him there and then, but experience had not prepared her for such an outcome, and besides, how could you *say* it, in the heat of the moment? It would have seemed so terribly cruel.

She sighed, closing the drawer on the letters. They had accompanied her through some challenging, exhilarating times. But if passion wasn't there, what on earth could be done? Well, for now, she'd better get back to work – or *try* to.

The way Blue spent her days had changed a great deal since finishing at the *Gazette*. She was spending long hours staring into space, chewing her fingernails, tapping her pen, ringing for coffee and getting nowhere.

She'd been very brisk for three whole days. She'd sent off her recent pieces to various nationals. She'd tried to take the professionalism that she'd learned at the *Gazette* into her freelance status, as she tried to think of it. But it was hard. Deadlines and word counts were all very well when Gordon was imposing them and she'd lose her job if she didn't meet them, but at home, when it didn't really matter on any given day, she found it hard to take herself seriously. Then Merrigan suggested that she might benefit from a short holiday after working flat-out for six months. That made sense, so Blue took a week off – and she was bored senseless. So she hastily wrote two more articles and sent those out too. That latest spurt of activity left her feeling lacklustre and wan. Nothing to do now but wait.

No, not *nothing*, she told herself sternly. There was The Novel. Blue had tried to motivate herself to write a thousand words each day, and when that didn't work she told herself to write a synopsis, character studies, plot outlines – various tasks she thought might ease her into the actual writing itself. They didn't. Apparently, she was a less effective boss than Gordon.

That was what really lay at the heart of this malaise. She *missed* Gordon breezing in and out, dispensing assignments, returning articles with a briar patch of red corrections on the pages. She missed Juno, with her turbans and her tough humour. She missed Will's quiet helpfulness and Sheila's glossy smile when she walked into reception in the morning. She missed being I. C., reporter.

She had thought the novel would prove a distraction, something into which she could escape, but it made her feel almost . . . *homesick*. And why should that be? She frowned at the garden from her bedroom window. Wands of lavender were flourishing; magnolia blossoms floated like dreams. The garden was festooned with satiny pink tulips and the tiny, tight clusters of grape hyacinth, the richest blue imaginable. *This* was home. The *Gazette* was only a job.

But the feeling persisted. What, then, was she homesick for?

It wasn't the tea dances, she knew that. It wasn't the discipline of early starts and long days. It certainly wasn't Cauderlie! But whenever she looked at the beautiful brown leather folder she'd chosen for her novel, whenever she saw the blank pages, all creamy and delicious, waiting to be filled, she thought of another novel in progress, a reporter's pad scribbled all over with arrows and crossings-out.

She saw the *Gazette*'s tiny kitchen. She saw a dusky evening with the street lamps glinting below. And she saw Barnaby, pushing his untidy manuscript towards her with that mixture of diffidence, hope and excruciating self-consciousness that as a writer she knew all too well. She saw Barnaby.

She saw *Barnaby*.

'What?' demanded Blue, out loud. '*What?* Oh no. No, no, no!'

This couldn't be. She was *missing* Barnaby. More than she missed Juno or Gordon or any of the others. Well, that was all right, she told herself nervously. They'd been quite good pals, really. Those after-work drinks, those lovely conversations. It was natural to miss a friend. She'd seen him every day for six months, after all, and now she hadn't seen him for three weeks. She was bound to feel it.

But, she realised, he was the reason for this feeling of homesickness. Suddenly she was swamped with memories of Barnaby, and each one was ten times richer, ten times warmer, than all her other memories. Sitting in the Roebuck dreaming of hidden treasure while he waited at the bar to buy her a pint of best mild. Barnaby hurrying into the hospital to chase a story and leaving empty-handed, because of a promise to Blue. Barnaby motivating her to finish her boring article so that they could go and talk. Barnaby scribbling his novel in a tiny, dark kitchen. Barnaby on that very first day, smiling and welcoming her in the corridor. The first time he had called her Blue. *Oh!*

They had felt like a double act, a conspiracy, from the first. Though it might be very different for him. He was a kind person; that didn't mean anything. They got on well, but he was a man with five sisters! Of course he got on well with women; he and Juno shared countless laughs. Barnaby had never given Blue any indication that he thought of her as anything more than a friend. Which was quite right and proper. But now . . . ? It hit her again, that wave of displacement, and she understood that it was because they'd made no plans to see each other again. There was no Barnaby in her days and weeks any longer. And actually, there was no one she liked talking to more. Oh Lord.

Well, she could saunter down to the *Gazette* whenever she wanted. He hadn't vanished; she could see him if she wanted to. But what then? Repeat the whole performance the following week? Ask him to go for a drink? Blue wasn't old-fashioned, but she couldn't bear the thought of him spending time with her only because he was *obliging*. She wanted him to feel . . . like this!

Good heavens! She got up and started pacing around her room. How had this sidled up on her? How hadn't she *noticed* it before? Was it – horrifying to consider – because Barnaby was not from her own background? Not the sort of fellow people thought of when they talked about a suitor for Blue? Or was it because they were colleagues and the whole time she'd known him she'd been preoccupied with learning to swim, not sink, in a new environment? Or was it simply that, from the very first day, he'd always been there?

She ran her hands through her hair, knocking out the mother-of-pearl comb with which she'd twisted up the back. She picked it up and stuck it back into her hair any old how. So there it was, she reflected, pacing about her room. Dorian had been all spark and no substance. L. W. had been a really decent sort but there was no spark at all – for her, anyway. Foster, dear Foster, was and remained like her little brother. And eight months after her father's absurd declaration, even though, despite herself, some sort of romantic candle had been lit in her heart, she was left with no beaux worth considering. All those dates, all those dinners, all that talking with the girls had come to nothing, like a damp firework.

Was that why her thoughts were turning to Barnaby now? Because all the other possibilities had been eliminated? Was she, after all, the sort of girl who simply must have some chap dangling in order to give her life meaning? But she knew it wasn't that. It was only because of Barnaby that she was trying to write this damn novel at all. It was thanks to him that she had not only survived the *Gazette* but thrived there. He had kept Foster from the papers. He was the reason Blue had withstood the difficult fag end of winter. Barnaby had somehow, gracefully, and without her even noticing, become the firm underpinning of her life.

She flopped down and stuck her feet out in front of her. They were clad in thick black socks – the house could still be chilly in April. She laughed. She didn't look very desirable now, with her passion-killer footwear and her hair scrunched up like a discarded sheet of paper. She blew out a weighty breath. Could Barnaby ever find her remotely attractive?

She'd been so intent on finding a man the way her father expected her to, the way Merrigan and Tab said she would. She'd waited for men to pay court to her, and she'd been swept away by admiration. For a time, it had seemed that that road could take her where she was meant to go. Then it had abruptly run out and she was glad that it had – glad, glad, glad – because one thing had been missing from her earnest conversations with L. W., and from all her thrilling gallivanting with Dorian, something elusive, indescribable and unimagined: a sense of rightness for her whole and true self. It was the way she felt with Barnaby. No one had ever talked to her about *that*.

The only trouble with it was that now the prospect of life without him felt unimaginably lacking. She groaned, and lay her head on her arms on top of her barely begun manuscript.

She was hauled from her melancholy by a roar from downstairs. Her father was calling her name, over and over again.

She leapt out of her chair. 'Daddy? What is it? Are you ill?' She stumbled in her loose socks as she ran down the landing. Oh please, God, not her father. She couldn't bear it if anything happened to him.

She ran down the stairs and found him in his study, tears streaming down his face.

'What has she *done*?' Kenneth demanded furiously. 'How can this be?'

Blue's whole being crawled to a standstill. She had no idea what he was talking about, but instinct told her that this was one of those moments – and she'd known a few of them – after which life would never be the same again, and forever afterwards you'd wish they'd never happened.

'Who, Daddy? Who are you talking about? What's happened?'

He looked at her like a man stunned, all the air knocked out of him. Then he lifted a limp arm and held out a piece of paper. Blue took it. It was written on Midge's lovely seashell paper.

'It's Midge,' said Kenneth, then added the one thing Blue had been certain he would never say. 'She's left us.'

# Chapter Sixty

Delphine ran up Richmond Hill, convinced that spring had actually taken up residence in her heart. It was early evening, and really she shouldn't have been out alone, but it was still light – the sky was the powdery lilac-blue of infinity. Birdsong scattered the air like sequins and Delphine decided to take the chance; it was a short distance and plenty of people were out and about, smiling and saying 'good evening'. A new princess, Princess Elizabeth, had been born just last week, and all was right with the world. It was hard to believe anything could ever go wrong again since Sid had kissed her.

She needed to talk to Blue. Blue would give her hope, help her see that everything could work out somehow. And apart from anything else, she just wanted to say the words: *Sid kissed me!*

But when she got to Ryan's Castle she had to knock a long time before Avis answered the door. Delphine started to think no one was home – what a let-down!

'Oh, it's you, miss,' said Avis, looking more harassed than Delphine had ever seen her. Her usually immaculate dark bun had slipped to one side. 'I suppose *you* can come in.'

'Is something wrong?' asked Delphine, stepping into the hall and taking off her gloves.

'Don't ask me,' muttered Avis. 'You'd better come through; they're in the study.'

'They' turned out to be Kenneth, Blue and Merrigan. Blue was sitting on the edge of her father's desk, her face tear-streaked. Merrigan had her arm around Blue. Kenneth stood looking out of the window, his entire posture radiating grief.

'Ha . . . have I come at a bad time?' asked Delphine, faltering in the doorway. 'I d . . . don't want to barge in . . .'

Kenneth turned and looked at her as though he couldn't quite place who she was. 'Oh, Delphine, it's you. Come in. Take a seat. We can tell *you* the truth, at least. Lord knows what we'll say to everyone else. Perhaps you might be able to shed some light . . .'

'On what? What's happened?'

He opened his mouth but no words came out. Delphine knew what that was like. This was bad then. Very bad.

'It's Midge,' said Merrigan. 'She's gone.'

'Gone?' Delphine frowned.

'Well, she's left us, in point of fact. Left Ryan's Castle. *Left* us!' She repeated the words, as though doing so might make the whole thing more comprehensible.

Delphine glanced at Blue. She looked terrible. To lose another mother – to lose *Midge*. Midge!

'B . . . but I don't understand. This family is everything to her. She loves you all so much . . . *Loves* you,' said Delphine inadequately.

'So she says,' said Kenneth crisply. 'Here.' He passed Delphine a letter.

She recognised Midge's handwriting. 'Are you sure?' she asked, aghast. What could be more private than a woman's farewell letter to her husband?

'Quite sure. I don't need to ask you to keep it confidential. I don't know what we're going to tell people – not *this*, that's for sure – but you, well, you must know everything. We've told Elf, of course. You've just missed him.'

Delphine nodded, hesitant. She'd known she held a special place in the household, but the Camberwells had always been the rescuers and protectors. This meant she could support them too; this made them equals. She felt honoured and appalled at the same time. She started to read.

*Kenneth, my darling,*

*I don't know how to tell you this. When I do, you will find it impossible to believe that I love you, but I do – as I always have – furiously and forever. I would lay down my life for you, for Merrigan, for Blue, in a heartbeat. Your happiness is more important to me than anything on this earth or beyond it. And yet, I have done a terrible thing to you. Love doesn't protect us from taking wrong actions.*

*I can't think now how it's even been possible for me to keep such a secret, but now it's all split open. Darling, when I was pregnant with Percy, I should have been happy, as you were, but I felt frightened and resentful. I was selfish, you see, burdened by a boundless, self-serving love. All I could think was how I was not beautiful. That Audra was beautiful. That Christie Dawson-Hobbs was beautiful. But I was not.*

*I was not love's young dream. I was not your heart's choice. I should not have let you marry me. You are honourable and you were in need and those are not reasons to pledge yourself to someone for life. You would not have chosen me under different circumstances. I have always known this. I have always felt guilty. I'm sorry.*

*When I became pregnant, all I knew was that I was steadily losing what little attractiveness I possessed. A woman of middle years in a society that prizes women for their looks, still, above all else. And I with the very handsomest of husbands. I couldn't bear it. You could surely never understand it, my darling, but so it was. Swelling belly, fattening ankles, then Percy came and I was leaking, flustered, limp and overwhelmed. We're supposed to find the tasks of motherhood easy and natural. Either that is a myth put about to torture women, or I am very deficient indeed. Either is probable.*

*The months that we had him were not joyful for me, I'm ashamed to say. They were nothing but a succession of days in which I failed at one task after another and revealed myself as inadequate over and over again before the very man I wanted to adore me. Until I could not tolerate it any more.*

# Darling Blue

*You were all away, my beloved husband and my darling girls. I readied Percy for a day out and it was as slow and obstacle-strewn and frustrating as ever. Eventually we made it onto the District, but we did not go to Esher, as I told you. I took him to the East End of London where I left him in a basket on the doorstep of an orphanage, like some tragic Dickensian pauper. I put a note in the basket saying his name was Terence. I knocked the door and hid, to be sure he was taken in safely. A girl answered the door and when she saw the basket she sighed, as though women put down babies like too-heavy shopping bags every day. They went inside and I went to Esher.*

*I carried another baby basket with a few books inside to give the appearance of a baby's weight. I then did everything I told you – bought a sandwich, picnicked in the park, lay down in the sunshine. Then I pretended the distress of a woman whose child has vanished. I lied and lied and lied.*

*And finally it has become unbearable. Never mind why, but at last I find I simply cannot go on like this. I cannot live with you any more. I cannot live with myself, truth be told, both for the fact of my own wickedness and because life away from Ryan's Castle will be unbearable. But I'm not the sort to end it all, so I'll have to endure somehow. My only comfort is that death, when it does come, will be so very welcome.*

*I am more sorry than I can say. I'm so sorry I could bleed from it. I could tell you over and over again and it would never be enough.*

*Midge*

Delphine laid the letter in her lap and found she was crying. She looked up at the family she had come to love as her own. Their eyes were trained upon her, as though she were an oracle. But how could anyone go forward from here? She didn't know what to say.

Blue started sobbing again. Delphine struggled with the enormity of it. Midge, gone. The family sundered, once again. Kenneth abandoned by his wife, who loved him to distraction. His son alive, most likely, but out of reach as ever, if he had been adopted. Even if he hadn't, if Kenneth could claim him and bring him back to Ryan's Castle, they had still missed years of his life. No one could ever undo the fact that Midge had robbed them of so much, and yet, Delphine couldn't hate her. She felt sorry for her. When life felt unbearable, people went to extremes, she knew that. She looked back down at the pages. It was inconceivable.

'Oh,' she said, and buried her face in her hands.

Kenneth came over and patted her shoulder. 'The deuce of it,' he said in a faraway voice, 'is not knowing how to feel. It's unforgivable, isn't it? By rights I should be glad to be shot of her. I could set the police on her. But we all just want her to come back. But how can she, now? Surely the Midge we want isn't really Midge at all, just a figment of our imaginations. The real Midge is a woman who could do this terrible thing. I can never forgive her.'

'Wh . . . when . . . ?' asked Delphine with difficulty. 'When did she . . . ?'

'The day before yesterday,' said Merrigan. 'We had a merry old to-do looking for her until we found the letter. Then Daddy went haring all over London trying to find her, but no joy.'

'I went to her mother's first,' he said. 'She clearly had no idea where Midge was, so there's another frantic woman. I tried all her old friends — pretty sure she won't have stayed in Richmond — but no luck. I can't ask the people she's close to here. I mean, how can I tell them something like this? I can't begin to guess where she might have gone. I don't suppose you . . .?'

'I'm so sorry.' Delphine shook her head. 'I've no idea.'

Kenneth sighed. 'No. Well, there we are then. She's lost. As lost as Percy all these years. I spent all of Tuesday chasing after Midge and all of yesterday traipsing around the children's homes of East London. The devil knew there were so many of them. He was adopted after just three months, apparently. I even managed to talk them into telling me where he is — not sure how I'd feel about that if I were his adoptive parents, but anyway. I went there, made a call under spurious pretences, and I saw Percy — or Terence, as they call him. He's happy, Delphine. They're a fine family, wealthy and kind. He has the best of everything, just as he would here. He's healthy and loved and I couldn't tell them who I really was. They're the only parents he's ever known and he's just a little boy. It would be cruel to disturb him now. *Could* we, even, legally? God!' He clutched his skull, sandy hair springing between his fingers.

Delphine remembered how Midge used to stroke his hair

all the time, as if she couldn't bear *not* to touch it. Oh, what a terrible, tyrannical love hers was.

'I'm so terribly sorry for you all,' Delphine whispered. 'It's hard to know where to start making sense of it. She's not my wife or mother and already I can't imagine life here without her. She's been so good to me. If there's anything at all I can do, you *must* tell me.'

Blue sniffed and held her arms out. Delphine got up and went to hold her, as Blue had comforted her so often in their short friendship.

'You find us in disarray, my dear,' said Kenneth at last. 'I apologise for receiving you with such shocking news and such an avalanche of emotion. Was there a reason for your call?'

'Heavens, don't say that!' said Delphine. 'No, no reason. I was just saying hello.' She could not speak to Blue of kisses now.

'I'm so glad you're here,' said Blue into Delphine's side, her voice muffled. 'Oh, Delph, how could she? How could she take my brother away from me, and now *leave* me? How could she?'

Delphine sighed. It was impossible to imagine. 'If it's any comfort, I think she probably wasn't herself at those times. Women who've had babies . . . very often they're all over the place. I've seen it more than once. I suppose she was in a state that drove her to do what she did, and then once she'd done it, well, how could you *tell* anyone?'

'But what I don't understand . . .' Kenneth frowned, then

he let out a short, joyless laugh. 'Well, one of the many, *many* things I don't understand, is this: why now? What you say makes sense, Delphine. I've read of such things. If some sort of temporary insanity set in all those years ago, driving Midge to take my son away, and then it passed, but she simply couldn't bear to tell us . . . Well, that was *years* ago. Why did it suddenly become impossible to keep the secret now? Why must she make the confession and leave us *now*?'

'Oh,' said Delphine again. Then she shut her mouth firmly. Should she tell them?

'What?' demanded Kenneth. 'Do you know something?'

Delphine bit her lip. She didn't want to betray Midge. But Midge was gone, possibly forever, and these people had suffered enough from her secrets. It wasn't right to leave them in the dark with another one.

'There is something,' she told them gently. 'I found out the last time we went for tea, but she said she was going to tell you.'

'What?' asked Blue fearfully.

Delphine took a deep breath and said it. 'Midge is expecting another baby.'

# Chapter Sixty-one

It made perfect sense, thought Blue, marching along the dusky river. Bursting with anger and hurt, she felt a painful energy surging within: a sort of tragic, unnatural strength. At some point during the years that had passed since Percy disappeared, it was as if the whole family, without discussion, had adopted the attitude that he was dead. It seemed almost easier than still imagining him out there somewhere, far away from them. Now, she didn't know what to think again. Could he ever be restored to them?

She realised that she shouldn't be out alone, but to hell with Foley. In fact, *let* him happen upon her tonight and try something. She would *pulverise* him. Destruction seemed like an appealing option just now; Blue only needed something she would be willing to destroy.

Delphine had been alone when she left them, too, Blue realised. None of them was thinking properly. God, she hoped this wasn't the night Foley chose to reappear. The threat of him seemed to have faded compared to the very present dramas unfolding in Ryan's Castle. Midge pregnant. Midge absconding. Midge, giving away their baby, her brother. If motherhood had been so unbearable the first time round, to the extent that she would stage Percy's disappearance and maintain her elaborate ruse for all those years, discovering that she was pregnant once again must have been . . .

Blue shook her head as a creamy moon rose in a dark lavender sky, her strides raking the length of the river. What were the odds? All the women in the world who longed to be mothers, and Midge, who didn't, had fallen twice. Discovering that she was pregnant again must have been ironic, infuriating, devastating . . . And it must have brought up her imperfectly buried guilt in spades. Blue didn't know how to feel about any of it. She didn't *want* to hate Midge, and yet she was full to the brim with fury and horror, plus a dose of childlike, self-centred woe that Midge had done this to *her*. How could she have taken Blue's brother away? How could she have let her fear he was dead? How could she have *left* her?

And more than anything, she felt confusion. Why, why, why? The word accompanied every footfall through the late spring evening. She stormed past Old Deer Park – or *Old Dear Park*, as Kenneth liked to quip in more carefree times. Why had none of them known how hard Midge found it back then? Why hadn't she told them? Why hadn't they noticed? Why had her blasted father flirted so much? Why, if it had all been so hard, hadn't Midge simply hired a nanny? Surely that would have been a lesser admission of weakness than getting rid of Percy altogether? *Why?* Blue liked to understand things. Elf had loaned her a book about post-partum disorders and Blue intended to read it – every word. But first, she must walk.

When Blue realised that she was in Kew, and it was dark, she turned round and walked back. She was still fizzing with painful energy, still bewildered and in need of working it out physically. As she headed for home, she wished she could see Barnaby. All through their acquaintance she had confided in him: about Foster, about her doubts about her work, about Midge and Delphine and Foley. And now a missing stepmother? He would think her life was nothing but drama. Perhaps it was. But she didn't want him to think she only wanted him for a shoulder to cry on. If she *did* ever pluck up the courage to call into the office, she wanted it to be so that their friendship could extend beyond their time as colleagues, pure and simple.

Soon she was back at the railway bridge and the turning that would take her into town, towards the office. She hesitated, picturing him there, working late, or perhaps scrunched into the kitchen, working on his novel. He might be there, all alone. He might be pleased to see her. Blue wanted more than anything to be with him, in the warmth and bonhomie of the Roebuck, instead of going home to Ryan's Castle where her father paced and raged and made endless telephone calls, Avis baked pointless pies and Merrigan came and went like a visiting constable.

Blue kicked at a stone and turned for home. She wouldn't visit Barnaby tonight.

It was surprisingly quiet by the river. Where were the late workers returning home? Where were the spring sweethearts loitering with passion on their lips? Blue was relieved when she heard a footstep behind her; there was something eerie about the silent shadows. But when she turned, there was nobody there. She quickened her pace a little.

And then, a footstep once more. She turned sharply. A man was walking a little way behind her, at a respectful distance. She carried on. As she walked, the glimpse of him was vivid in her mind's eye. Medium height, slight build, cap pulled low. Sharp features, if she wasn't mistaken. That could be a hundred men, she told herself, but as she neared Richmond Bridge she couldn't resist looking around again. He was gone. That was odd. They'd passed the last of the tall, proud gateways along the river walk; there was nowhere for him to go, unless he'd turned back. But there was no receding figure in the distance.

Blue found herself hurrying up the stone steps by the bridge. And she heard footsteps again, running, taking the steps behind her two at a time. She whirled round to see the same slender fellow hurtling after her. Her foot slipped on the pearly stone but she sped up still more until she reached the top, where motor cars passed and people milled about and it felt safer again. All in an instant she spotted Foster and Tab and called out to them.

She couldn't know whether it really was Foley, for he only tugged his cap and walked on. He might be nothing more than a chap in a hurry who happened to be going her way. But there was a boldness about the way he held her gaze that was at odds with his deferential gesture, and he hesitated for just an instant, as though acknowledging something. Or was she imagining things?

The relief of seeing her friends was immense, for so many reasons. She was safe, Foster was looking a thousand times better and it was a distraction from the ghastly debacle of her home life.

'Cocktail at our place?' suggested Tab, and Blue accepted.

In Foster and Tabitha, Blue could confide. She told them about Midge and they were both horrified and sympathetic. Then they distracted her with their news. Tabitha was seeing a new chap of whom she spoke in rather glowing terms. She had seen him five whole times – a record.

Things were looking up for Foster. Mr Mathews had left the school, and though Foster missed him, it made it easier to spend time in the music department again. The nasty comments continued, he admitted, but only from one or two people, and they didn't have the same power now that two people he cared about knew and loved him anyway. He'd decided to work on overcoming his stage fright, hence the violin solo in last week's concert.

They talked so long that it was later than Blue had intended before Foster and Anthony walked her home. She should have phoned Delphine to warn her that Foley might be in the area again, she realised in alarm. Horrors — she wasn't thinking straight since Midge had left. Eleven o'clock was late to telephone a private home, especially that of an elderly couple, but it was too important to wait until morning. She telephoned Paul and Sylvia, hoping she wouldn't wake the babies. Paul understood.

'Delphine's fine,' he reassured her. 'I've just come back from there and she went to bed while I was there. I said goodnight to her myself.'

'Oh, thank goodness,' said Blue. 'I'd never forgive myself if anything had happened.'

'It's the last thing she'll want to hear at this time of night,' said Paul. 'I'll let her have a good night's sleep and I'll go round first thing to tell her to be extra careful. We've all become a bit slack lately. It's been so long since he made an appearance. We'd better redouble our efforts.'

'I agree,' said Blue, sighing inwardly. As if there wasn't enough to fret about.

# Chapter Sixty-two

———◦⌒◦———

The following morning, Kenneth passed on Blue's news to Inspector Cromley. Then Blue telephoned the Greenbows.

'I haven't seen her like I planned,' said Paul, sounding harassed. 'Oscar's been sick all night. He's screaming blue murder and hot as a clam. Sylvia hasn't slept and we were trying to get hold of the doctor and we lost all track of time. By the time I remembered, she'd gone out, but it's all right, Miss Blue, she's not alone. Sid's with her. We'll tell them as soon as they come back.'

'Well, that's something. Thank you, Paul. I hope Oscar's better very soon.'

Blue felt more frustrated than ever. Feeling powerless was the most soul-destroying thing. There was nothing she could do about Midge; there was nothing she could do about Foley. Jobless, she was like a Victorian heroine, wringing her hands and pacing the halls. It didn't suit her very well. The worst of it was that she couldn't write. It had been hard enough before, but now, confronted by a blank page, her mind flapped in every direction like a trapped bat, preventing her from attaining the cool, still stream of mental peace that was needed to write even an article. Of the novel, there was not a whisper from the muse.

She flung herself on the new sofa in the drawing room, so much more comfortable than the old one, she had to admit. It made her think of Midge and she suffered a painful stab of tenderness, nostalgia and fury all over again. How were you supposed to come to terms with something when every single thing in your home reminded you of it and scrubbed at the wound? She took up the newspapers.

The outside world mirrored Blue's personal chaos. It was the fourth of May. The General Strike had begun. It was unsurprising. There had been negotiations over the last three days, debate and preparation for the last nine months, and rumblings for a long while before that. For two days now, a million coal miners had been locked out of their mines. The mine owners wanted them to work longer hours for less money. Kenneth had laughed when he first read that.

'Seriously?' he marvelled. 'With the poverty that's already strangling this country and the disarray since the war? And now they want them to work for *less*?' That was before Midge vanished. Kenneth hadn't taken much interest in current affairs since.

But Blue found that here at last was something to take her mind off her own concerns. Some of the newspapers were intent on branding the strikers as revolutionaries. Of course there would be some who would take the opportunity to cause as much trouble as possible, but as for the rest, Blue couldn't see how their cause could be seen as anything but reasonable. No one could help that coal production had dwindled, but there seemed to be a distinct refusal from the owners to weather their share of the ups and downs of the industry; a family couldn't live on the wages they were proposing.

So today was the first full day of action. Between 1.5 and 1.75 million workers were striking, read Blue. Which of the *Gazette* reporters would be covering it? No doubt Cauderlie would have bagged himself the choicest stories. Perhaps Griggs would be out there, seeing this strange new world. She doubted *he* would be sent to tea parties!

A light rap on the door brought Avis before her. 'Visitors for you, Miss Blue. Miss Forrester and a Mr Tanner. Do you want me to make your excuses?'

Blue sat up hastily, the broadsheets slithering all over the floor. 'No! No, thank you, Avis. I'll see them. Please bring them in!'

It was as if her thoughts had conjured them! Their arrival felt like a river in the middle of a desert. She felt like greeting them by declaiming, 'Hail, life-bringers!' That might send them packing pretty sharpish!

She leapt off the sofa and hastily tidied her hair in the mirror over the mantel, tucking long strands into some sort of order. She patted her cheeks, wishing she were wearing a little make-up. Barnaby had only ever seen her dressed for work before. Thank the Lord she'd changed her silky robe for actual clothes, albeit a slouchy old skirt and blouse of the variety so despised by Merrigan.

'Would you like me to bring some tea, Miss Blue?'

'No thanks, Avis. I'll ring if we want some.' Instinct told Blue that if two reporters were on her doorstep today of all days, it wasn't so they could sit around and drink tea.

'Blue, *darling*!' Juno, in one of her more outlandish turbans, a sort of sage green with silver embellishments and a small ornamental pony tucked into the folds, enfolded her in a cloud of Emeraude by Coty. 'How *are* you? How's your divine family?'

'Er . . .'

'Ishbel. Blue.' Barnaby smiled and shook her hand. 'I hope you don't mind us descending like this.'

'I'm so far from minding you can't imagine!' said Blue. Feeling herself blush, she bent to pick up the newspapers. 'Would you like to sit?'

'Just for an instant,' said Juno, sitting on the very edge of a chair as though, if she relaxed into it too much, indolence might swallow her. Barnaby perched on the end of the sofa.

'What brings you? And how are you both? It really is awfully good to see you.'

'You too,' said Barnaby. 'And what's brought us is the strike, of course.'

'I was just reading about it.'

'We knew you would be. Now, Blue, have you been commissioned to cover the strike? Have you plans to go out and interview the workers, anything of that sort?' demanded Juno, businesslike.

'No, nothing. I wish I did. It's intolerable to be sitting here with something so important going on. I could just *go* of course, write something speculatively, but well, things here . . . It hasn't been possible, that's all.'

'Well, quite right!' said Juno, looking appalled at the very thought of it. 'A strike is no place for a woman alone – even I know that! Gordon's all for keeping us out of the line of fire altogether, dinosaur that he is, but I say send us in with a colleague and let us do our jobs! That's why we've come for you.'

'For me?'

'Gordon was saying the other day that he wished you were still with us with all this going on,' Barnaby explained. 'I think he wanted you to come in for a week or so – an extra pen, so to speak – but the budget didn't allow. That's what gave me the idea. *Us* the idea.'

*It was Barney's idea!* thought Blue.

'We knew you'd want to get stuck in, so of course we came.' Juno beamed.

'Of course you did,' said Blue, with her first real smile in days. 'I should change, just quickly. Can you wait two minutes?'

'Just two,' agreed Barnaby.

Blue took the stairs two at a time and threw on something more substantial, then hammered back down again. 'Let's go!' she said, grabbing the nearest hat from the hall. One of Midge's, as it happened. Another pang.

# Chapter Sixty-three

Delphine loved having Sid accompany her on her errands. He carried her basket and walked at her side. As they strolled from shop to shop, she indulged in a little daydream that they were man and wife and this a regular occurrence. When she'd woken up she felt sad, remembering that Merrigan wouldn't be joining her today because she was beside herself about Midge. And Midge couldn't join her because she was gone. It had posed a practical problem, too, until Sid appeared, wanting breakfast and a refuge from a poorly Oscar's screams. He had a day off because he'd worked all weekend planting some imported saplings from Japan. And Delphine's problem was solved.

It all took longer than usual, partly because they loitered, enjoying this time together, and partly because in every shop, in the post office and the bank, they became embroiled in discussions about the General Strike.

'Revolutionaries, every last one!' said Mr Pike the cobbler Delphine needed to have two pairs of Fanny's shoes reheeled.

'We'll all be murdered in our beds before long. I shouldn't wonder if none of us sees the week out.'

'Courageous folk!' commented Mr Frobisher at the bank. 'A line must be drawn; a point must be made. Not easy to stand up to the system.' And he sighed and went back to stamping loan applications.

'It's all very well,' exclaimed a well-dressed lady in the milliner's. 'One does feel terribly sorry for these poor folk and all that. Only it's playing merry hell with my plans! I was going to visit my cousin in Reigate tomorrow, but they say the trains might not be running then *either*!'

Delphine paid Sylvia's bill and she and Sid grinned at each other.

Then a mundane little succession of events occurred, so unremarkable in themselves that afterwards Delphine could hardly believe they led to the outcome they did. First of all, Sid noticed the time. 'We must go back,' he said ruefully. 'I promised Paul I'd be home by twelve. He wants my help with something.'

On their way, they happened across one of Sylvia's friends, Annette Bryce, who was trying to wrestle a fractious baby into a pram. The baby was writhing so spectacularly that Delphine suspected he would buck right out of Annette's arms and crack his head on the pavement. If he survived that, he'd likely grow up to be an Olympic gymnast.

Annette had to take the furious child to the baby clinic and begged Delphine to go with them.

'I can't handle him all alone,' she said, flustered. 'So help me, I can't. We've got five dogs – huge Great Danes – and I walk them all at once without turning a hair. But one small baby and I'm unmanned. Say you've got time, Delphine. I'll buy you cake afterwards.'

'She can't,' said Sid. 'I have to walk her home.'

'*I'll* walk her home!' promised Annette wildly. 'It's a nice day for a walk. No problem there!'

'I don't mind,' said Delphine to Sid. 'Annette does look as if she could do with a hand, and it won't take long. As long as Annette takes me home, what harm can it do?'

'You're *sure* you'll be able to accompany her afterwards, Mrs Bryce?'

'Lord, yes! Off you go, Mr Birch, and leave her to me.'

But, as it happened, Annette couldn't walk Delphine home. On their way out of the clinic, one of the pram wheels caught on the doorstep. It skewed in its socket and Annette couldn't push it any more. So it was decided that she should leave it at the clinic until it could be repaired, and she would carry the baby home. When she lifted him out, he started yelling and wriggling once more. They were five minutes from Annette's home and ten minutes in the opposite direction from Delphine's. It seemed cruel to insist that Annette walk so far out of her way under the circumstances, and Delphine feared for baby Bryce's skull if she did.

'Go,' she said. 'Forget about the cake and get him home.'

'Are you sure? But Mr Birch . . . I promised!'

'It's fine,' said Delphine firmly. 'We'll have cake another day. Go on, Annette, truly.' It was broad daylight, and Richmond was busy. What harm could it do?

But as she walked, she suspected she'd done the wrong thing. She should have telephoned someone to come and meet her from the clinic. Or asked Annette just to walk her as far as the police station; someone there would have seen her right. But it hadn't occurred to her, because a simple walk home really shouldn't present such an enormous difficulty.

Well, it was done now. She was halfway there. She'd be back in a few moments and Fanny would smile from her comfy chair in the parlour and all would be well.

She was passing the Cricketers when a sudden burst of male laughter, nasty and belligerent, made her jump out of her skin and whip round. But it came from inside, it was nothing to do with her, and she laid a hand over her heart in relief. She sped up her footsteps and ran smack into a hard body. Immediately a hand gripped each of her arms, above the elbow, and her husband's voice said:

'Still a nervous little thing, ain'tcha, Delphine? Still a frightened little sparrow.'

Delphine looked up and laid eyes on Foley. So it had come. He had come. For a brief, deceptive moment, she felt calm. So be it. He had harassed and hounded her all through those months without even showing his face. It was almost a *relief* that

that was over. Perhaps her new life, her new-found confidence, would prove a match for him; perhaps she could stand up to him at last. But when she opened her voice to speak, nothing came out. That was how she knew she was terrified after all.

# Chapter Sixty-four

In the event, Blue's day as an intrepid freelance reporter was rather anticlimactic. The principal effect of the strike on its first day was to paralyse the transport systems. Barnaby had managed to borrow a car from a friend to drive into central London, but everyone else who needed to be there had had the same idea. The roads were busy; plans were in chaos; people were in uproar. So they contented themselves with interviewing whomever they could find within a small radius once they got as far as Piccadilly.

Even so, it was a relief to Blue to be out of the house and away from Richmond altogether. Without the imperative of a specific assignment, she could adopt a different focus from Juno and Barnaby. She gathered as much human-interest detail as possible, from the points of view of both the strikers and those affected by the strike. She wasn't sure yet how she would use all this information, but it felt good to have a project again, something to push her cares away. But when they returned to Richmond that afternoon, all her worries came flooding back. They dropped Juno at the office and then Barnaby drove Blue home.

'They haven't found your friend's husband, I suppose?' he asked when they were alone.

'Sadly not,' said Blue. 'It all went very quiet for a time, but I think I saw him the other night . . .' The drive up the hill was short; they were at Ryan's Castle already. 'Well, thanks very much for the lift,' she said. 'And for today. I'm really very glad you both thought of me.' She wondered about inviting him in, but her father was as bad as he had been in the days after her mother died – sometimes silent and staring, sometimes raging, sometimes pacing the rooms, laying out plans of action. Sometimes he appeared to be absent altogether, closeted away in his study or bedroom, only to appear suddenly and startle Blue half to death. He railed at Midge's behaviour throughout, swearing that he would never forgive her. It wasn't the best climate for entertaining – not anyone you might wish to return, anyway.

'A pleasure. I'm sorry it wasn't more useful. I say, Blue, do you need to get back right away or shall we snatch a quick drink? I miss our chats in the Roebuck.'

'Do you? So do I, as a matter of fact. I'd love to.'


Back in the Roebuck, Barnaby went to the bar. Waiting at a small window table, Blue felt a sudden unexpected spurt of happiness. How could she feel happy amidst the carnage of her beloved family? Was it even allowed? At last she under-stood, or caught a glimpse into understanding, what people meant when they talked about living for the moment. After this, she would go home to a gloomy, Midge-less house, and tomorrow Foley would still be at large. One hour in the pub with Barnaby wouldn't change that. Yet it felt like such a rich and welcome reprieve that the enjoyment of it would sustain her for quite some time.

He reappeared with a pint of mild for himself and a lemonade for Blue. 'Shall we sit outside? We've never had the weather to do it before. And it's not your typical view, is it?'

Blue agreed. They took their drinks and crossed the road, Barnaby holding her elbow lightly. It was the same sort of soft, dusky late afternoon as yesterday, though she hadn't been in any mood to appreciate the weather then. She shivered, remembering the running footsteps behind her. She wouldn't be taking that sort of risk again in a hurry.

The view certainly was spectacular: an expanse of meadows far below; the bow and bend of the silver river, thick at the edges with willow and oak. Blue knew it well, but it was all the better for being absorbed with a drink, in good company. They sat on a bench and nodded at the other folk admiring the gauzy beauty of a late spring afternoon. The Star and Garter Hotel, with its pointed tower, gave the vista a fairy-tale quality.

Blue sighed and sat back. 'So tell me about the office,' she said. 'How is Griggs settling back? Is Cauderlie as obnoxious as ever? Who's covering the tea parties?'

Barnaby laughed. 'Griggs is glad to be back. Grateful to

Whisky for keeping his job; grateful to you for keeping it warm. He's a nice lad, but we all miss you, Blue. And yes, Cauderlie *is* as obnoxious as ever, so you're not missing anything there. The tea parties . . . Well, Juno did a few. Then she put her foot down and they've been divided between Will and Spencer ever since.' He grinned at the thought. 'Can you imagine *Spencer* observing the niceties? It could be the end of social reporting as we know it.'

'And how is your family? And the novel?' Blue found herself firing questions at him, hungry for the continuity of their old friendship, wanting to recapture a time when Midge had still been home and things made some sort of sense.

Barnaby started telling her a few funny stories about his sisters that actually made her laugh. A miracle. But when it was Blue's turn to say something, she realised she didn't have any funny stories *or* much good news – a depressing state of affairs.

'Foster is much better,' she said, looking hard for positives. 'I truly dare to hope he's turned a corner now. I won't go into it all, as it's his business, but he does seem happier.'

Barnaby nodded. 'I'm very glad to hear it. And what did you start to tell me earlier about Foley?'

Blue filled him in about her nerve-wracking walk by the river.

'I'm so glad you're safe,' he said. 'I know it's hideous to be curtailed and fearful, but Blue, if I can ever escort you anywhere, I hope you know I'll do it gladly. Too many people need you to be safe and happy.'

Blue nodded. Happy was a bit of a stretch at the moment, but she should be able to manage safe, at least. And Barnaby was so kind, she wasn't sure she trusted herself to speak. *Genial. Benevolent. Caring. Wonderful!* She sipped her lemonade.

'And dare I ask . . . How is the story of Richmond's darling's courtship by letter progressing? Cauderlie's devastated at the loss of an inside track – not to mention the chance to torment you about it daily. Needless to say, I ask as a friend, not a columnist!'

Blue blushed. How embarrassing that Barney knew about all that. Then again, everyone at the *Gazette* did. 'Nothing to report. It's all gone very quiet. The two chaps I was seeing a bit of are friends, nothing more. Oh, will I ever live this down?' Although, in truth, she had much bigger worries now.

Barnaby grinned. 'Possibly not. And how's your family?'

The question she'd been dreading. 'My sister's expecting a baby in two months.'

'That's lovely news.'

'It is.' There was a telling silence where Blue would normally have elaborated. Barnaby was looking out over the meadows, where cows meandered between the oaks, little black dots. 'The rest is complicated. But I'm afraid you'll think everything is complicated with me.'

He turned to look at her. 'Not at all. You've had a run of bad luck lately though, haven't you? Not more trouble, I hope?' His dark eyes were warm and concerned.

'Yes, I'm afraid so.' And so Blue told him about Midge, and Percy, and how the family had become a reduced, splintered version of itself. When she'd told him she felt . . . not better, exactly, but more detached.

'Here it is,' he said, sketching a rough ball in the air with his hands. 'Everything you've told me, the whole situation and all the feelings it gives you. Now it can float off over the meadows and disappear over the horizon. In fact, let's help it.' He started to blow, noisily, as if he were blowing a balloon away. Blue watched in astonishment for a moment but when he nudged her, she started blowing too, one puff after another until the whole sad story was far away and she was completely out of breath and laughing again. The other drinkers, the strollers and birdwatchers, looked at them rather strangely, which, when Blue noticed, made her laugh all the harder.

'There,' said Barnaby. 'See, it's just a cloud of *stuff*. It won't feel like this forever, Blue.'

Blue looked at him. It was true, she knew. For the present it was impossible to see how any of it could resolve, but somehow, one day, it would. And, despite everything, there were still blessings to be counted. She had her father, Merrigan, Lawrence, Cicely and the new baby. She had Ryan's Castle and her ambitions and her friends. She lived in a beautiful place, was materially abundant and could walk in three minutes from her house to this magical spot. And there was this moment with Barnaby. He was like a lucky charm.

She looked straight at him. 'You're a very kind man,' she told him.

He smiled. 'I hope so. And you are a very special lady, if I may say so. Don't forget that. If you ever need a friend, please don't hesitate to call on me.'

'Thank you, Barney. I really do appreciate that and I may very well take you up on it. Do you . . . do you perhaps have a telephone number I might take?'

'We don't, no. But you can always call me at the office, or leave a note. Perhaps I could have your number?'

'Absolutely.' Blue scribbled it down on the dainty silver-clasped notepad that she always carried and handed him the slip of paper. He put it carefully in his breast pocket.

'And if you wanted to,' he said, 'although it might not suit with all you have going on at the moment, we could maybe make another arrangement. Say for a week's time? Something to look forward to?'

'It would be, yes.'

He smiled, looking pleased, though not half so pleased as Blue, she would have been prepared to wager. Something to look forward to? It felt like a lifeline.

'Can I ask you something else?' he said.

'Of course!'

'I've been wondering – and you did say you'd tell me one day – why do they call you Blue?'

Blue laughed, amazed that he somehow didn't already know.

He felt so much a part of her life that it seemed he must know everything about her. But of course that wasn't the case at all.

'Oh yes, I'd forgotten about that. Well, when I was very small, my parents used to take me to Richmond Park in the summer. We still go – we Camberwells are mad for picnics. Anyway, when I was little I was just obsessed with the common blues.'

Barnaby cocked a questioning eyebrow. 'Oxbridge athletes from a working-class background?'

Blue snorted, choking on her lemonade. Bubbles shot up her nose. 'It's a butterfly.'

'Ah. I don't know much about butterflies.'

'Oh, they're beautiful. Small and pretty and the most *wonderful* colour – a very soft, misty, sort of blue, with a hint of lilac. Princess blue, I used to call it as a child, because I thought that was the exact colour that a princess ought to wear. Midge, bless her, hunted down some fabric in that very colour to make me a dress for my twenty-first . . .' Blue trailed off, frowning.

'She had a lot of love in her heart,' observed Barnaby, 'alongside all her troubles.'

'Yes. Apparently it took her *months* to find the right colour, so she had to make the dress in five days or something. She was at it all hours, sewing on these tiny, glittering beads . . . A real labour of love.'

'You mean the world to her.'

Blue felt like crying, thinking of Midge working her

fingers to the bone for Blue to have the perfect colour to wear, just once, on her special occasion. A dress as fragile as a butterfly wing, with love in every stitch. Never mind her father's toast, thought Blue, there had to be magic in *that*. But months later, Midge had run from the house, never to return. All the furious things Blue had thought about her lately came rushing back. Then she rallied. She had been telling Barnaby about her name.

'When I was small, I used to run around in the park chasing the butterflies – not the white ones or the brown ones, only the common blues. I used to shout, "Blue! Blue!" And I'd get very annoyed at picture books where the princesses wore pink or yellow. I'd smack the books and say, "Blue! Blue!" So it stuck. Pretty soon they were all calling me Blue and I was only ever Ishbel when I was naughty. "Ishbel Christina! Stop that at once!"' She grinned, remembering how often she'd heard that.

'That's a wonderful story,' said Barnaby. 'And Blue suits you. Far better than Ishbel, I think. I'd love to see a common blue, so I can picture this colour that had you so besotted as a child.'

'We could go for a walk in the park sometime, if you like. It's May, so they should be just starting to emerge, and they'll be around for a few months yet.'

'You're on.'

He dropped her home and Blue ran through the arch of yew that framed the gateway of Ryan's Castle. She wanted to linger and daydream, but she knew Barnaby would watch until she was inside, so with a quick wave she went in.

She would go into the garden, she decided, drift under the apple trees, think about their conversation and what it might mean. But there was Elf, pacing in the hall, and there was her father, his face ashen. So it was to be one of those nights again.

'My darling,' Kenneth said, coming to hold her close – her strong, dependable father once again. 'I'm so sorry to be the bearer of yet more bad news. It hardly seems possible that so much could go wrong.'

'What?' asked Blue, stricken with fear. 'Is it Midge?'

'It's Delphine. She's vanished. I've just been at the police station. They're pretty sure Foley's got her.'

# Chapter Sixty-five

The road was busy with cars because of the strike. Progress was slow and it would have been easy for Delphine to jump out and run but for two things. The first was that she knew she couldn't move as fast as Foley. The man was like lightning striking. Delphine knew this from a hundred punches delivered invisibly; recoil and strike in a splinter of a second, like a cat unleashing a paw on an unsuspecting mouse.

The other thing that kept Delphine glued to the front seat of the black Lancia was that Foley had Midge. Apparently she was locked up in their old house in Whitechapel, where she would remain until Delphine was back where she belonged. Foley had told her so as they'd stood on the green in the sunshine.

'Then I'll let her go.' He'd shrugged. 'She's no more use to me after that.'

*But Midge will run straight to get help*, Delphine wanted to say. *She'll find a constable, call Kenneth and they'll rescue me.* But all she managed was, 'B . . . b . . . b . . .'

Foley laughed. 'Bravo, Foley?' he suggested. 'Bright boy,

master plan, I know, I know. Come on then, love, let's get you home. Oh, how I've missed your smiling face.' His sarcasm had always been especially cutting.

It disgusted Delphine that, after all this time and so much change, she still let him take her so easily. He had the Lancia parked nearby, at the edge of the green. It took maybe a minute to reach it, then he opened the door and helped her inside, the picture of the solicitous husband. She was stunned and disbelieving, even though they'd all been expecting exactly this. It went to show how powerful a level of denial had been at work, allowing her to get through her days. If it *were* true, if he really did have Midge, and Delphine somehow managed to escape . . . he might go straight back there and hurt her. So she sat, docile, while he ran around to the driver's side and hopped in. Then, without fuss or bother, he just drove them away.

He looked the same. He had the brownest eyes, which she had liked when they were courting, but they turned black with intent when he was angry with her. They were black now, despite his smile and easy tone of voice. No one on Richmond Green would have guessed he was bent on trouble – unless they'd happened to notice his fingertips digging into her arms. His brown hair had a few fine strands of grey, but they weren't new, and his features were foxy as ever, slim and definite.

In her mind, Delphine heaped blessings on the General Strike; the time on the road was a reprieve. The longer that lay between now and whatever awaited her, the better.

She was glad, too, that he didn't say very much. After a few remarks early on in the journey, prodding her to admire the Lancia that he'd 'borrowed', sneering at the gracious houses and grassy spaces of Richmond, he fell into a gritty silence. 'No conversation to be had with you,' was his last comment. 'Takes too long for you to spit something out.' As if he'd ever had the faintest interest in what she had to say. It gave Delphine time to think. She tried to tell herself that the situation wasn't that bad, though really she knew it was.

She reminded herself that she had friends now, that the police were looking for Foley and that she would soon be missed. But how would they find her? And by the time they did, who knew what Foley would have done to her? She shuddered, remembering her old life.

The memories stood alongside images of her new life: walks along the riverbank, tea in the drawing room at Ryan's Castle, the magnolia tree outside her window and her journal on the little desk. Images of beauty, dignity and a way of life based on kindness and becoming the best you could be. They made the violence and degradation look all the uglier by contrast. In the old days, Delphine had been able, somehow, to endure. Now she couldn't imagine how she had. Before, she'd switched off every part of herself that had ever wanted love, that had ever dared to dream the world could be a beautiful place. Now she knew too much of how life *could* be to do that again. But she wouldn't unlive these last nine months, even so. Whatever happened to her now, she would hold those memories close; something to treasure when the world went dark again.

Crowding buildings, grumbling automobiles, grey roads. She couldn't really tell where they were. She had never negotiated the city by car before. Without tube stations and bus stops, the journey made no sense to her. A dozen times she imagined grabbing the door handle, flinging herself out and running, losing herself in the crowds. But that she would stay felt inevitable. The very fact of being beside him made her feel as small as one of the common blue butterflies that Blue had once shown her in the park, and just as crushable. She'd been afraid of Foley a long time, and bad habits didn't die easily.

And now Midge's fate depended on Delphine accepting her own. Midge was trapped in that ghastly house where unhappiness radiated off the walls and the roof pushed down on a person, bruising their soul. Strange that he would take Delphine there, she thought suddenly, when that would obviously be the first place they would look for her. A cold dart shot through her. He wouldn't make that mistake: he was too clever. And if he was taking her somewhere else, where was Midge? Had he even taken her at all? He'd needed something to persuade her to come without making a scene, in case fear wasn't enough. If he'd seen Midge leave with a suitcase, that would have been something he could use.

She was coming back to herself now, remembering how clever, how cunning, he was. She sat up straight but before she'd finished adjusting her position his left arm shot out and he grabbed her.

'You ain't goin' anywhere, darlin',' he said.

Darling. For years it had been Delphine's least favourite word. He was the only person who ever called her that, and of course there was no love in it. She hated it when he mocked her, calling her darlin', sweetheart, love. In Richmond it had taken on a new resonance. Terms of endearment were thrown out casually among the Camberwells and their friends. Everyone was a darling in their world. Blue, most of all.

The Lancia turned right and left and it became clear, finally, that they weren't going to the house at all.

'Y . . . y . . . you don't really have M . . . M . . . Midge, d . . . do you?' she asked painfully.

He threw her a scornful glance. 'Course not. What do I need with a skinny bitch like that? Up her own arse and havin' the vapours. I thought about it though. Watched her at the station for half an hour crying while she waited for the Reading train. Thought about whether she might be useful. But all the use I needed was just in tellin' you. Well, don't think you can run away just because you don't have no friend to save. I'd have you on the ground before you crossed the road and don't you think I wouldn't. A soft little head like yours would crack easy as eggs, and wouldn't that be heartbreakin', if a lovin' husband like me accidentally killed his wife while he was chasing after her, begging her not to leave him. Even if she had been cheating on him with a hopalong cripple.'

Of course he knew about Sid. Delphine prayed fervently that when Foley was done with her that would be enough, that he wouldn't go after Sid. A little later they turned between the high stone columns of an imposing entryway and travelled down a long, straight strip, reminiscent of an aeroplane runway that she'd seen in one of Kenneth's books. She knew where she was without asking: Foley's place of employment, the Royal Albert Dock. It was late afternoon, she supposed from the mood of the sky. And because of the strike, the docks were deserted. She swallowed. She wasn't going to return to her nightmarish old life. She didn't need to worry about being another of those grey, downtrodden wives that no one spoke about, whose horror-filled lives went on right under everyone's noses yet were somehow invisible. No. Because Foley didn't want his wife back at all. Foley was going to kill her.

# Chapter Sixty-six

—❧—

'The thing of it is, blasted Cromley's disappeared too!' exclaimed Kenneth, pacing back and forth before the fireplace, almost bursting out of his skin. 'The one time something really happens and no one knows where he is! What worries me is that he hasn't been seen all day, so he doesn't even know Delphine's gone yet!'

'Bad,' said Elf. He was sitting on the edge of a chaise, leaning forward and tapping his fingers ceaselessly on a side table. 'Bad, bad, bad.' *Tap, tap, tap.*

Blue was slumped on the sofa, dizzy with despair. Midge being gone was hard enough, but at least they could hope that she was safe, however unhappy she might be. Leaving had been her choice. With Delphine it was a completely different kettle of fish. Blue wanted to hunt for her, wanted to fight. But how? No one knew where to start.

'To be fair,' Kenneth went on, 'the other chaps at the station seemed pretty clued-up. They knew who I was at once, knew all about it. Cromley's certainly kept them in the picture.

So they've sent men off to all the obvious places: Delphine's former home, her mother's, her sister's. But for heaven's sake, from what she's told us of him, he's not going to take her there, is he? That's why we need Cromley – he'll think a bit more broadly. Hell, I could wring the man's neck. I hate being useless, Blue!'

'Tell me again what happened. I can hardly take it in.' Being flung from the pleasure and respite of her time with Barnaby into this was a stupefying transition.

Kenneth recounted what the police had told him: about Sid needing to rush home and Delphine staying with Annette Bryce and her troublesome baby. When an hour had passed with no Delphine, Stephen had telephoned Ryan's Castle to see if she was there. Kenneth had immediately rung the police. A constable had gone straight to see Annette, and she explained about the pram breaking and Delphine insisting she walk alone. She was distraught, blaming herself.

'As well she might, dizzy woman!' said Kenneth with some wrath.

Sid was beside himself, Elf added. The whole family was in shock. Between them, and despite all their precautions, they'd let her slip through the net. *Tap, tap, tap*.

This time Blue forced herself to listen calmly, to take it in. 'And no one saw her walking home? No one saw her talking to him?'

'They haven't found any witnesses yet. There are a couple of ways she might have walked, but I assume she would've taken the most direct route from the clinic and cut over the green.' Kenneth shrugged. 'But we don't know anything, really.'

'Can we go out anyway?' asked Blue. 'I know the police are looking, and I know it won't be light for very long, but just in case we see something. I can't sit here all night, Daddy, I really can't.'

'Of course we can. We'll look and we'll look. Are you staying here, Elf?'

'Like hell,' said Elf. He stopped his tapping and stood up.

Kenneth nodded. 'And I'll tell you something else, Blue. I'm sick of people disappearing. If we find Delphine, I'll be overjoyed. If we find Midge – and I have to think she'll get in touch at some point, *surely* – she's coming home. I don't care *what* she's done. We'll work it out somehow. Our beautiful life is getting torn to pieces. I've had enough of it.'

'And if we find Cromley?' said Blue, fetching her coat somewhat wearily.

'I really will wring his neck.'

'I only hope Delphine's still nearby,' sighed Blue. 'It's our only chance of finding her before something terrible happens.'

# Chapter Sixty-seven

'Nice of you to take an interest in me place of work,' said Foley with amusement, as Delphine craned her neck to look behind them. She was wishing wildly to see Kenneth's royal blue Duesenberg puttering after them, that *somehow* he might know where she was. But of course, there was no one. It was early evening, the sky mauve. For other people, in other places, it might be quite lovely.

The docks were eerie: a huge, purpose-built expanse of moorings, storehouses, machinery, jetties and walkways, all utterly without purpose on this strange day; fallen motionless, as if their time had passed. Delphine could see a huge square building with covered conveyers leading to the water's edge, and a collection of boats crowded into squared-off sections of water so still that they didn't even bob. These were the lighters, Delphine knew, small barges on which the lightermen, like Foley, carried goods between quay and ship. She remembered the dream she'd been having on the day she arrived by accident in Richmond: bobbing on a boat with Esther, safe and content, then being tipped into the water to drown.

Foley pulled up outside the big square building. Its windows were blank, unkind eyes. He had a key; he opened up and hauled her inside. She didn't offer much resistance: her legs had turned to jelly. She started to absent herself, as she had done so often before, and barely noticed her surroundings. It was cold. There were high ceilings.

'Cold storage,' said Foley. 'Where we keep the carcasses.'

He dragged her down a corridor to an office, shoved her inside and slammed the door. Then he hit her hard across the head and she flew off her feet. She landed on her side and slid across the floor, brought to a halt by a wall. She wanted to stay curled on her side, facing the wall, so that she wouldn't see whatever was coming. But slowly she wriggled around, the pain in her head making her feel sick, and looked up at him from the floor, as she had so often done before.

From underneath a large desk, he heaved a metal safe, and from his pocket he drew a razor blade, wrapped in a hanky. Casting a quick glance at Delphine to make sure she wasn't going anywhere, he started jiggling the lock. Waves of nausea and dread rolled through Delphine as she lolled against the wall. He broke open the safe. Money. A large wad of notes, which he gripped and shook at her.

'My boss,' he announced, 'has been makin' me very annoyed. I'm a professional, a member of me guild. He'd be nowhere without men like me. But do we get a pay rise? No. So I'm taking what I'm owed and I'm leaving on the next boat. Not from here, not with the strike on, but down the river a ways, and from there, the world's me oyster. A young, strong man with money, newly widowed – there'll be lots of opportunities for the likes of me. See, Delphine, you done me a favour when you run away. Made me start questioning me lot. Realised I deserve much better.'

He tucked the money into a deep pocket inside his jacket and came to stand over her. 'Up you get, love.' He pulled her up by the hair and struck her another quick backhander across the side of the face. She felt her eyebrow split. Blood ran down, obscuring her vision. She'd always loathed the feeling of blood in her eyes. She shut her right eye against it, knowing what came next, and sure enough, he shut his own eye, twisting up his mouth, Quasimodo-esque, mimicking her again.

'Cor, you ain't a looker, though,' he said wonderingly. 'What did I ever pick you for?' A quick punch to the stomach – he was nothing if not efficient – and Delphine's legs gave out.

'What you got to realise,' he said patiently, pulling her up by her hair, 'is that for better or worse, you're me *wife*. We took vows, love! That means you don't get to run away from me. That means you don't get to start a new life, or get a job, or kiss other fellas. Just because I don't want you no more don't stop you bein' mine.'

Delphine's ears were ringing, yet over this internal noise she heard a sound outside. Her heart leapt with hope. Foley heard it too and tensed. But it was only the machine-gun rattle of a magpie. She saw the feathered shape flashing at the window, as if it were trying to get in and reach her.

'Daft bird,' said Foley, and she wasn't sure whether he was referring to her or the magpie. 'Come on, sweetheart. I've got to get downriver.'

He frogmarched her out of the office and along the corridor, her feet scrabbling for purchase. Delphine's head was starting to clear. What had he said? Newly widowed? Cold storage? A dock on strike. He was going to leave her here, and who knew when her body would be found. She'd always known, deep down, that he was biding his time, waiting for the perfect moment. And what could be more perfect than this: a city in chaos, a deserted warehouse, even Midge's flight had played a part. Foley had an instinct for these things. He was an outstanding poker player. The fragile, lovely life she had built could never have lasted, she realised. Sooner or later, his moment was always going to come.

Even so, when she saw the door looming at the end of the corridor, she knew she couldn't go quietly. She just couldn't. Although she wanted it to be over and she knew it was hopeless, she *needed* to fight back, even just once. She'd die happier for that. His hold on her arm was quite loose, really – well, she was hardly fighting fit – and suddenly Delphine had the fancy that the door to the cold storage facility, with its silent sides of meat hanging in the darkness, was at one end of the corridor, while Blue and Sid and all the rest were at the other, behind her, waiting in the fading light.

Holding them in her mind's eye, she stamped on Foley's foot, jabbed an elbow in his stomach, as hard as she could, then twisted out of his grip and ran. Her head wound was pouring and her legs felt only loosely sewn on, yet fury gave her speed. Perhaps she'd landed a lucky blow on a sensitive spot, for it was a full minute before she heard his footsteps pounding after her. Delphine was nearing the door, she could see the purple sky beyond, and a plan flashed fully formed into her mind. If she could just get *out*, she could hide in the water, amongst the jumble of boats. If he went searching far enough for her in the wrong direction, she might run to the road . . . Then she fell heavily, with Foley on top of her. She felt him turn her over, his whole weight pinning her.

So far, he'd been quite pleasant, for Foley. But now the face of her nightmares was back, as if whatever shred of humanity had lingered in him had vanished. He was holding the razor blade he'd used to jimmy the safe. Delphine closed her eyes. Thought of Blue. Of Sid. Of all the Greenbows and Camberwells. She felt herself starting to fade away again, but she pulled herself back and looked right into his eyes. 'I hate you,' she said, without a trace of a stammer. And then she heard another noise outside. Not a magpie. An engine.

Foley rocked back on his heels, wearing an expression of real shock. And Delphine knew it must be someone coming for her, for why would anyone else come here today? But how? And were they too late?

A car door slammed right outside the warehouse and dark shadows fell across her. Her eyes were full of blood and Foley still gripped her. Then she did slip away, away from Foley, from the fear and pain, and now, most terribly, the hope. Everything went black.

Delphine had always loved the relief of fainting. When she came to, something had always changed. Usually it was just that Foley had left the house for a while, but back then even that was a blessing. Today though, she was heartbroken to find that she was still lying on the cold warehouse floor, with the high grey ceiling above. She wondered what had happened to whoever arrived in that car. She turned her head slowly and winced at the pain that crackled down her neck and across her skull. She tried to wipe her eyes, but everything hurt.

'You're awake.' The voice was familiar, but she couldn't place it. 'Don't try to move. I've called for an ambulance. You'll be fine, but you've got some nasty injuries. Just stay still for now.'

Definitely not Foley. But it was too much to believe that she was safe. Just then, Delphine wanted two things more than anything in the world: to be out of that cold, square building, and to understand.

'Wh . . . where's . . . ?' It wasn't her stammer causing her trouble, but the fact that her mouth was swollen and sore.

'Your husband? Gone. Just stay still – not much longer now.'

'I c . . . can't . . .' She struggled to sit up. She needed to know. 'Who are you?'

'Wait. If you must move, I'll help.' Strong arms came under her armpits and helped her to sit; a hand supported her head. A man's overcoat was thrown over her for warmth, she noticed. 'I'm sorry, I thought you'd know me. It's Inspector Cromley.'

'Inspector?' she mumbled. Of all the people in this world *least* likely to be watching over Delphine, cradling her head and reassuring her, Foley was top of her list and this man was second. 'I can't see very well. But . . . when you say he's gone?'

'Foley's dead, Mrs Foley.'

'Dead? *How?*' It took her a moment to absorb it. Foley being dead was better than Foley being in prison. You could come back from prison. If it were true, then it really *was* over. It didn't seem right to be happy about someone dying, and yet it was too good to believe. For a wild moment, she feared she might have killed him in the struggle, that her fear and loathing and desperation had somehow *made* this come about. She wouldn't ever choose to end a life, however rotten. But if it had just *happened* . . .

'It's a long story. Let's get you to the hospital, wait till you have some family around and then I'll tell you – official, like.'

'But he's really dead?'

'Really.'

463

'Then I don't care what happened. As long as I didn't do it, I don't care if he got hit on the head by a flying pineapple.'

Through the haze she saw his lips twitch. 'Close,' he said. 'But won't you rest now?'

Delphine next awoke in hospital, with morning sunshine falling into an unlovely ward. Blue, Kenneth and Inspector Cromley were all sitting round her bed, as well as another man she didn't recognise. She squinted in his direction and he leaned forward to shake her hand – gently.

'Hello, Delphine. It's Barney. Barnaby Tanner from the *Gazette*. But I'm definitely *not* here in a professional capacity, rest assured.'

'Blue's Barnaby?' she murmured.

'If you like.' She thought she heard a smile in his voice at the thought of being Blue's Barnaby. She'd had a feeling.

'We shouldn't have let you out of our sight, not for one minute,' said Kenneth. 'My dear, I'm so sorry you had to go through that. I'll never forgive myself for handling it all so badly.'

He looked old, suddenly, thought Delphine. He'd aged dramatically when Midge left, and now, instead of looking young and debonair for his age, he looked tired and grey.

'Your poor face,' said Blue. 'Your poor arm, your poor head. It's all our fault.'

'What? No!' Her lips still felt fat and painful, but Delphine was determined to make them understand. 'You've all been wonderful. You *are* wonderful! And it's over. Inspector Cromley said he's . . .?' She remembered the wonderful, improbable truth that she'd learned lying on the warehouse floor. *How?*

'Yes, he's dead,' confirmed Kenneth. Delphine could hardly hear it enough.

Inspector Cromley cleared his throat. 'Mrs Foley, I need to speak to you about that, when you're up to it.'

'As long as I'm not in any trouble,' said Delphine. She still could hardly believe that an outcome so beneficial to her had been reached and she wasn't to be blamed or held accountable in any way. Foley had made her feel that *everything* was her fault.

The inspector shook his head. 'Not you, Mrs Foley. But he was your husband, after all. I must tell you what happened.'

Delphine nodded. 'Whenever you like, Inspector. But please don't call me Mrs Foley any more. I haven't thought of myself that way for a very long time, and now it's legal, isn't it? I can be Delphine Painter again. And you' – she looked at Blue and Kenneth – 'must realise you have *nothing* to apologise for. It was always going to happen – that's what I realised when I was trapped with him. You did everything you could. And it could've been much worse,' she concluded, remembering his blow sending her flying across the office, her conviction that she was going to die there. Yet here she was with a new day dawning and friends around her bedside. 'I got off lightly, really.'

'It wouldn't have been very light if we hadn't got there when we did,' observed Cromley. 'He'd have killed you. I wouldn't call that light.'

'Neither would I. But that's just it: the worst of it was thinking I'd never see any of you again, not . . .' She gestured vaguely at her wounds. 'Where are we anyway?'

'The Poplar Hospital, my dear,' Kenneth said. 'It was too far to take you to the Mile End, even though that's nearer your mother. She's on her way here now, though it may take her a while, with the strike.'

Blue helped Delphine to sit up. There were pillows behind her and Blue's cardigan was draped around her shoulders. She encouraged her to sip a little water, then a nurse came to check her dressings and finally they told her what had happened.

It transpired that while Kenneth had been cursing Cromley for going missing just when they needed him most, Cromley had actually been one step ahead.

'That man followed you everywhere, Miss Painter,' he explained. 'When you walked to Kew with that young relative of your employers, when you visited the Camberwells at their home, when you lunched with Mrs Camberwell or Miss Merrigan – *everywhere*.'

Delphine shuddered.

'I believe he must have been trained as a tracker during the war, miss. No other way he could've learned the skills he had. You were completely unaware, I daresay.'

'I was.'

'In different circumstances, I might have admired his methods. Only one mistake he made, only one thing tripped him up.'

'What was that, Inspector?'

Cromley smiled a little complacently. 'He was so intent on being the perfect hunter that he failed to notice he was also the quarry. All the time he was following you, I was following him.'

'*Everywhere?*'

'Everywhere. I haven't slept in days. It was just like you said, miss. He was biding his time.'

'Waiting for the perfect moment.'

'Just so. I could see it in everything he did. He was calculating, calculating all the time. I knew his moment would come and I wanted him to have it. If I'd arrested him before, what would I have got? Trespassing? Loitering? Even if we'd gone historical and got him on assault and battery, it wasn't enough to put him away like I wanted to. I wanted to give him enough rope to hang himself, as they say.'

Delphine shivered. He had very nearly hanged her along with him.

'Only thing I didn't reckon on was how quickly he'd strike when he did. One minute he was talking to you outside the Cricketers . . .'

'You were there?' The thought gave Delphine a kind of

wonder. Guardian angels came in all shapes and sizes, it seemed, even six foot two and burly, clad in a blue uniform.

'I was. One minute you were talking, the next minute you were in the car, driving off. He moves fast – *moved* fast – your husband. No time to fetch a colleague, no time to let anyone know where I was going. I commandeered a vehicle and followed.'

'You did? Oh, *thank* you, Inspector. Thank you so much. If only I'd known. I thought there was no way anyone could find me.' To think that she had always believed Cromley was disapproving and unsympathetic, and here he had put himself out to the nth degree and stuck with her doggedly to the final grizzly outcome.

She learned how the inspector had crawled out of Richmond, three cars behind Delphine and Foley. He'd spotted Eric Stanley, the newest recruit from the police station, walking along the street. He wound down the window and bellowed at the young constable to get in. 'Not who I would've chosen to support me in a mission like that,' he admitted, 'but he did a sterling job, I must say. Just as well he was there, the way things panned out. I was very glad to have a witness.'

'Where is he now?' wondered Delphine.

'Still at the dock, clearing up the scene – taking care of . . . everything.' He cleared his throat. Delphine swallowed. Here it came.

'We got held up near the docks, miss, and lost you for a

while, but by then it was clear that he was taking you to his place of work. When we arrived at Royal Albert, miss, we saw the car outside the cold storage facility. You'd been there alone with him too long. We ran in to find you lying on the floor, badly beaten. He was crouched over you, holding a razor blade . . . I'll never forget the look on his face. He knew he was clever, didn't he? He couldn't believe he'd been caught out. I've seen some nasty sorts in my time' – Cromley shook his head – 'but I've never seen a cold soul like that.'

Blue sighed and squeezed Delphine's hand.

Foley had taken off. With Cromley and Stanley blocking the doorway, he sped back towards the cold storage. It was dark in there, and Foley knew the layout while Cromley did not. Cromley shot at him – but missed. He shot again and grazed his leg; Foley came tumbling down. The policemen ran but Foley was up and fleeing again.

'Half the speed this time, mind you. Blood pouring. But he still got there before us, disappeared from sight in a minute. I was beside myself. I'd followed him too long to let him get away now. Then I saw him again, darting between the carcasses hanging from the ceiling, heading for one of them conveyors that lead out to the ships. If he'd reached it, miss, he'd have been straight down it and out of there. A million places for him to hide, between the piers and the lighters and the dolphins.'

'Dolphins?' said Blue, frowning.

Delphine smiled. She could see Blue's writerly imagination

conjuring pictures of beautiful sea creatures cavorting between the jetties of the London docks.

'It's what they call the boat moorings there, Miss Camberwell. Now, Mrs F— Miss Painter. Those carcasses are heavy. They're hung from iron hooks. But a few of them were hung with rope. I don't know why. I wouldn't have noticed it myself, I must confess – I was so intent on keeping sight of your husband. But Stanley pointed it out. Good lad, bright future. So I shot at the ropes. I didn't want to shoot your husband – from that range I couldn't be accurate and I didn't want to be hauled up for killing an unarmed man. I just wanted to stop him, Miss Painter. Two of the carcasses fell. And one of them fell on your husband. Flattened him. Dead. Worth his weight in gold, was Stanley yesterday.

'And now that I've told you, I must go and join him, Mrs— Delphine. It's not how I'd imagined things turning out, but I can't say I'm sorry.'

He stood to go, a huge shape blocking the light. Delphine's eyes filled with tears at the thought of what he had done for her. She held out her hand and when he went to shake it, she hung on to him, pressing her face against his huge paw. 'Thank you,' she whispered, and kissed his hand. 'A thousand times thank you for following him, for not giving up, for saving my life. I can never repay you.'

'Nor do you need to, miss. I'm just glad you can start your life properly now. Good day. So long, all.'

After he left, Blue stepped forward to hug Delphine gently. Delphine laid her head back and closed her eyes, still struggling to understand that she really was free now, that Foley would never darken her days again. What an appalling end he had met.

'Goodbye, Foley,' she murmured. 'May you find a greater peace in death than you did in life.'

Just before she slid into peaceful, healing sleep, she heard Blue say, 'Delphine, darling, that's the first time I've ever heard you say his name without stammering!'

# Chapter Sixty-eight

Two days later, Blue woke from the first good night's sleep she'd had in ages. It was such a wonderful feeling that for a moment she felt happy. She could tell without opening her curtains that the day was sunny. She could hear her sister's voice somewhere downstairs and that made her smile. Merrigan had come for breakfast.

In the last few days and nights, she'd hardly slept. They'd come back from the Poplar late yesterday, utterly worn out. Blue had fallen into bed and into a deep sleep, eased by the resolution of at least one enormous worry. Now she woke to the knowledge that Delphine was healing. Anne and Esther were with her and she'd be back in Richmond in just a few days.

Blue would make up the guest room – not that there was much to do. Midge always kept everything so beautifully in readiness. And just like that Blue's mood changed; the sadness was back, lodged into the depth of her being like a solid brick. Midge.

Midge had taken Percy away. Midge was expecting another child. Midge had gone. Blue was now the woman of the house.

She got out of bed and threw on her robe. She knew that if she sat in bed wallowing, the anger and sadness would swallow her spirit for the entire day. It was easy, Blue had learned, to let whatever was wrong, or lacking, colour everything muddy and dark. Far, far harder to keep counting your blessings when everything inside you wanted to shrink away from the outrageous hurt. But counting her blessings was what Blue *had* to do, not because she believed in a stiff upper lip, but because it was the only thing that was going to get her through. And that was what mattered. She would go down to see Merrigan and manage a little breakfast if she could.

She brushed her long blonde hair vigorously. And there *were* blessings, still. Delphine was safe. Not just for the moment, but for good. That was a better outcome than she'd ever dared hope.

And there was Barnaby. On the evening when she'd learned Delphine was missing, she, Elf and her father had raced off in senseless action, because they couldn't do *nothing*. After an hour or two of pounding the streets, asking people the same questions the police had already asked and learning nothing new, they'd passed the *Gazette* office and seen a light on upstairs. Blue had needed to see Barnaby. If he wasn't there, she thought, she would leave him a note. But he was there, of course, writing up his notes from the day into a story about the strike. As it turned out, Barnaby was about to go looking for *them*. He'd just heard from Inspector Cromley, who'd called him when he couldn't reach the Camberwells. Elf went back to Ryan's Castle and Barnaby drove Blue and Kenneth to the Poplar on East India Dock Road. He hadn't left her side for a moment. And when Delphine called him 'Blue's Barnaby', well, Blue could have died! But he didn't seem to mind.

She held her hair back, examining her face. Maybe Merrigan was right. Maybe she did look old-fashioned. What on earth would Midge say if she cut it? But Midge wasn't here, was she?

Blue splashed water on her face from the old ewer on her table. The water had lost its winter chill in the mornings. May was drawing on. The strike was stretching out. Summer was coming.

Blue smiled. All would be well. As long as she concentrated on Barnaby and Delphine, on her father and on Merrigan with her baby on the way . . . But Merrigan wasn't the only one in that position, was she?

Her father had said, in the height of his panic about Delphine, that if he found Midge he would bring her home, no matter what she'd done. Blue wasn't sure how she felt about that. She couldn't bear the thought of seeing Midge at the moment, but that didn't mean she wanted to be without her. And she wondered how it would be for her father, to continue a life with a woman who had robbed him – robbed them all – so cruelly.

Blue scowled into the garden. Midge had done a terrible thing. Two terrible things. But how was it possible to conceive of life at Ryan's Castle without Midge appearing in a doorway, a parcel of fabric under her arm, saying, 'I just ran this up for you, dear, I hope you like it.' Without Midge presiding over a drinks party, quietly elegant in the background, checking Kenneth's madder impulses, making sure Blue was happy, watching over them all. Without Midge's great, great love for them all. Surely that love would bring her home? But then what? She was the reason Percy was gone! How could they trust that she wouldn't hurt them again?

Another part of the problem, Blue suspected, was that Midge didn't know that they loved her just as much as she loved them. Perhaps she never really had known that. She might be thinking at this very minute that they were furious with her, which was true, and that they didn't *want* her, which wasn't.

Where on God's earth was she?

# Chapter Sixty-nine

There was a little square – you couldn't call it a park – just a street away from the boarding house, and now that spring was in full flourish, Midge went there as often as she could. She would sit on the bench under the cherry tree, hands in her lap, listening to a blackbird sing out its full-throated joy. The cherry blossom had fallen and lay at her feet, trampled into a pale pink mat. Tulips stood in a fierce blaze before her, and she stared into the mass of dark purple, cinnamon and cerise like someone watching flames in a fire. She talked to no one.

It had been over a week since she'd left home. She had telephoned her mother and heard that Kenneth had been round there looking for her. To lacerate her with fury, no doubt. She supposed one day, many years hence, she'd have to face him. But she couldn't yet. A tiny voice inside her whispered that he might have gone looking for her in love, or at least concern. But she wouldn't listen to that voice; it would get her hopes up and break her heart. She knew Kenneth was a kind man, but he had a highly developed sense of right and wrong and what Midge had done was wrong, plain and simple.

Her mother was Vesuvian in her wrath. 'Why have you left your husband, you stupid girl?' she demanded. 'I suppose he's had an affair. Well, men just *do*. Swallow your pride and get back there before you find the door's closed behind you. You're not irreplaceable, you know!'

Midge had hung up the receiver quietly, thinking it typical that this was the only explanation her mother could conjure. Even her own mother didn't think Midge could hold him. On the positive side, Kenneth obviously hadn't told her what Midge had done, and she was grateful for that. She didn't know if she would ever be able to tell her mother the truth about Percy, but she would have to see her at some point, and then the new pregnancy would be revealed.

As yet, it was still barely showing. Midge was five months along, but tall and slim as she was, she hadn't ballooned, only swelled a bit, like a bud. The spring breezes made a coat a reasonable thing to wear and the shapeless fashions helped. She wore a pale blue knee-length coat cut in an A-line from the shoulders. It swung like a bell and covered a multitude. She still wore her wedding ring. She'd do better presenting herself as a widow than as a pregnant single lady, so at the boarding house she was Mrs Smith, and there she had a small studio on the second floor.

The girl above her was a ballerina and Midge was frequently

woken by the flumps and thumps of her practising jetés and fouettés at ungodly hours. The woman below had the biggest set of rooms, with her own kitchen from which the smell of roasting beetroots drifted upwards. But at least it was an all-female establishment and at least her studio had two small windows. Even so, she came to the public square whenever there was sun. It was a million miles from Ryan's Castle, but when she sat there she felt numb and that was the best she could hope for these days.

The rest of the time was torture, really. She missed Kenneth and the girls unspeakably. Their absence felt like heavy beams trapping her in a collapsing building. The baby growing inside her caused little trouble, but the fact of it was inescapable. Night-time saw Midge tossing and turning, unable to sleep for the great mill wheel of questions turning and churning in her head. She could take it to a home again, but the thought of doing so a second time was the emptiest, most barren prospect of all. She'd even wondered about bringing it up herself, but it felt like too foul a betrayal of Percy to keep another child when she hadn't kept him. So she had decided to have the baby and then take it to Kenneth. She knew he would want it. And at least then the baby would have its father, its sisters. Yes, she would be saddling Kenneth with the conundrum of what to tell the child about its mother one day, but he would think of something.

Nor would he struggle to bring it up – he had Avis,

Merrigan and Blue. And once the women of Surrey learned that Kenneth Camberwell was available again, he wouldn't be on his own long.

They must divorce. Perhaps they could do so by correspondence; she could make it a condition of the divorce that he mustn't seek her out. Then he would be free. And she would be a divorcee . . . What on earth would her life hold then? Would she ever go home to her mother? She couldn't see it. She would have to find work, perhaps as a seamstress or in a department store. And she would have to move far away, because she couldn't bear for a single person she knew to recognise the fugitive Midge Camberwell of Ryan's Castle.

She might go to Yorkshire. That was a long way, and the moors and great skies might offer solace. She would have to be Margaret again, because the name Midge was now unbearably associated with love and affection – betrayed and thrown away. It was a shame, because Margaret had been a passive soul, grey as a Dulwich Sunday. She would miss being Midge.

But first the baby must be born. She had enough money to last these few months and a little beyond . . . She should arrange a doctor; she wasn't young to be pregnant . . . And so the nights passed in ruminations and conclusions which left very little room for sleep.

As for the days, she simply sat in her room, or stared into the tulips and thought of the people she loved. She was haunted by memories of home and her family. Oddly, Midge was haunted by Percy as much as any of them. Over the years, it was her imagined pictures of him that had preoccupied her: what must he look like now, aged four? How was he dressed when he took his first steps? Were his eyes bright, like Kenneth's, or brown and thoughtful like her own? Now, though, it was the real Percy she saw, as she had briefly known him. She remembered the fine, damp curls stuck to his scalp; she felt his little head, round as an orange, resting in her cupped palm. She saw his gummy grin and longed for him. At last she had shifted into right feeling for her son, now, when it was all too late. And the remorse and guilt that she felt were unbearable.

Then she'd see Kenneth's springy gold hair, turning just a little salty in the last year or so, rising up from his forehead in that dear, irrepressible way. His intelligent eyes and graceful figure. The laughter that lurked about the corners of his mouth and in his eyes. The humbling, blood-rushing pride she always felt at the sight of him.

She saw Merrigan with her sleek, nut-brown hair and bright, stylish clothes, a mischievous Tabitha almost always in tow. Opinionated, huge-hearted Merrigan, chiding Blue, chasing after Cicely, stepping into the kitchen and helping Avis. She always knew just what needed to be done without asking.

And Blue, dear, sensitive Blue, who struggled to make sense of life, but had such strength running through her, motivating her to hold on to magic and beauty and optimism even when it seemed hardest. Midge saw her frowning over a notebook;

striding out of the house in her long, old-fashioned skirts; the way she tilted her head when she listened, as though absorbing everything you were saying and quite a bit that you weren't. Blue's good opinion would be hardest of all to lose. She'd endured too much grief for someone only twenty-one, and now Midge had meted out more to her. She'd give anything to take that back.

But how – *how* – could she have stayed with them once she was pregnant? How could she have gone through the panto-mime of delight, knowing what she had done last time around? This baby spelled the end of that dishonest existence, which she had so treasured despite its warped nature. 'Oh, baby,' she whispered, 'you've ruined everything.'

# Part Five

## Summer

*The weather was startlingly fair
and all was golden and blue*

# Chapter Seventy

A new, Midge-less era had set in at Ryan's Castle. Over the weeks, Blue's fury at her stepmother had dulled to a sullen bruise. Holding on to hatred of Midge felt just as bad as the rest of it. As much as she continued to struggle with what had happened, as much as she mourned Percy – all over again – her memories of Midge were so plentiful and so full of love that she couldn't help but wish she would just come back. Love. That was what it all boiled down to in the end.

Life seemed so slow, like a river that was silting up. It was as if the place was under a sad spell, Blue thought, a haze of resignation and disappointment was settled over them all, when outside the world was as beautiful as ever.

July was ablaze in Richmond, with roses clouding garden walls and laughter drifting along the riverbanks once again. On Richmond Hill, the gardens tinkled with crystal and china as families took tea on the lawn. In the park, the grass was starting to get that slightly parched look, and it would only get yellower and more strawlike as the days wore on.

One afternoon in late July, Blue, Merrigan and Cicely took a picnic in the park, for Cicely's sake. Under bright skies, the child toddled about, chasing soft blue butterflies and picking grasses with which to tickle her mother and aunt. Blue ran after her while Merrigan lay under a parasol like a beached whale. Blue had lowered her gently down, and when it came time to leave, had to haul her not-so-gently up.

'How is it possible to be so big and not actually give birth?' she demanded, puffing, as she pulled her sister to the vertical.

'Don't blame me!' said Merrigan crossly, taking a moment to find her balance. 'I'm not holding on to it for the fun of it, am I? "Any minute," Dr Harcourt said. That was eight days ago. He should damn well try hauling it around in this heat.'

'Are you all right now?' asked Blue, daring to let go at last, and darting after Cicely, who had sensed the picnic was at an end and made a run for it.

'Ready,' nodded Merrigan, waiting queenishly while Blue gathered everything up. 'Lord, but it's not the same around here without old Midge, is it?'

Blue paused in folding the rug. 'No,' she said. 'It's not.' It was usually Blue who lamented the loss of Midge while Merrigan was tough and stoic and looked to the future. She had the baby coming, after all, which gave her rather a significant focus. Blue was relieved to hear that her sister missed Midge too. They'd talked about it a lot, in the beginning, about Percy and the new pregnancy and how on earth Midge, whom they all knew to be so kind and caring, had come to make such choices.

'Would you want her to come back now?' Blue asked cautiously. You could scare Merrigan off a topic she didn't want to discuss if you pushed it too hard.

'Of course I would,' said Merrigan. She shook her head in disbelief. 'She lied to us, took our brother, hurt us beyond imagining . . . But she's part of us, isn't she? And we know she's so much more than the woman who did those things. She wasn't in her right mind when she did them and it's obvious she's been hurting just as much as we have. More, in some ways, I don't doubt. Imagine being responsible for the damage she's caused! The thought of me doing that to Cicely . . .' She shuddered. 'It doesn't bear thinking about. But I remember when Cicely was tiny – there were times when I thought *I* was losing my mind. No one admits how hard motherhood is. I just thank God that I didn't experience what Midge did. Somehow, I think, we all need to be back together for the hurt to heal. But I don't think it's going to happen, Blue, because *she* doesn't realise that, the silly woman.' She started fanning herself with a magazine. It wasn't as hot as last summer, but the pregnancy was making Merrigan horribly sensitive to warmth.

'And do you . . .' Blue paused, wondering what she really wanted to ask. 'Do you think it would *work*, having her back? I mean, they're not small things to forgive, are they, what she did?'

'They're not. But people fail to forgive far smaller things, don't they? It's not the size of the misdemeanour that dictates the future, but what everyone *wants*. And what they're prepared to do. It would be hard for Daddy. She took his *son* away, for heaven's sake! He's a chap of his time for all that he's open-minded and has a heart the size of America. He wanted Ryan's Castle to have a prince. But if he misses her as much as we do . . . and if we all tried really hard . . .'

Blue nodded. She thought so too. It wouldn't be easy, but then nothing about human life was.

Merrigan sighed. 'I think the person who'd have the most trouble forgiving Midge would be Midge. Still. It's all academic anyway, isn't it?'

In all this time, they'd had word from Midge only once, via her mother. Midge had asked her to let them know she was well. 'Don't ask me where she is,' Mrs Fawcett had said, 'because I don't know. Can't get in touch with my own daughter! I have to wait for her to telephone if I want to ask her anything. And then I'm taken by surprise and I forget what it was, so I've taken to keeping a list by the side of the telephone.'

In vain, they had plied Mrs Fawcett with messages for Midge, begging her to contact them, telling her they could work everything out. They'd even written letters, and Blue had taken them to Dulwich, but Midge's mother only shrugged.

'I never see her and I don't have an address,' she said flatly. 'I'll take them if you want, in case she does turn up, but who knows if she will?' Blue left with the uncomfortable feeling that Mrs Fawcett somehow held them all accountable for her daughter running away. Perhaps, somehow, they were.

'Come on, rhinoceros lady,' Blue said, tucking her arm through Merrigan's. 'Back we go, before this child drops out. I'm not at all game for an impromptu outdoor delivery.'

They went slowly, slowly down the hill, walking at Merrigan's pace. Blue – and everyone else come to that – questioned the wisdom of Merrigan still going out and about at this late stage, but try stopping her when she had an idea.

'How's your writing going?' asked Merrigan, in an obvious attempt to distract Blue from thoughts of Midge. 'And have you had any word from that L. W. chap?'

Blue had written one last letter to L. W. after that soul-dousing kiss, then they met in a coffee house in Hammersmith. She wanted to tell him in person that she liked him immensely but only wanted to be friends. 'If that's all right with you,' she'd added, feeling tremendously uncomfortable. It wasn't an easy thing to tell someone you felt no attraction to them whatsoever.

He'd looked upset, poor man, and bewildered. He said that he'd like to be friends but that it might be difficult now, his hopes having been raised for so long. Blue felt guilty. 'May I think about it?' he asked. 'If I feel that I *can* think of you that way, I'll write.'

'That would be fine,' Blue had said gravely and never heard from him again.

She read his letters once more, then burned them. They had meant a great deal to her. But love was not, after all, something to be confined to words on paper. Letters were not enough.

She had quoted L. W. to her father though, one night during a heart-to-heart about Midge. They were talking about how difficult it was to come to terms with discovering that the Midge they thought they knew was capable of such things. 'But then I reread this,' she said, 'and it helped: "If we only ever acted in character, what a narrow range our lives would span." It's true, Daddy. Life's too big for someone to be one way all the time. Remember when you came back from the war and told me that reality has room for all sorts of things in it, good and bad? Well, so do people, that's what I've decided.'

Kenneth chewed on a thumbnail and considered. 'I like that, darling,' he'd said at last. 'Plato?'

'L. W.,' said Blue.

'I don't see him any more,' she told Merrigan now.

'Oh?'

'No. In the end, I realised it was only friendship I felt, but he wanted more. He was disappointed, but the magic just wasn't there for me.'

'You had dollops of magic with Dorian.'

'Dollops of *something*, yes, but no real friendship; or at least, only the most superficial sort. I want both. You have both with Lawrence,' she added, lest Merrigan say she was being unrealistic or something of the sort.

'Yes,' agreed Merrigan. 'But I've been so jolly lucky.'

'Well, I want to be jolly lucky too.'

Merrigan looked at her and squeezed the arm that she was hanging on to. 'So you should, darling, so you should.'

Blue smiled and wondered whether to tell her about Barnaby. She hadn't said a word to anyone – though Delphine had guessed. Two months on, her feelings for him were stronger, if anything. She'd seen him a few times and could tell that he liked her very much, but she didn't know more than that. Perhaps he felt about her as she did about L. W. Somehow, with Barnaby, Blue didn't know how to flirt or fish . . . Maybe it was because they had started out as colleagues, or maybe it was because he was so direct and straightforward. Or maybe it was just because she was afraid of getting the response she didn't want, and preferred to keep it in her head, where everything was still possible. She wasn't sure she wanted to confide such tender feelings to her strong-minded sister.

Back at Ryan's Castle, they found Delphine visiting. After leaving the hospital, she'd stayed with them for a month. Her abduction and the dramatic dispatch of Foley weren't things she could forget overnight. Both Inspector Cromley (showing unsuspected depths of empathy) and Dr Harcourt recommended a good long rest to come to terms with it. But Delphine had been back with the Greenbows for several weeks now and was fully recovered, physically at least. Emotionally, it would take longer. Blue knew from several long conversations that Delphine felt hugely guilty that Foley's death signified such a marvellous change for her. Blue understood: it was hard to accept that someone's death could be the cause of joy – of great, cavernous relief. Yet so it was.

'How lovely to see you, darling.' Blue hugged her, then kissed her father on the cheek and poured herself a cup of tea.

'Merrigan, you're enormous,' said Delphine. 'It can't be long now, it just can't.'

'Tell the baby,' said Merrigan shortly, reaching for the teapot and failing – her belly prevented her getting close enough to things.

'I'll pour,' said Blue.

There was a little silence. Sometimes even something as happy as Merrigan's baby made them feel sad, because it reminded them of the other baby, who would follow this one so closely, but whom they wouldn't see. But they *would* see this one, Blue reminded herself fiercely, handing her sister a cup with a bright smile.

'Delphine and I were just reflecting on how time flies,' said Kenneth, cutting a tiny piece of fruit cake. He used to be a man of huge enthusiasms and hearty appetites. He would never have cut such a stingy piece of cake when Midge was here. Looking at him now was like looking at a pressed flower in an album. 'Two months since her dreadful ordeal, and doesn't she look well?'

'She does,' agreed Merrigan. 'Lord, Delphine, every time I

get upset about Midge, I think of how bad things were, but how wonderfully free you are now, and it helps me to feel lucky again.'

Blue smiled. She hadn't realised her sister made the same ruthless daily decision not to surrender to sadness that she did.

'I still can't quite believe it,' said Delphine. 'Sometimes when I'm walking around I suddenly think, oh hell, I've forgotten to get Merrigan or Sid or someone to come with me, and I get such a fright. Then I remember it's fine for me to be alone now. This morning I was walking past the Cricketers and there was a gang of men in there – shouting, no-good types, just like that day. And it gave me such a turn, remembering how he just appeared in my path. But I told myself that can never happen again. Then I felt bad for feeling so relieved, because the relief comes from him being dead, of course.'

'I still can't believe that you didn't scream or run or anything, because he told you he had Midge,' said Blue. 'You're such a darling to put yourself in such danger to try to help her. I wish we could let her know what you did.'

'I was stupid,' said Delphine. 'We were nearly at the docks before I realised he didn't have her at all.'

'"Courage is fire, and bullying is smoke,"' said Kenneth. 'Benjamin Disraeli. Foley was smoke, Delphine, and you were all fire. And *we* all think you're terribly brave. We all think . . . what? What is it, my dear?'

Blue looked at Delphine, who had gone white. Involuntarily

she glanced to the window, half expecting to see Foley standing there. She could understand why it would take time for his absence to sink in fully with Delphine.

'Oh,' said Delphine, 'I can't believe it. I've just realised, I know something! Oh, I should've told you ages ago, only I'd completely forgotten. It's only now it's come back to me.'

'Well what?' asked Merrigan, pausing with her cup half raised.

'Foley said about Midge, didn't he, that he'd seen her leave. He followed her to the station and thought about snatching her, but he didn't. He said, I'm sure he said – yes, he *did* – that he'd watched her sitting and crying, waiting for the Reading train. Foley saw Midge catch the Reading train.'

Blue's heart leapt. A lead! At last! She watched her father frowning, trying to make a connection.

'Reading? What's in Reading?' he asked at last.

'Maybe nothing,' said Blue excitedly. 'Maybe that's the point.'

'A neutral place, where there's no one we know,' agreed Merrigan. 'Did he say anything else, Delphine?'

Delphine shook her head. 'No, I'm certain of it. Now it's come back to me I remember it clearly.'

'Of course, she might not have gone as far as Reading. There are other stops on that line,' mused Kenneth. 'And Reading's not a small place, after all . . .'

'But still, it's something to go on, isn't it, Daddy?' said Blue.

'Will you check . . .' But Kenneth had bolted from the room. 'Oh, he's gone. I haven't seen him move so fast in ages.'

He flew back in, wearing his hat and a light summer jacket. 'Ladies,' he said, kissing each of them in turn, 'I'm off.'

'Another one vanishes,' said Blue softly, as they heard the front door slam. The room slid to a standstill. She sighed. There was the click of Delphine's cup returning to its saucer. There was a sound of barking from over the wall. Could he ever find Midge after all this time?

'Girls,' said Merrigan, her voice strangled. 'Um, sorry to bother you, but I rather think the baby's coming.'

# Chapter Seventy-one

Midge's baby was making his or her presence felt now. She'd started to think in terms of 'his or her', despite determined efforts to stick with 'it'. She was getting off lightly this time; she remembered a very different pregnancy with Percy. Odd that now, when she was alone and living in a single room, everything else should be so much easier. Perhaps that was the way of life – always to compensate for one thing with another, always to keep balance.

The landlady of the boarding house had raised an eyebrow when her shape began to show, but she said nothing. Midge was a quiet, no-trouble tenant who never missed her rent payments. Whether she believed Midge's story of a Mr Smith, recently deceased, Midge couldn't be sure, but she wouldn't be here much longer now. She still took daily walks to the park, made weekly telephone calls to her mother and continued to lay plans to take the baby to Ryan's Castle and then move to Yorkshire.

Her broken heart hadn't even begun to recover. She still thought of them all, every day, and the memories surged over her like sun bursting over a hillside. In fact, memories were the most vivid thing she had; after that, there was only colourless speculation. Merrigan may or may not have had the baby by now. Blue may or may not have found another writing job. She may or may not have chosen a suitor. Delphine may or may not be safe from Foley. Kenneth may have started to make his peace with what had happened, and perhaps even to forgive her a little. Or, he may not.

She wished she could reassure him that she would take the baby to him. But hearing his voice would cause all her resolve and purpose to shatter. So she remained in isolation, in agony.

One warm July day, she sat before the tulips, which had faded and fallen. At Ryan's Castle they would have been pruned and cleared away long before now. Their pale, sappy stems lay across the ground and the diminished heads rested in the earth. She couldn't help remembering the first time she and Kenneth had made love. It was a memory that kept chasing her and she wished it would let her be. She was trying so hard to accept that sometimes in life you made mistakes so awful that you couldn't hope for healing. If you took yourself far enough away, perhaps there could at least be a measure of peace. But how could she believe that when she knew what it was like to love someone so much and so dearly that the very sight of them lit up your world? When the thought of their face made you smile even when nothing inside you felt like smiling? What was the point of life without that?

The baby kicked. He or she would be born next month. Blue's birthday month. Midge wished she could organise a party for her. Perhaps Merrigan would, but she wanted to be there, doing the work, doing the loving. A memory, swift as a swallow: Blue in her blue dress on her last birthday, beautiful and on the cusp of everything. *I wish I'd asked her about that Barnaby*, thought Midge. *He seemed to mean a lot to her. Dorian was never right for her. You don't like to interfere, but perhaps I should have said something.*

She was starting to wilt in the sun, like a tulip. Over the last two months, Midge had come to identify closely with those tall, willowy flowers that so easily bowed under the weight of their own blooms. Now their flowering season was past too.

She stood up and started meandering through the rose beds to the east gate, which was nearest her studio. As she walked, she saw a man who was looking all around, and her heart skipped. He looked like an older, thinner version of Kenneth. The resemblance made her gaze at him tenderly, hoping he wouldn't notice; he would think her mad, staring at a stranger that way.

But the man did see her, and stopped in his tracks. His looking about came to an abrupt end as he stared back at her. A horrible, wonderful thought occurred to her. *Was it?*

It was. She could see now. It was Kenneth, here in her exile, looking terrible.

She wanted to run away. It seemed the only bearable thing.

Yet now that he was before her, she couldn't actually tear herself from him. It had always been that way: no amount of gazing had ever quenched the thirst of her eyes; no amount of love-making had ever slaked her belly's desire; no amount of conversation with him had ever come even close to boring her. So although her mind screamed at her to run, her whole being wanted nothing more than to throw her arms around him and drink him in for one last moment.

'Midge.'

His voice, so familiar, brought tears to her eyes. He seemed equally transfixed and they stood looking at each other across the rose beds. Then he started walking towards her. When he reached her, despite herself, she flinched. In a moment, she would hear all the things she most feared.

'Midge . . .' His voice was a gentle reproach. He reached to tuck a lock of hair under her hat. 'You're not afraid of me?'

She stared at him, speechless. *Not of you, exactly, but of how you make me feel. I've always been afraid.* That's what she would have said, if she could. Instead, she just gazed at his dear, grey eyes, his careworn face. Her eyes rose to two golden curls that had slithered out from under his hat. He whipped his hat off, as though self-conscious, and pushed his hair back in the old way. She lifted a hand but stopped herself halfway.

'You hate me,' she said. 'I know; I understand. I hate me, too. Please, Kenneth, just get it over with and go. I'm going to bring the baby to you when it's born, you know. I won't deprive you of another child. I know it's not much of an amend, but it's all I can do now.'

He frowned. 'You think it's that easy?'

'Easy? Kenneth, nothing about us has been that, not from the very beginning. But what else can we do now? I understand why you had to find me. I should have told you where I was, but I'm a coward. But it's nearly over now. And I'll divorce you, Kenneth, I promise. I know it's too late for Christie, but there'll be someone, you know there will. And she'll make you happy.'

'Divorce me?' His voice rose, and a few sparrows flew out of the bushes. 'The hell you will, woman. You're my *wife*! Midge, come on. Let's shake ourselves out of this trance and talk properly. Seeing each other is a big shock to both of us after so long, but I came for a reason, so let's get on with it.'

'What reason?' she whispered.

'To take you home, of course!'

Her head started spinning. 'No! Kenneth, you can't mean it.'

'I do. I don't say I haven't been angry. There was a time when I thought I could never look at you again. But time goes on, Midge – life does. I need you. I don't care what's happened. Come back!'

She could get lost in his eyes. She knew it all too well; she'd done it a million times. He wanted her back. The word *yes* jumped into her mouth, but she swallowed it back. She'd spent two whole months ruminating on the way things were – the way they had to be. She couldn't just pick up the threads of their life as if nothing had happened. But knowing that didn't stop her wanting something quite different. She swayed a little and he caught her.

'I need to get out of the sun. And a little water.'

'Let's find a tea room. We must talk. Then we'll go back to that absurd place of yours and pack.'

'*No!* Well, we can talk, but I'm not coming back.'

'*Why?* Tell me I know everything now, Midge, that you don't have any other secrets to thrust upon me? You haven't met someone else? You weren't married to someone else before me? The child is mine?'

'*Kenneth!*' She stared at him in shock. He *was* angry, still. Well, of course he was.

'You're not in a position to ask how I could think such things of you, Midge. I never thought you'd taken Percy away. I never thought you'd run out on us. I don't know *what* to believe. So tell me.'

'No,' she whispered. 'No other secrets.'

'Well then,' he said impatiently. 'If I'm in possession of all the facts, and I say we can do this, then surely that's all there is to consider. I forgive you, Midge. What more do you want?'

She dug her feet in, a child resisting her nanny. 'A great many things, Kenneth. A great, great many things besides that. And they are impossible things, which you can never give me.'

He looked at her in mute frustration. 'We'll talk anyway,' he said at last. 'And you can tell me what these things are that you want so badly. And I'll see if *I* think they're impossible or not.'

'Oh, that's all that matters, is it, what *you* think?' demanded Midge pettishly, but she trailed along behind him anyway, despite the fact that she knew the area and he didn't. As a result, they wandered for longer than necessary before settling into a table at the back of Crawshaw's Coffee House. The daylight didn't reach them all the way back there, and Midge found the dim corner in some way comforting. By then she had composed herself a little. From Kenneth's face, it didn't look as though he had.

He helped her out of her coat and caught sight of her swollen belly. The bump was small and neat, still, but unmistakeably that of a very pregnant woman.

'*Midge!*' he murmured and laid his hand, briefly, on the bump. They stood like that for a second, a husband touching his wife, a tableau of marital bliss, before she pulled away and they sat down.

'For the love of God, woman, why won't you come home?' he asked when tea had been poured and cake served. Midge looked around and marvelled at the ordinariness of it all – china and people having conversations and unmannerly service – as a backdrop to this extraordinary conversation. 'I thought you were staying away because you thought I was furious and didn't want you. But I'm telling you you're wrong. So why can't we go back to normal?'

'Kenneth, *darling*!' she marvelled, his naiveté making her feel like her old sensible self by comparison. 'How could we *ever* go back to normal? I took our son away from you. I preferred to have you all to myself rather than keep him with us, where he belonged! For heaven's sake, what sort of a woman am I? You never loved me much, but with what you know about me now . . . You deserve so much *better*!'

'Why do you say that I never loved you much? Of course I loved you. I married you.'

Midge frowned. 'Lots of people marry without love, darling, you know that. A woman senses these things. Anyway, let me finish. It's not easy to talk about. When I discovered I was pregnant again, Kenneth, there was no joy, no excitement. It was the straw that broke the camel's back, the thing that meant I couldn't sustain my life of lies any longer. But just because you *know* now doesn't alter the fact that I *did* those things. You wanted to know what else could matter besides your forgiving me. Well, I don't forgive myself. I never will. And that's far more fundamental. I can't live with myself, Kenneth, with being this person. Oh, don't worry, I won't do anything drastic. I'm not Foster. I'm seeing a doctor and eating well and getting fresh air and resting. I'll keep myself healthy and bring your baby into the world, and then I'm going far away, to live out my days as best I can. You can have a fresh start, Kenneth, with someone who makes you feel the way Audra did.'

'Audra? Is *that* what all this is about? Midge, you are a *fool*!

Of course I loved Audra. But I love you too. You *knew* I was a widower when you married me; you knew that we'd been happy! How can you cast that up now? It's not fair.'

Midge looked at him and saw that it wasn't a real question. He didn't really want to understand how it had all happened for her. He wanted to get what he wanted, which was for her to go back to him. A week ago, she would have said that if, impossibly, he asked her, she would go, but she understood now that it wasn't as simple as that.

She was taking a piece of cake apart with her fingers, then jamming the crumbs back into a lump, then picking it apart again, over and over. She tried not to notice the heartfelt plea in his eyes, tried to ignore all the small things she wanted to do to care for him: smooth the worry lines away from his eyes, pour him a whisky, make him promises.

'The life we would have, if I do as you want,' she said slowly, 'would be unbearable, Kenneth. You'd try to be good to me, because that's the kind of man you are, but you would hate me, somewhere deep down. You say you're not angry, but you are, I can feel it. I don't blame you for that – how could I? – but for you to live pretending otherwise would twist you into a different man. I know what I'm talking about – I've lived a life of pretence, remember.

'And Kenneth, this child raises so many questions. I've been grappling with them since I came here. Like, how could I keep it with me, if I didn't keep Percy? Would that mean I loved it more than him? Because believe it or not, I do love Percy, desperately. I only realised after it was too late. If we were together, whatever would we tell it? Could you let it grow up knowing that I ran away from you when I was carrying it? Would we tell it about Percy? Could you lie? Kenneth, this isn't the sort of tale that you can tell a child about its mother. But if I'm not there, if it never knows me, it will be easier for you to explain.'

'Midge, these are the very questions I've been asking myself. Every day since I read your letter. But I don't care, Midge. I just don't care. I want you to come home.'

'*Why?*'

'I just . . . *do*! It's what I want, Midge, why isn't that enough? If you love me – us – so much, you should come back! Don't you miss the girls? They miss you *dreadfully*.'

Midge closed her eyes. 'Darling girls. Oh, Kenneth, of course I miss them. I miss you *all*, every minute of every day. It's sheer hell. But it's my punishment, don't you see? It's loving you so much that made all this happen. Fear of losing you made it happen. And wanting you to love me the way I love you made it happen. If I come back now, it'll all be worse. I'll feel I'm there on sufferance. And God knows what would happen next; I don't trust myself, Kenneth! Please go. I look at you and want nothing more than to come with you, pretend we can start again. But it can never be the same, so please *go*! I won't change my mind.'

They went on in this vein for some time longer, and eventually Kenneth admitted defeat.

'Promise me one thing, if I go, as you ask,' he said. 'Promise that you won't disappear again. Stay here, or better yet, go to your mother's so that you're not alone. I won't keep pestering you, if that's what you need, but I *must* know where you are. Please, Midge. Vanishing is *cruel*. Promise!'

'All right, I promise. I'll go to Mother. You're right. It's not a time to be alone.'

'Thank you. Good. Will you let me take you there now? I have the car.'

'No, thank you. That would be too hard. I can get myself there. You needn't worry. It won't be a bad thing to save a month or two's rent, either,' she mused, thinking of the new life she must set up and sustain when the baby was gone.

Kenneth exploded. 'Rent! Don't you talk to me about *rent*, woman, or *money*! As if I would ever be ungenerous. You should know me better than that. No matter *what* you've done!'

'I know, Kenneth! But it's not that. I don't deserve . . .'

'Will you be *quiet* about what you deserve!' he roared, and the other customers looked up. The waiter frowned in their direction. Midge had never seen Kenneth lose control like that. 'Will you please stop thinking about it all from your point of view,' he continued, in a more reasonable tone, 'and realise that no matter what has occurred between us, I am not a man who could bear to see his wife struggle or suffer, even if she *has* done some unforgivable ill, which is after all *your* view of it, not mine. I don't like your choices, but that doesn't mean I want to add penury to your list of troubles.' He pulled out his wallet and emptied it – literally turned it upside down, held it open and shook it, so that all the notes fell onto the table and nothing was left. Midge watched, horrified.

'Pay your damn rent,' he said in a low voice that shook with strain. 'Get a train to Dulwich. Take a cab. Ride there on a white unicorn! Just don't struggle while you do it. And if you insist upon this ridiculous divorce nonsense, you must take *everything* you're owed. I won't *give* you a divorce unless you accept full financial recompense, how's that? I've obviously been the very worst of husbands, but I'll be the best damn ex-husband you've ever seen!' He stood up and snatched his jacket from the back of his chair. 'And see that you keep your promise to me, Midge Camberwell. It's the bloody least you can do.' Then he stormed out.

Midge sat oozing silent tears for a while. Despite the warm July afternoon, she started to shiver. Eventually she gathered up the notes from the table and patted them into a neat sheaf. Then she folded it and put it in her pocket, leaving enough to cover their bill. She hadn't asked him any of the things she wanted so badly to know. She hadn't asked about Merrigan's baby, or Blue. She hadn't even asked about Delphine and Foley. She would never know now.

He'd arrived begging her to go home and be his wife again, but left talking about divorce – and this had come about entirely due to Midge's single-minded determination. 'Well done, Midge,' she whispered bitterly. 'Well done.'

# Chapter Seventy-two

———— ✦ ————

Tears poured down Blue's face and her heart expanded like a balloon. It was the most utterly joyous thing . . .

In the maternity ward at the hospital, Avis sat in a corner, sobbing happily, while Blue stood clinging to Lawrence. Merrigan, who had roared like a trooper throughout the birth, lay in bed, sweaty and smiling. The new baby was a little girl.

As yet unnamed, she nestled into her mother's collarbone, her tiny nose buried in Merrigan's neck, her eyes screwed up with good dreams. Blue ached to hold her. So diminutive! So squidgy! Brand new, bright and pure, like a rainbow.

The door behind her opened and Delphine arrived with Kenneth. Merrigan's labour had lasted six hours and Delphine had been in and out for the duration. First, she'd seen Merrigan safely settled in the hospital. Then she'd raced to the Greenbows' to tell them Merrigan was in labour. They'd insisted she go back and be with the Camberwells, so she returned, then she'd dashed out to leave a note for Kenneth at Ryan's Castle, so he would know to come straight to the hospital when he got back from Reading; it was something they'd all forgotten when Merrigan's waters broke. After the birth, Delphine had gone out to telephone the Greenbows with the news, and Kenneth had arrived at that very moment.

'Another granddaughter?' he said, racing to the bed. 'And she's fine and healthy? Oh, Merrigan, my darling! Are you all right? I can see you are – you look positively luminous. Oh, well done, darling. Well done, my girl.'

'Daddy!' Merrigan grasped his hand and burst into tears. He kissed her brow and gently stroked the baby's small head. Delphine sat down beside Avis, who put an arm around her and pulled her close. Oh, joyful, joyful day.

'What time did she come?' Kenneth asked, sounding awed.

'Barely an hour ago,' said Lawrence. 'Merry did awfully well. The whole thing went like a dream.'

Merrigan snorted. 'If that's your idea of a dream, Lawrence Miller, you have the next one. In fact, I'm still not sure you'll ever touch me again. But yes, it went very smoothly on the whole, Daddy. I'm so lucky.'

'And now you have two little girls,' Kenneth marvelled, his face awash with emotion. He looked like a man taking refuge in a moment, thought Blue, just as she had with Barnaby, over-looking the meadows that day.

'Sisters,' smiled Merrigan. 'Just like Blue and me.'

'Lucky them,' said Blue. 'It's a fine arrangement.'

Blue wiped away tears with her scarf and Lawrence passed her a handkerchief. It probably wasn't the right moment to ask . . . but she couldn't wait, after all. 'Daddy? No Midge? Didn't you find her?'

He sighed and didn't look at her. 'No, darling, I didn't. But it would have been a miracle, wouldn't it, with no clue beyond an entire town?'

'But you'll look again, won't you?' asked Blue. 'Or I could go? Or we could go together?'

Kenneth hesitated. 'No, darling. Midge left because of our marriage, you see, not because of you. It's me who has to find her. And yes, I will look again. Of course I will. But I don't want you getting your hopes up.'

Blue nodded. She wouldn't let that disappointment touch her now. Not more than she could help. She gazed intently at the bed. Her sister; her niece. Her family gathered around her. After a while, a nurse came and asked them all to leave so that mother and baby could rest.

'Back home for some bubbly, then,' said Kenneth. 'Come on, troops.'

'Beasts,' grumbled Merrigan.

'I'll come back later,' said Blue.

'You'd better. Hey, Blue, come here,' Merrigan ordered, hanging on to her sister's hand as the others kissed her and trickled out reluctantly. When the room was empty, she pulled her close. 'I know what I'm going to call her.'

'Really? Tell me.'

So Merrigan told her, and Blue smiled sadly. 'It's gorgeous, Merry. Perfect.'

# Chapter Seventy-three

Delphine and the Greenbows eventually gave up the pretence that theirs was any sort of usual employer–servant relationship.

'Despite our best intentions,' beamed Stephen, half standing, half sitting on the kitchen table while Delphine made dinner, 'it's all gone horribly wrong. We find ourselves overstepping all bounds of professionalism, and simply put, Delphine, we love you.'

'We do,' agreed Fanny, sitting at the table and sipping ginger tea. Delphine placed the lid on the pot, wiped her hands on a towel and turned to look at them.

This had been prompted by her flurry of apologies about needing yet more time off. First there had been Christmas, then recovery time after Foley and most recently another two days to be with Merrigan and Blue and the baby. 1920s Britain wasn't a place where those fortunate enough to find work could play fast and loose with their jobs. Without utter dedication, you could easily find yourself replaced.

'I feel as if I'm taking advantage of you,' she'd wailed when she came home from the hospital, wrung out with emotion. 'It's been one thing after another with me for months! I'm the worst "capable girl" in the world!'

'The worst . . .? Oh! Our advertisement! Well, that's simply not true, dear,' Fanny had argued. And then she'd insisted Delphine go to bed and recover.

'Nothing's changing,' Stephen continued now. 'You'll still live here for as long as you wish, still carry out your duties and we'll pay you accordingly. But there's just no point pretending that you're merely our "capable girl". You're like a daughter to us, Delphine.'

Delphine put down her towel and went to hug them. 'I love you, too,' she whispered. 'I do.'

'Oh, mind the towel, dear, it's a little bit on fire,' observed Fanny. Sure enough, Delphine had left the end trailing and now modest flames were leaping from it. She shot across the kitchen and doused it under the tap.

'And we wouldn't at all mind,' Fanny continued, 'if you were to become family *really*. We just wanted you to know.'

'If I were to . . .? Oh!' They meant Sid, of course. Delphine blushed and didn't know what to say.

A knock at the front door rescued her. She threw the burned towel away, took another from the cupboard and went to answer it. It was Kenneth. The Greenbows started fussing about tea in the parlour but he frowned the offer away.

'I don't want to disturb you,' he said. 'I'll come through.'

And he joined them at the kitchen table while Delphine continued preparing the trout.

'Will you eat with us?' asked Fanny.

'Yes. Please.'

Delphine wondered why he'd called. When Kenneth had flown out of Ryan's Castle like a migrating goose that day, she'd been so hopeful. He'd arrived back to meet his brand-new granddaughter, but with no Midge in tow. When he told them he hadn't found her, Delphine had watched him, and wondered if it were true.

They ate dinner in relative silence, then he got to the point.

'I did find Midge,' he said.

'I knew it!'

'I found her and she refused to come home.' He sunk his head into his hands, then looked up with a wretched expression. 'I don't know how it went so badly wrong. It was an appalling conversation. I thought that *finding* her would be the hard part, that if I could only do that, then I could tell her I forgave her, and she would be happy and that would be that. But she said she needed more. And I ended up shouting at her! In a coffee house! How does that happen?'

'Men and women trying to understand each other over something important,' said Stephen. 'That's how.'

'But . . . but . . .' Kenneth spread his hands, looking helpless. Delphine wanted to hug him. He was her protector. He'd opened his home to her when she was just a stranger, a waif dripping with pondweed. He'd made it his personal mission to ensure the police captured Foley; he'd devised plans to keep her safe. He had fought for his country and now he quested for social justice and everyone looked up to him. Yet faced with a recalcitrant wife, he was just a man, confused and impotent, and Delphine could have laughed if it hadn't been so pitiful.

'Yes, exactly!' said Stephen, nodding enthusiastically as though Kenneth were making real progress. '*Exactly!*'

'That's all very well, old chap, but understanding that we don't understand each other isn't going to bring her home. What do I *do*? Is there anything I can say that will change her mind? Two people come together, marry, then five years later . . . this! How did we come to this?'

'As to that, perhaps you'd be better off talking to Mr Elphwick,' said Fanny, looking troubled. 'We can't claim any special wisdom to help you.'

'Yes, what *does* Elf say?' wondered Delphine.

'He said I should talk to *you*!' cried Kenneth, looking indignant. 'At least, he said I should talk to someone who knew about love, about women. And I thought of you because you two . . . love each other . . . and Delphine, you're a woman.'

'I suppose that's one qualification I do have,' she agreed. 'But we're all different, you see. I can't tell you what Midge is thinking or feeling . . .'

'But you can *guess*, can't you? Speculate? What do you *think* might help? I won't hold you accountable if you're wrong, my dear.'

Delphine had never seen him so uncontrolled. Desperate, actually.

'I want to see her again,' he said. 'But I can't keep turning up after she's asked me not to. I don't want to hound her; I don't want to disrespect her wishes. So the next time has to count. I have to get it right.'

It was true, thought Delphine. If he just kept plaguing Midge, shouting at her, and going round in the same old circles, it would only make everything worse. If there was to be any hope at all, something must shift. She sighed.

'I'll try,' she said. 'I know she loves you very much. Perhaps if you tell us what you said to her in Reading, and what she said to you, we might think of something. Why don't you tell us everything?'

# Chapter Seventy-four

Blue's birthday was fast approaching. She had always thought of birthdays as a marker in the year, a time to take stock and reflect, but she didn't really want to do either just now. So much was veiled. Her future as a writer, Midge, Percy . . . and she still didn't know how Barnaby felt about her. She could hardly ask!

She knew from Delphine's occasional looks and comments that she too was waiting for something to happen. But friends Barnaby and Blue appeared to remain, and she would take that, if that was all they could be. Life without him in *any* shape or form would be intolerable. Still, she kept hoping and wondering.

There might be any number of reasons why he didn't declare himself. Perhaps he felt the difference in their upbringing and financial position too keenly. Perhaps he didn't know how she felt about him. Perhaps he thought a romantic advance would be unwelcome when she was so preoccupied by Midge. Or perhaps he was simply too busy.

He had written an article about Foley's last actions and death for the *Gazette*. He wouldn't have, if Delphine hadn't agreed, but they all knew the papers would pick it up one way or another. Due to the dramatic nature of Foley's end, it had the potential to become a sensational story in the wrong hands. Barnaby had ensured it was a sensitive and thought-provoking piece instead, one that would stir discussion about violence within the legal framework of a marriage. Since then, he'd been approached by several magazines and newspapers and was working harder than ever.

'Well, I didn't want to jog along in the same safe job forever, did I?' he would say. 'These are the opportunities I've dreamed of. I can't turn my back.'

One Sunday when he decided *not* to write, for once, he took Blue to his home to meet his sisters. They rattled over to Acton on a bus and he led her into a house so small she honestly couldn't imagine how it housed all the people Barnaby had listed. As it was Sunday, even the Tanners who didn't live there were visiting. It was, as Barnaby put it, 'a baptism by Tanner'.

'You're brave,' was his sister Ella's first comment as she shook hands with a quick grin.

Mrs Tanner was grey-haired and thin and looked worn out but cheerful. She shook Blue's hand and exclaimed over the jars of Avis's home-made preserves that Blue had brought as a gift. Blue offered to help with lunch, but Barnaby's mother was aided by an efficient crew of daughters who bustled about in a revolving constellation so that Blue could hardly fix on who was whom.

Mr Tanner was buried in a book in the corner of the kitchen. When Barnaby brought Blue in, he looked up, took his pipe from his mouth to say a friendly 'how do?' then returned to his book with grim determination.

'It's the only day of the week he has a chance to read,' explained Barnaby. The others stepped around him, reaching over him when necessary. He kept turning pages through it all. Blue could relate to Mr Tanner.

Barnaby's two brothers said hello then went out to the front step to smoke. That made a little bit more room. Eventually they congregated in a dining room where a second table had been squeezed in next to the dining table with about an inch to spare on either side.

Blue was seated next to Barnaby's youngest sister, Polly. 'It's so lovely to meet you,' she said, squeezing Blue's hand. 'Barney talks about you all the time.'

'Not all the time!' he protested, looking slightly flushed. 'I do have other topics of conversation.'

'*All* the time!' repeated Polly, and a couple of her sisters sniggered and nodded.

'And I could say the same about you,' said Blue, to cover his embarrassment and her own delight. She decided now was the moment to fetch the ballet-shoe pink roses she had brought for Polly. She squeezed out of her seat, climbed over a few legs and brought them in from the hall. Polly beamed.

'I'll put them in water,' said Grace, who was nearest the

door. Mrs Tanner was buried behind family and furniture at the far end of the table. Grace returned with the roses in a glass bowl and set them on the table. 'There,' she said with satisfaction. 'Elegant.'

'They're from my garden,' said Blue.

'Oh, how lovely,' said Polly. 'Nicer than shop-bought.'

Independent Ella grilled Blue on being a working woman at the *Gazette*. 'Do you miss it?' she asked when Blue had told her everything she could.

'Every day,' said Blue honestly. 'I never thought when I started there that I would come to feel like this.' She caught Barnaby watching her carefully.

Mavis admired Blue's simple ivory day dress, and Blue, feeling a twinge of sadness, explained that her stepmother had made it.

'Lucky,' said Mavis. 'Ma's a fine cook but she can't sew to save her life, can you, Ma?'

'Cheeky devil. You ain't exactly Michelangelo with a needle.'

'Well, seeing as he was a *painter*,' sighed Mavis, 'he probably wasn't much with a needle either.'

'You know what I mean, madam. Eat your roast.'

After a busy, noisy, delicious lunch, Barnaby took Blue for a walk. 'It's not scenic.' He smiled. 'Not like Richmond.'

'Lots of places aren't,' said Blue. 'Where would you live, Barney, if you could live anywhere?'

He looked at her. 'Oh, I think Richmond is as good a place

as any.' He paused, then rushed on. 'I mean, it's beautiful, and that's come to matter to me. I like the space. And it's near home, so that's good. I wouldn't want to have to travel hours to visit the family. It's pricey, though; I can't afford it *just* yet.'

Blue smiled. That pause had been telling. She was starting to think . . . In fact, she was *almost* certain that . . . But still they walked side by side, not touching, while he pointed out the scenes of youthful memories: fights and kisses and his old school. He told her stories of family and friends, several times mentioning someone called Sam who now lived in Petersham.

'Oh, is he the friend you were meeting in the Roebuck that night?' asked Blue. Barnaby looked blank. 'Remember the first night you walked me home? You said it wasn't out of your way because you were meeting a friend for a drink in the Roebuck.'

Barnaby looked deeply uncomfortable.

'Don't you remember?' she persisted.

'Yes, I do. Um, to be honest, Blue, I wasn't meeting anyone for a drink that night. I'd never been in the Roebuck. I just wanted to walk you home and I thought it sounded more casual that way.'

Blue tingled. 'You did?' she asked innocently. 'Why?'

He shrugged. 'Thought you looked like an interesting girl,' he said, offhand. 'Now look, that's the pub where Lewis used to work, and over there . . .'

That night, when Blue went to bed, she paused on the fifth

stair. This was where Kenneth had stood almost exactly a year ago to make his extraordinary birthday toast.

'What qualities do I, doting father, hope for in a son-in-law? Well, they may be easily hazarded. Honour, kindness, strength . . .'

That summed up Barnaby to a T, thought Blue. In fact, Barnaby and Kenneth were as similar deep down as Kenneth and Dorian had been on the surface. Barnaby wasn't the polished, wealthy young gent Kenneth might have imagined for her, but he was a man of integrity and warmth, and when things weren't as they should be, he would strive to better them, for himself and others. She knew that Kenneth liked him. Surely he would give them his blessing – if only there was something to bless.

Kenneth passed her on his way to bed. 'You're thinking of your last birthday, aren't you?' he observed. 'Once again, Blue, apologies for the foolishness.'

Blue smiled. '"I am content to be a fool, if foolishness might open up an unexpected avenue,"' she quoted.

'Plato?'

'L. W. again.'

'And did it? Open up an unexpected avenue, I mean. *Is* there someone, darling?'

'I don't know, Daddy. Perhaps. But do you mind if I don't talk about it yet?'

'Take your time,' said Kenneth, barely containing his satisfied beam. 'So can I take it I'm once and for all forgiven?'

Blue considered. Actually, it had been that toast, indirectly, that had brought her to Barnaby. For if she hadn't been so infuriated, so busy protesting that her interests lay elsewhere, she might not have mustered the pluck to send those articles to Juno. Which led to her job at the *Gazette*, which had led to her meeting Barnaby. But if she told her father *that*, he would be insufferably smug. So for now, she just wound her arms around him and kissed his cheek. 'Completely forgiven, Daddy, darling.'

In one week, her birthday would come around again. Here she was, on the cusp of twenty-two. Compared with how things had been when she was about to turn twenty-one, her life seemed much worse at first glance: Midge had gone; Blue was too distracted to write; and a lot of her girlhood dreams were looking rather ragged. But . . . a year ago she hadn't met Delphine. She hadn't met Barnaby. She hadn't worked for the *Richmond Gazette*. And she hadn't known her own mind half so well about all sorts of things.

Blue didn't want a party. She couldn't feel excited about one after everything that had happened, and a jolly old bash didn't seem to suit the climate. The heart had gone out of the house without Midge. Yet she had always felt that rituals at significant times were important. To acknowledge that, however bad things got, there was always something to celebrate. To measure where one had been and where one was going. To participate in the festivals of the year . . .

Perhaps, instead of a party, she would have a special birthday dinner. Avis had offered to prepare one, and Blue had said no at first, but now she was changing her mind. Despite the large splinter that was Midge's absence, there were still plenty of people to share the day: Kenneth; Merrigan and Lawrence and their little girls; Avis and Elf; Delphine and the Greenbows. Oh, and Sid of course. Barnaby and maybe Juno – *if* she promised to come as a friend, not a reporter. And the Foxtons. It would be a big dinner. But they could keep the menu simple and she would help Avis. Yes. It mattered that these people were together on her birthday, all gathered in love. Otherwise she would quite simply dread the day. She had to choose something better than that.

# Chapter Seventy-five

Visitors to the Greenbows' kitchen were coming thick and fast these days, thought Delphine as she made a pot of tea for Barnaby, feeling touched that he'd called to see her. He was Blue's friend, after all – though how disappointing they were still nothing more. Delphine was longing to ask him about it. She'd been sure, after seeing them together in the Poplar that day, that it was only a matter of time. Did he not love Blue? It seemed unthinkable! But she restrained herself. It was Blue's business, after all, and Barnaby had called to apprise Delphine of the epilogue to Foley's story.

Foley's funeral had taken place a week after what they all delicately referred to as The Incident. It had been a shabby affair on a drizzly day, attended only by Barnaby, Cromley and a woman who claimed to be a sister that Delphine had never known Foley had. How she'd even known to come, no one could fathom.

The strike had lasted nine days. Agreements had been reached and the docks continued to flourish as a place of employment. 'For now, anyway,' said Barney, who had a feeling more troubles lay ahead. He took an appreciative slug of strong, black tea and told her that the Royal Docks had 750,000 frozen carcasses stored in those warehouses. The strike meant no electricity, and they'd nearly lost a fortune, but the navy had come along in the nick of time with two submarine generators and saved the day.

It made Delphine's head spin to think that her own personal drama had taken place against a backdrop of such national importance. The thought of such a great number of carcasses all hanging there in a cold, dark warehouse – and she had so nearly been one of them – gave her chills, as if she could feel that icy air from here. *Courage is fire,* she reminded herself. It meant the world to her that Kenneth thought of her that way.

'As fitting ends go,' Barnaby pondered, 'well, he did get hit by a falling carcass.'

And suddenly it was all too much for Delphine. Her astonishment that he was gone, and in such a way, and her stifled, guilty joy at being free, spilled over in a wild and completely inappropriate bubble of laughter. She clapped her hands over her mouth, shocked at herself.

'What?' Barnaby grinned.

'Well, it's just that Foley . . . he was always so *proud* of the docks! The fact that he was in a guild, the fact that they always had jobs when others didn't . . . And the goods they handled! He was always on about them, boasting. "Timber, wine, tobacco," he used to say. "Wool, grain, sugar, rubber, fruit . . ." He used to rub his hands in glee, as if those cargos were somehow all credit to him. But when it come to it, it wasn't the timber or wine that got him, was it, or anything exotic? It was a chunk of old meat!'

Barnaby guffawed. 'Poetic justice,' he agreed, composing himself at last. 'Please don't waste your life feeling guilty about this, Delphine. It might so easily have been you lying there that day, instead of him. And the world would be a worse place for it. This second chance you've got, this blank slate, you only got it by the margin of a second, by a miracle. You were meant to have it. Make the most of it.'

'Don't you worry, Barney. I do know. I've been feeling . . . a bit numb, I suppose. But you're right, and I'll live a good life now, you'll see.'

# Chapter Seventy-six

Midge kept her promise to Kenneth. She paid her landlady until the end of the month, but moved to Dulwich the very next day. Her mother, despite Midge's doubts about the arrangement, was welcoming – pleased, perhaps, that her daughter had turned to her at last in her time of trouble. Two weeks had passed.

Rose Fawcett didn't ask any questions for the first few days, didn't even comment on the now-visible pregnancy besides asking if Midge needed to see a doctor. A tender sort of peace grew between them, based on little conversation but small shared rituals: crumpets in the parlour on dull evenings; morning walks through the streets – early, when everything was quiet; afternoons spent reading, side by side. It felt more of a refuge than Midge had imagined.

She was right about one thing, though. Seeing Kenneth in Reading had made everything worse. It just dredged all her longings back to the surface, made the memories of him all the fresher. And it had raised contrary hope. For although she'd ordered him to stay away, now every knock at the door made her heart jump, and when they went out, she kept thinking he was walking up the street towards her. But he wouldn't, she reminded herself. She had seen to that. She had sent him away.

He telephoned once and spoke to Rose, who assured him that Midge was now with her. He sounded relieved, Rose reported. He also asked Rose to tell Midge that Foley was gone and Delphine was safe. He said nothing of how, but it was sublime news. He hadn't asked to speak to Midge. He must have taken her at her word – or decided he was better off without her after all. It should be a relief, to know that no further emotional tussles were to ensue.

And then he came. Rose showed him into the parlour and left them to it. Midge had never suspected her mother of such discretion.

When he saw her belly, straining at the seams at last, his face was flooded by emotion. 'Oh, my darling,' he said, and rushed to hold her. She allowed herself to cling to him, to draw the feeling of him into her very pores. It would help nothing, but she had only so much strength to resist what she so badly wanted.

'When . . . ?' he asked, gesturing at the bump.

'About a week, we think.'

'It might have the same birthday as Blue.'

'Perhaps.'

'Won't you sit down, Midge, dearest? I should very much like to talk to you again, and do a better job of it than last time.'

Midge sighed. 'Very well.'

'First of all, I want you to tell me something. Several things, actually. Last time we met, I was so afraid I wouldn't find you that it never occurred to me you wouldn't come home with me if I did. The relief of seeing you, and then the shock that it didn't solve everything . . . Well, I didn't handle it well and the conversation was . . . as you remember it.' His rueful, boyish smile made her heart melt.

'I asked you a great many questions and I didn't really wait for the answers. I'd like to listen now, truly listen. What would you need, to come home with me? And why, Midge, *why* do you think I don't love you? Why has all this happened, really? I won't shout; I won't argue. I just want to understand.'

At first, Midge couldn't say a word. So much had been cycling through her mind for so long, unshared. To have an opening to let it out was daunting. Terrifying, actually. What on earth would he think about some of the petty, mean thoughts she had had? But then again, she had very little left to lose.

So she told him everything that had troubled her since the early days of their marriage: her guilty conviction that she'd somehow taken advantage of him, that he'd only married her because he was distraught, her belief that he was too gentlemanly to admit he regretted it. She told him how every pretty young woman who reminded her of Audra felt like a threat, and how she'd always felt herself to be so different from them. She tried to explain how undignified it felt to be a woman of forty-five still jealous and uncertain in her love, and how he hadn't helped, with his boundless charm and flirtatious manner and ridiculous good looks. She told him how hideous she had felt during her pregnancy and how useless and stupid she'd felt after it, and her great, great fear that these undesirable qualities would cost her his regard.

She told him as much as she could think of as the August sun circled the house and the patch of yellow warmth on the rug moved from one side of the room to the other. When she had finished, he sat quietly and nodded, and looked as if he were thinking. He was holding her hand, she noticed.

'I want you to know that I've listened very carefully to all you've said, and I think I've taken it in,' he said. She nodded. It felt that way. 'I feel as if you've told me a sad story about some other chap who married in haste, in the throes of grief, and came to regret it later, when he realised he wouldn't have chosen that woman for his wife had he been in his right mind. From this error, all sorts of difficulties ensued for the both of them.'

Midge nodded again. That summed it up.

'May I – while I accept your version of events totally, my dear – may I just say that I don't recognise those characters as you and me. May I tell you how it's been for me?'

Midge shuddered. In all honesty, it was the last thing she

wanted, but how could she deny him the chance to express his deepest truths when she had just done that very thing? 'All right,' she said in a small voice.

'You know the prologue to this story,' he said. 'There *was* a chap who was mad with grief. He'd lost his wife, whom he'd loved dearly, just as you said. But the mad-with-grief bit came *before* he met the strange and lovely creature called Margaret Fawcett. By the time he – oh, dash it, by the time I met you, Midge, I wasn't mad any more. Of course I was still suffering, but not *mad*. I was also a little numb at times, which meant I wasn't very observant. There were things I missed.

'The remaining damage probably would have taken a very long time to heal, except that I met you. Light came back into my world again. It started melting whatever was still frozen in me. And I *liked* you. Very much. You were a kind, intelligent, attractive woman with boundless compassion for others and conversation that never grew dull. You were someone I would have liked under *any* circumstances, Midge. As time passed and we grew closer, liking turned to love. Where I had thought you attractive, I came to see your beauty.'

Midge lifted her eyebrows. *Beauty?*

He nodded. 'We became intimate, while still unmarried, and yes, that bothered me. I'm old-fashioned, as you know. But would I have married you simply to be gentlemanly? Goodness, Midge, I'm afraid you have me on rather a pedestal if you think that. I would *never* have married you if I hadn't wanted to. And no, you aren't Audra. But don't you see, no one is. Christie Dawson-Hobbs wasn't Audra; *none* of the women you've fretted about were her. And none of them is *you*, either. You and Audra are very different, but one thing you do have in common is that you're both unique, both irreplaceable. Love isn't finite – you know that! My past with Audra doesn't stop me loving you too. I married you because you were the only woman I could see myself making a life with then, and I *wanted* that life! I still do.' His face was intense with the effort of trying to say things properly, explain his heart, and Midge wanted to throw herself into his arms already. But she sat firm; there was much more to be said.

'The only regret I have about marrying you is that it was too soon,' he continued, 'because in all these years, you haven't felt we were on a firm foundation. But I didn't know, then, that you felt that way. That's one of the things I missed, because of the numb bits. I wish now we'd waited another year, then you'd have seen for yourself that I *wasn't* out of my mind, that I *wasn't* proposing out of obligation. That's the only thing I would change.'

Midge frowned. 'But then why did you flirt the way you did? You still *do*. I always thought it was because you're not truly satisfied with me, because I don't live up to Audra.'

'Oh no, Midge, you're quite wrong there. To be perfectly honest, I don't know *why* I do it. Audra was a flirt, you see. Oh, devoted to me, and it was all harmless, but she was. As was

I. But it never caused either of us a moment's doubt. We met when we were very young, you see. We had that sort of young, carefree, glamorous marriage that you thought I wanted again. It was the pattern I'd learned, that's all. I didn't realise how different you were in that way, how the flirting made you feel. I feel a fool for it now, but it was simply another blind spot. Another thing that might have been different if we'd waited to get married. The bits of me that were still numb may have thawed out and I may have been more sensitive to you. I'm sorry that I wasn't.'

Midge looked at him tremulously. He had really loved her? Never regretted it, or yearned elsewhere? She'd had his heart all along? For one blindingly beautiful moment, she believed him and understood that she was loved. Then she remembered Percy and felt him slip through her fingers all over again. She'd ruined it, done those terrible things, for no reason at all. 'But Percy, darling Percy . . .' she whispered, starting to cry.

'Shh, shh,' he said, wiping her eyes with the back of his hand and then holding her firmly as if to fortify her. 'There's more. For five years I lived with you, Midge Camberwell, and you were everything I wanted in a wife. I have never known a woman so gracious, so passionate, so intelligent, and you opened your heart to my daughters like a water lily. We had our ups and downs, our share of strange arguments and inexplicable moods, but I honestly thought – and perhaps this truly does make me the most unobservant fellow in Surrey – that

that was normal in a marriage. We also had a terrible tragedy when we lost our son.

'Then suddenly, one day you were gone. And I learned that we hadn't lost our son at all, but that you had taken him away, hidden him from me, and constructed a whole scaffold of lies around that day in Esher. Look at me, Midge.'

She looked, fearfully, into his eyes. 'It was a terrible thing,' he acknowledged softly. She nodded. It was almost a relief to hear him say it. 'You did a bad thing, Midge. Very wrong.' She nodded again.

'For a while, I thought it was unforgivable. I was sure of it. I've been like an angry animal, wondering what to do with such a preposterous turn of events. But you know me, Midge, don't you? I'm not the sort to fly into a rage and never look at a thing again. Deep down, I always knew that you weren't a bad woman. So why had you done it? What was my part in it? Did I somehow drive you to it? I talked to Elf and he gave me some reading – on post-partum disorders in women. Remember when Delphine . . .'

Midge gasped. 'Oh, Delphine! Is she really safe, Kenneth? Is it truly over, as Mother said?'

'Entirely, thank God. But let's concentrate on *us* for now, darling. I hope to have the chance to tell you *that* story another day.

'Remember when, because of Delphine, we talked about the effects of the war on returning soldiers? About how some of the extraordinary things they do can be explained by the effects of the trauma on the nervous system and brain? I found that fascinating, as you know. It made me ponder what it must be like to have your own personality altered by external circumstances and not be able to do a thing about it. Because of what I saw in the war, it isn't hard to understand how that can happen.'

She reached across and kissed him; she couldn't help it.

He smiled, and kissed her cheek in return, but he was not to be distracted. 'Not so easy for me to understand a woman, to imagine what it's like to have your body, and I daresay your brain, taken over for a while! But do you think I would make efforts to understand suffering soldiers, and not my own wife? Hardly. Midge, I'm not being gentlemanly and I *don't* say this lightly: I've given it a great, great deal of thought, and I still believe that you are the wonderful woman I fell in love with, that there were many reasons you did what you did, some of which were out of your control. You have to take responsibility, of course. But responsibility isn't the same as self-flagellation, darling. The latter gets us nowhere. So here I am, reiterating my plea. I want you to come home, still. That's *my* story, Midge.'

Midge could hardly make sense of anything. The sun was falling directly onto her face now, and it dried her tears as fast as they fell. When Kenneth pulled her into his arms, she melted against him. She could feel his heart racing, the vulnerability beneath his strength. He held her for a long time in silence and she almost felt she could go to sleep like that; it was so peaceful to have come to the end of the words, and the end of this long, dark road she had travelled.

'You must be . . . the most remarkable, magnanimous man in the world,' she sighed.

'Undoubtedly.'

She wanted to smile, but . . . 'Percy,' she whispered.

He nodded and sat back. 'Percy,' he agreed. 'You said in Reading that one of the impossible things you wanted was to forgive yourself. Well, maybe that *is* impossible, I don't know. But darling, I have things to tell you, if you're willing to hear them. Yes? Well, I found the children's home where you left him and persuaded them to tell me where he is. I went there under some spurious excuse and I've seen him. He's a beautiful boy and so happy. It broke my heart all over again to see our child and not be able to claim him. Of course it did; I won't lie to you, Midge.

'What right course of action can there possibly be in such a situation? I don't have any answers to that. But can't we please try to decide together? At least we know where he is now, and that he's well. The family he's placed with are prosperous, open-hearted and clearly give him the best of everything. It wouldn't be right to take him away, Midge. But at least he's not dead! He's not suffering. It's more than we had before.'

She nodded. 'But so much less than you deserve.' She'd

always known Percy wasn't dead, but she hadn't known where he was, how he was living, if he was happy . . . She sighed.

'I've wondered whether we should tell them who we are,' he continued. 'Assure them that we won't try to claim him back but ask if they would send us the occasional photo, perhaps every now and then some news. I couldn't do anything without talking to you, Midge, but they do seem like the sort of folk who might be decent that way, if that was what we decided.'

'And then, maybe one day, when he came of age, we could meet him,' Midge murmured, frowning. Her whole world was transforming itself, over and over again. Perhaps all was not lost. But surely, after such a dark and desperate tangle, it couldn't be that easy. Could it?

'Darling, this isn't easy.' He smiled, as if reading her thoughts. 'But I think all that matters now is that we make up our minds what we want and then act on it. We'll go and talk to Percy's new family. I promise. We'll find some way forward, somehow.'

'Because I felt our getting married was dishonest somehow,' she whispered at last, 'I think that it set a tone for our whole marriage. From that foundation, it was quite easy to lay down more and more layers of dishonesty. How could I have got everything so muddled? How could I have understood you so wrongly?'

He smiled sadly. 'You'd never had a romance before, had you, darling? Certainly not with a complex fellow like me,' he teased. 'So what did *you* know?'

'Very little, it seems,' murmured Midge. 'Well, nothing at all, in truth. But oh, Kenneth, what about Blue and Merrigan? And whoever else knows. Elf? Our friends? *You* might forgive me, but can they? How could I simply step back into our world and go on as if nothing has happened? Oh, the dear, dear girls. I always tried so hard to do right by them, but in this most important thing I *wronged* them.'

'Yes,' he said, looking at her steadily. 'You did. But it's done now. Are you likely to do so again? I highly doubt it. You know our girls, Midge. They have the biggest hearts in the world. They love you. They miss you. They want you back desperately.'

'And Elf?'

'Darling, remember his profession. Besides, as he said to me, what view can *he* take on the troubles of a marriage? He lives in a shed at the bottom of a garden. He has great wisdom, does Elf, but he's too afraid to use it to change his life. But you're not, and I'm not, Midge. We chip away, the pair of us, jump in, get things wrong, try to put them right and make them worse. I think that's what living a life *is*.'

'Are we like that, darling? Courageous?'

'We are,' he said firmly. 'This conversation wasn't for the faint-hearted! As for our friends . . . I haven't told many people the truth. Only Delphine and the Greenbows know. And Tab. Needless to say, they all love you still.'

Midge gazed at him. He was systematically dismantling her

every objection, one by one. 'So . . . where does everybody else think I *am*?'

'I told them all you've gone to stay with a distant cousin who's been taken ill. I didn't want *everyone* knowing – people who might not understand. You see, darling, there's no reason whatsoever why you can't come home and be with us again and order an electric oven.'

Midge gave a great laugh of distress, relief, disbelief and hope all mixed into one. His flippancy had always entertained and tormented her. 'Oh, Kenneth. The bloody stove! I'm so sorry about all the decorating. I think I was trying to create some sort of . . . blank slate for us.'

'Well, good!' He seized her hands and stared into her eyes.

In that moment, she felt her own love change, just as her perception of his love for her had done. She could have sworn she felt it slow and deepen right there and then. Her old love had been a forest fire; this new one might be an oak tree.

'You made a good start,' Kenneth continued earnestly, 'but now I'm involved too, in creating that blank slate. Let's do it, Midge. Don't give up on us now. I want you back. The girls want you back. But the most important thing in this whole picture is whether *you* want it. Whether you choose to let yourself have it. Do you, Midge?'

# Chapter Seventy-seven

Three days before her birthday, Blue was returning from an afternoon walk around Richmond Park with Barnaby. To her disappointment, they hadn't seen a single common blue.

'Butterflies are magical creatures, so I've always thought,' she said. 'You can't just summon them. You have to wait.' *Like love*, she added silently.

'I'm not too disappointed.' Barnaby shrugged. 'Just means we'll have to take another walk before long.'

As they neared Ryan's Castle, Blue saw a familiar figure walking towards them, a figure that walked with an easy stride and unburdened air.

'Barnaby!' she exclaimed. 'Here's my friend Foster. Floss, darling! Were you coming to pay me a call?'

Foster smiled and kissed her cheek. 'I was. I've been studying all day and I needed to get out. It occurred to me that I used to swing by quite a bit and I haven't done it for ages.'

Blue's heart swelled at this evidence of a continuing return to normality between them. 'How lovely. Foster, let me introduce you to my good friend and former *Gazette* conspirator Barnaby Tanner. Barney, this is my old friend Foster Foxton, Tabitha's brother.'

'I'm pleased to meet you, Mr Tanner.'

'Call me Barnaby. And likewise. How are the studies going? I think Blue said you're going in for the law?'

'I am, yes, and they're going like a great sludge of mud, to be perfectly honest. But I think it'll all make some sort of sense in the end. And how is life at the *Gazette*? I know Blue misses it immensely.'

'It's very good, thanks. Busy, infuriating, and not half so much fun since Blue left, but I love what I do, so I can't complain.'

Blue took further delight in the easy rapport that seemed to exist between them in an instant. 'Floss, come in, take tea. Barney, will you come too?'

'No thanks, Blue, I really do have to get back to it now. But I'll see you soon, I hope. Goodbye, both.'

Foster watched him go. 'He seems very pleasant,' he remarked.

'He is,' said Blue, busying herself with her key. 'Come on.'

They took tea in the garden, with magpies flashing back and forth and a bank of pink dahlias against the wall to delight the eye. Blue frowned at them. 'Not too ragged,' she observed. 'Midge would be happy. The earwigs get them, you know, and it drives her mad. Drove.'

'Still no word?' asked Foster.

Blue shook her head. 'But never mind that now. Tell me what's new.'

'Everything's jolly good, as a matter of fact. Thanks to you. Thanks, Avis, how are you?' he added, as Avis brought the tea.

They chatted for a while, and Blue was pleased to see that her earlier impression was correct. Foster seemed better and happier in every particular.

'I still feel afraid when I remember that kiss, and how right it felt,' he said quietly. 'What it might mean, you know. I've been seeing a bit of Primrose Ashton lately – cracking girl and jolly pretty – but I'm afraid to . . . do anything, you know . . . in case that feels *wrong* – and then I'll know. And I don't want to hurt her. But somehow, I'm all right. Is there anyone who *doesn't* have some huge part of their life that they just have to set aside for a while in order to carry on? Look at Delphine when her husband was alive. Look at you Camberwells, with Midge gone. I'll face all that when the time is right. And meanwhile, at least I've learned from the whole mess how lucky I am to have you and Tabitha. I may not understand much about . . .' He blushed. 'You know. Sex. But at least now I know what love is.'

Blue squeezed his hand and dropped lemon slices into the Earl Grey. 'I'm so proud of you, Floss. I couldn't be more so. And I truly know that you have a good life ahead of you, whatever happens.'

His face turned serious. 'One thing, Blue. I have to ask. Are you still seeing Dorian at all?'

'No,' answered Blue in surprise. 'Not for a couple of months now. Why?'

'But you're good friends still, the two of you?'

'Not good friends, no. We're cordial if we bump into each other, of course. But that's only happened once or twice. I've been so busy with Delphine and the new baby. I've even started my novel, at last! But no, despite Dorian's endearing qualities, he doesn't really have the sort of character I can admire, the sort that I want in my friends just as much as in a beau. So no, we're not.'

He looked down at the wrought-iron table, spread with a pink floral cloth. 'Well, good. I'm glad.'

'Why? What difference would it make now?'

'There's something else I want to tell you. I didn't think it was right before. The men in your life are your business, after all. But it's the last piece in the story of me and Mr Mathews. Remember I told you about the unkindness from one or two of the boys in school? The nasty remarks, the innuendos, the veiled threats?'

Blue nodded. 'Of course I do. But you've kept clammed up about it ever since.'

'Well, they're easing up now. I suppose it all blew over after Mathews left, and they've lost interest. Wonderfully, things seem to have gone back to normal, though I never thought they could. But I wanted to tell you who it was.'

'Tell me, so I can go and wring their necks.'

'No, don't. But Blue, it was Mallory Fields.'

'Dorian's little brother? Good heavens! The foul little *beast*! And who else?'

'There wasn't another boy from school, Blue, just Mallory. The other person who used to taunt me and . . . and push me about a little bit, sometimes, was Dorian.'

'Dorian? *Dorian?* Foster, are you serious? What did he do? When? I can't *believe* you haven't told me this before now.'

'I wanted to! I was so worried about you, Blue. I knew, you see, that all that charm, all that sunshine, was only skin-deep. I was afraid you'd fall for him and get caught up in a life with him and then find out what he's really like. If it had gone that far, I would've told you, Blue, no matter what. But at the time, I was too afraid. If you knew Dorian was being unkind, you would have wanted to know why. If you'd asked him, then *he* would've told you about me – and put it all so hatefully. It was before I told you, and I was afraid you wouldn't like me any more. *And* I was afraid you might not even believe me. Everyone likes Dorian. You might have thought it was sour grapes on my part, that I was just trying to come between you.'

'Yes, I can see all that. Of course.'

Blue shook her head, letting it sink in. So much made sense now: Foster's strange letter about the cruelty in the world and wanting her to be safe; Foster saying that Dorian wasn't good enough for her; her own discomfort when Dorian had spoken of Foster in so cavalier a way – gossiping about him with Carlton James, of all people! And she understood. Oh, *now* she understood. All that time he'd been paying court to her, filling her head with lavish compliments, kissing her, he'd been bullying someone he *knew* she cared about. All that time he'd been duplicitous and fork-tongued and Janus-faced and . . .

'I'm going to kill him,' she said calmly, standing up.

'No, Blue! You can't! Don't say anything. He's eased up now! Mallory too. They've got bored. And I survived it; I don't want to stir it up. Promise me.'

She sat down again, her mind racing. 'All right, Floss, I promise. Well I'm glad you've told me now, that's all.'

When Foster left, she stayed in the garden, staring into the dahlias, recasting everything that had passed between her and Dorian in this new light. Heavens, how *could* he? Such a smug, self-satisfied, complacent, lazy, selfish *weasel*! When she remembered the autumn party, she couldn't contain herself. Blasted Dorian had stood in this very garden, *baiting* Foster, under her very nose! Insinuating that he and Blue were serious, saying what a loss it would be for the ladies when he settled down, offering Foster tips on how to deal with girls! All the while knowing . . . what he knew. Oh. Blue stood up again. She had kept every confidence Foster had made in her, honoured every promise. But this one she would have to break.

She stormed down the hill to Dorian's riverside flat. His older brother Harrison let her in. Just as well that snivelling little Mallory wasn't there. Harrison fetched Dorian, who emerged from a bedroom with his braces dangling and a champagne cobbler in hand. Through the open door, Blue could see Cassandra Tilley sitting on the bed, wearing a pretty green dress. Blue shivered, remembering the last time she'd been in this apartment. Oh, what a lucky escape.

'Blue! What a smashing surprise! You look like the ducky's quack.' Dorian paused, and closed the bedroom door behind him. 'I've jolly well missed you, you know. What brings you?'

'Just this, Dorian,' she said. 'I think you're a loathsome, spiteful, two-faced piece of excrement and if I ever hear that you've been tormenting Foster, or anyone I care about, or anyone at all, you'll have me to deal with.' His face paled and his jaw dropped, but Blue rolled on. 'You loll here in your ivory tower – which isn't very nice by the way; the architect must've been sozzled when he designed it – and you don't even care how hard life is for some people. Actually, for *everyone*, sooner or later. One day you'll struggle with something, Dorian, and I hope you encounter more compassion than you showed to Foster. But either way, I don't ever want to see you again – and stay away from Foster. Or else.'

She turned on her heel and slammed the door, hard as she could. There was a clunk behind her, as though a painting had perhaps been shaken off the wall.

She ran down the stairs and slammed the exterior door as well. Then she charged along the river. Her steps had slowed and her breathing and heart rate steadied by the time she got to Isleworth.

# Chapter Seventy-eight

Without the cloud of Foley threatening to break at any moment, the friendship between Sid and Delphine had blossomed. Slowly and tenderly, it became apparent to them – and to everyone else – that the pair of them *were* a pair, just like the swans nesting near the White Cross.

For a long time, nothing changed. They didn't talk about anything but the small moments of life: daily plans and changes in the weather and people they knew. All these things, unshadowed, were like treasure to Delphine. And sharing them with Sid was an unspoken pleasure.

One morning, they sat on a bench looking at the river for over an hour, talking. Big heads of foamy cow parsley and spikes of sorrel crowded around them like guardian angels, and somehow it came about that their heads leaned together and their fingers were intertwined. Delphine felt her heart speed up pleasantly. They hadn't touched like this before, not for more than a fleeting instant, yet now it felt as if they should always sit this way.

'I want you to know, Delphine, that I want to marry you,' Sid said, gazing over the green water. 'But this isn't a proposal. It isn't time yet.'

'Well,' said Delphine, watching an octet of ducks squabbling in the reeds, 'I want to marry you, too. And I agree, it isn't time.' She pressed her lips together to contain her joy. There was a solemnity to this moment, with the green water shimmering before them and the hushed rustle of the trees all about.

'When do you think the time might be?' wondered Sid. 'For me, it's when I've saved up enough money that we can make a decent start. Another year ought to do it. But what's your opinion? I know you're not in mourning, exactly, but you are a widow. I don't know how much time is decent after losing a husband who was no sort of a husband. Or how much time it will take you to get used to it all.'

'I don't know either.' Delphine smiled. 'Another year ought to do it.'

Small words, lightly spoken, but not intended lightly at all. They looked at each other and squeezed hands. Delphine laid her head on Sid's shoulder. 'We'll be happy, won't we, Sid?'

'Yes. I wish everyone could be as happy.'

'There's another thing I'd like to wait for. I'd like for Midge to be home. She's been so good to me. I'd like her to be at the wedding.'

Sid gently lifted her head and looked into her eyes. 'But

we don't *have* to wait for that, do we?' he asked, and Delphine knew that he didn't believe Midge would ever come home. She shook her head and sighed, settled back onto his shoulder and gazed at the water.

# Chapter Seventy-nine

They decided to make it a luncheon in the end. It seemed more appropriate and less newspaper-worthy than an evening soirée. After careful consideration, Blue invited Juno, but only on the condition that she came in a strictly personal capacity. 'A twenty-second birthday lunch hardly counts as news, darling,' she pointed out.

'True enough,' said Juno. 'But it's not just *anyone's* twenty-second, is it? It's Blue Camberwell's. The occasion at which her renowned papa will give her hand in marriage to some lucky suitor. The paper's been following this story all year. I *have* to come, whether you want me or not. And if I *don't* write something, they'll fire me.'

'But Juno, you know as well as I do that Daddy won't be giving my hand to anyone! None of the letters I received have led to anything – the suitors fizzled out. What do you want me to do, conjure a man from apple boughs?'

'You could try,' said Juno reproachfully. 'I don't see how

I can make a story out of "they all ate sultana cake and had a jolly time".'

'Try,' said Blue.

Firm in her resolve that it wasn't to be a *party*, Blue told herself that she could wear whatever she wanted and just be comfortable. She needn't bow to Merrigan's fashion dictates like last year. Then she remembered that Barnaby was coming and consulted her sister, after all.

'I have a brand-new baby, Blue, darling,' said Merrigan, contrary as ever. 'I hope you don't expect me to abandon her in her infancy to go shopping?'

'That's exactly what I expect,' said Blue. 'Come on.'

Blue was suspiciously amenable when it came to following Merrigan's advice this year. At least, Blue was amenable and that made Merrigan suspicious.

'I expect it's that Barnaby fellow you're trying to impress,' she said in a bored tone as she flipped through dresses with a critical eye.

'Yes,' said Blue, stroking some long satin gloves. 'It is.' She waited for the lecture.

But all Merrigan said was, 'We'd better go all out then, I suppose.'

They left the boutique an hour later with the most wonderful dress. It would have been even more wonderful had it been made with love by Midge, but still, it was a dress that was sure to seal the deal, Merrigan declared, and that was something. Then, for good measure, Blue went to the hair-dresser and bobbed her hair. Merrigan, uncharacteristically emotional since the baby's birth, shed actual tears of joy.

On Blue's birthday, the weather was startlingly fair and all was golden and blue. It was less violently hot than last year; Blue was confident that her guests would be able to breathe *and* eat. Kenneth and Elf carried tables onto the lawn; Blue and Avis spread them with linen and set them. Then Blue went to change.

Her dress was a brick-red satin sheath with an overdress of the brightest scarlet chiffon. Between them they created a colour somewhere between a rose and a flame. Tiny scarlet gems in fire-burst patterns around the neck and shoulders threw winking lights onto her face. The hem boasted an extra layer of froth scattered with the same tiny ruby beads, as though they had simply tumbled from the pattern above and come to rest there. She wore long scarlet gloves – they wouldn't last long in this heat – and a scarlet and gold headband, narrower than a ribbon, which gleamed in the waves of her newly bobbed hair.

'Lord, Blue,' sighed Merrigan when she saw her. 'I'd give my babies back in a second to be able to wear a dress like that, I swear I would. But now my figure's all mumsy and stout. Thank heavens for elasticated corsets,' she added, smoothing gorgeous steel-blue silk over her hips. 'Whoever invented them should be knighted.'

Blue snorted. 'If you're stout, I'm an armadillo. Golly,

Merrigan, but it's rather much for a luncheon, isn't it? Mine, I mean.'

'It isn't meant to be appropriate,' Merrigan reminded her. 'It's meant to be irresistible.' Adding red lipstick and then applying black kohl to her eyes, Blue dared to hope that it was.

When she emerged onto the lawn, she was greeted with oohs and aahs, as if she were a firework display.

'My darling, you're ravishing,' said her father. 'I couldn't be prouder of you – not just of your beauty, but of the woman you've become.'

'I say, I'm glad we didn't get together,' murmured Foster. 'I'd be rather terrified, I think.'

Amidst the jokes and kind remarks, Blue looked around for Barnaby in the little throng. When she saw him, he just smiled at her and nodded.

Everyone who was invited came. By one o'clock, the hors d'oeuvres had circulated three times. A little champagne had been drunk on arrival, but was followed by ice-cold elderflower cordial, since this wasn't to be an occasion of *that* sort.

Then they all sat down to lunch. In between the roast beef salad and the gooseberry fool, Kenneth stood and dinged his glass with a teaspoon.

'My lords, ladies and gentlemen,' he announced with a bow and a flourish. 'If I may have your attention for a moment, I should like to propose a toast.'

'Oh Lord,' groaned Tabitha, vampish and sleek in black satin and jet. 'Should we stop him now?' Juno, resplendent in aqua dress and cerise turban, brightened.

But Kenneth was sober, as they all were. 'I have no startling announcements to make,' he began. Some people whooped, others groaned. Whatever else Kenneth might be when he was drunk, he was always interesting. 'I merely want to wish my darling daughter Blue a happy birthday and to thank you all for coming today. It's been a difficult year for many of us, yet we have stuck together and that is a fine thing. True friends are hard to come by, and Blue, Merrigan and I feel blessed in ours. Blue has absolutely vetoed a party, but a gathering with those we love can be nothing but a pleasure. So, thank you for coming to celebrate with Blue. And thank you, Blue, for being one of the two equally very best daughters a father could wish for. To darling Blue.'

'Darling Blue,' they echoed.

She blushed and raised her glass. 'Thank you, Daddy. Thank you, everyone.'

'Remarkably painless,' said Merrigan with some relief.

Blue gazed around the table and thought that, after all, they hadn't done too badly. Delphine was wearing a new cream linen dress with blue embroidery and kept darting glances at Sid as though he might vanish in a puff of smoke. No one looking at her now would dream that she'd spent the last years under the black spell of a violent man. Foster looked relaxed and even less gawky. That Adam's apple wasn't quite so prominent, and he tucked into the food with gusto. Humans were remarkable, thought Blue. They could suffer such terrible things. They might need years to heal. But add love into the equation and everything got better far more quickly. Love, and a decision to be happy. Her father was looking better, too; he wore an air of buoyancy and hope that Blue didn't understand but was pleased to see. He'd become involved in a new project, creating affordable housing in Battersea, so perhaps that was giving him a renewed sense of purpose.

He caught her eye and smiled. Watching him, Blue felt so proud. No matter what he went through, he kept springing back, looking after people, living life, trying. He was a fine example for a girl to have, she thought, and made a mental note to tell him so later. Then she saw him look towards the house and his whole face lit up. His grey eyes turned golden with sunshine and happiness. Blue turned to see what had delighted him and gave a little cry. She couldn't help it. For leaning in the drawing-room doorway was Midge. She was wearing a loose brown and gold brocade jacket with pale pink lining, an expression of immense fondness on her face. She was slim and elegant as ever, with one pronounced curve, front and centre.

'Midge!' Blue shrieked, making everyone jump. 'Midge!' She was out of her chair and across the lawn in a second. She threw her arms around her stepmother and they hugged as if their lives depended on it.

'Midge, darling,' she implored in a whisper, 'you aren't just visiting, are you? Tell me you've come home.'

Midge's eyes were misty with tears. 'I've come home, darling. I'm so sorry I went away.'

'Oh, never mind that now. We can talk all you want when you're settled, but for now won't you come and have some lunch?'

'I should love to. Happy birthday, Blue.'

And Blue led Midge to the table, where she was greeted all round with hugs and handshakes and heartfelt welcome. Kenneth poured her a little fizz.

'I shouldn't really,' Midge protested, patting her neat baby bump.

'*Very* unfair,' sniffed Merrigan.

'Never as long as I live,' shuddered Tabitha.

'A thimbleful, my darling. A mere sip,' said Kenneth, and Midge smiled.

'Well, perhaps I will, after all.'

'Now *that's* news,' Juno observed, of Midge's homecoming. Then, seeing Barnaby's shrewd eyes on her, added, 'But I won't, darling. Of course I won't.'

# Chapter Eighty

When Midge had arrived on the doorstep of Ryan's Castle, she had paused, feeling like a visitor. But she wasn't a visitor; she belonged. She took a moment to absorb it. Then she took out her key and let herself in. She knew they would all be in the garden.

When Kenneth had visited her in Dulwich, she'd known at once that she would come home. 'But may I have a day or two to adjust, my darling?' she'd asked. 'I've spent the last six years thinking things were one way. Now you're telling me that everything is different, and my head is spinning. And I think I should like a few more days with Mother now that I know I can be happy again; maybe tell her a few things. She's been awfully good to me.'

'But you won't change your mind?' he'd urged.

'No, I won't change my mind.'

She'd telephoned Kenneth this morning, unsure whether Blue's birthday was the right time to come home. It would be the very perfect time, Kenneth had insisted. Midge had wondered about waiting until the evening, so that her home-coming could be a private affair. Kenneth's reassurances were one thing, but she still feared censure from everyone else.

'But remember, darling, the people who are coming today are not the sorts to judge,' he'd reminded her. 'All I know is that you'll be the best birthday present Blue could have. She'd want you to be there for her day.'

And he was right, of course. If she were to resume her life and position, then she would see all these people again, so why not see them all at once, at a happy event? She stood watching from the drawing room for a moment or two, still wearing her light summer coat, and marvelling at the beauty of the world – *her* world. Then Blue had flown at her, and now she was being offered dessert and cold cuts and potatoes in no particular order.

'About time,' said Merrigan. 'Don't think we could've gone one more day without you, actually, Midge.' She embraced Midge, who noticed in her merry brown eyes the tiredness of the sleep-deprived new mother.

'I'm sorry, darling,' Midge whispered, then said aloud, 'Kenneth said a little girl . . .'

'Let me fetch her. Give you a taste of things to come.'

She collected her daughter, who was slumbering in her father's arms, and brought her over to Midge. Meanwhile, Cicely toddled over from the apple trees and tried to scale Midge's legs.

'Cicely,' said Merrigan. 'Be careful with Midge. She's about to have a baby.'

She placed her new daughter in Midge's arms, and Midge, never the most maternal of women, took in a high forehead, two fringed crescents of lashes and a rosebud mouth. She blinked hard, remembering Percy. Was it possible after all that he may not be quite as entirely lost to them as she had always imagined?

'She's rather sweet,' she murmured. 'What's her name?'

'Midge, darling,' said Merrigan, 'I'd like you to meet Francine Margaret Miller.'

'Oh, that's pretty. Wait, Francine *Margaret*?'

'Of course. Cicely is Cicely Audra, so Francine had to be named after my other mother. So it's jolly convenient she's a girl, as a matter of fact.'

'They were going to call her Felicity Margaret,' explained Tab. 'But I told them absolutely not. Cicely and Felicity – sounds like some sort of ghastly vaudeville double act.'

'Horrors,' smiled Midge. 'That wouldn't do at all.' But all she could think about was that, despite everything, Merrigan had named her daughter after her.

# Chapter Eighty-one

The afternoon wore on. Wraps and gloves and jackets were shed, and Midge fished out the old gramophone so there could be dancing on the lawn. Blue danced with her father, and Foster and Lawrence, and then Barnaby asked for a dance. Her shoes were pinching dreadfully by then, so she kicked them off and danced barefoot on the grass. A lively Charleston left them breathless and laughing.

'I still can't fathom that dance,' she heard Midge saying. 'Not at all.'

Then Midge put on a slow song, an old-fashioned song. Blue looked at Barnaby hesitantly, not wanting to presume, not wanting to let him go. But Barnaby pulled her into his arms and she felt herself melt a little bit.

'No announcement from your father today?' he murmured. 'He won't be bestowing your hand on anyone?'

'No.'

'I feel bad for Juno. It'll be devastating for her to leave with no scoop at all. Cauderlie will never let her live it down. I was just thinking . . . maybe . . . we should give her *something* to write about?'

Blue looked into his dancing eyes and grinned. 'How thoughtful,' she said wryly.

He smiled. 'I'm all heart.'

'I've said it before, Barney. You're a very kind man.'

They swayed together on the spot, then he started waltzing her in lazy circles, further and then a little further away from the others, until they found themselves in the privacy of the trees. Then he bent his head to kiss her. She felt the world spinning gently around her.

*Oh!* thought Blue. *That's what kisses should be like.*

When they broke apart, she gazed up at him, starry-eyed and weightless in his arms.

'Darling Blue,' he said softly. 'I've never written you a letter, and I'm not sure there's much about me to capture your imagination. I'm just an ordinary man, with an ordinary, too-large family and an ordinary, low-paid job. But although you're kind and clever and brave, not to mention the most beautiful woman I've ever seen, some magical fate made me cross paths with you and now . . . well, I love you. You do see that, don't you?'

She looked at him in wonder, and stroked the side of his face, the plane of his cheekbone. Now she understood at last why Midge was always touching her father. Impossible not to, when you felt like this.

'Well, thank goodness for that,' she breathed. 'I was worried you just wanted to be friends.'

'No, that wouldn't do. I need you in my life, Blue, for good. As my wife. I don't have much to offer, yet, but you know I'll change that. You know I'll work hard and make good things happen for us. Splendid things. We'll make it an adventure. I've wondered and wondered if I shouldn't stand back and watch you make a better match. Only, we *are* a match, aren't we? We just are.'

'We just are,' she agreed dreamily. 'And by the way, there is *nothing* ordinary about you, Barnaby Tanner. Oh!' she exclaimed. 'Look! I can't believe it!'

She pointed, her finger circling around them, up and down, in a teasing, tilting arc.

'A common blue,' she whispered. 'I've *never* seen one down here before. Not once.' *Serendipitous, propitious, auspicious . . .*

'That *is* a beautiful colour,' he said, whispering too. 'Princess blue.' And together they watched the tiny scrap of colour fluttering around them, his arm tight about her waist.

'Blue!' her father shouted, bursting into their leafy paradise. 'Oh! Sorry, Barnaby, old man. Carry on in a sec, won't you? Blue, I've sent out for more champagne, and Midge has only gone and bought a cocktail shaker, so we should probably give it a try. A cocktail shaker at Ryan's Castle – how thoroughly modern! But is that all right with you? You said you didn't want a party.'

Blue laughed. 'It's perfectly fine, Daddy. I feel rather differently about it now. We have one or two things to celebrate after all, don't we?'

'That we do, my darling, that we do.' Kenneth paused only to shake Barnaby's hand. 'I'm happy for you both,' he added. 'Barnaby, you're everything I could have wanted for Blue.' Then he rushed off, his old irrepressible self again.

'Look out,' said Blue. It was to be a party after all.

# Acknowledgements

Every book I write is different from the ones before, and *Darling Blue* is no exception. It was an absolute joy to soak myself in 1920s history, fashion and dialogue in my research for this book and such a pleasure (if not a little nerve-wracking) to find the narrative splitting off into three very different strands. Beverley Rogers was an absolute star when it came to helping me with research. Her enthusiasm and persistence in finding out every last tiny detail I queried were invaluable and I am deeply grateful.

Come to that, huge thanks to all my friends and family, as always, for the support, company and distraction they offer through the intense and isolating process of bringing a novel to birth. Thanks too, to my earliest readers who gave input at first draft stage: Jane Rees, Marjorie Hawthorne, Ellen Pruyne and, for the first few chapters, Stephanie Basford-Morris. Thank you too, as always, to my parents for putting up with the stresses and outlandish flights of fancy of having a writer in the family and for constant love and support and cheerleading of each new project of mine.

It was wonderful to set the book in my old home of Richmond and to spend days wandering around this lovely place in the name of research. The Richmond Local Studies Library and Archive was a tremendous resource. Thank you to all the staff there for friendly assistance and for letting me browse old local newspapers from the mid-twenties for hours on end.

Huge thanks are also owed to Katy Green at the London Transport Museum and the LTM's team of expert volunteers who patiently answered a succession of questions about Delphine's journey when she escaped from Foley and accidentally ended up in Richmond! You were absolutely brilliant.

Thank you to Fleur Johnson at the Fashion Museum in Bath for another fascinating study session. It really does make the world of difference being able to see and hold clothes from another time instead of merely reading about them.

And last but by no means least, thank you to my amazing publishing team: thank you to my agent, Eugenie Furniss, for keeping me inspired, encouraged and supported, for brilliant insights and fabulous meetings. And thank you to my new editor at Quercus, Emily Yau, who has been a pleasure to work with – I hope *Darling Blue* is the first of many we publish together. And to the wider team at Quercus: Cassie Browne, Jon Butler, Corinna Zifko, Alainna Hadjigeorgiou, Frances Doyle, Emma Thawley and everyone else who does such an amazing job for my books across the divisions. You are all brilliant, and so much appreciated.

# Bibliography

*Britain in the 1920s*. Fiona McDonald. Pen and Sword Books Ltd, Barnsley. 2012.

*The 1920s Scrapbook*. Robert Opie. Museum of Brands, London. 2003.

*Fashion in the 1920s*. Jayne Shrimpton. Shire Publications, Oxford. 2013.

*1920s Britain*. Janet Shepherd and John Shepherd. Shire Living Histories, Oxford. 2010.

# AMY SNOW

## TRACY REES

Abandoned on a bank of snow as a baby, Amy is taken in at nearby Hatville Court. But the masters and servants of the grand estate prove cold and unwelcoming. Amy's only friend and ally is the sparkling young heiress Aurelia Vennaway. So when Aurelia tragically dies young, Amy is devastated. But Aurelia leaves Amy one last gift. A bundle of letters with a coded key. A treasure hunt that only Amy can follow.

**A life-changing discovery awaits . . .**
**if only she can unlock the secret.**

Available now

# FLORENCE GRACE

## TRACY REES

Florrie Buckley is an orphan, living on the wind-blasted moors of Cornwall. It's a hard existence but Florrie is content; she runs wild in the mysterious landscape.

**She thinks her destiny is set in stone.**

But when Florrie is fourteen, she inherits a never-imagined secret. She is related to a wealthy and notorious London family, the Graces. Overnight, Florrie's life changes and she moves from country to city, from poverty to wealth. Cut off from everyone she has ever known, Florrie struggles to learn the rules of this strange new world.

And then she must try to fathom her destructive pull towards the enigmatic and troubled Turlington Grace, a man with many dark secrets of his own.

Quercus